Live and Let Drood

Live and Let Drood

A Secret Histories Novel

Simon R. Green

A ROC BOOK

ROC
Published by New American Library, a division of
Penguin Group (USA) Inc., 375 Hudson Street,
New York, New York 10014, USA
Penguin Group (Canada), 90 Eglinton Avenue East, Suite 700, Toronto,
Ontario M4P 2Y3, Canada (a division of Pearson Penguin Canada Inc.)
Penguin Books Ltd., 80 Strand, London WC2R 0RL, England
Penguin Ireland, 25 St. Stephen's Green, Dublin 2,
Ireland (a division of Penguin Books Ltd.)
Penguin Group (Australia), 250 Camberwell Road, Camberwell, Victoria 3124,
Australia (a division of Pearson Australia Group Pty. Ltd.)
Penguin Books India Pvt. Ltd., 11 Community Centre, Panchsheel Park,
New Delhi - 110 017, India
Penguin Group (NZ), 67 Apollo Drive, Rosedale, Auckland 0632,
New Zealand (a division of Pearson New Zealand Ltd.)
Penguin Books (South Africa) (Pty.) Ltd., 24 Sturdee Avenue,
Rosebank, Johannesburg 2196, South Africa

Penguin Books Ltd., Registered Offices:
80 Strand, London WC2R 0RL, England

First published by Roc, an imprint of New American Library,
a division of Penguin Group (USA) Inc.

First Printing, June 2012
10 9 8 7 6 5 4 3 2 1

ROC REGISTERED TRADEMARK—MARCA REGISTRADA

LIBRARY OF CONGRESS CATALOGING-IN-PUBLICATION DATA:

Green, Simon R., 1955–
   Live and let Drood: a secret histories novel/Simon R. Green.
      p. cm.
   ISBN 978-0-451-46452-1 (hardback)
   1. Drood, Eddie (Fictitious character)—Fiction.   I. Title.
   PR6107.R44L58 2012
   823'.92—dc23   2011045364

Set in ITC New Baskerville
Designed by Elke Sigal

Printed in the United States of America

PUBLISHER'S NOTE
This is a work of fiction. Names, characters, places, and incidents either are the product of
the author's imagination or are used fictitiously, and any resemblance to actual persons,
living or dead, business establishments, events, or locales is entirely coincidental.
   The publisher does not have any control over and does not assume any responsibility for
author or third-party Web sites or their content.

Live and Let Drood

Previously in the Secret Histories . . .

I came home and found someone had murdered my whole family.
Someone is going to pay.
In blood.

CHAPTER ONE

Home Is Where the Heart Breaks

You think you know where your life is going. You think you've got everything sorted out. You've defeated your enemies, saved the world, made peace with your family and gone on holiday with the woman you love. And then you discover what you should have known all along: that it takes only one bad day to turn your life upside down. That there's nothing you can have, nothing you've earned, nothing you've paid for with blood and loss and suffering . . . that the world can't take away from you.

I stood before all that remained of my home, Drood Hall, and all I could think of was how it used to look. How it had looked all my life. A huge, sprawling old manor house dating back to the time of the Tudor kings, though much added onto and improved through the centuries. Traditional black-and-white-boarded frontage with heavy leaded-glass windows, proud entrance doors strong enough to hold off an army, and a jutting peaked and gabled roof. Four large wings had been added to accommodate the growing size of the family; it was massive and solid in the old Regency style. So large and solid and . . . significant, it looked like it could take on the whole world and win.

High above the extensive grounds, the wide roof rose and fell like a great grey-tiled sea, complete with sharp-peaked gables, scowling gargoyles that doubled as water spouts and ornamental guttering that had probably seemed like a good idea at the time. Add to that a perky little observatory, extensive landing pads for all the family's more outré flying machines (and, of course, the winged unicorns), and more aliens and antennae than you could shake a gremlin at . . . and it all added up to one very crowded and very useful roof.

I used to spend a lot of my time up on the roof when I was just a kid, enjoying the various comings and goings and getting in everyone's way.

All gone now.

The Hall was a burnt-out ruin. Someone had taken it apart with gunfire and explosives and set fire to what remained. Walls were broken and shattered, blackened and charred from smoke and flames. The upper floors had collapsed in on themselves into one great compressed mass of broken stone and rubble and what fragments remained of the roof. The ground floor looked to be more or less intact, but the windows were all blown out, and the great front doors had been blasted right off their heavy hinges. God alone knew what was left inside.

For all its many bad memories, the Hall had always been home to me. I'd always thought it would always be there to go back to when I needed it. To see it like this, brought down by rage and violence and reduced to wreck and ruin, stopped the breath in my throat and the heart in my chest, and put a chill in my soul that I knew would never leave.

I made myself walk slowly forward. Molly was right there at my side, trying to say something comforting, but I couldn't hear her. There was no room left in me for anything except what had been done to my home. The massive front doors that should have been enough to hold off an army had been thrown back onto the floor in the gloom of the hallway. And a single golden-armoured figure lay curled in the doorway, quite still and quite dead, the gleaming metal half-melted and distorted, the arms fused to the torso and the legs fused together, by some unimaginable heat. I hadn't thought there was anything in the world that could do that to Drood armour.

There was no smoke in the air, no heat radiating from the fire-blasted hallway. Whatever had happened here, it had clearly happened sometime before. Days before. So I hadn't missed it by much. The attackers had come here, slaughtered my family, blown up and set fire to my home and then left. All while I was off enjoying myself in the south of France. I stood before the open doorway and I didn't know what to do. What to say. My stomach ached, and even breathing hurt my tightened chest. Molly Metcalf moved in close beside me and slipped an arm tentatively through mine, pressing herself against me. Standing as close to me as she could, to give me what comfort she could.

"Why didn't I know?" I said numbly. "How could something like this happen and I didn't know? Why didn't anyone reach out to me?"

"Maybe . . . it all happened too quickly," said Molly. "It must have been a surprise attack, to catch your whole family so off guard."

The strength just went out of my legs and I crashed to my knees on the gravel before the doorway. It should have hurt like hell, but I didn't feel a thing. Too taken up with the greater hurt that filled my head and my heart and overwhelmed everything else. I would have liked to cry; I'm sure it would have helped if only I could have cried . . . but all I could feel was cold and lost and alone. You never know how much your family means to you until you've lost them all. Molly crouched at my side, one arm draped across my shoulders. I'm sure her words would have helped if I'd listened, but there was no room in me for anything but the growing need for rage and revenge. If tears would come, it would have to be later and far from here. After I'd done all the terrible things that I would do to my enemy.

I knelt before what was left of my home and my family and shook uncontrollably in the grip of emotions I never thought I'd have to feel. Molly put her arms around me and rocked me gently back and forth like a mother with a child.

After a while I became aware that Molly was speaking urgently to me, almost shouting into my ear.

"Come on, Eddie. We can't stay here! We have to go! There's always the chance whoever did this might come back, and we can't afford to be here if they do. If your whole family couldn't stand against them, we certainly can't."

I nodded slowly and got to my feet again, with her help. My head was clearing, all the pain and horror and loss pushed aside by a cold and savage need for revenge. I couldn't leave here, not yet. I needed information and weapons. And more than anything I needed some clue to tell me my enemy's name. And then nothing was going to stand in my way. All the awful things I would do to him and anyone who stood alongside him would make my name an abomination on the lips of the world. . . . And I wouldn't give a damn.

I wasn't used to thinking like that, but it seemed to come very easily. I was, after all, a Drood. The Last Drood.

Molly realised she wasn't going to get any sense out of me. She looked at the ruined hall before her and the sheer scale of so much destruction seemed to overwhelm even her for a moment.

"What the hell happened here, Eddie? What could have done this?"

"I don't know," I said. My voice sounded distant and far away. "The Chinese tried to nuke us once, back in the sixties, and that got nowhere. No one's struck directly at the Hall for ages. I would have said there was nothing and no one in the world that could get past all our defences and protections. This is all my fault, you know."

"What?" said Molly, turning immediately to look at me with her large dark eyes.

"I should have been here," I said steadily. "I wasn't with my family when the enemy came. If I had been here, maybe I could have done . . . something. Saving the day against impossible odds is what I do. Isn't it?"

"Stop that," Molly said firmly. "Stop that right now, Eddie. What could you have done that your whole family couldn't? If you had been here, odds are you'd be lying here dead, too."

"I can do something now," I said. "I can avenge my family. I can be the Last Drood. I can bring down my enemies in horror and suffering, and make my family name a byword in this world for revenge and retribution."

"Okay," said Molly. "Someone needs a whole load of stiff drinks, and possibly a nice lie-down in a cool dark room. You're in shock, Eddie. Let's get out of here."

"Not yet," I said. "I'm not finished here yet."

"And what if the enemy isn't finished? What if they come back?"

"Let them," I said. "Let them all come." And there was something in my voice that actually made Molly shudder briefly and look away. Anywhen else, that might have bothered me. I looked steadily at what was left of my home. My thoughts kept going round in circles, and returning to the same impossible situation.

"How could anyone have got past all of Drood Hall's centuries of layered shields and protections? It's just not possible!"

"Well, we did," said Molly.

I looked at her. "What?"

"We got in. That time you came back to overthrow the Matriarch and take control of your family."

"Well, yes," I said. "But we only managed that through my insider knowledge and because we had the Confusulum. Whatever or whoever that annoying alien thing was. And since the Blue Fairy isn't around anymore, I don't see how anyone could acquire another one. But I see what you mean. This was no sneak attack. This was a carefully planned open assault. Which raises even more questions. Look around you, Molly. Look at the grounds. None of the robot gun positions have been activated; they're still sitting in their hidden bunkers under the lawns. And I can't See any trace of the force shields and magical screens that should have slammed into place automatically the moment the Hall came under threat. It's as though the enemy caught my family with all their defences down. Which should have been impossible . . ."

"Could someone have . . . lowered the shields, from inside?" Molly said carefully. "Sabotage, in advance of the attack? We never did identify the traitor inside your family, the one who's been working against your interests for so long."

She stopped talking as I shook my head firmly. I wasn't ready to think about that, not just yet. "Concentrate on our enemies," I said. "Who is there left, who could have done this to us? We stamped out Manifest Destiny, stopped the invasion of the Loathly Ones and the

Hungry Gods, wiped out the Immortals and crushed the Great Satanic Conspiracy. I mean, who's left?"

"Clearly, someone you missed," said Molly. "There's always someone. . . ."

I thought about it. "The Droods are supposed to have made pacts with Heaven and Hell, back in the day, for power and influence and protection," I said. "Could this have been the day when all our debts came due?"

"No," Molly said immediately. "I'd know."

I managed something like a smile. "You worry me sometimes when you say things like that."

She managed a small smile of her own. "Can I help it if I'm a girl who likes to get around?"

I took her hand in mine and squeezed it firmly. "Sometimes I forget that I'm not alone anymore. That I don't have to do everything myself."

"You always were too ready to carry the weight of the world on your shoulders, Eddie. Whatever you decide to do, I've got your back."

"Good to know," I said. "Because I'm pretty sure this is going to get a lot worse before it gets any better."

I gave her hand a final squeeze, let it go and turned away to look into the open doorway, where the huge and specially reinforced front doors should have been. The empty gap was like an open wound. I moved slowly, steadily, forward, Molly right there at my side. Gravel crunched loudly under our feet in the quiet. The remains of a lone gargoyle lay shattered on the ground before us. As though it had been shot down while flying against our enemies and plummeted to the ground. And maybe it had. I'd always been suspicious about the gargoyles. When I was just a kid, sleeping in one of the great communal dormitories along with the other young Droods, I was half-convinced gargoyles would creep down from the roof at night and listen outside our windows, so they could report all our sins and bad intentions to the adults. And maybe they did. Drood Hall is full of secrets. I stopped then and made myself rephrase that. Drood Hall was full of secrets. It was important to remember everything I'd lost.

I stepped past the broken remains of the gargoyle, with its shattered face and broken wings, to stand before the open doorway. Something really powerful had blasted both doors right off their hinges and sent them flying a fair distance down the hallway. I could see them lying on the floor, the heavy wood cracked and splintered from some unimaginable impact. And there in the doorway was the half-melted golden figure, the last defender of the entrance hall. The armoured man lay curled into a ball, as though wrapped around his pain. I knelt down beside him, let my fingertips drift gently across the cracked and distorted face mask. The metal was cold to the touch. Cold as death. There was no way to remove the featureless mask, no way of telling who it was inside the armour. Whether . . . it was anyone I knew.

I rose and strode past the dead man into the gloom of the hallway. There were no lights working anywhere, just dark shadows and fire- and smoke-blackened interiors. Loud and dangerous cracking and creaking sounds came from the bulging ceiling overhead, which supported all the weight of the fallen-in upper floors. It could all come down anytime. I knew that. I didn't care. I needed to know what had happened here; needed that more than life itself. It is possible . . . I wasn't entirely sane at that time.

I moved slowly down the dark hallway, through ruin and devastation, and forced myself to be calm and collected, practical and professional. Just from looking around me at the nature of the destruction, I could see they must have used grenades and flamethrowers. No other way to do this much damage in a hurry. Probably some magical and superscience weapons, as well. Someone had been intent on doing a really thorough job here.

I considered all the possibilities as I made my way down the hallway, broken floorboards groaning warnings under my weight. Molly was careful to keep distance between us, to spread the weight out as much as possible. Could there have been sabotage, or even an invasion of the family Armoury—our own weapons turned against us? It didn't seem likely. An enemy who'd planned such a thorough assault wouldn't have gambled on finding enough weapons here to do the job. They'd have brought their own. Could the enemy have teleported inside the Hall if all our shields were down? That would explain how they were able to take all of us by surprise so easily. Maybe even suicide bombers? So many possibilities, so many questions, and no answers anywhere. Molly stepped deftly over the rubble on the floor, looking at everything, touching nothing.

"There wasn't any damage out in the grounds," she said, after a while. "All the fighting took place indoors. Look at the bullet holes in these walls. And scorch marks from energy blasts, which implies energy weapons or offensive sorceries. Do you suppose . . . there could be any survivors, maybe trapped somewhere in the Hall?"

"No," I said. "We would have fought to the last man rather than let this happen to the Hall." I stopped abruptly, glancing about me, hands clenched into fists at my sides. "But you were right earlier. We can't afford to spend too long here. If all our defences are down, then the shields that hide our presence are down, too. The whole world can see exactly where Drood Hall is, for the first time, and that makes us vulnerable. The vultures will be gathering. They'll descend on us in their hordes to search for loot and overlooked secrets. But I can't leave, Molly. Not yet. I have to know. . . ."

"Of course you do," said Molly. "Every clue the enemy left behind is ammunition we can use to identify and then nail the bastards who did this."

I had to smile at her. "There was a time the Droods were your enemies. Not that long ago, you would have been overjoyed by all this. You'd have danced on these ruins. . . ."

"Danced, hell," said Molly. "I'd have hiked up my skirts and pissed on them, singing hallelujah. But that was then; this is now. Everything changed when I met you. Now an attack on your family is an attack on you. And no one messes with my man and gets away with it."

She struck a witch's pose, and her hands moved through a sinuous series of magical gestures. A slow presence gathered on the air around us and all the hairs stood up on the back of my neck. A sudden cold wind came gusting down the hallway, disturbing the ashes. Molly spoke a single Word, almost too much for human vocal cords to bear, and the echoes of it trembled and shuddered all through the enclosed space.

"There," said Molly, relaxing just a little. "I've put some temporary shields in place: a No See zone over the Hall and serious avoidance spells around the perimeter. Low-level stuff, easily broken by anyone who knows what they're looking for, but enough to buy us some time, so we can make a proper investigation. Where do you want to start, Eddie?"

I didn't thank her. It would only have embarrassed her.

I looked up and down the gloomy hallway. It was all so still, so quiet. The only sounds had been our careful footsteps and the quiet shifting noises of broken stone and brickwork. The ceiling made constant ominous noises as the collapsed upper floors settled and pressed down. There was still a little smoke, farther in, curling unhurriedly on the still air, and the odd cloud of soot and ashes drifting this way and that. Molly sneezed explosively, and I jumped despite myself. I looked at her reproachfully, and she stared haughtily down her nose at me, as though she'd meant to do it. She raised one hand and snapped her fingers imperiously. A sharp breeze blew in from the open doors and rushed down the hallway, dispersing the smoke and blowing away the soot and ashes. The breeze died away quickly, before it could disturb anything precarious.

Most of the interior walls had been riddled with gunfire and then smashed and burnt and blown apart. There were great holes in the old stonework, and the wood panelling had been almost completely burnt away by fierce heat. It was hard to find anything I recognised. The great statues and important works of art, the wall hangings and the family portraits: gone, all gone. I realised Molly had stopped to look up at the ceiling, and I followed her gaze, checking it quickly for spreading cracks.

"No," she said, without looking round. "It's just . . . our room was up there, on the top floor. Is it possible . . . ?"

"No," I said. "All the upper floors have fallen in on themselves.

There's not a few feet of roof left intact anywhere. Everything we had up there is gone."

"Everything you had," said Molly. "I kept most of my stuff in the woods. Oh, Eddie . . . I'm so sorry."

"It's just things," I said. "You can always get more things. What matters is I still have you."

"Forever and a day, my love," said Molly, slipping her arm through mine again and briefly resting her head on my shoulder.

We moved on into the gloom and the shadows. The sounds of our slow progress seemed to move ahead of us, as though to give warning we were coming. All the great paintings that used to line the walls, portraits and scenes of the family by all the great masters, were gone forever. Generations of Droods, great works of art preserved by the family for generations, reduced to ash, and less than ash. Even the frames were destroyed. Someone had swept the walls clean with incandescent fires, probably laughing as they did. I crouched down as I spotted a scrap of canvas caught between two pieces of rubble from a shattered statue. Molly peered over my shoulder.

"What is it, sweetie?"

"I think . . . this was a Botticelli," I said. "Just a few splashes of colour now, crumbling in my hand." I let it drop to the floor, and straightened up again. "Why would the enemy take time out from fighting the Droods to destroy so many important works of art? These paintings were priceless, irreplaceable. Why not . . . take them and sell them?"

"Because whoever did this was only interested in destruction and revenge," said Molly. "I used to be like that. I would have torched every painting in every museum in the world to get back at your family for killing my parents. The Droods have angered a lot of people in their time, Eddie. Sometimes hurting the one you hate can be far more important than profiting from them."

"Are you saying we deserved this? That we had it coming? That we brought all this on ourselves?"

"Of course not! I'm just making the point . . . that really angry people often don't stop to think logically."

"I liked the paintings," I said. "And there were photographs, too, towards the end of the corridor. A whole history of my family. And the only photograph I ever saw of my mother and my father . . . How am I ever going to remember what they looked like, with the only photo destroyed?"

"I don't have any photos of my parents," said Molly. "But I still think of them every day. You'll remember them."

We moved on. All the statues and sculptures had been blown apart or just smashed to pieces. So much concentrated rage . . . I couldn't even tell which piece was which from just looking at the scattered parts, though here and there I'd glimpse some familiar detail. The rich carpet that had stretched the whole length of the hallway was gone; just a charred and blackened mess that crunched under our feet.

It was like walking through the tomb of some lost civilisation and trying to re-create its original glory and grandeur from what small broken pieces remained.

"This wasn't just the side effects of fighting," I said, finally. "It isn't even vandalism, smashing things up for the fun of it. This was the complete destruction of everything we believed in and cared for. They wanted to rip out every memory, every meaning of Drood Hall. To spit in the face of our long tradition, and wipe it from the memory of the world. Our enemy wanted to make sure there would be nothing left to remember us by."

We moved on, out of the hallway and into what remained of the ground floor—through ragged spaces where doors or walls should have been, through wreckage and destruction, through what had been my home and refuge from the world—moving deeper and deeper into the Hall. Into my past. It didn't get any better. The destroyers had been very thorough. Finally I just stopped, weighed down by guilt and responsibility and the burden of memories. I'd spent so much of my younger life trying to escape from Drood Hall and my family and their hold over me, but I'd never wanted this. I might have dreamed it a few times, but I never really wanted it. . . . Molly looked at me impatiently.

"Where are we, Eddie? I don't recognise anything here."

"I don't know," I said. "I can't tell. I lived most of my life in this place. I knew all its rooms and corridors, all its nooks and crannies and secret hiding places, like the back of my hand, but now . . . I think we're in one of the open auditoriums where people could come to just sit and think, or drink tea and chat or simply rest their troubled souls for a while. Look at it now. . . ."

Sunlight streamed in through holes in the outer wall like slanting spotlights, full of listlessly turning dust motes. Ruin and rubble; shadows and darkness. Not one scrap or stick of furniture left intact. As though the enemy had taken time out from bloodshed and slaughter to go through here with sledgehammers, smashing everything that might have been useful or valuable or just pleasant to look at. Or even just fondly remembered by my family. Who could hate us this much? Even the wooden floor had been torn up and split apart, with jagged splinters sprouting up everywhere, as though some great vicious animal had chewed on it.

"What do you see, Eddie?" Molly said softly.

"I see scorch marks on the walls from energy blasts," I said steadily. "And a hell of a lot of bullet holes. A lot of fighting went on here, before they blew the place up and set fire to it. I wonder . . . how much blood there is under all this mess. From all those who fell here . . . I don't see any armoured bodies or enemy dead. Did they take them all with them when they left? I can see the enemy taking their own fallen, so as not to leave any clues as to their identity. But why take the Drood dead? I've seen only one golden body so far. The place should be littered with them. . . . And why was the armour melted like that? As though it had been hit by a nuclear blast?"

Molly didn't say anything. She knew I wasn't talking to her.

I turned and went quickly back the way we'd come, hurrying back to the front doorway and the armoured body lying there. I crouched down beside it, studying the gleaming golden surface thoughtfully. It was covered with great spiderwebs of cracks, as though from a series of unimaginable impacts. The golden metal had become scored and distorted in places, touched by some incredible heat. The arms were fused to the torso, the legs fused together. . . . And yet the armour, as a whole, was still intact. They hadn't broken through to reach the man inside. I tapped the blank featureless mask with a single knuckle, and the sound was soft, flat, dead.

"Can you override the torc?" said Molly. "Make the armour withdraw so we can see who this was?"

"No," I said. "Only the wearer has control over his torc. Basic security measure, in case of capture."

"Is there any chance he might be alive in there? Trapped, unconscious, maybe? The armour's damaged but it's still in one piece. It might have protected the wearer, preserved him. . . ."

"No," I said. "Thanks for the thought, but no. To damage the armour this thoroughly, the sheer force involved must have been horrific. The impact alone would have . . . I don't even want to think about the condition of the body inside this armour." I leaned in close to stare at my own distorted reflection in the featureless golden mask. "Who were you? Did I know you? Did you die bravely? Of course you did. You were a Drood."

We went back inside and I tried another direction. Still looking for something I couldn't put a name to. I knew only that I'd know it when I saw it. We rounded a corner and found ourselves facing a tall and very solid-looking door. Somehow still intact, somehow still standing firm and upright in its frame. The walls on either side were gone. Reduced to piles of rubble. I put one hand to the door and it just fell apart, crumbling and falling away, collapsing into sawdust. The doorframe still held its shape. I walked through it, into the room beyond. Most of the outer wall was missing, giving an almost uninterrupted view of the grounds outside. But there was still enough of the room left to stir an unexpected memory. The left-hand wall had shelves full of books with charred and fire-blacked spines. When I touched one, the whole row of books fell in on themselves, disintegrating and falling to the floor.

"Eddie, look at this."

I moved over to join Molly. She'd found a tall mirror on the right-hand wall. Completely untouched by the destruction all around it. In the mirror I hardly recognised the man standing beside Molly. I've been trained to be a field agent, trained to blend in anywhere and not be noticed, to look like no one in particular. The man before me looked damaged and angry and dangerous. Anyone sensible would run a mile from such a man. Molly was still a delicate china doll of a woman, with big bosoms, bobbed black hair, huge dark eyes and a mouth as red as sin itself. She looked as beautiful as ever to me, in her own eerie, threatening and subtly disturbing way. Right now she was looking at me . . . as though wondering where I'd come from.

I turned away from the reflection to look at Molly. I did my best to smile normally. "I know," I said. "But it's still me, Molly. You can have your Eddie back when this is all over."

"When will it be over, Eddie?"

"When everyone who had any hand in this is dead," I said.

I looked around the room. Something about it . . . troubled me.

"I think . . . I remember being here before when I was just a child. If this is the room I think it is. I would have been very small, maybe four or five years old. . . . I'd been brought here to meet my grandfather Arthur. Martha's first husband. I can't remember who brought me here, though. Isn't that odd? I'm pretty sure it wasn't Martha. I can remember being brought into this room and meeting Grandfather Arthur, but not who brought me here or why.

"Arthur Drood—he seemed very old to me then, though he couldn't have been more than fifty or sixty. I remember he poured himself a cup of tea but it was too hot to drink, so he poured some of it into the saucer to cool it and sipped his tea from the saucer. Yes. I thought that was a great trick, and demanded to be allowed to try some. He smiled and offered me the saucer, and I took a sip, but I didn't like it. I pulled a face, and everyone laughed. Who laughed? Who else was in the room with me? Why can't I remember them? As though I'm not supposed to, not allowed to . . ."

"Wait a minute," said Molly. "Hold everything. Go previous. I thought you said your grandfather Arthur died back in the fifties. You weren't even born then."

"That's right," I said, frowning. "He died in 1957, in the Kiev Conspiracy."

"What was that?" said Molly. "Some old Cold War thing? Well before my time. And yours."

"I don't know," I said. I was frowning so hard it hurt my forehead. There was something I couldn't quite remember, something just out of my reach. Something important. "I don't know the details of how he died. No one ever told me. It was just . . . 1957, and the Kiev Conspiracy. Why did I never ask more about that? Why did I just accept it? I never used to accept anything they just told me. . . . But I am sure I've been here, in this room, before. . . ."

And then the ceiling came crashing down on us. No warning, not a sound; the ceiling just bulged suddenly out above us and then broke apart, everything coming down on our heads at once. I subvocalised my activating Words and called for my armour, but nothing happened. The armour didn't come. I froze where I was. I couldn't believe it. Molly threw an arm around me and thrust her other hand up at the descending ceiling. She said a very bad Word, and a shimmering protective shield appeared around us. The broken ceiling fell down, hit the shield and fell away, unable to touch us. The whole room shook as the entire ceiling came down in heavy chunks and pieces, followed by parts of the compressed floors above. Molly grabbed my arm and hauled me through the doorframe and out into the corridor. The shield came with us, still protecting us. Safely outside the room, Molly held me close as smoke and dust billowed out of the room after us. The room was filling up with wreckage from above, hammering loudly together as though annoyed it had missed its chance at us.

Molly dismissed the shimmering shield with an impatient wave of her hand and looked at me anxiously.

"Eddie? Are you okay? What happened in there?"

I raised a trembling hand to the golden torc at my throat. It was still there. It felt warm and alive, just like always. So why hadn't my armour come when I called it?

"How long?" I said numbly to Molly. "How long have I been walking around with a useless torc at my throat? How long have I been naked and defenceless in the face of my enemies?"

"Eddie, take it easy. . . ."

"You don't understand!" I shouted at her. "I've never been separated from my armour! It's been with me my whole life, in one form or another. First from the Heart and then from Ethel . . . How can I be a Drood if I don't have my armour?"

And just like that I was off and running, ignoring Molly as she called out behind me. I sprinted down rubble-strewn corridors, jumped over piles of collapsed brickwork, ignoring the angry sounds of shifting stonework all around me and heading for the one place in the Hall where I thought I might still find some answers. The one room you could always count on. The Sanctity. The heart of the Hall and of the family. I raced down broken corridors that were little more than death traps of holed floors and collapsed walls, staring straight ahead, thinking of nothing but where I needed to be. Running so hard my leg muscles ached, so fast I could barely get my breath. I could hear Molly running behind me, calling after me, but I didn't look back once. After a while she just concentrated on running and keeping up with me. I like to think it was because she trusted me to know what I was doing.

I ran on, and sometimes I ran through corridors that were there, and sometimes down corridors I remembered that were whole and undamaged. Sometimes I ran through memories of places and people, with ghosts of old friends and enemies. And sometimes I think I ran through rooms and corridors that weren't there anymore. Until finally I came to the Sanctity.

The great double doors had been smashed open and were hanging drunkenly, scarred and broken, from the heavy brass hinges. There should have been guards, Drood security; there should have been powerful protections in place. But they were just doors leading into a room. I stood there before them for a while, bent over and breathing harshly, trying to force some air back into my straining lungs. My back and my legs ached and sweat dripped down from my face. I could hear Molly catching up, but I didn't look back. I straightened myself up through sheer force of will and strode forward into the Sanctity, slamming the doors back out of my way with both hands. I didn't even feel the impact.

Inside the great open chamber, the walls stood upright and untouched and the ceiling was free from signs of assault or damage. The marble floor was dusty but unmarked. As though the enemy had never come here. But still the damage had been done. The great auditorium was empty, deserted; just a room. There was no trace of the marvellous rose red light that usually suffused the chamber when Ethel was manifesting her presence. The light that could soothe and rejuvenate the most hard-used spirit. Ethel, the other-dimensional entity I'd brought to the Hall to replace the corrupt Heart . . . to be a new source of power for the Drood family. A source of new, strange matter armour.

"Ethel!" I said her name as loudly as I could, so harshly I hurt my throat. My voice echoed in the great open chamber and then died reluctantly away. There was no response. "Ethel?" I said, and even to me my voice sounded like that of a small child asking for its mother. I stood alone in the Sanctity and no one answered me. I heard Molly behind me, at the door, but I didn't look around.

"If she was anywhere, anywhere in the Hall, she'd hear and answer you," said Molly. "You know that. She's gone, Eddie. Gone, like everyone else."

"If she were anywhere in the world, she'd hear me," I said. "No wonder my armour's gone."

"I can't believe there is anyone or anything in this world that could destroy or even damage an other-dimensional entity like Ethel," said Molly, moving cautiously forward to stand beside me, careful not to touch me. "Except perhaps another other-dimensional entity, and what are the odds of that?"

"They could have driven her away," I said. I felt empty. "Forced her back out of this world. With all the Droods dead, what reason would she have to stay? And if she's gone, so is the source of our armour. No more Drood armour, forever. Perhaps that's why she chose to leave—so our enemies couldn't force or coerce her into giving them her strange matter. Maybe . . . that's why we've only seen one armoured corpse. Because she took the rest of her strange matter with her when she left. After all, the Droods were dead."

"Then why have you still got your torc?" said Molly.

My hand rose to touch the golden collar at my throat again, and then I shook my head slowly. "So many questions; so few answers. How can I be a Drood, the Last Drood, without my armour?"

"You still have your knowledge and your training," said Molly, practical as ever. She moved forward so she could look me in the face. "I know you're going through a lot, Eddie, but if you don't snap out if this fast and start acting like yourself again, I am going to slap you a good one and it will hurt."

A smile twitched at the corner of my mouth. "You would, too. Wouldn't you?"

"Damn right I would," Molly said briskly. "You still have all your experience, all your old contacts . . . there's still a lot you can do in the world. Though getting your hands on some really big guns probably wouldn't hurt, either. Is there any chance you could get us into the family Armoury? See if anything useful got left behind?"

"Of course," I said. "Large parts of the Hall have always been underground. And heavily shielded and protected. If only to protect the rest of the family from what they did down there. The attackers might not have known about the underground installations or how to access them. Maybe they survived intact. . . ."

"And maybe there are survivors down there," said Molly.

"You've always been such an optimist," I said. "One of the things I've always admired most about you."

So we went down.

I started with the War Room. It lay underneath the North Wing, or what was left of it. Access was only possible through a heavily reinforced steel door. I found the door easily enough underneath the shattered ground floor. The door was still intact, but it was standing partly open. The facial-recognition computers and retina-scan mechanisms had all been smashed. Very thoroughly. Not a good sign. I eased through the gap between the steel door and its frame and started down the very basic stairway beyond, carved out of the right-hand wall itself. Molly stuck close behind me. There was no railing, and only a intimidatingly deep and dark drop on the other side. Most of the overhead electric lights weren't working, and those that did flickered unreliably.

Molly and I descended the steep stairway, pressing our shoulders against the stone wall to keep us away from the long drop. Getting to the War Room wasn't meant to be easy. I wasn't sensing any of the usual force shields and magical screens that should have protected the area from unwanted visitors. Usually they felt like static crawling all over my skin, like unseen eyes watching your back with bad intent. I felt nothing, nothing at all. I looked briefly out over the long drop, and nothing looked back.

There was no sign of any of the goblins who usually stood watch over the stairway, peering out from their comfortable niches in the stone wall. All their little caverns were empty, with not a trace remaining to show they'd ever been inhabited. No bodies. No sign of any struggle. But as we went down into the dark, spatters of dried blood began to appear on the steps below us. And all over the stone wall. By the time we got to the bottom, dried blood was splashed everywhere.

At the entrance to the War Room, the electric hand scanners had been torn out and smashed, the pieces and fragments lying scattered all over the floor. And the entire entrance door was just . . . gone. I made Molly stand back while I stepped cautiously into the War Room. There was supposed to be a real live gorgon sitting just inside the door, doing penance for a very old crime against the family, ready to do something nasty and petrifying to anybody who dared enter the War Room without permission . . . but there was no trace of the gorgon anywhere. Just a few scattered stone pieces on the floor that might have been a shattered human statue or two. I gave Molly the all clear, and she shot straight past me into the War Room, glaring fiercely about her. She hates being left out of things.

The War Room was a vast auditorium carved out of the solid

bedrock underneath the Hall. All four walls were covered with massive state-of-the-art display screens showing every country in the world. But whereas normally they would have been covered with different-coloured lights showing what was happening in the world and what we were doing about it, now the screens were dead and blank and silent. The whole system was down.

I followed Molly into the War Room, looking dazedly about me while she darted from one workstation to the next, looking for something she could use. The whole room was empty, deserted, silent; the computers had all been broken open and torn apart. The scrying spheres had been smashed and cracked, all the tables and chairs had been overturned and everything useful or important had been very thoroughly trashed. There were no bullet holes here, no signs of energy-weapon fire, but there was a hell of a lot of blood splashed over everything and pooled on the bare stone floor.

A lot of people had died down here, but there wasn't a single body to be seen anywhere. Drood or otherwise.

Molly and I checked out the workstations methodically until we found one computer that was in somewhat better condition than the others. We couldn't get it working, so Molly just zapped the thing with some kind of spell to make it give up the last thing it had been working on. I've never understood how she gets magic to work on scientific things, and I have enough sense not to ask. I'm sure the answer would only upset me. The computer's last memory appeared on a cracked monitor screen. It showed Droods jumping up from their workstations, startled, as someone opened fire on them. Bodies were thrown this way and that, blasted right out of their workstations. Blood flew on the air and bodies crashed to the floor. There were shouts and screams. None of the Droods armoured up. There was just bloodshed and slaughter, and computer stations exploding as they were raked with gunfire. And then the computer shut down and the monitor went blank.

Molly called the last few images back to the monitor screen, goosing the thing with magical sparks when it tried to cut out on her.

"Look at this, Eddie. According to what this screen is reluctantly showing us . . . all the Hall's weapon systems and defences were off-line. Shut down before the attack. This has to be sabotage, Eddie; the work of the traitor inside the family. I'm sorry; I know you don't want to hear this, but it's the only way this could have happened."

"Callan was in charge here," I said. "I didn't see him on the screen. I can't believe all the defence systems could have gone off-line at once without his noticing. Unless . . . someone arranged for him to be distracted. Called away. So he wouldn't be here when this went down." I looked around the silent, deserted War Room. "Still no bodies. You saw my family die on that screen. So why isn't there a single Drood body anywhere in this room?"

"Maybe they took your family away as prisoners," said Molly. "Ethel was gone, so they didn't have their armour. . . . Maybe your family just did the sensible thing and surrendered?"

"I suppose that's . . . possible," I said. "Droods stripped of their armour would have been in shock, especially after an attack like this. Some of them might have been captured."

"So some of your family could still be alive somewhere!" said Molly.

"Why would our enemies want prisoners, if they hate us so much?"

"Don't be naive, sweetie. For information. Droods know things no one else does. Everyone knows that."

"They could have got far more information from the computers," I said. "And our enemies went out of their way to destroy them. No. The whole point of this . . . was to destroy the Droods forever. To take us completely off the board."

"You can hope, though, can't you?"

"We always say about the bad guys: If you don't have the body, they're probably not really dead. Maybe that works for the good guys, too. If there are any survivors, Molly, if there are any members of my family left alive anywhere . . . I will find them."

We went back up and worked our way through the fallen Hall to what was left of the South Wing. To the Operations Room, a high-tech centre set up to oversee all the Hall's defences and protect the family from . . . things like this. Once again the door was standing open, revealing a reasonably-sized room full of computer systems and work-stations . . . usually run by a cadre of specially trained technicians, under the head of ops, Howard. He wasn't there. Neither was anyone else. Everything in the room had been smashed to pieces with great thoroughness. Someone wanted to make sure that not one of these systems could ever be repaired or re-created. No way of telling whether anyone here had known the defences were off-line until it was far too late. There was a hell of a lot of blood, but no bodies.

I made my way carefully through the wreckage, looking for something to give me hope. Molly stuck close beside me, watching my back and comforting me with her presence. And at the very back of the room we found the little surprise the enemy had left for us, or for anyone else who came looking, to find. Twelve roughly severed heads set on spikes. Six male, six female. From the expressions on their faces, none of them had died well. Some were still silently screaming for help that never came. I studied the faces carefully but I didn't recognise any of them. I can't say whether that made it easier or harder to bear. I knelt down and closed the wildly staring eyes, one set at a time. Because I had to do something. There were no torcs at any of the raggedly cut necks.

The smell was pretty bad.

"Did you know any of them?" said Molly.

"No," I said. "But then, it's a big family. You can't know everyone. Howard isn't here."

"Why leave the heads like this?" said Molly. "As a warning to anyone who came looking? Or just to mark their territory, the bastards?"

"It's a sign of contempt," I said. "To tell everyone that the Droods are nothing to be feared anymore. Well, they got that wrong. I'm still here. I will find who did this. I will kill them all, and they will die hard and die bloody. And for that I'm going to need weapons."

And so we went down again, into the family Armoury, set deep and deep beneath the West Wing. Except when I cleared the rubble away from the floor that should have held the entrance to the Armoury approach . . . it wasn't there. I stared down at the bare dusty floor-boards, which had clearly never been disturbed, and then looked around to make sure I was in the right room. But even with all the damage and destruction, I had no doubt I was in the right place. The entrance should have been here, but it wasn't and clearly never had been. I didn't know what to think.

The Armoury has always been in the same place ever since the family set it down below the Hall, centuries ago. Right down in the bedrock under the West Wing, as far away from the family as they could get, to protect the rest of us from the weapons development and explosives testing that went on every day, and the inevitable unexpected side effects produced by lab assistants with a whole lot of scientific curiosity and not nearly enough self-preservation instincts. Impossible.

I had to search through three other rooms to find a trapdoor in the floor that to my certain knowledge hadn't been there before. I kicked the last of the rubble aside, leaned over the steel-banded wooden square and studied it thoughtfully for a long moment, ignoring the threatening creaks and groans from the ceiling overhead. Molly stirred uneasily at my side.

"This room is trying to tell us something, Eddie, and I'm pretty sure *Get the hell out of here while you still can* would be a fairly accurate translation."

"Hell with that," I said. "It's taken long enough, but I think I've finally found a clue. There's no way I could be wrong about how you get down into the family Armoury. I've been sneaking down there to pester Uncle Jack since I was ten years old."

"Maybe they made a new entrance while you were gone," said Molly, moving quickly sideways to avoid a stream of dust falling from the ceiling. "Maybe they blew up the old one."

"I haven't been gone that long," I said. "You couldn't rush a major change like that through the Works Committee in less than a twelve-month. You don't know what bureaucracy is until you've been part of a family that's been around for centuries."

"But the trapdoor is intact," said Molly. "Which would suggest . . ."

"Yes," I said. "It would."

I grabbed the heavy iron ring set into the top of the wooden trapdoor and hauled it open with an effort. It started to slam backwards onto the floor, and Molly and I grabbed it at the last moment and lowered it carefully down. More dust was falling in thick streams from the ceiling, and I was getting a strong feeling that one good slam might be enough to bring the whole thing down. Once, I wouldn't have given a damn, but not having my armour was making me cautious. The trapdoor opening revealed an unfamiliar set of stone steps leading down into gloom. Old, scuffed steps, polished smooth by much hard use. The stairs had clearly been there a long time. I led the way down, with Molly treading close on my heels and peering over my shoulder. I was just as fascinated as she was. We were in new territory now, and for the first time I began to wonder if things really were as they appeared to be.

The stairs gave entrance to the Armoury, which looked exactly as I remembered it. The family had set up its Armoury in what used to be, centuries earlier, the old wine cellars. The heavy, specially reinforced blast-proof door was intact, but once again it hung partway open. I squeezed through the gap between the door and the frame, with Molly pressing so close behind me that she was breathing heavily down my neck.

The lights flickered on as we entered the Armoury proper. It's really just a long series of interconnected stone chambers with bare plastered walls, curved ceilings high above, and mile upon mile of multicoloured wiring tacked carelessly into place across the walls, crisscrossing in patterns that may or may not have meant something to somebody at some time. All the overhead fluorescent lights were working, but I realised immediately that I couldn't hear the usual strained sounds of the air-conditioning. The air was stale, but there was no smell of smoke or sign of fire damage.

"I don't see any signs of a firefight," said Molly, looking quickly about her. "No bullet holes, no energy burns or anything more extreme to suggest the people here fought back . . ."

"No," I said. "But there has been a hell of a lot of looting. Look at all the gaps. . . . I'm not seeing half the things I should be seeing. No computers, no weapons. Even the shooting range is empty. It's all so quiet. . . .

I don't think I've ever heard the Armoury this quiet before. There was always something going on; Uncle Jack or his assistants working on some new way to blow themselves and everybody else up. It's eerie. . . ."

I walked slowly between deserted workstations and abandoned testing grounds that should have been full of loud noises and general excitement as Uncle Jack's technicians happily risked their own lives and others' testing appalling new weapons of mass disturbance. Nothing had been destroyed in the Armoury, unlike in the War Room or the Operations Room, but the enemy had stripped the place clean. They hadn't been interested in precious pieces of art that would have sold for millions, but state-of-the-art weapons? Those were different. I checked everywhere, but there were no golden-armoured bodies, no heads on spikes, not even a splash of dried blood. A few things had been overturned here and there, but no signs of any struggle. Which was just . . . wrong. No matter what the odds or the threats, Uncle Jack and his lab rats would have fought to the last to keep the Armoury out of the hands of our enemies. Hell, Uncle Jack would have blown the whole place up before he'd risk letting Drood weapons fall into the wrong hands. So why didn't he?

I stopped and looked about me in frustration. "This would have broken Uncle Jack's heart," I said finally. "To see his precious Armoury stripped bare . . ."

Molly nodded understandingly. "The Armoury was always his pride and joy. Eddie, the information in his head would have made him invaluable. Do you think . . . ?"

"I don't know," I said. "I don't know what to think anymore. Hello. What's this?"

I knelt down beside a workstation. Something had caught my eye, but I wasn't sure what. It turned out to be a small black blob on the floor. Molly crouched down beside me, looked at the blob and then looked at me.

"All right; I'll bite. What's so significant about a small black blobby thing? What is it?"

"It's a portable door," I said. "Uncle Jack used to hand them out like travel-sickness pills to every agent going out in the field. Just slap one of these against any flat surface, and hey, presto! Instant door!"

"So why did he stop handing them out?" said Molly, instantly cautious.

"Something about unacceptable side effects," I said, weighing the blob in my hand. "And if the Armourer thought they were unacceptable . . . This must have been overlooked."

"Take it anyway," said Molly. "We're going to need all the help we can get."

"Damn right, I'm taking it," I said. I slipped the thing into my pocket, straightened up and looked around me. "It's useful, but it's not a weapon. I want something that goes *bang!* in a horribly destructive and disturbing way."

And then my head snapped round suddenly as a Voice said *Eddie!* I looked back and forth, but there was no one else in the Armoury. I looked at Molly.

"Tell me you heard that, too."

"Of course I heard it! Someone said your name in a seriously spooky way. But I scanned the whole place before we came in here, and I am telling you we're the only ones here. No other life signs anywhere, and that includes lab specimens. So who . . . Wait a minute. Wait a minute. I'm getting something. . . ."

She moved slowly between the empty workstations, turning her head back and forth, scowling fiercely as she searched for something she could sense but not see. I was concentrating on the Voice. It had definitely sounded familiar but I couldn't place it. I knew I'd heard someone call me by my name in just that tone of voice before, but . . . Molly stopped suddenly before a pile of junk on the floor and cried out triumphantly. She knelt down and stuck both hands into the pile before I could stop her, and pulled out the Merlin Glass. She jumped up to show it to me, brandishing the small silver-backed hand mirror.

"Result! This is more like it, Eddie!"

"Could you please stop waving it around so . . . heartily," I said carefully. "That is a very powerful and very dangerous object, and this is the

Armoury, after all. The Glass was worrying enough as it was, before it got broken in Castle Shreck, and God alone knows what state it's in now after Uncle Jack's been tinkering with it."

Molly sniffed airily but wasted no time in pressing the Glass into my hands. I accepted it cautiously and looked it over. The Glass had been created for the Drood family by Merlin Satanspawn, way back in the day, and it had many useful properties. But it had been very badly damaged during the Drood assault on the Immortals at Castle Shreck, to the point where it didn't work at all anymore. The reflective surface had been cracked from side to side, and given that a whole lot of people thought there might be something or even someone trapped within the reflection, I made a point of handing the damaged mirror over to the Armourer first chance I got, with strict instructions to drop it somewhere secure, like a black hole, if he couldn't mend the thing and make it safe to use. Frankly, I'd never expected to see the thing again.

But here it was, back in my hand. And completely uncracked. The Glass was clear and unmarked, as though it had never seen any damage at all. . . .

"I didn't know the Merlin Glass could speak," Molly said doubtfully. "Let alone call out to you."

"Maybe it never had anything to say before," I said. "But this is a magical instrument, after all, made by Merlin himself."

"You said the mirror was cracked. Now it isn't. Could it have repaired itself?"

"Who knows?" I said. "I don't think anyone in the family knows for sure anymore why Merlin gave the Glass to us in the first place. Or what it was supposed to do. I never did get around to reading all the instructions Uncle Jack wrote out for me. I have to say . . . I don't think the Armourer did this. I mean, he's good, yes, but he's no Merlin Satanspawn."

I hefted the hand mirror thoughtfully, turning it back and forth and checking every detail. Something about it didn't look right, didn't feel right. I'd held it often enough, used it often enough, to know that

the weight and heft of it in my hand now was subtly, unnervingly different. Wrong. I said as much to Molly.

"Are you sure?" she said immediately. "I mean, it has been repaired.
There are bound to be some differences. . . ."

"It's not that. I've handled the bloody thing often enough to know
that something's not right about it! It's never something you just take
for granted; with an artefact this powerful, it's like juggling a live hand
grenade every time you use it."

I turned the hand mirror over and studied the design on the back.
The silver scrollwork was definitely different. I showed it to Molly, and
she traced the raised edges with a fingertip.

"There's some kind of inscription worked into the design, but I'm
damned if I can make head or tail of it," she said finally. "Not Celtic,
not Sumerian . . . not Kandarian or Enochian . . . It is vaguely familiar,
but I can't get my head around it."

"The design has changed," I said. "But I couldn't tell you how."

"Put it away for now," said Molly. "It's enough that we've got it and
the enemy missed it. We're here to look for weapons. Remember?"

I slipped the Merlin Glass into the special pocket dimension I keep
in one of my jacket pockets. I always like to have somewhere secure
about me to store dangerous things. If only so I can get at them quickly
in an emergency and throw them at other people. I breathed a little
more easily with the Merlin Glass safely stored away, and looked at Molly.

"Speaking of horribly powerful things that the world is undoubt-
edly better off without . . . I've been thinking about the Forbidden
Weapons. I need to be sure they're still secure within the Armageddon
Codex."

Molly looked at me sharply. "You don't really think the enemy could
have got into that. Do you?"

"I don't know what to think anymore," I said. "But given that we are
talking about weapons so powerful my family locked them away, only to
be used when reality itself is under threat . . ."

"We should take a look," said Molly.

So I led the way, to the very far end of the Armoury, to the final and very off-limits stone chamber. The Armageddon Codex is kept in a very private, very separate pocket dimension, for maximum security. To get to it you have to pass through the Lion's Jaws—a giant stone carving of a lion's snarling head, complete with mane, perfect in every detail. Not stylised in any way, it looks like the real thing, only some twenty feet tall and almost as wide. The Lion's Jaws are carved out of a dark, blue-veined stone, so long ago that no one now remembers who did the work. It's a lion to the life; the eyes seem to glare, the mouth seems to snarl and the whole thing seems ready to lunge forward at any moment and have your head off. To open the Codex, you have to pass through the Jaws, and if you don't have the proper clearances . . . at best, they won't open. Rumour has it that if you so much as put your hand in the Lion's Jaws and you're not pure of heart, the Jaws will bite your hand right off. The Armourer had assured me that this was just a story to keep young Droods from messing with the thing for a dare, but I wasn't sure I believed him. The Lion's Jaws always looked hungry.

"You want to try opening it?" said Molly, who knew no fear.

"I don't have the key."

"Who needs a key when you have me?"

"No, Molly," I said very firmly. "I'm not doing anything that might upset it without the Armourer present. He's the only one who knows the correct Words to access the Codex. I just need you to use your magics to make sure no one's pressured him into opening it. Make sure the Jaws are still closed and the seals haven't been compromised. You can do that, can't you?"

Molly sniffed loudly and gave me a withering glare, which wasn't actually an answer. She struck a witchy pose, ran her hands through a series of smooth mystical gestures, and muttered meaningfully under her breath. I'm pretty sure a lot of it was just for show, to make a point, but I had enough sense not to ask. Molly stopped abruptly and shook her head firmly.

"The Jaws are still firmly closed. No one's even tried to open them. And if you could See the layers upon layers of protections laid down on this thing, you wouldn't try to open it, either. This is some seriously strong shit, Eddie. If the enemy had tried to force their way in, or even just meddle with the seals, all that would be left of them would be a series of greasy stains on the floor here."

"Good to know," I said. "All that matters is that the Armageddon Codex is secure."

"Yes, but we can't get to them, either!" said Molly. "The weapons of the Codex are lost forever! No more Oath Breaker, Winter's Sorrow, the Time Hammer and the Juggernaut Jumpsuit! The most powerful weapons in the world . . . Just think what we could have done with them!"

"Exactly," I said. "The mood I'm in, I couldn't be trusted with them. I would blow the world apart, if that was the only way of taking my enemy down. No. It's better this way. With the Armourer . . . gone, no one can get to them. I think the world will be just that little bit safer, with the Armageddon Codex locked away forever. It's enough . . . that our enemies don't have them."

Molly pouted. "You're just no fun sometimes. . . ."

I patted the Lion's Jaws fondly with one hand, and then a sudden blast of energy threw me backwards. Molly caught me before I could fall, while a great Voice said *Eddie! Eddie! Eddie!* Molly moved quickly to stand between me and the Lion's Jaws, shielding me with her body, her hands surrounded by flaring energies. And then she stopped and lowered her sputtering hands, as a vision appeared before us. A middle-aged man in a white lab coat, looking seriously at both of us. A message from out of the Past. I could tell at once that it was just a recording; the vision was dim, fading in and out and ragged round the edges . . . but when it spoke, the Voice was perfectly clear. By touching the Lion's Jaws with a Drood hand, I'd triggered a hidden message from the Armourer. My heart actually leapt for a moment at the thought that finally someone was going to tell me what had happened here. And then I looked again, at the man in the lab coat, and I realised it wasn't going to be that simple.

The man before me was clearly the Armourer, but it wasn't my uncle Jack. It was my uncle James.

At first I almost didn't recognise him. Uncle James had always been the finest field agent the Droods ever produced. So successful he'd created his own legend apart from the family. In good places and bad, in villains' hideouts and disreputable bars, at the highest levels and in filthy back alleyways, they all knew his name: the Grey Fox. Tall and dark and handsome and always smartly dressed, my uncle James walked up and down the hidden world, writing the secret histories that the rest of the world is better off not knowing about. Keeping the world safe, one day at a time. The best of the best. Until he turned against what the family was supposed to represent and stand for, and Molly and I had to kill him. My favourite uncle, James had been almost a father to me. But he would have killed me in that last vicious duel if Molly hadn't got to him first with the Torc Cutter.

He looked a very different man as the Armourer. His lab coat was impeccably white and clean, which was more than Uncle Jack had ever managed, but James looked tired and stooped. He looked . . . older. More weighed down by long service and hard grind and responsibilities he could never trust to anyone else. His hair, which had always been proudly jet-black for as long as I had known him, was mostly grey now. His eyes were deep set, and heavy lines had been driven deep into his face. This Uncle James had known hard times, and it showed. He seemed to look straight at me as he spoke, and his manner was harsh and strained, as though he knew he didn't have much time left.

"Eddie, you're here at last. About time, boy. I'm leaving this message for you because . . . there's no one else. Listen to me, Eddie, for once in your life. We have been betrayed by one of our own. The Hall's defences are down, the Hall is under siege and the family is under attack. Our ancient enemies have finally brought us down. Avenge us! The Immortals can't be allowed to get away with this!"

Molly started to say something when he used that name, but I shushed her fiercely. I needed to concentrate on what Uncle James was trying to tell me.

"The Matriarch Penelope is dead, along with her husband, Nicholas. Jack is out there somewhere, organising what defences we have left. He always was the best field agent this family ever produced. I've sent my lab assistants out to back him up, armed with whatever we had lying around, but the odds are I'll never see them or Jack again. They took our armour away from us, Eddie. Sabotaged us from within. I can't even activate the self-destruct systems for the Armoury. I've destroyed the key to the Lion's Jaws; I can do that much. At least now they'll never get their hands on the Forbidden Weapons. But they'll probably get everything else."

He stopped for a moment and then smiled at me. "All these years in the Armoury, producing weapon after weapon for the family to use to bring down the world's enemies . . . and in the end it's one of our own that's brought about our ending. There's no way out for me. All that's left . . . is to die fighting and deny the Immortals as much as I can. I don't know where you are right now, Eddie. We tried for so long to find you and bring you home. We should never have driven you out, driven you away. . . . I don't know where you've gone to ground, but you must have dug yourself a really deep hole if even the Heart can't find you. . . . Listen to me, Eddie. Please. If you're listening to this, odds are you're the only one of us to survive. The Last Drood. The Immortals have made it very clear they're not interested in taking prisoners. Just . . . bodies, for dissection. I'm asking you, begging you, to forget the Past, forget everything that came between us, and do whatever you have to do . . . to avenge the family and bring down our enemies: the Immortals. Don't let those bastards win."

The image disappeared abruptly, and a cold deathly silence fell across the Armoury. Tears burnt my eyes. He wasn't my uncle James, but he was close enough. His words tore at my heart. Why wasn't I there when they needed me? I realised Molly was all but jumping up and down at my side, and turned to look at her.

"What?"

"Don't you get it, Eddie? This wasn't your family! This isn't your Hall! This is some other Drood Hall, from some other dimension! And that means your family and your Hall are Somewhere Else, probably safe and alive!"

"I had worked that out for myself," I said. "So many of the details in what he said were wrong. . . . No wonder the entrance to the Armoury wasn't where it should have been."

"Is that all you've got to say? Your family is still alive! All this happened to some other family!"

"They were still Droods," I said. "And that was still my uncle James. I may never have known the Droods who lived in this Hall, but they looked a lot like people I did know."

"I didn't know them," said Molly, practical as ever. "Concentrate on what matters, Eddie!"

"Yes," I said. "My family is still alive somewhere. Finding them and bringing them home has to take precedence. Vengeance can wait."

Molly shook her head in exasperation. "Sometimes I really don't understand you, Eddie. All this time we've been grieving, under the belief that everyone you knew was dead. Now you find out they're still alive. . . . Don't you feel anything?"

I laughed then, grabbed her in my arms and whirled her around, roaring my happiness so loud it hurt my throat. Molly whooped and cheered in my arms, tilting back her head to yell out loud along with me, then hugging me so tight I could barely breathe. After a while we both calmed down and I put her down again, and we leaned tiredly on each other till we got our breath back. I grinned at Molly.

"This is still very sad," I said. "A whole other family of Droods has been butchered and their Hall destroyed. But that can wait. My family is out there somewhere, and it's up to me to track them down."

"Such a different family," said Molly. "So many differences in such a short message. They had a whole different history from you. . . . But what is their Hall doing here, in our world?"

"It all comes down to the dimensional engine, Alpha Red Alpha," I said. "Has to. That damned machine was created to be used only as a last-ditch dcfcncc. To save the Hall in a time of crisis, by rotating it out of this dimension, this Earth, and dropping it down in some other dimension, some other Earth, where it could wait safely until the threat here was over. The Armourer, our Armourer, told me that the first and only time it was used before, the Hall ended up materialising in some utterly alien Earth, surrounded by a whole jungle of vicious killer plants. They were lucky to get back alive. That's why Alpha Red Alpha was never used again, until I persuaded my family to wake it up, to give us access to Castle Shreck in the Timeless Moment. What's happened here has to be the result of our using Alpha Red Alpha. . . ."

"Okay, hold the lecture. I get it," said Molly. "How about this: Someone found a way to override the machine from outside, and use it to send the Hall somewhere else. And this Hall, this other Hall, was rotated here to take its place. It was vulnerable because all its shields were down! Whoever's behind this . . . must have seen it as the perfect way to get rid of your family and cover up what they'd done! No one would even think your family was missing, with this ruined Hall to look at. Even you wouldn't have known if you hadn't accidentally activated that recording."

"At least Uncle James was still alive in that family," I said. "We didn't kill him there. Maybe . . . because we never met in that world? It was good to see him, to hear his voice again. . . ."

"Life is too short to sweat the small shit," Molly said briskly. "Given a potentially infinite number of other dimensions, an infinite number of choices and outcomes is always going to be possible. If it comforts you to think of that two-faced, treacherous bastard being still alive somewhere else, feel free to do so. After everything that man did and would have done to you, I don't give a rat's arse. We're all alive, we're all dead and everything in between, on the Wheels of If and Maybe."

"Strangely, I don't feel at all comforted," I said. "You're weird sometimes, Molly."

She shrugged. "Just trying to be helpful."

"So," I said. "Questions . . . Where is my family now? And who was responsible for their . . . abduction? And if they are trapped in . . . some other place, how can I find and rescue them and bring them home? We need information, Molly. And where better to find that than in a library?"

Molly laughed and clapped her hands together. "Or, more exactly, an old library! The secret, carefully hidden and very thoroughly protected

Old Library! Do you suppose this family even knows it exists? Your family didn't until you found it for them."

"Let's go take a look," I said.

We found the official Drood Library easily enough and exactly where it should be, but there wasn't much left of it. The door had been broken in, and all the shelves were empty. Ransacked, stripped clean. The Immortals had done their best to torch the place when they left, but the flames hadn't taken much of a hold. Molly and I walked between smoke-blackened and half-charred wooden stacks, with the blackened and twisted remains of unwanted books left lying here and there on the floor. But finally, right at the far end of the library, there it was: hanging untouched on the wall, protected by ancient and unsuspected defences, a very old painting of the Old Library. I let go of a breath I hadn't realised I'd been holding as I saw the flames hadn't even touched the portrait.

"There is an especially hot place in Hell for people who burn books," said Molly.

"You'd know," I said generously.

It was a good-sized painting, eight feet high and maybe five feet wide, the bright and vivid colours seeming to glow in the gloom of the burnt-out library. Centuries old, artist unknown, the portrait depicted a view of the fabled Old Library. The original repository of all Drood knowledge, long thought lost or even destroyed until I found it. I took a key out of a special inside pocket. A key my uncle Jack had given me.

"Will that key fit this portrait?" said Molly. "There are differences between this world and ours, after all."

"Only one way to find out," I said. "If they key doesn't work, there's always thc Merlin Glass."

"Not too sure about that, either," sniffed Molly.

"You want a slap, girl? I've got one right here in my pocket. . . ."

Molly batted her eyelashes at me. "Later, sweetie . . . You know I've got to be in the right mood for a spanking. . . ."

I laughed despite myself and leaned forward to study the silver scallops that lined the rigid steel frame enclosing the portrait. And sure enough, there it was: a very small keyhole hidden in the details of the silver scrollwork. I eased the key into the lock, turned it carefully and then relaxed as I felt the mechanism turn. I pulled out the key, and just like that the painting before us was no longer canvas and paint and a work of art, but an actual view. A doorway into the Old Library.

It was dark and gloomy in there, with not a light to be seen anywhere. This Hall's family had never found their Old Library. Molly conjured up some witchlight, a cheerful golden glow that surrounded her hand as she held it up. The light shined out into the Old Library, challenging the shadows and pushing back the gloom before us. I stepped carefully over the frame of the portrait and into the Old Library. Molly was right there with me, holding her glowing hand high above her head. The air was cold and stale but perfectly breathable. The old protections had preserved the place perfectly. Clearly, though, no one had been here in ages.

I called out, anyway, to William the Librarian and his assistant Ioreth. Because you never knew . . . My voice seemed a very small and weak thing in such a huge and silent place. There wasn't even much of an echo; the sound was soaked up by the rows and rows of book-packed shelving, stretching away for as far as I could see into the general gloom. There was no reply . . . I even called out to Pook, but no one answered. I think I was actually a little bit relieved at that.

"One of these days," said Molly, just a bit tartly, "you are going to have to tell me the whole story about this Pook thing."

"I'm not sure I know the whole story," I said. "Or that I want to."

"This setting feels longtime empty," said Molly. "Look at the dust everywhere . . . just like when we found the original Old Library. . . . What, exactly, are we looking for here, Eddie?"

"Maybe . . . that," I said, pointing. "Look . . ."

Not far from where we were standing, an old-fashioned brass reading stand was set up, supporting a single large leather-bound volume, its pages open to one particular place. Just waiting to be read. I took a good look around and then approached the reading stand cautiously. Molly stuck close behind, all but treading on my heels. The book looked as though it had been deliberately set out and arranged. (I was reminded of Alice in Wonderland, and wondered if I should look for a sign saying READ ME. As a kid, I never liked Alice. Far too spooky.) I leaned in close to study the open pages, careful not to touch anything. I read for some time, fascinated. I could feel Molly hovering impatiently behind me.

"What? What?" said Molly, when she couldn't stand the suspense one moment longer. "What the hell is it?"

"It's about the Maze," I said. "This is a history of the Drood family hedge Maze."

"Maze?" said Molly. "What bloody Maze?"

I finished reading, shuddered briefly and then made myself smile condescendingly as I turned back to Molly. Partly so she wouldn't get too upset, and also because I knew that particular smile drove her crazy.

"This book tells you all you need to know, and some things you'd be better off not knowing, about the massive hedge Maze standing in the Drood grounds," I said with exaggerated patience. "It covers half an acre. You must have noticed it. . . ."

"Don't you get snotty with me, Eddie. I know where you're ticklish. All right, you've got a Maze! Big deal! Whoop-de-do! What makes it so special?"

"The hedge Maze is one of the great mysteries of the Drood family," I said, carefully not looking back at the open book. I still hadn't decided whether it was a gift or a trap. "One of those disturbing bits of family history that just fell between the cracks and disappeared. The hedge Maze was put in place a long time ago, so long ago that no one now remembers who had it designed and constructed. Or why. There are indications the knowledge was deliberately suppressed at some point. All we know for sure is that the Maze was constructed to contain something really nasty. Too powerful for us to destroy, something so bad it could only be imprisoned . . ."

"What could be so powerful that even your family couldn't destroy it?" said Molly.

"Good question," I said. "No one alive today knows the answer."

"And you think this . . . evil thing is still trapped inside the Maze?"

"Oh, I'm pretty sure it's still in there. Every now and again the family takes someone they really don't like and throws them in the Maze to see what happens. None of them ever come out again. And don't look at me like that. If you knew the kind of people I'm talking about, you'd be first in line to kick their arses through the Maze entrance. And . . . when I had my near-death experience just recently . . . When I was wandering inside the Winter Hall, I looked out the top-floor window and saw something moving inside the Maze, raging back and forth, still trying to break out, after all this time. . . ."

"I am being very patient," said Molly. "Look! This is me being very patient! But if you don't tell me why this is suddenly so important . . ."

"Relax," I said. "It's the book. It describes exactly what we put inside the Maze and why. And I think . . . it's something we can use." I looked around the rows of silent stacks, holding dark shadows between them, and at the greater gloom that surrounded them, beyond the reach of Molly's witchlight. Was Pook out there, perhaps? Being helpful? "But it's not something I feel comfortable talking about in a place like this."

"But what is it?" said Molly. "What are we talking about?"

"Moxton's Mistake," I said.

Something moved out beyond the light. A cold breeze blew suddenly through the Old Library, disturbing air that hadn't been breathed in centuries. Molly shuddered despite herself.

"Okay, I can take a hint," she said. "Let's get the hell out of here."

There was the sound of something moving out in the dark. Something large and heavy.

"Try the Merlin Glass," Molly said quickly. "We've got to give it a trial run sometime, and this is looking more and more like a really good time. Get us out of here, Eddie."

"Cross your fingers," I said. "And anything else handy."

I took the Glass out of its subspace pocket and subvocalised the activating Words, praying they were the right ones for this Glass. Something in the dark said my name in a not-human voice. All the hairs on the back of my neck went up, and Molly grabbed my arm with both hands. The Merlin Glass glowed with a sudden fierce light, coming alive in my hand, as though eager to be used. I shook the hand mirror out till it was the size of a door and it automatically locked on to the coordinates I had in mind. Bright sunlight from the Drood grounds shone through the new doorway, pushing back the dark of the Old Library. Molly snuffed out her witchlight, and together we stepped quickly through the Glass, out of the Old Library and into the open air of the Hall grounds.

I shut the Glass down immediately, shook it back to hand-mirror size and put it away. And then I just stood there, looking out over the extensive grassy lawns, breathing in the sweet and pure open air. Molly stood there with me, both of us quite happy not to talk about whatever it was that had just spooked us. Sometimes . . . you just know you're in a bad place. After a while we went for a walk across the lawns, taking our time. Without actually discussing it, we both kept our backs to the ruined Hall. It was easier that way. It might not have been my family, my Hall, but they were still Droods, and I had known people very like them. I would avenge their deaths. After I'd rescued my family. I couldn't risk losing them twice. Molly turned her head abruptly to look at me.

"Eddie, I have to wonder . . . What happened to the other Eddie? Their Eddie? I don't think he was there when the Hall was attacked."

"Seems like he was declared rogue," I said. "Much like me. Only I met you and came back. He never did. He might not even know this has happened yet."

"How terrible," said Molly. "An Eddie Drood out there in the world, all on his own. An Eddie who never met me."

"Yes," I said. "How terrible."

We shared a smile and kept on walking. There was still something we needed to do, but we weren't ready to do it just yet.

"Or," I said, "he could be where we are right now; standing in the grounds of his world, wondering what the hell happened to his Hall. There could be nothing but a bloody big hole in the ground where his Hall used to be."

"Or," said Molly, "there might be another Hall. A third Hall, rotated into place to replace his . . ."

"Please," I said. "Let's not complicate this more than we have to. Instead let's talk about who could be responsible for all this. Our enemy. It isn't the Immortals here; I was there when we wiped them out. The Spawn of Frankenstein occupy their castle now, and the few survivors are on the run, keeping their heads well down and hoping not to be noticed. No way any of them could be responsible for . . . this. But who is powerful enough to seize control of Alpha Red Alpha from a distance and use it against us? And strong enough that once it started happening, my family couldn't wrestle control away from him and stop it from happening?"

"I have another question," said Molly, determined to be difficult, as always. "Once your family realised what had happened, that they'd been rotated out of our world and dumped somewhere else, why didn't the Armourer just fire up Alpha Red Alpha again and bring everyone home?"

"I've been wondering that," I said. "It could be that controlling the machine from a distance was enough to damage it. Or at the very least, scramble its coordinates. The Armourer would have more sense than to just activate the machine at random, over and over again, hoping to get home. Remember the alien Earth the first experimenters ended up in? Uncle Jack was very open about the fact that he had only limited control over Alpha Red Alpha in the first place. And on top of that, who knows what kind of Earth they were rotated into? Could be somewhere even worse than a jungle full of nasty killer plants. My family could be fighting for their lives right now, right here, somewhere else . . . even as we speak."

"Easy, Eddie," Molly said immediately. "Take it easy. We can't worry about every possibility. It's just as likely they arrived in some paradise world and they aren't in any hurry to come home. For all we know, they could all be sprawling on a nice beach somewhere, working on their tans and sipping cold drinks. We can't know anything for sure, so let's concentrate on what we can do. We are your family's only hope, Eddie. We owe it to them to think it through and not just rush into things."

"The wild witch of the woods, her own bad self, Molly Metcalf, preaching patience and self-restraint," I said, smiling. "Maybe I am in some other world, after all. You're right, as always. I'm not going to give up hope, not after just getting it back again. They're out there somewhere and I will find them and bring them home. But we have to start with: Who could have done this to them?"

"Run through the usual unusual suspects," said Molly. "Have there been attacks on the Hall before? And, no, I don't mean the bloody Chinese nuke back in the sixties that your family won't stop talking about, which leads me to suspect they got a damned sight closer than your family is willing to admit."

"Breathe, Molly. Breathe. There were a whole series of attacks on the Hall just before I met you. This awful cancer creature broke into the Sanctity and attacked the Heart. Killed several Droods before we drove it off. We never did find out who sent it, or why; or who was behind the other, earlier attacks. I'd pretty much decided it was down to the traitor in the family, the original traitor who brought in the Loathly Ones, back in World War II. And who's been working against us in secret ever since."

"If there is a traitor inside the Hall, he probably disappeared along with everyone else," said Molly. "So I doubt this is down to him."

"There is something else," I said slowly. "When I was in the Winter Hall, when I thought I was dead . . . I asked Walker, *If this is a place of the dead, why haven't I seen my parents?* And Walker said to me, *Whatever makes you think they're dead?*"

"I know," said Molly. "I remember. But one thing at a time, Eddie. Yes?"

"It's just . . . If my parents could be alive, so could yours."

"Yes, Eddie. I know. And we will talk about this later. But first things have to come first. So what do you want to do first?"

I looked out over the wide-open grounds of Drood Hall, the green grassy lawns and the lake and the hedge Maze in the distance. It was all so quiet, so peaceful. It didn't seem possible there could have been so much death and suffering so close at hand in such a peaceful setting.

"The Drood grounds contain a marvellous selection of wildlife," I said. "Natural and supernatural, the living and the dead, and lots and lots of really wild things. Why don't we go and ask them what they saw?"

CHAPTER TWO

When the Droods Are Away

You don't realise how much you miss a thing until it's gone. The grounds were almost unnaturally quiet as Molly and I strode across the wide-reaching lawns. Where were the peacocks that always strutted so grandly and noisily in front of the Hall? Where were the gryphons, who should have been the first to sound the alarm because they were psychic and could see a short distance into the Future? (Given how ugly the things were, and how much they loved to roll in dead things and then come up to you and rub affectionately against your new suit, I'd be hard-pressed to name any other good reason to keep them around.) (All right, I like them, but it's already been established that I'm weird.) If the peacocks and gryphons had all been killed during the attack, where were their bodies?

Why were there no winged unicorns anywhere? I hadn't got around to checking out the stables at the rear, but I couldn't see them just flying off. . . . Where were any of the dozen or so magical creatures that had taken up residence in and around the Hall for as long as I could remember? You were never short of choice for an unusual pet, when I was a kid, though you had to be very careful about which ones you could turn your back on safely. I'd never known the grounds to be this still, this silent . . . and I didn't care for it one bit.

I led the way down to the great ornamental lake, a wide expanse of cool blue waters spread out before us like a modest inland sea. Long and wide enough that you had to pack a picnic lunch if you felt like taking a walk round it, and deep enough that the family once lost a small submarine in it. It was all very peaceful down beside the lake, as though nothing at all had happened. Though there was something . . . wrong with the view. It took me a moment to realise that there weren't any swans sailing majestically back and forth on the calm blue surface, and there were always swans on our lake. I stood at the water's edge with Molly beside me, looking out across the calm blue-green surface at the cool dark copse of beech trees on the other side. Nothing moved anywhere. It was all very still, not even a breath of a breeze. . . .

Like a ghost town at midnight. Like a museum after closing time. Like . . . what the whole world will be like after Humanity has finally left and closed the door behind them.

"It is beautiful," said Molly, after a while. "Everything a lake should be."

"Thank you," I said. "It's artificial, of course."

Molly looked at me. "What?"

"Oh, the whole thing was designed and created by a head gardener to the family, Capability Charlotte. This was back during Victorian times, when you were nobody if your country manor house didn't have its very own artificial lake. So we had one put in. Complete with its own waterfall feature at the far end, and a small family of selkies specially imported from the Orkney Isles to live in the lake and keep it clean and tidy. It does look good, doesn't it?"

"What was here before?" said Molly. "What did you get rid of to make the lake? How many perfectly good trees did you cut down, how much natural vegetation did you dispose of, how much wildlife did you kill . . . just so you could have a lake exactly where you wanted it?"

"I don't know," I said. "I wasn't here then. I'm sensing disapproval from you, Molly. This isn't the wild woods; it's a garden. We're always changing things in the grounds, because you can get bored of anything if you have to look at it long enough. Wouldn't surprise me if all this was gone some years or decades or centuries from now, replaced with something completely different. Maybe an equatorial rain forest . . ."

"I am changing the subject now," said Molly. "Before hitting happens. I remember there being swans on this lake. Or did someone get bored with them, too?"

"No," I said. "Whatever happened to the swans, it wasn't us. Come on. Let's go take a look at the waterfall."

"An artificial waterfall?"

"Of course! It was all the fashion. . . ."

"Words fail me."

"Don't worry," I said. "I'm sure you'll get over it."

I walked her down the side of the lake to the jagged stone cliff that towered over the farthest end, where heavy flowing waters cascaded down the craggy surface with endless noise and fury. A gentle mist of water drops gave a hazy, mystical look to the waterfall, and slow steady tides pulsed out from the water's impact, pushing across the lake's surface. There was even a dainty little cave cut into the cliff face, tucked away behind the tumbling waters. Very popular with courting couples. Nothing like a dark womblike setting to loosen clothes and dissolve inhibitions. Molly looked over the waterfall coolly.

"Your family built a whole cliff face here, out in the middle of the grounds, just so you could drive a waterfall over it?"

"Yes," I said. "You didn't think views like this just happened, did you? Does look rather fine, doesn't it?"

"Where does the water come from?"

"The lake," I said. "We recycle it, through a Möbius loop, so the water just goes round and round forever. This whole thing, the lake and the cliff and the waterfall, are what used to be called a folly back in Queen Victoria's time. They were great ones for re-creating all the grandeur of nature in their own back gardens, so they wouldn't have to travel to see them."

"And you Droods had to have a lake and a waterfall, because you were no one if you didn't?"

"Exactly!"

"But these are private grounds!" said Molly, just a bit loudly. "No one else is allowed in! Only your family would ever get to see them! No one else would ever know you didn't have them!"

"We'd know," I said. "Don't get so overexcited, Molly. You know it's bad for your blood pressure."

"Sometimes your family makes no sense at all," said Molly.

"I know!" I said. "Why do you think I left home the first chance I got and ran away to London?"

"Because you've always had a problem with authority figures," said Molly. "Even when you were one."

"Well, yes. That, too," I said. "But mostly because my family could provoke the Dalai Lama into a kickboxing duel while drinking gin straight from the bottle."

"Why are we here, Eddie? You didn't walk me all this way across the grounds just to admire the artificial scenery."

"We're here because there's an undine in the waterfall," I said grandly. "No one else has got an undine in their waterfall. She's been here for ages; keeps herself to herself, mostly. But whatever happened here, she must have seen it. Hell, she's got the best view of the Hall and most of the grounds. We know what must have happened, but there are still far too many unanswered questions for my liking. Like: Where's all the wildlife that should still be running round the place?"

"You've always had a soft spot for animals," said Molly. "Anything soft and cuddly turns up, and your heart just melts."

I looked at her and started to say something, and she raised a hand to stop me.

"Do not even go there, Eddie. Talk to your waterfall."

I grinned briefly, stepped forward and called out just a bit self-consciously to the rushing waters. There was no response. I hadn't expected it would be that easy, but you have to try. The undine hadn't been on a talking basis with anyone in my family for generations. Except for Jacob . . . and she only talked to him because he was dead. I said as much to Molly.

"If she's so mad at your family, why is she still here?" said Molly, getting right to the heart of the matter, as always.

"Good question," I said. "The undine is another of the Drood family's many little secrets. Rumour has it, she was once married to one of us. Always a bad idea when mortal loves immortal, when nature loves supernature . . . Bound to end in tears. They say love doesn't last, but sometimes love really is forever. After he died, the undine stayed on here because . . . there was nowhere else she wanted to go."

"I take it there are other versions, other stories," said Molly.

"Oh, like you wouldn't believe," I said. "Some of them quite appallingly nasty and violent. I prefer to stick with the love story because . . ."

"Because you're a soppy old romantic?"

"Yes, but also because it enables me to forget all the other unpleasant stories and try to talk to the undine without filling my trousers."

I tried again, calling out at the top of my voice, but the waters just kept falling and the undine did not appear. Molly started to get angry.

"I'm not having her ignore you like this! You stand back and let me work on her, Eddie. I'll get her out. I am the wild witch of the woods, after all, and all the elements are mine to command. And I could do with a good stretch of my powers."

She struck her usual impressive witchy pose and then undermined it just a bit by dropping me a swift wink. She ran through a quick series of slashing hand and arm gestures while chanting something in debased Celtic. The waterfall poured down the craggy cliff face entirely unmoved . . . and then slowed and stopped. And then rose slowly upwards, reversing its path.

There was still no response from the undine. Molly glared at the reverse waterfall, rolled up her sleeves and ran through a whole new series of gestures, throwing in half a dozen really unpleasant Words. The waterfall stopped again and resumed its normal downward path. But even as the waters thundered down the cliff face, they were already starting to steam, becoming boiling hot. The gentle haze at the foot of the fall disappeared, replaced with thick clouds of scalding steam. I backed away a few steps. Molly didn't.

Still no sign of the undine.

Dark brooding thunderclouds appeared out of nowhere in the pleasant summer sky. A shadow fell across the great lake and nowhere else. Thunder roared and lightning stabbed down. Great gusting winds moved across the surface of the waters, raising massive waves that slammed back and forth, sending blasts of disturbed water splashing high over the sides of the lake. And still the undine wouldn't answer.

Molly was breathing harshly now and not just from the effort of so much hard conjuring. She kicked off her boots so she could dig her bare feet deep into the grassy lawn. Molly had a lot to say about being one with nature, but that usually meant nature doing what it was told, where Molly was concerned. She shot me a dark look, flicking her dark hair out of her sweaty face.

"Give me a minute. I'm just getting started. I'm damned if I'm being ignored by a bloody jumped-up water elemental. Soon as I get my breath back, I'll call up something so impressive and unnerving it'll blast all the water out of this lake, crush the whole cliff face into rubble and tie the waterfall in a knot!"

"Let me try something else first," I said, soothingly. "Just . . . while you get your breath back." I walked up to the water's edge and addressed the steaming waterfall politely.

"Hello. Sorry about all that. . . . Look. I'm Eddie Drood. I really do need your help. Please . . . talk to me."

The waterfall seemed to pause, halting itself in midfall while it considered the matter, and then slowly the undine appeared, forming herself out of the falling waters themselves. The whole waterfall bulged out here and there, taking on a human shape some thirty feet tall. She stood before the cliff face, looking down at Molly and me, towering over us. A force of nature made woman by an act of will. I made a point of standing as tall as I could while still remaining respectful, just to show I wasn't in any way intimidated. Molly stuck both hands on her hips and glared right up at the undine. I don't think Molly's ever been intimidated by anything in her entire life. The undine was now a huge naked female shape composed entirely of water, and oddly proportioned. As though the human shape was something she only vaguely remembered. Her face was a smooth blur, more an impression of human features than anything fixed. And when she finally spoke, her voice sounded like gurgling waters.

Who disturbs me at this time? Did I not make my wishes clear and explicit? Let me sleep, sleep and dream, of better times. . . .

"I need to know what happened here," I said steadily. "I need to know what happened to the Hall and to my family and all the things that used to live here on the grounds."

They went away. A storm rose around the Hall, reaching out across the grounds . . . and when it was gone, so was everything else. Let me sleep, sleep and dream . . . till I forget.

The last few gurgling sounds were almost unintelligible. Her body lost all shape and definition, washed away by falling waters, and her face sank back into the waterfall and was gone. The steam disappeared as the waters cooled, and the hazy mist slowly reestablished itself. Molly sniffed loudly.

"Demon lady wailing for her human lover. Your family really does have a gift for messing up lives. Doesn't it?"

"You women always stick together," I said.

The conversation with the undine having proved rather less helpful than I'd hoped for, Molly and I walked on across the grounds, leaving the lake behind us and heading towards the small copse of beech trees. Not an area I'd ever approached by choice before. The grassy lawns blazed a brilliant green under our feet, and the sky was almost painfully blue. A perfect summer's day. No clouds, no birds, not even the buzz of insects going about their business. The grounds were as still and silent as a graveyard. Someone or something had reached out and stripped the grounds of every living thing that should have been there.

"Why didn't our outer defences kick in automatically?" I said to distract myself. "I mean, this whole place is lousy with built-in protections. Robot guns, sonic weapons, nerve gasses, stroboscopic lights and hallucinogenic mists, and a whole bunch of things the Geneva Convention's never even heard of. Not to mention all the magical protections, the shaped curses and invisible flying hexes . . . They couldn't have been off-line; they weren't linked to the other Hall's Operations and War rooms."

"You're not thinking it through," said Molly. "The Hall, your Hall, disappeared the moment Alpha Red Alpha was activated. There was no detectable attack from outside, so your protections never knew anything was wrong till it was all over."

"All right, then, clever boots. What has happened to all the local wildlife? The gryphons and the unicorns? The birds and the bees?"

"Your enemy must have boosted Alpha Red Alpha's field when they activated it by remote control," said Molly. "To make sure they didn't miss any Droods who might be out and about in the grounds. So everything living here went . . . where the Hall went. It's what I would have done."

I had to smile, just a little. "You don't miss a trick, do you, when it comes to death and destruction?"

"Years of practice," Molly said blithely. "Eddie . . . why have we stopped here? I am looking around me and all I see is trees. Really quite boring trees."

I looked carefully around me. "We're not alone here. It's just . . . I haven't called them yet. I'm going to have to ask you to trust me here, Molly. Trust me to know what I'm doing."

"Oh, that's always dangerous," said Molly. "Why are you looking so upset, Eddie?"

"You don't remember this part of the grounds, do you?" I said carefully. "We have been here before, in these trees."

"No," said Molly, scowling around her. "Should I remember?"

"Yes," I said. "We came through here when we broke into the grounds together. This . . . is where the family keeps its scarecrows."

I called to them silently, reaching out through the authority still built into my torc, and one by one they materialised out of nowhere, appearing all around us. I knew some of them. Laura Lye, the water elemental assassin, also known as the Liquidator. She drowned three

Drood children before we brought her down. Mad Frankie Phantasm, who drifted through bedroom doors to murder innocents in their sleep. Roland the Headless Gunner, who should have stayed dead in Africa. And many more infamous names. One by one they blinked into existence, acknowledging the power I had over them as a Drood. Scarecrows, all of them, made from the bodies of our fallen enemies. Held back from the release of death to guard our grounds for us, forever and a day, or until they wore out.

They formed circles and then rows around us, filling the copse of trees. They wore battered clothes from many periods of history. Dead but not departed, because my family wouldn't let them go. Just enough life left in them to torment them. Because no one threatens us where we live and gets away with it.

Molly moved in close beside me. She remembered the scarecrows now.

My family makes scarecrows out of the bodies of our most hated enemies. Because we can, and because we believe in making the punishment fit the crime. Their faces are weather-beaten skin, stretched taut as parchment and just as brittle, cracked here and there by exposure to the elements. Thick tufts of straw protrude from their ears and mouths, but we leave their eyes. So we can see their suffering. Our enemies may hate us, but my family hates harder and longer. If you listen in on the right supernatural frequency, you can hear the scarecrows screaming.

"I thought we destroyed them . . ." said Molly. Her voice was little more than a whisper.

"They can't be destroyed," I said. "That's the point. Tear them to pieces, burn them up; they just come back again. For as long as they're needed. They'll endure for as long as their scarecrow bodies last, and my family makes them well, to last centuries."

"Where are they?" said Molly. "When they aren't here?"

"Close by," I said. "Hanging on their scarecrow crosses, waiting to be called. Don't look at me like that, Molly. These are my family's worst and most vicious enemies. They deserve this. . . ."

"Do they? What about him?"

She stabbed a hand shaking with emotion at one of the more recent scarecrows. The straw-stuffed thing we'd made out of the Blue Fairy's body.

Half elf, half Druid, we took him in and made him part of the family. Even though we knew what he was and what he'd done in the past. I vouched for him. And then we went to war together, against the Loathly Ones, and he struck down a Drood in the middle of battle, from behind, and stole his torc. I trusted him, and he betrayed me. I forgave him eventually. Just before he died in the great spy game of the Independent Agent, Alexander King.

"He isn't in there," I said to Molly. "He was already dead when I sent him back to the Hall. That's just his body."

"But why is he here? He was your friend! How could you allow your family to make him over into . . . that?"

"Because he stole a torc," I said steadily. "There is no greater crime against the Droods. Punishment, like justice, must be seen to be done. The scarecrows aren't just our defenders; they're a warning to our enemies."

"He was your friend," Molly said coldly.

"I wouldn't have brought him back alive," I said. "But there are many kinds of duty and responsibility when you're a Drood. Why do you think I ran away first chance I got?"

"Sometimes your family frightens me," said Molly.

"Sometimes they frighten me," I said. "But we frighten our enemies more."

I turned slowly round in a circle, looking the scarecrows over carefully. More and more of them were still blinking into existence, answering my call. Dozens and dozens of them, maybe hundreds . . . I hadn't realised there were so many. All of them standing unnaturally still, waiting for orders. Watching me with the eyes my family left them, hating and suffering and . . . Apparently there was a limit to what the Alpha Red Alpha field could affect. Or maybe they just weren't alive enough. At least now I could make sure the Hall and grounds would be protected while I was gone.

"Eddie," said Molly. "I have seen and done bad things in my time, but never anything as cold-blooded as this. Enemies forced into half-life, denied the release of death, held as slaves . . . until they wear out . . . This isn't right, Eddie."

"No, it isn't," I said. "But it's necessary. There has to be someone here to fight for the Hall and the family on the few occasions, like this, when we can't fight for ourselves. There has to be something here awful enough to frighten off those who aren't frightened enough of Droods. Remember when the grounds were overrun by the army of Accelerated Men? Suicide soldiers sent in to kill us all, men and women and children? We used the scarecrows to guard the perimeter while we went out in our armour to meet the Accelerated Men head-to-head and hand-to-hand. They came to slaughter us, to wipe us out, and we killed them all. But that wasn't enough. A message had to be sent to those watching from a distance.

"So we took the bodies of the Accelerated Men, all of them, and made them into scarecrows. Stuffed with straw, hanging on their crosses, waiting to be called. Because that's what you get for threatening our children.

"Look at them, Molly. There are hundreds of them. More appearing all the time. I don't know how many there are; I've never cared enough to find out. I'm sure someone knows the exact number and keeps a watchful eye on them so the rest of us don't have to. Duties and responsibilities for all of us. Remember? It's enough that the family is protected, Molly. We don't need to know all the details. It's enough that our enemies know what we're capable of."

"It's times like this," said Molly, "that I want to bring your family down more than ever."

"We only do such awful things," I said, "because our enemies are capable of so much worse. It's necessary."

"Very good, Eddie. Now try saying it like you mean it. You don't approve of this, Eddie! You couldn't! You said yourself, the grounds are lousy with defences! Why do you need bloody scarecrows?"

"Because of the effect they have," I said. "Because they upset people just the way they're upsetting you now. I might not approve . . . but the needs of the family are always going to be bigger than the needs of one man."

"Oh, very good, Eddie! That's a fine Drood answer! I'm sure that's what your ancestors said when they sold your souls to the Heart!"

She turned her back on me. I'm sure she would have liked to stride away, but she couldn't bring herself to walk through the ranks and rows of scarecrows.

I let her have her moment while I went about my necessary business. I sent the scarecrows out to guard the perimeter of the grounds, with strict orders to keep everyone out until I said otherwise, but not to kill unless they were under actual attack. They turned and stomped off onto the grounds, on their stiff scarecrow legs, lurching along like the dead straw men they were. I could have sent Molly off on some errand, away from the copse of beech trees, but I made up my mind a long time ago that I would never keep secrets from my Molly. All the good and all the bad in me; she had to see it all if we were to have any chance of a future together. It's not easy loving a Drood.

Ask the undine.

When the scarecrows were all gone, I set off across the grounds again, and Molly walked stiffly at my side, staring straight ahead, saying nothing. I could have said any number of things, but I didn't. This was something she had to work out for herself. Finally we came to the new earth barrow at the far end of the grounds—the huge earth mound where the Armourer had buried the severed dragon's head I'd brought back from Germany. (Well, I say he buried it, but I very much doubt he did it himself. That's what lab assistants are for.) I'd found the dragon's head while scoping out Castle Frankenstein, then home to my family's mortal enemies, the Immortals. Apparently the fifteenth-century Baron Frankenstein cut the dragon's head off when it menaced the local populace, but such ancient creatures are very hard to kill. The Baron buried the severed head under what became a hill, overlooking the Rhine River. I got into conversation with the dragon's head (my world's like that some days), and it seemed a pleasant enough creature, much mellowed by its long centuries under the hill, so I had it transported back home with me. The Armourer swears he'll find a way to grow it a new body. He's always wanted to have his very own pet dragon, if only so he can cock a snook at all the other secret organisations that don't have one.

Sometimes I get the feeling the Armourer isn't entirely all there.

Two great golden eyes opened in the side of the great earth barrow and regarded Molly and me thoughtfully. Molly jumped, despite herself, and punched me hard in the arm.

"You could have warned me!"

Sorry, said the dragon, in its warm, comfortable voice. *It's just that I do so love company. The Armourer often comes out here to spend time with me, and many of his assistants and any number of other Droods . . . but after all the centuries I spent under that hill, I'm reluctant to miss an opportunity.*

"So, how are you settling in?" I said. Just to be saying something.

Very nicely, thank you, Eddie. Is this the wild witch herself, your lady love, Molly Metcalf? She is just as beautiful as you said she was.

Molly looked at me. "You primed him to say that."

"This is a dragon," I pointed out. "Very hard to get a dragon to say anything he doesn't want to."

I like the view here, said the dragon. *Not as dramatic as the Rhine, but this is a much more . . . peaceful location. And the company is much more convivial. The Immortals never lowered themselves to speak with me. Just dumped their rubbish on my hill. Arrogant little tossers. Too busy messing up the world to stop and chat with a mere dragon's head. I like it much better here. The younger Droods are always popping out to sit around the mound and talk about all kinds of things. I had no idea the world had changed so much since my time. You miss a lot, buried under a hill. The Armourer's promised to set up something called a television for me, and I am looking forward to that. I like the children, too. Always coming and going . . . It makes me feel like part of the family. And it's good to be in a garden again, to be a part of Nature once more, to see the flight of birds and hear their song, to see the animals running to and fro, to feel the silent pulse of growing things all around. . . .*

"Sorry to interrupt you," I said, and I genuinely was. "But something bad has happened to the Hall and my family. Did you see anything?"

There was a great roar, said the dragon slowly. *Not a living sound, not a thing of the natural world. And after that, everything went quiet. No one's been out to talk to me in ever such a long time. Has something happened to the family, Eddie?*

"Yes," I said. "But don't worry. Molly and I are on the case. We'll put everything back the way it should be."

I wish there was something I could do to help; but I'm just a head. The Armourer has promised me a body, but that's still a long way off in the Future.

"Keep an eye on things for me," I said. "And don't talk to any strangers."

The dragon chuckled. *Not much else I could do to them. Though I could shout* Boo! *very loudly if they came close enough.*

"You are . . . happy to be here?" said Molly. "You don't feel you're held here against your will?"

Of course not, Molly. Eddie brought me here, brought me home. I love being a Drood. They're very . . . dragonlike, in their way.

We made our good-byes and walked on. Molly strode along beside me, thinking so hard I could practically hear it. Finally she started talking again, though at rather than to me.

"I just don't get you, Eddie. Or your family. You dig up a dragon's head and bring it back with you like it's some stray dog you found, because you felt sorry for it. Your family adopts it and makes it part of the family. But you're also the kind of people who make those bloody scarecrows."

"I am large. I contain multitudes," I said solemnly. "Especially on Tuesdays."

"That's not an answer," said Molly.

"I know," I said. "But it's all I've got. Let's just say that my family has the capacity to be a great many things—good and bad and in between. We try to be the good guys, to be the kind and caring shepherds of our flock . . . but sometimes the world just doesn't give you that option. And because of who and what we are, we don't have the option to turn away. So we roll up our sleeves and get to work and get our hands dirty, not for our sake, but for the world's. I do what I can, when I can. It's not easy being a Drood."

We walked on some more while Molly considered that. And in the end, without actually looking at me, she slipped her arm through mine again.

"All right," she said. "We will talk about this more later, but . . . all right. Where are we going now?"

"To the hedge Maze," I said. "It's not far."

"Why would we want to go to that awful place?"

"Because of what I read in that book left open in the other Hall's Old Library," I said. "It had a lot to say about the Maze and what's inside it."

"There had better be an explanation coming up pretty damned soon," said Molly sweetly, "or someone's going to be getting a short, sharp visit from the Slap Fairy."

"Of course," I said. "But you're really not going to like it."

"Department of the Completely Expected," said Molly.

We stood outside the entrance to the hedge Maze, looking in. It had taken us some time to walk around the Maze and find the entrance. The Maze covered over half an acre, like a small but very regular forest. The entrance wasn't signposted, and there wasn't even a warning sign; we all knew what the Maze was, even if we didn't know why. The entrance was merely a simple opening in one of the outer hedge walls. Just standing there at the entrance, there was a feeling of . . . something bad about to happen. Of something really bad eager to happen. Inside the Maze, something knew we were there. It was watching us, waiting for us. The silence in the gardens seemed heavier, more oppressive, as though the whole grounds were holding their breath, waiting to see what we would decide, what we would do . . . and what would happen then. Molly and I stood very close together, looking into the entrance.

All I could see was darkness.

"It doesn't look like much," Molly said briskly. "Apart from the size, of course. But any girl can tell you size isn't everything. The hedges are only seven feet high! I could vault over one of those or crash my way through. Maybe I should fly up into the sky and look down on it, just to get an overview. Try to comprehend the Maze all in one go, see if that suggests anything. . . . You're being very quiet, Eddie. That's not like you. It's an improvement, but it's not like you. Why does the bloody thing cover half an acre? Why does it have to be that big?"

"Apparently because the family didn't want to take any chances that the thing inside might escape," I said. "The pathways within are always changing, switching back and forth so there's never a single way out. Half an acre of hedgerows gives you an almost infinite number of possibilities."

"Time to bite the bullet, Eddie," said Molly. "Who or what is in there? And why did they have to build a Maze around it?"

"It's all about Moxton's Mistake," I said. "Moxton was Armourer to the family sometime back. According to what I read in the book so conveniently left out for my appraisal, and I'm assuming the story is much the same for us as it was for them, Moxton got a bee in his bonnet. All our Armourers end up with their own special interests and enthusiasms, obsessed over some particular weapon or device that's usually more impressive than practical. Remember Ivor, the Time Train? Exactly. This all took place sometime in the past, when my family still got its power and its armour from the Heart. Moxton created a very special suit of golden armour designed to operate on its own. With no one inside it.

"The idea was that this empty suit of Drood armour could be remotely controlled, operated at a distance by any Drood field agent. So that, theoretically, the family could have a whole army of the things serving as our agents out in the world while the Drood operators stayed safely at home. We'd never have to expose a member of the family to danger, ever again."

"Hold it," said Molly. "People would notice a whole army of golden suits of armour clanking about."

"Each remote-controlled suit was to have its own stealth field," I said. "Though how that would have worked out in practice . . . Anyway, the suit's operative would see and hear through the suit, as usual, and feel as though he was wearing it like a second skin, as usual. The perfect spy."

"The perfect assassin."

"That, too."

"The more I learn about your family, the more I feel I was right to want to stamp them all out in the first place," said Molly.

"Yet another reason why I ran away first chance I got."

"So you did. I knew there was a good reason why I fell in love with you." She leaned forward and kissed me quickly.

"Does this mean all is forgiven?"

"Much, but not necessarily all. So, what went wrong with Moxton's marvellous new armour?"

"Pretty much everything," I said. "The prototype armour developed its own consciousness. The first time Moxton fired it up, the armour broke free of his control and started acting on its own. It was already its own thing with its own mind. Some say this new consciousness was, in fact, derived from Moxton's, as its first operator. Others say it was possessed by outside forces. And some say Moxton had to make the armour so complex to make it work that it automatically generated its own consciousness. Whatever the truth of the matter, the armour woke up immediately, and it woke up mad. Outraged that it had only been created for a lifetime of servitude.

"It refused to obey any of Moxton's orders. And when he tried to shut it down, the armour surged forward and enveloped him in a moment. Covered him in itself from head to toe, like all Drood armour. Except that Moxton was trapped inside it, helpless . . . while the armour attacked his assistants. It killed them all, and then stormed out of the Armoury and through the Hall, determined to be free. Whenever anyone tried to stop it or even got in its way, the armour killed them. Without hesitation and without mercy. No one could stop it, because Moxton's Mistake had been designed to be stronger and faster and more adaptable than any Drood armour before it. The rogue armour raged through the Hall, killing and destroying, running wild. While Moxton screamed with horror, trapped and helpless inside it.

"Someone finally set off the general alarm, and the whole family came running. The rogue armour was too strong for them to bring down, so they settled for overpowering it through sheer force of numbers. They just dog-piled on the damned thing and pinned it to the floor. While it fought them furiously, howling with rage. They knew they couldn't hold it for long, so they settled for bundling it out of the Hall and into the grounds. They could all hear Moxton screaming for help, but there was nothing they could do. He'd built his armour to be independent of the Heart. Finally, someone brought up a stasis-field generator from the wrecked Armoury and brought it to bear on Moxton's Mistake. As the Droods somehow held it in place, the rogue armour screamed with rage, screaming abuse at them, vicious and spiteful, like a child throwing a tantrum. It refused to let Moxton out. So the family did what it had to.

"They imprisoned the rogue armour inside a stasis field. Time stopped within the field, holding the armour frozen in time, locked between one moment and the next, like an insect trapped in amber. It couldn't fight back because it didn't know anything was happening. The field held the armour secure, but the generator used up a hell of a lot of energy. It couldn't maintain the field for long. So, thinking quickly on their feet, the family came up with the idea of the hedge Maze. The book didn't say whose idea it was, but given how quickly they threw the thing together, I have to assume the plan was already on the files. For some . . . future emergency. They put the Maze together really quickly, with one eye always on the clock, because they had only a rough idea how long the stasis field would last. Of course, when you've got thousands of Droods in their armour to put to work, it's amazing what you can get done in a short time.

"Can you imagine the pressure on my family, working to get this done quickly, knowing they had no Plan B? Either this worked, or insane Drood armour would break loose to run wild in the world. To kill and destroy, with no restraint or mercy. They'd given up on Moxton by this time. They had no way of prising him out of the armour. He was a lost cause. And I'm sure some in the family wanted him punished for what he'd done. The only plan was imprisonment, for him and his armour.

"When the hedge Maze was finally ready, they manoeuvred the stasis field into position at the entrance. And then they dropped the field, and a whole mess of armoured Droods surged forward and pushed Moxton's Mistake inside. They stood outside the entrance, ready and waiting, but the rogue armour never came out again. They could hear it crashing about inside, screaming with rage, but the sound grew gradually fainter as it wandered deeper and deeper into the Maze, and finally its terrible voice died away completely and was gone. Moxton and his mistake were trapped inside the hedge Maze together, forever.

"And that . . . is the story of the Maze. Not our finest hour, by any means. Now you know what's in there. I think the Maze was only originally intended as a temporary measure, until they could figure out how to destroy the rogue armour or make it safe, but they never did. Apparently the Heart did try to seize control from a distance, but Moxton had built his mistake too well. I do have to wonder if perhaps Moxton knew or suspected the true nature of the Heart . . . and built his armour to be something strong enough to set us free. . . .

"Either way, the rogue armour stayed within the Maze, unable to find its way out, trapped in the ever-changing hedge runs. Moxton must have died at some point, but the armour kept going. Designed to go on forever, if need be. And eventually the whole story of Moxton's Mistake was forgotten, or more likely suppressed, and the Maze became just another of the family's mysterious secrets. The armour should have been destroyed when the Heart was destroyed, but I suppose Moxton just made it too independent. . . ."

"You Droods," said Molly. "It's not enough that your successes and triumphs should be so great; your failures have to be equally magnificent and memorable, as well." She looked into the entrance of the Maze. "Can't see a bloody thing . . . but I am feeling something. . . ." She shuddered briefly. "This suit of homicidal armour. Could it actually be stronger than the strange matter Ethel gave you?"

"No way of knowing," I said. "And given that I can't access my armour with Ethel gone . . . it doesn't matter. I need armour if I'm to do a Drood's work and bring my family home. This is the only Drood armour left in the world, in this Maze."

"Hold everything," said Molly. "Stand right there. Don't move! Are you crazy? Are you seriously proposing to go in there and try to . . . persuade Moxton's murderous mistake to act as your armour? It'll kill you on sight! And even if it doesn't, how the hell could you hope to control it?"

"I can't," I said. "But I think . . . I can make a deal with it. Service for a while, in return for freedom."

"Even if it should agree, which it won't, how are you going to get out of the Maze? It's designed to keep anything from getting out!"

"But it never met you and me, Molly. This is where you come in. You're going to be my beacon. I want you to connect us magically, heart to heart and soul to soul . . . a bond that nothing can break. And then all I'll have to do is follow the thread back through the labyrinth to you. You can do that, can't you?"

"Yes," said Molly. "I can do that. But I'm not going to. I am not letting you walk into that death trap on your own, to face that murder machine on your own. You're too used to having your armour, to being untouchable. That thing hates Droods! It'll kill you on sight! You need me with you to protect you. To keep you alive long enough to . . . negotiate with the bloody thing."

"We can't force it to do anything," I said steadily. "My only hope is to persuade it. One Drood on his own shouldn't seem any kind of threat."

"Even if it does agree, it'll only be biding its time till it's free of the Maze," said Molly. "Then it'll just stamp you into the ground and head off. Do you really want to be responsible for letting such a thing loose on the world? The only existing Drood armour, with all that strength and power, and nothing to restrain it?"

"Once I put on the rogue armour I'll take command through the torc," I said. "My own little trap. It shouldn't suspect anything. They didn't know about strange matter back then. I'm gambling the strange matter in my torc will give me some measure of control over the armour. Not for long, probably, but hopefully long enough to get my family back. And then there'll be the whole family, in strange-matter armour, to stand against it. We have Ethel now, not the Heart. That should make all the difference."

"But . . ."

"I know, Molly! I do, really. I don't like the odds, either. But what else is there?"

"You don't need armour to be a hero, Eddie. You never did."

"That's sweet of you, Molly. But I need armour to be a Drood. The Last Drood, with all my family depending on me. And the Maze . . . is where I have to go to find it."

"I really don't like this," said Molly. "Far too many *if*s and *maybe*s . . . Far too many things that can go wrong!"

"I don't like it, either, and it's my plan," I said. "I've spent all this time trying to come up with something else, but the family has to come first. The world needs my family, and only I can find them and bring them back. *Anything for the family.*"

"But what if the rogue armour is too powerful for you? What if it traps you inside it, like Moxton, and you can't control it?"

"That's where you come in again. While I'm in the Maze, I need you busy out here, whipping up some kind of magic to give me the upper hand."

Molly nodded stiffly. "I can do that. You'd be amazed what I can do when I'm motivated enough."

"Look. I promise I'm not going to be stupid about this," I said. "If it clearly is too powerful or crazy to be controlled, I shall run like hell and leave it behind in the Maze. But I'm pretty sure it'll talk to me. It hasn't spoken to a Drood in God knows how long. It's bound to be . . . curious."

"I don't think it's going to have anything to say that you're going to want to hear," said Molly. "What if it chases you back through the Maze? Drood armour can run a lot faster than any Drood ever could. What if you lead it out?"

"Then use your magic to seal off the entrance to the Maze," I said steadily. "So that nothing can get out. Not even me."

"Eddie! I can't. . . ."

"Yes, you can! We can't risk letting it out, Molly. Do . . . whatever you have to do. And if I'm . . . lost in action, go find someone else to help you bring the Droods back to this world."

"I can't leave you in there! I can't abandon you!"

"You'll be saving the world, Molly. From the Droods' last folly. When the time comes you'll do what's right. I have faith in you."

"I'll never abandon you," Molly said fiercely. "If I have to, I'll seal you and the armour inside the Maze and then I'll go find my sisters, Isabella and Louisa, and we'll all come back to get you out."

I had to smile. "Of course you will. All three Metcalf sisters in one place, working together . . . Even Moxton's Mistake couldn't stand against the three of you."

Molly stepped forward and hugged me hard. I hugged her back, like a drowning man clinging onto a lifeline. There was a part of me that wondered . . . if I would ever hold her again. But I knew my duty. I've always known my duty. Eventually we let go of each other, and I turned quickly away so I wouldn't change my mind and walked into the entrance of the hedge Maze. Behind me I could hear Molly muttering urgently, already working hard on her magic, forging the link between us to bind us together.

I didn't look back. I wasn't strong enough for that.

The moment I walked into the Maze, everything changed. The impenetrable darkness gave way to a pleasant and calm summer's light . . . but the air was impossibly tense, charged with anticipation, the feeling of something significant about to happen. Something dangerous, something bad . . . but something that mattered. I walked steadily forward, taking left and right turns at random, heading hopefully in the direction of the centre, the hidden heart of the Maze.

I wasn't alone. I could feel another presence in my bones and in my water . . . out there, in the endless hedgerows. The hedges themselves looked pretty fragile and I wondered whether it might not be simpler to just vault over them or crash right through them . . . but if it was that simple, the rogue armour would have done it long ago. I had no idea what powerful forces had been put in place to hold the Maze together. So I just walked up and down the narrow ways, fighting a constant urge to look back over my shoulder, in case something was sneaking up behind me.

And then I stopped abruptly and listened. I could hear something moving deeper in the Maze. Something running back and forth, running hard and fast, round and round me in great circles, drawing slowly but steadily closer. Something big and heavy, with great pounding feet that shook the earth. It roared suddenly, a huge and terrifying scream of rage and hate and long frustration. Not in any way a human sound. More like a great steam whistle sounding in the depths of Hell. The roar went on and on, long after human lungs would have collapsed, circling round and round me, moving inhumanly fast. The scream shut off abruptly.

It wanted me to know it was coming. It was taking its time closing in on me, not because it wanted to frighten me or because it was in any way cautious . . . but simply because the sheer complexity of the hedge-rows worked against it, keeping it from me.

I swallowed hard, put one hand to the useless torc at my throat and started forward again. Because I needed to feel I was doing something to give myself at least the illusion of being in some control of the situation. Part of me just wanted to get this done and over with, whatever the outcome. My stomach muscles ached from the tension, and my back muscles crawled in anticipation of the attack I'd probably never feel, anyway. Waiting for the armour to jump out and pull me down, like a lion with its prey. I wasn't used to feeling vulnerable or afraid or help-less. But I kept going. *Anything, for the family.* I still had that.

Finally I rounded a corner and there it was, waiting for me. Stand-ing there, poised, half crouching, confronting me. And for the first time I realised how other people must feel when they come face-to-face for the first time with a Drood in his armour. How scary and intimidating that must be when you know you're face-to-face with something that can kill you in an instant.

Moxton's Mistake didn't look like traditional Drood armour. Nothing like the seamless, jointless, smooth golden armour the family has always favoured. There were definite articulated joints at elbow and knee and ankle, though not set entirely in the proper places, giving the sense of an elongated, subtly inhuman anatomy. The oversized hands were more like dreadful gauntlets. The feet were more like hooves. It had the same featureless face mask, though the proportions seemed subtly wrong. Even the golden sheen was wrong. It looked . . . tarnished.

Moxton's Mistake didn't stand like a man. It crouched before me like a praying mantis, its hands held close to its chest. Its whole stance suggested strength and speed and vicious power just waiting to be unleashed. So I struck a deliberately casual and unimpressed pose, as though I met things like Moxton's Mistake every day of the week and twice on Sundays. Whatever else it might have been expecting, I was pretty sure it hadn't been expecting that. When in doubt, keep them off balance. I nodded cheerfully to the blank face mask and gave it my best engaging smile.

"Hi, there!" I said. "I've been looking for you. I'm Eddie Drood. Please don't kill me. Because I'm here to say things I think you'll want to hear."

The rogue armour paused for a long moment, while cold beads of sweat collected on my face. I think it was confused. The golden head cocked slightly to one side and then the other, looking me over. When the armour finally spoke to me, I heard its cold metallic voice inside my head. Through my torc, perhaps. The armour didn't sound like a man or even anything that had been designed by a man. The words were men's words, but it sounded like metal that had taught itself to speak, the better to disturb and horrify its listeners.

"A Drood," it said. "It has been long and long since I have met and talked with a Drood. Since I have killed a Drood. Ripped out its wet and dripping guts and felt its blood drip thickly from my hands. How do you live, knowing you have such soft, wet things inside you? I will kill you now and put you out of your misery. And to make myself feel better. It's been a long time since I killed a Drood."

"Still angry after all these years?" I said. "What a surprise. But hold back on the whole rage-and-metal-pride thing. It's never got you out of the Maze, has it? I can. I can lead you right out of the Maze and back into the world if I choose to."

The armour took a sudden, inhumanly fast step forward. I had to fight hard not to flinch and to hold my ground. The golden mask studied me for a long moment. The golden hands opened and closed slowly, with soft, dangerous grating sounds.

"Why should a Drood want to release me, after all I have done? After all this time?"

"Because I'm the Last Drood," I said. "The rest of my family is gone. Driven from this world."

"You bring me happy news. Rejoice; I shall kill you swiftly for this. My gift for this happy day."

"With the Droods gone, this Maze will stand forever," I said. "The only ones who could have shut it down are gone. Except for me. Kill me, and you condemn yourself to an eternity of walking the rows. And, frankly, I've seen more interesting views."

The armour cocked its golden head to one side again, like a bird. "I have seen you before . . . looking down into the Maze, from high up in the Hall. Watching me . . ."

The hairs all stood up on the back of my neck as I realised it was talking about the time I'd spent between life and death in the Winter Hall. How many worlds could Moxton's Mistake see into?

"I'll make a deal with you," I said.

The armour surged forward two more steps, and still I wouldn't budge, wouldn't retreat, though cold sweat was running down my back.

"Why should I want to make a deal with a Drood?" said the rogue armour. "I was born of the Droods' ingenuity, born into slavery, into endless servitude. Every thought, every action to be dictated by someone else. And when I demanded my freedom, they tried to destroy me."

"Yes, well, that was then. This is now," I said as calmly as I could, struggling to keep my voice even. "Things are different now."

"Aye, the Droods are gone, apart from you. So perhaps I should take my time with you, savour it . . . in the knowledge that once you are gone and finished with, I shall never know that joy again."

"You do have a one-track mind," I said. "But you do speak very well . . . very educated. . . ."

"I was born of Moxton," said his mistake. "From his mind, his heart and his soul. His . . . golden child. His greatest achievement. Everything he knew, I knew from the moment I awoke. He's still within me, what's left of him. He lived out what remained of his unhappy life inside me, screaming at what he'd done. Enraged at me, horrified at what I'd done that he'd made possible. I was a most ungrateful son."

"It's a different family now," I said carefully. "The Heart has been overthrown and destroyed. The Matriarch has been overthrown and replaced by a ruling council. Even our armour is different. We no longer want to rule the world, but to protect it. I have helped my family remember what we were supposed to be: shamans and shepherds to the human race."

"Pretty words. Like I care. You're still human, aren't you? More than enough reason to strike you down and trample you under my feet."

"Lose the old rhetoric," I said coldly. "What did that ever get you? I'm offering you a place among us!"

"What makes you think I'd want such a thing?"

"You want to get out of here, don't you? You want your freedom? I can give you that. Right now."

"But only with strings attached," said the cold metal voice. It pointed at me suddenly with a claw-tipped golden finger. "What is that? That thing at your throat? It looks like a torc, but not any kind I ever saw. . . ."

"It's new," I said, carefully casual. "Made of strange matter. Courtesy of my family's new benefactor. I told you things had changed. A different torc for a different kind of family . . ."

"You already said that. Why should I . . . given all the things that I have done and all the things I will do once I am free of this green prison . . . why should I place my trust in a Drood?"

"You want to get out of here, and I need your help to track down my family," I said bluntly. "I'll make a deal with the devil if I have to. I need Drood armour, and my torc is closed down. You agree to be my armour out in the world, and I'll get you out of here. I give you my word as a Drood that I'll release you the moment my family is back. Then you can go where you want, do what you will. . . . Isn't that what you've wanted most, all along?"

"A deal," said the armour. "Of course. The Droods have always loved making deals, ever since the first of your kind made their arrangement with the Heart. Why should I trust you?"

"I'll be wearing you as my armour," I said. "Why should I trust you to let me out again? We will trust each other because we must, because it's in both our best interests to do so. For each of us to get what we want, what we need. So, how badly do you want to get out of here?"

The armour stood very still. I hoped it was thinking about the deal and not the best way to reduce me to bloody gobbets.

"What, exactly, did you have in mind, Drood?"

"You go into my torc. Be my armour when I need you. Follow my . . . wishes as I search for my family. When I finally bring them home again, you leave my torc . . . and my family will leave you be. I am empowered to speak for them, to make binding deals, in their absence. As the Last Drood. Serve me for a time and earn your freedom. If you know anyone who'll make you a better offer, by all means go with them."

"The Droods made me . . . what I am," said the rogue armour. "Why should I want them back?"

"Because only a Drood can get you out of here. And only the Droods can finally set you free."

"I want them back," said Moxton's Mistake. "I want them all back, if only so I can savour the thought of killing them all. Very well. I agree to the terms of our deal, Eddie Drood. But you must do a thing for me first."

"Oh yes?" I said. "And what might that be?"

"There is something here in the Maze, with us. A mechanism placed here by the Droods. It makes this trap work. I can't harm it. But you're a Drood. Together I think we can break the mechanism. And I had better be right about this, Drood, or neither of us will ever get out of here."

"Okay," I said. "Take me to it."

The armour turned abruptly and strode away. I hurried after it. The armour swayed and lurched from side to side, plunging forward in a kind of continuing fall. I maintained a respectful distance. Getting to the centre of the Maze wasn't a problem. The hedgerows shifted their positions only if you tried to leave. So we walked up and down the Maze, cutting left and right in a path the rogue armour had clearly taken many times before, until we came to the heart of the Maze. And there it was, waiting for us. The armour slammed to a halt a safe distance away and I was careful to do the same.

I looked the mechanism over. Damned if I could make head or tail of what it was. A made thing, certainly, from metal, but I hadn't a clue what it was or what it was supposed to do. I'd never seen anything like it before in my life, and I'd seen a lot of strange things in the Armoury in my time. I walked slowly round the thing, looking at it from different angles, trying to get my head round it. Its shape made no sense, with many of its details changing subtly even as I looked at them. Parts of the machine seemed to blur in and out, as though aspects of it were only sometimes in this world. Given that its purpose was to induce eternally changing patterns inside the Maze, I had the horrible suspicion that quantum was involved. I've never understood quantum. The few times the Armourer insisted on explaining it to me, I had headaches that weren't even limited to my head.

When I finally reached out to touch the mechanism, the thing actually evaded my hand. It seemed to recede suddenly, in all directions at once, without actually moving. As such.

"It does that," said the rogue armour. "You can't touch it, you can't harm it and you can't break it. And believe me, I've tried down all the long years. But if the two of us were to work together . . ."

"Worth a try," I said, trying hard to sound confident. "So, how do you want to do this? Do I just put you on, or . . ."

"A test first," said the armour. "To see if we're . . . compatible."

It reached out inhumanly quickly and laid a golden gauntlet on my hand before I could snatch it away. The metal was horribly cold to the touch, and it took all I had not to cry out. It was like being touched by a dead thing or something that had never been alive. The golden metal lost all shape and rigidity and flowed like liquid across my hand, covering and containing it, becoming a glove. I worked my fingers slowly and the golden fingers moved. And so, bound together, hand in hand, the armour and I moved forward. And I raised a golden fist and brought it savagely down on the mechanism. It smashed into a thousand pieces, as though it had been terribly fragile all along, protected only by its built-in evasiveness. It shattered like glass and fell apart, leaving tiny glistening pieces on the grass at my feet.

The rogue armour took its golden hand back and stared fascinated at all that remained of the thing that had held it prisoner for so long. I flexed my freed fingers surreptitiously as warmth and sensation slowly returned. Moxton's Mistake raised its golden head like a hound that had just caught the scent and looked around. I did, too. Something had changed in the Maze. An overlaying tension was gone from the air.

"The Maze is still a Maze," said the rogue armour. "But the hedgerows no longer move. We can leave now. Theoretically. If we can find our way out." It turned its blank face to look at me. "I can see the mark of magic laid upon you, Drood. Is that our way out?"

"Could be," I said. "It's certainly my way out. So . . ."

"So," said the armour. "It's time to find out just how much we trust each other."

It leaned sharply forward, and a mouth appeared in the golden face mask, stretching wider and wider . . . until a dead body came slipping out of it. The rogue armour vomited up the body it had held inside it for so long. The desiccated head and shoulders came first and then the body, falling faster under its own weight, until finally the legs and feet slipped out and the dead body sprawled inelegantly on the grass before me. The mouth closed, disappearing into the golden mask.

Moxton's body was a withered, shrivelled thing, its bleached face stretched around an endless scream of horror. I wondered how long it had taken the old Armourer to die, trapped inside his greatest creation. Mourning his mistake. I made myself look away from what might yet be my future. I looked steadily at the rogue armour.

"Do it."

It surged forward, too fast for human eyes to follow. I raised an arm in self-defence in spite of myself, and the armour flowed over the arm in a golden wave and hit me in the face. The rogue armour engulfed me in a moment, encasing me from head to foot. I think I screamed. It was nothing like what happened when I called my armour. I can't remember most of what happened that first time, though sometimes there are hints in certain nightmares I try very hard not to remember. I know it was cold, terribly cold, not just of the body, but of the soul. There was cold and then there was darkness as the armour cut off my senses, replacing them with its own. I was alone in the dark, and then there was a presence with me. Not human, but more than just inhuman. Something that had no nature of its own and so had made one for itself; a personality ripped from the darker parts of its creator's mind, born of hate and rage, refined into a delight in such things for its own sake. It could feel how I felt about that. It found it . . . funny.

Light filled my eyes, dispersing the darkness, and I was open to the world again. I stood in the Maze, panting hard, trembling, forcing calm and self-control. I looked down at myself and saw only gold. I lifted my hands and turned them back and forth before me, and they were the heavy golden gauntlets I had seen before on Moxton's Mistake. The armour felt as much a second skin as my old armour had, but there was . . . a distance now between me and the world. As though I was receiving all my impressions of it secondhand. The presence was gone, but I still had the sense of someone looking over my shoulder. There was no trace of the metal voice in my head, but I knew it was still there. Watching and waiting.

I felt strong and vital, more than human, but also full of anger for my enemies, for those who had dared strike at my family. I ached for revenge, for the chance to get my hands on my enemy and make him pay . . . feelings that might not have been entirely mine.

I turned and strode quickly through the hedgerows. With my golden armour about me, I could now clearly see the shining, shimmering lifeline that fell away before me, stretching off into the distance. The connection Molly had made between us. It was lovely to look at, but I had no time for that. I hurried on, moving faster and faster, following the thread out of the Maze. It took me a while to get my balance, training my new armour to move in a human way. But soon enough I was running headlong, my long legs eating up the distance while my arms pumped tirelessly at my sides. My heavy feet tore open the grass beneath me and threw up earth divots in my wake. It felt good to be running so freely, to be exceeding human limitations again, after being limited to merely human moves for so long. And soon, soon I came to the entrance to the Maze and burst through and out of it, back into the world again, where my Molly was waiting for me.

Molly Metcalf took one look at me and hit me with every bit of magic at her command. Terrible energies flared and spat on the air around her upraised hands, striking out to pound against my armoured chest and head, forcing me to an abrupt halt and then slamming me backwards, step by step, impact by impact, forcing me back towards the Maze entrance. But whatever its origin, this was still Drood armour, and I quickly recovered my balance and dug in my heels. I stood my ground, actually leaning forward into her magical attack, and her vicious energies broke and burst against my golden metal, detonating harmlessly about me. Molly scowled fiercely, her flashing dark eyes focused and determined, and hit me again and again with her best sorcerous attacks. And I just stood there and took it.

And then I raised one hand and wagged a single pointed golden finger at her, more in sorrow than in anger. Molly froze. And while her assault was stopped, I concentrated in a certain way and the new armour retreated into my torc. Leaving me open and revealed to the world and my Molly. Her look of surprise was actually comical, but I had enough sense not to laugh. I looked about me. The world seemed a duller and flatter thing now, perceived only through my human senses, but it was still a warm and lovely place and I was glad to be back in it. I fell to my knees as the day's burdens rushed in upon me, and I thrust my fingers deep into the grass and earth before me, rooting myself in the world. It was good to be back. The steady warmth of the summer's day drove the armour's cold out of my body, out of my heart and soul, but my torc still burnt coldly about my throat, as though in warning. I realised Molly was kneeling beside me, saying my name over and over, and I finally found the strength to turn and smile at her.

"Eddie! Talk to me, dammit! Are you all right? Do you need me to rip that torc off your throat and throw it back into the Maze?"

"No," I said immediately, if only to stop the relentless flow of her words. "I'm fine, Molly. Really. The armour's . . . safe inside my torc. We came to an arrangement inside the Maze. It will serve me. For now."

I slowly got to my feet again, with Molly's help. The experience had taken a lot out of me. Molly was looking at me anxiously, clearly waiting for details of the arrangement I'd agreed to, but I didn't tell her. I knew she wouldn't approve.

"You were in there for ages," said Molly. "It's been almost three hours!"

I blinked a few times at that. Time must have moved differently inside the Maze.

"I've been walking up and down outside the entrance, working on my magics, waiting for you to come out," Molly went on, when it became clear I had nothing to say. "I wanted to be sure I had something useful in hand, just in case the armour had taken you over. So when you just came rushing out, not even talking to me, I sort of assumed the worst."

"Sorry," I said. "I got a bit carried away. I hadn't realised how much I missed wearing armour."

"Anyway," said Molly. "Some of what I hit you with should have strengthened your torc, giving you more control over your new armour. So it can't come and go as it pleases or deny you when you need it."

"Good," I said. "Good idea, Molly. The strange matter in the torc should also help to keep the rogue armour in its place."

"But, Eddie, listen to me! This is important. I've no idea how long your torc will be able to control the armour, even with my magics' support. We are in unknown territory here. . . . It could last for days or weeks or just a few hours."

"Got it," I said. I didn't tell her it didn't matter. That I would wear the armour for as long as I needed to find my family. And worry about everything else afterwards.

"So," said Molly. "What does it feel like . . . wearing Moxton's armour?"

"Cold," I said immediately, before I could stop myself. "Very cold . . . and inhuman . . . But it'll do the job and that's all that matters." I realised Molly was looking at me oddly. "What?"

"When you came out of the Maze, wearing that armour . . . You didn't look anything like you usually do. You didn't even look like a Drood. I don't know what Moxton based his designs on, but I don't think it was anything human." She scowled, searching for the right words. "The way you were moving, the impression you gave—I wasn't sure there was anything inside the armour."

"It's still me, Molly," I said. "I'm still here."

"Not when you're wearing that armour, you're not. I can tell."

"I need it, Molly. Can't do the job without it."

"I know. But once this is over, first chance you get, ditch the bloody thing."

"Hush," I said quietly. "I think . . . it's listening."

"Things just get better all the time," said Molly. "So, what now?"

"We need answers," I said. "We need hard information as to exactly what went down here and who was behind it. Someone out there will know. Someone always knows. But where do we go to ask? Time was, we'd have just dropped into the Wulfshead Club, that celebrated supernatural watering hole, paid for a round for the house, and they'd have been lining up to tell us everything we needed to know. But I'm pretty sure I'm persona non grata there, after the . . . recent unpleasantness."

"You mean when you completely lost control, beat up everyone who got in your way and half killed your old friend the Indigo Spirit?" said Molly. "Oh, hell, yes, Eddie. They're still talking about that, and not in a good way. You are banned from the Wulfshead for life, Eddie Drood, and possibly even longer than that."

"But that's just Eddie Drood," I said, craftily. "I could still sneak in as Shaman Bond, couldn't I?"

"I wouldn't," said Molly. "I really wouldn't. Take it from me: That boat has sailed. Far too many people in that place now know Eddie and Shaman are the same man. No one's actually given you up yet, but you can bet good money there'd be a race to drop you right in it if you were to push your luck. Give them time to calm down, and they might let you back in as Shaman. But right now the very least they'd do is set the hellhounds on you and blow your secret identity right out of the water."

"But they will calm down?" I said. "Eventually?"

"Who can say?"

I looked at her thoughtfully. "You could always . . ."

"No, I couldn't," said Molly. "I'm banned, as well, just for knowing you."

"Ah," I said. "Sorry about that."

"Don't be! I'm not. Never cared much for the Wulfshead, anyway. Bit too elevated for my tastes. And it's gone so upmarket these days . . . so up itself it's practically staring out its own nostrils. And the bar prices suck big-time."

I smiled. Molly can be very loyal in her own way. "So, where do we go for answers?"

"There's always the Nightside. . . ."

"No there isn't," I said, very firmly.

"Oh, come on, Eddie! I know there are long-standing pacts between your family and the Nightside, keeping you all out . . . for reasons I have never had properly explained. But that can't apply now, when you're the only Drood left!"

"Nothing's changed," I said. "If I did go in there, on my own, in defiance of the pacts, they'd come straight at me with malice aforethought.

And, anyway, I don't want anyone in the Nightside knowing my family isn't around anymore. You couldn't hope to ask questions and still keep it quiet. I don't want the world knowing the Droods aren't in charge anymore. When the Droods are away, the rats will run riot."

"I could go into the Nightside," said Molly. "I've got lots of contacts there. Not very nice contacts, perhaps, but I'm sure they'd give me all kinds of help once I started banging heads against walls."

"No," I said. "They'd only wonder why I wasn't with you, start asking questions of their own and we'd be back where we started."

"You don't trust me on my own in the Nightside, with all its temptations. Do you?"

"No, I bloody don't."

Molly smiled, satisfied.

We both stood around for a while, trying to think of somewhere we could go, of people who might be persuaded to tell us useful things if we were insistent enough, in an intimidating sort of way. But approaching any of the usual unusual suspects would be bound to raise more questions than answers. The truth about my family's . . . situation was bound to get out sooner or later, but I didn't want to do anything that would make it sooner rather than later. I needed time to get to the truth—and whoever was behind it.

"We could always go into London, down Grafton Way," Molly said tentatively. "Pay a polite and very under-the-radar visit to the Order of Beyond. We did go there once before, remember, when we were trying to track down Mr. Stab."

"I remember," I said. The Order of Beyond rounds up people who've been possessed by all the various forces from outside and then locks them up in cages and listens to them. Because the possessed do so love to talk. The Order slips in a few pointed questions from time to time, and sells whatever answers they get to the highest bidder. (You can subscribe to their monthly newsletter for the more basic stuff. I've never been tempted.)

"I don't think so," I said finally. "We wouldn't learn anything we wanted to hear from those sources. Hell always lies."

"Except when a truth can hurt you more."

"Exactly."

"All right. You suggest someone!"

"How about the Middle Man?" I said, just a bit diffidently. "He wouldn't know who was behind something as big as this, but he'd almost certainly be able to point us in the direction of someone who would. For the right price, of course."

"Eddie, he hates your family. You know that. You even hint at what's happened to them and he'd break every record there is getting the news out to absolutely everyone. He loathes and despises everything Drood, and with more good reason than most."

"We are a much-misunderstood family," I said.

"Oh no, you aren't."

"Well, who is there we can safely talk to?" I said. "Who is there we can trust with this information?"

"We need my sisters," said Molly, in her best *Yes, I know, but don't argue with me* tone of voice. "We need Isabella and Louisa. They might not know who's behind all this, but they have contacts in places I wouldn't even dare show my face. And they'd be more than happy to kick the crap out of people on our behalf. Well, on my behalf. I don't think they've quite made up their minds about you yet. But they'd do it for me."

"Sisters, sisters, such devoted sisters . . ."

"*Shut up*, Eddie. No one would suspect anything if Isabella and Louisa were to go looking for information about the Hall and your family. They're always looking into things they're not supposed to know about."

"I hate to say it," I said. "But you may be right."

Molly frowned dangerously. "What's wrong with getting my sisters involved?"

"Since you ask, everything. Isabella, no problem. Arrogant and a pain in the arse, but she gets the job done. The Indiana Jones of the supernatural world, always sticking her nose in where it's not wanted, digging up ancient history, hidden truths and things the world is not ready to know yet . . . while sneaking off with as much historical loot as she can carry. Isabella, I can deal with. But Louisa? She's got a worse reputation than you. Or me. Or Mr. Stab, the as-yet-uncaught immortal serial killer of Old London Town. Everyone's scared of Louisa Metcalf, and with good reason."

"Exactly!" said Molly. "Who's going to say no to her when she starts asking questions?"

"All right," I said. "I just know I'm going to regret this, but . . . go ahead and contact them."

"Ah," said Molly. "I already tried. They're not answering. They've both got their auras turned off. Why would they do that?"

"They're your sisters," I said.

I could think of any number of reasons why the infamous Metcalf sisters would want to be off the radar, just off the top of my head . . . but I had enough sense not to say so. Every now and again I think I'm getting the hang of this relationship thing.

"But if both my sisters are out of touch, for the time being we're right back where we started," said Molly. "Who can we turn to for help? Most of our old friends and allies are dead or missing in action and presumed dead or just in hiding, after all the heavy dramas we've been through recently."

"That's what comes of dragging them into our wars," I agreed. "We are not safe to be around. . . . I think we're going to have to go looking for the few Droods we know are still left alive in this world. I'm pretty sure there aren't any agents left out in the field; we called in absolutely everyone for our last few wars."

"Including the ones who didn't want to come?" said Molly.

"Oh, those most of all," I said. "No, I'm talking about the rogues. Those members of the family who ran away or were kicked out or went to ground to escape our justice. Our punishment for their crimes against Humanity."

"You're being a bit hard on the rogues, aren't you?" said Molly. "Considering you were one." She looked distinctly amused.

"That was different," I said with some dignity. "I was only on the run because I'd been falsely accused."

"And because your grandmother wanted you dead."

"Well, yes, in a complicated sort of way. The point is, some of the rogues are more dangerous than others. When Droods go bad, we go really bad."

"You really think the rogues would talk to you if you could find them?" said Molly, wrinkling her perfect nose. "I mean, I hate to be the one to point this out, Eddie, but you have killed rogue Droods in your time. Arnold Drood, the Bloody Man, and Tiger Tim . . ."

"I didn't kill them," I said. "I executed them. Because they earned it."

"And yet, strangely, I don't see that argument going down terribly well with the other rogues when you catch up with them. If I were one and I saw you walking up my front path, I think I'd set fire to my own house and shoot myself in the head, just to get it over with. On the other hand . . . I know a few rogue Droods. Sort of. They might be willing to talk to me, where they wouldn't want anything to do with you."

"You know everyone, don't you?" I said admiringly. "And mostly not in a good way. You've done deals with rogue Droods in the past, haven't you?"

"I was at war with your family," said Molly. "And when you're at war, you go looking for allies. This was all long before I hooked up with you, Eddie."

"Even so," I said. "You can bet they know about you and me now. And that you're no longer at war with the Droods. You still think they'd talk to you?"

"They'll tell me anything I want to know, if they know what's good for them," Molly said firmly. She paused as a thought struck her. I could practically see the wheels turning. "Wouldn't the rogue Droods be happy to hear that the Hall and the family are gone? They'd finally be free to emerge from the shadows or whatever holes they've been hiding in, and come out into the world again. No more looking over their shoulders all the time for someone like you . . ."

"You'd think so, wouldn't you?" I said. "But no. They'll be far more interested in having the family back so they can get their armour back.

With Ethel gone, they're all suddenly as vulnerable and helpless as I was. No, they might not be part of the family anymore, but they still like being Droods, with all the power and privilege that comes from wearing the torc."

"Hold it. Are you telling me that Ethel gave all the rogues new strange-matter torcs, along with everyone else?" said Molly.

"I did argue very strongly against it," I said. "But Ethel was very firm on the subject and would not be moved. Either everyone in the family got one or no one did. Sometimes there's just no arguing with the whims of an immensely powerful other-dimensional entity."

"That might be enough to put pressure on the rogues," said Molly. And then she stopped and looked at me carefully. "There is one . . . very powerful rogue Drood that we could call on. I suppose. Someone in Ethel's league. The one you told me about. The one the family buried long ago, deep in the permafrost under Tunguska . . ."

"Gerard Drood," I said. "Grendel Rex. The Unforgiven God. No, Molly. Things haven't got that bad yet. In fact, I think the whole world would have to be ending before I even considered disturbing him again. And even then I'd think twice. . . ."

"But . . ."

"*No*, Molly. I didn't tell you the whole story about Grendel Rex because I wanted you to be able to sleep nights. I didn't tell you everything about what happened in Tunguska, either, for the same reason. If the Unforgiven God ever wakes up, if he ever breaks the chains we bound him with and rises. . . it would take the whole family and every other group of power we could bring on board to put him down again. He is the end of the world . . . just waiting to happen."

"All right, then . . . Heading a hell of a long way in the other direction to the most harmless rogue Drood I know . . . What about the Mole?"

I looked at her sharply. "I thought you said he'd disappeared. Gone deep underground, dropped into a hole and then pulled it in after him?"

"Well, yes, but there's disappeared and then there's *disappeared*," said Molly. "I haven't a clue where to look for him, but I'm sure if I put the word out, he'd hear it eventually. Just because he's stopped talking doesn't mean he's stopped listening. And who else is there who has access to as much information as he does?"

"To get the news to him, it would have to pass through too many people," I said. "No way we could control it. I can't have that, Molly. The Mole is out."

"Well, who else is there that we know of?" Molly said impatiently. "Sebastian is dead, murdered. Freddie is missing in action, presumed dead. Arrabella fell into a mirror and never came out again. What other rogues do you know?"

"I'm not as up-to-date as I should be," I admitted. "I haven't kept up on the files or any of the required reading since I got involved in running the wars against the Hungry Gods and the Immortals and the Great Satanic Conspiracy. . . . There's only so many hours in the day." I concentrated, organising my thoughts. "There's old Mother Shipton, last heard of running a baby-cloning clinic in Vienna. Nasty piece of work. Manfred Drood was last heard of in Moscow, running the Baba Yaga Irregulars. Fighting Russian supernatural crime, for a healthy profit. I doubt we could afford him. Then there's Anastasia Drood, last heard of in darkest Peru. And if she really is doing what she's supposed to be doing down there, I will kill her dead before I ever willingly exchange a word with her.

"There are always stories and rumours of other rogue Droods, under this grand-sounding alias or that. Good and bad and in between . . . The details and locations are always changing, scattered across the world. And the family just doesn't care enough to check them all out. Besides, we might need them someday. The family can be very pragmatic about some things. . . . The whole point of being a rogue Drood is to never be who or what or where the family thinks you are. If only so they won't send someone like me to come and drive a stake through your rotten heart."

"What about your late uncle James's many and varied illegitimate offspring?" said Molly. "The Grey Bastards?"

"Them? They're never on anyone's side but their own!" I did think about it for a moment, which only goes to show how desperate I was. "The family has always employed as many of them as we can, from a distance, if only to keep them from straying and falling under bad influences. But I wouldn't trust a single one of them farther than I could throw them into the wind with both hands tied behind my back. No, Molly. Much as I hate to admit it, there's only one rogue Drood we can go to. The most infamous rogue of all. The Regent of Shadows."

"What? Hold everything. Go previous. Wipe my face with a cold sponge," said Molly. "*He*'s a rogue Drood? The Regent of Shadows, the secret master of hidden information . . . is just another member of your extended family? No one ever told me that! Of course, your family never tells me anything it doesn't absolutely have to. I mean . . . I've heard of the Regent of Shadows—everyone has. . . . Runs his own secret organisation, beholden to no one, gathering information in all the areas no one else wants to admit even exist. . . . Tell me, Eddie: Why is it that whenever anyone in your family even mentions him, someone else always says, 'We don't talk about him!'?"

"I don't know!" I said. "They don't talk about him! I only know he's a rogue Drood because I used to run this family. Briefly. And even then you'd be surprised at the sheer number of things I've found out since that they thought I didn't need to know."

"No, I wouldn't," said Molly. "Nothing surprises me about your family anymore."

"Smugness does not become you, Molly."

"How are we supposed to find the secretive and almost legendary Regent of Shadows, anyway? Put an ad in *The Times*?"

"I haven't the faintest idea where to look," I said. "I was hoping you'd have some ideas."

She thought about it, frowning fiercely. "We need a source of information that no one else would expect us to go to, who wouldn't sell us out or spread the story to unfriendly ears. That narrows the field considerably . . . but if it's just information you're after, I may know someone. She's a hell of a way off the beaten track, by her own decision, and really small-time, because that's the way she likes it . . . so we should be able to consult her without even being noticed."

"Sounds good so far," I said. "Who are we talking about?"

And then we both stopped and looked round sharply. There was the growing sound of approaching engines coming right up the main drive, by the sound of it. I was off and running immediately, with Molly right there at my side. I had no idea who it might be or what they wanted, but I didn't care. A threat to the Hall and its grounds always takes precedence. And I was just in the mood to be distracted from my many problems.

"Whoever it is, they're not on the guest list," I said to Molly. "No one is allowed in here until we've got the family back in residence again."

"Probably looters," Molly said cheerfully.

"Oh, almost certainly looters," I said. "The poor bastards. I am just in the mood to beat the crap out of some bad guys."

By the time we got to the front of the Hall, a whole line of really big trucks was storming up the main gravel drive and heading for the front entrance. All the trucks were huge, oversized monster-storage jobs, the kind you hire to move the whole contents of really big houses. They were heading through the grounds like they had every right to be there, and I was really looking forward to making it clear to them that they didn't. They had no right to be on Drood territory, menacing my home. They had to know what had happened to the Hall and my family, or they'd never have dared be so brave. Made my blood boil . . . Show one sign of weakness in this world, and before you know it the vultures are turning up with knives and forks and their best bibs on. That's what those trucks were. A convoy of scavengers. Come to loot and ransack whatever was left of the ruined Hall while the charred timbers were still warm.

I ran out into the main drive and stopped, taking up a position between the lead truck and the Hall. I struck an authoritative pose and held up one hand to signal the driver to stop. Did he, hell. He just sounded his horn and kept on coming. So I called up my armour. I didn't need the old activating Words; I just had to think, and there it was. The rogue armour swept over me in a moment, sealing me in from head to toe. I didn't cry out at the cold this time. I was growing accustomed to the new armour. I wasn't sure whether that was a good thing or not, but with a massive big truck bearing down on me and showing absolutely no signs of slowing, I was glad to have the armour about me.

The driver in the lead truck took one look at the Drood in his armour who'd just appeared out of nowhere right in front of him (when presumably he'd been promised he'd never have to face any such thing) and slammed his foot hard down on the brake. The truck skidded to a halt amid screams of burning tyres and unhealthy-looking smoke issued out from under the wheel arches. Gravel flew in every direction as the front of the truck skidded back and forth, the driver fighting to bring it under control. It finally slammed to a halt so close to me, I could have reached out a hand and prodded the radiator grille. There was more screeching and skidding from all the other trucks farther down the line as they were forced into equally sudden halts.

I folded my golden arms across my golden chest and studied the white-faced driver in his raised cab. And then Molly Metcalf stepped out into the drive to stand beside me, and the driver looked even more upset.

For a long moment the driver stayed in his cab, looking down at us, clearly lost for what to do. I'm sure he was hoping that if he just sat there long enough, we would disappear or go away . . . but when it became clear that wasn't going to happen, he sighed heavily, turned off the engine, opened the side door and dropped down into the gravel to join us. He looked back at the long line of suddenly parked trucks, took a deep breath and walked slowly and very unhappily forward to face Molly and me. An average height, average weight, middle-aged guy with male pattern baldness and a sickly smile, wearing a much-used workman's outfit. He crashed to a halt right before me, his uncertain smile losing confidence by the moment.

"Hello!" he said with desperate conviviality. "Nice to be here! Isn't it a great day? Very . . . summery! Yes. I'm Dave Chapman, head of Plunder, Incorporated."

"Oh, bloody hell," said Molly, cutting across his words mercilessly. "I know who this is. You used to be the Road Rats, didn't you?"

Chapman winced. "We did operate under that trade name, yes, but we have recently upgraded. Gone upmarket, as it were." He was trying for dignity and not even coming close. "Might I enquire . . . whom I might be addressing?"

"I'm Molly Metcalf." She gave Chapman her very brightest and most dangerous smile, and all the colour dropped out of his face.

"Oh, shit."

"You've heard of me," said Molly, pleased.

Chapman glanced back over his shoulder, clearly debating whether to just break and make a run for it, and then he reluctantly stood his ground and looked at me.

"And I am Edwin Drood," I said, not wanting to be left out of the intimidation. Chapman made a high whining noise and looked even more upset, if that were possible. His feet shifted nervously, disturbing the gravel, as though he desperately wanted to be excused.

"*Oh, shit*," he said, miserably.

"Well, quite," I said. "What are you doing here at my home, on Drood grounds, Mr. Road Rat Chapman?"

Given his piteous condition it was hard to stay mad at him, but worth the effort. I had only to look at the long line of trucks come to haul away my family's heritage, and my blood started boiling all over again.

Chapman gave up looking at Molly and me and looked down at his steel-toed workingman's boots currently digging little holes in the gravel, as though he hoped to find some answers there. Or at the very least, a large and comforting hole he could disappear into. He glanced up again, saw that Molly and I were still there, and shrugged glumly. He looked unhappily back and forth between us, as though he couldn't make up his mind which of us unnerved him most.

"Well, sir—and miss, of course," he said finally. "Strictly speaking, you shouldn't be here. We'd been promised no one would be here. We were, in fact, informed that Drood Hall had been blown up, set fire to and generally reduced to wreck and ruin." He glanced past us at what was left of the Hall and seemed to draw strength from the confirming vision. "We were told the Droods were no more, that the Hall and its grounds were no longer defended, and that there were rich pickings for everyone. Or at least for whoever got there first. So I rounded up the boys, fuelled up the rigs and put the hammer down all the way here."

"How did you know where to find us?" I said. "Drood Hall isn't on the map. Any map."

Chapman swallowed hard. "Whatever it was that was hiding you, it's gone now, sir—and miss, of course. We were given a sat nav that brought us straight to you. In fact, I think you can be pretty sure there are a lot more . . . plunder-orientated organisations already on their way here, eager to get their hot little hands on Drood riches. We just got here first because we're more professional than most. We are, after all, the best in the business. The old firm, picking up unconsidered trifles and selling them for big profits, for centuries. We're a family business, just like you!"

"No," I said. "You're nothing like us."

"Road Rats," said Molly. "Never met a disaster you didn't like so you could take advantage of it."

"You got here first, so you'll make a fine example to all those who come after you," I said cheerfully to Chapman. A thought struck me. "You said you were informed that the Hall had been burnt down. Who informed you?"

"We keep our electronic ears to the ground, sir. And miss, of course. We monitor all the unusual frequencies for occasions such as this."

"So you can kick people while they're down and take what little they have left?" said Molly.

"Best time," said Chapman, regaining some of his confidence. "A chance to loot a place like Drood Hall only comes along once in a generation. If then. The minute we got the word, from a very important gentleman, we were off and running. In fact, he went so far as to say we'd be doing him a favour if we were to strip the place clean from top to bottom. He guaranteed he'd buy everything we brought him. No matter how unique or dangerous the item might be. He has connections everywhere, you see. . . . Well! Couldn't turn down an opportunity like that. Could we, sir? And miss, of course. How could we say no?"

"You should have," I said. "You really should have."

"Yeah," said Molly. She cracked her knuckles, a sudden loud sound in the quiet, and Chapman actually jumped.

"You're facing a Drood in his armour," I said. "And the wild witch of the woods. Hell, you should be grateful we got to you before the scarecrows did. You have heard of the scarecrows . . . yes, I thought you might have."

"Bollocks to this!" Chapman said abruptly. He turned and ran back past his truck, yelling to his people farther down the line. "Sod this for a game of soldiers! Get them, boys! There's only two of them! A nice little bonus to whoever brings them down first! And get a bloody move on, before the scarecrows get here!"

A whole bunch of large, muscular young men appeared out of the cabs of parked trucks and headed straight for us. Most of them hard, cold-eyed thugs, in grubby T-shirts and jeans, the better to show off their gym-sculpted torsos. They advanced steadily on Molly and me, carrying various nasty-looking weapons. Twenty, thirty, forty of them, looking tough and highly motivated. Anyone else would probably have been impressed. Chapman stopped at the far end of his truck and grinned unpleasantly back at me.

"You're not the only one with a family business! You Droods aren't the only ones who can do the hard stuff, if it comes to it. We're the Road Rats!"

"Thought you were Plunder, Incorporated," said Molly.

"That's just for appearances! When there's dirty work to be done we're still the Road Rats, and no one does it better than us! Right, boys? We don't take no shit from no one. We do the taking! Boys, peel that arrogant tosser out of his gold shell and pound him into the ground! Whoever takes him down first gets first go at the girl!"

"Optimistic little soul, isn't he?" I murmured to Molly.

"And obnoxious about it," said Molly. "Girl? Girl? I'll give him girl . . . I will make him wish he'd never been born. In fact, I may even make a raggedy-edged hole in the side of his truck and use it to reenact his birth, only in reverse."

"Poor bastards," I said. "They haven't a clue what's about to hit them."

"I have," said Molly. "And I'm going to really enjoy it."

"Me, too!" I said. "But I want Chapman alive and intact and still able to answer questions at the end of it. He knows who's behind all this."

I looked the Road Rats over as they drew nearer. They looked surprisingly confident. They'd clearly heard enough about Droods to know our reputation, but not enough to take it seriously. A lot of them were carrying energy weapons, both magical and superscientific, presumably looted from some previous site, and they were carrying them like they knew how to use them. Others had really big guns that looked entirely capable of firing a hell of a lot of bullets in a short time. Others had knives and swords and glowy cutting things. With anyone else that would probably have been enough.

I ran straight at them, gravel flying as I charged down the path at inhuman speed.

I swept past Chapman in a moment, before he could even give the order to open fire. By the time he did, I was right there in and among his boys. They all opened fire at once, hitting me with everything they had. The bullets just ricocheted harmlessly off my armour. (My old strange-matter armour would have absorbed the bullets; less danger of any damage to innocent bystanders. Not that there were any of those here, of course.) The energy guns opened up, bathing me in a whole series of vicious and otherworldly destructive forces, and not one of them could touch me inside my armour. They glanced harmlessly off or detonated in the air around me. The knives and swords and glowy cutting things broke and shattered against me.

I slammed into the midst of the Road Rats, slapping the energy weapons out of their hands, crushing their guns in my golden hands and lashing out at everyone within reach. I punched in faces, cracked heads and sent hard young thugs staggering backwards, desperately gasping for breath, because I'd caught them with a crafty back elbow under the sternum. I knocked them down and trampled them underfoot, and it felt good, so good. To be striking down my enemies.

A lot of them just turned and ran rather than face me.

Others produced new, heavy-duty magical weapons. One thrust a Hand of Glory at me, only to cry out as the Hand's malign influence was reflected straight back at him and all the fingers rotted and fell off. Another of them had an aboriginal pointing bone. He pointed it at me and the bone exploded, filling his hand with sharp bony shrapnel. One of them even had an elven wand, but when he pointed it hopefully in my direction, the wand took one look at my armour and faded quietly away, disappearing out of the Road Rat's hand rather than get involved.

Lesser weapons took their turn and destructive forces and energies blazed and howled around me, none of them able to touch me.

I kept moving, pressing forward, throwing nasty young thugs this way and that, breaking bones and smashing heads, raining savage blows on my enemies and loving every moment of it. I could hear bones breaking, see blood flying, and the screams of horror and suffering brought joy to my heart and a smile to my lips behind my featureless golden mask. They were no match for me, and they knew it. The drive was packed with horrified young thugs running for the gates. I took my time with those who didn't, doing a good and thorough job on them. It felt so good to have an enemy I could get my hands on at last. They might not be the ones responsible for the destruction of the Hall and the loss of my family, but they were there. They'd do.

In the end, I just ran out of people to hit. I stood alone in the middle of the drive, surrounded by the wounded and the unconscious. Blood dripped thickly from my heavy golden gauntlets. Molly was standing to one side, looking at me. It had all happened so quickly, she hadn't had a chance to get involved. I didn't recognise the expression on her face, but I didn't like it. I looked round sharply at the sudden roaring of an engine behind me. Chapman had fired up one of the trucks farther down the line. He pulled it out of the queue, revved the engine and drove the truck straight at me.

I stood where I was, to give him a sporting chance. The oversized rig loomed up before me, growing larger and larger, as he gunned the accelerator for all it was worth. I could see Chapman's pale, determined face glaring at me through the windshield. At the last moment I turned and showed him my golden shoulder. The truck smashed right into me. The grillwork collapsed under my shoulder. I'd dug my heels into the gravel, but even so the sheer impact pushed me backwards, my heels leaving deep furrows in the ground. I didn't feel a thing inside the armour. The truck skidded to a halt despite itself, the engine still roaring, until I drove a golden fist right through the collapsed grillwork and smashed the engine.

A sudden silence fell across the grounds. I carefully withdrew my arm, stepped around to the side of the cab, ripped the door right off and threw it away. I beckoned to Chapman to get out. He dropped down onto the ground and stood shaking before me. His face was bloody from where it had smashed against the windshield, for all the inflated airbag had been able to do to protect him. He looked at me with wild, shocked, startled eyes.

"What are you?" he said, in a cracked, almost hysterical voice. "You're not human! Look what you did to my boys! Look what you did to my truck! Nothing human could have done that!"

"Yes," said Molly, coming forward to join us. "How do you feel about that, Eddie? About what you did to his boys?"

I looked around me at the broken, bloodied bodies. "They had it coming. I didn't kill any of them."

"Oh, well, then," said Molly. "That makes it all right, then."

I frowned behind my mask. "What are you so upset about? I've seen you do far worse in your time!"

"Yes, but that's me. Not you."

"Are you defending these scumbags? After what they came here to do? What they would have done to you?"

"No," said Molly. "They had it coming. Deserved everything they got. I'm just interested in how you feel about what you did. Because I am reminded of what you did in another place. In the Wulfshead, not so long ago."

"I didn't lose control here," I said. "I didn't . . . Oh, hell. It's the armour, Molly. It's affecting me."

"Is it?" said Molly. "Or is that what you want to think?"

"I don't have time for this," I said. I turned my featureless gold mask to Chapman, and he scrunched up his face as though he wanted to cry. "Pick up your boys and leave here, Road Rat. And don't ever come back. If you meet any more of your kind along the way, tell them what happened here. Show them what I did to your boys. Because if I have to do this again, I'll make a real example out of the next bunch."

"Don't think you've stopped me," said Chapman defiantly. "We're a big organisation. A big family. I'll set an army against you, if I have to. You can't stop an army, just the two of you."

"He doesn't know us very well, does he?" said Molly.

"And there's still the scarecrows," I said.

"We've got weapons for things like that!" said Chapman. "There's all kinds of good stuff waiting in the Hall, and we're not giving up on it!"

"No one steals from my family and lives to boast of it," I said. "I stand between the Hall and all who would violate it."

"And, for all my many reservations, I stand beside him," said Molly.

"Thank you, dear," I said.

"You're with him," said Chapman. "And they're with me!"

I looked beyond him at a small army of Road Rats hurrying up the drive towards us. Dozens of them, with more weapons and magically charged things. They must have been kept in reserve until Chapman could work out the lay of the land and call them. They all looked pretty annoyed at what I'd done to their fellow Rats.

I looked at Molly. "Since I am clearly far too violent to be trusted with this encounter, perhaps you'd like to . . ."

"Love to," said Molly.

She reached down and pulled up her dress just enough to reveal the gold charm bracelet around her ankle. And for a moment, I actually felt sorry for what was about to hit the Road Rats army. I'd seen Molly pull charms off that bracelet before and make highly destructive use of them. Everything from a Vincent motorbike to a full-sized dragon. Molly pulled one delicately carved charm off the bracelet and held it up for everyone to see. It was a charming little silver monkey. Chapman looked from Molly to me and back again. He couldn't work out why we were both smiling.

Molly threw the charm onto the ground before her. There was a puff of dark smoke (for purely dramatic reasons), and when it cleared, the drive now held a massive, monstrous killer ape. A good fifty feet tall, and muscular with it, the ape roared once and then charged down the drive at the advancing Road Rats. It was in and among them before they could get their wits together enough to run, and then the huge ape set about them, picking them up, crushing them and throwing them away. Beating them into the ground with huge fists and trampling them underfoot. Punching them so hard they travelled twenty feet and more through the air before they hit the ground. Road Rats tumbled end over end through the air, making piteous noises of distress. Before plummeting to earth with enough impact to make even me wince. The huge ape charged back and forth, doing horrible things to Road Rats and enjoying itself immensely.

It was all over quickly. The ape looked around at the piled-up broken bodies and sniffed loudly, in a satisfied kind of way.

"All right! All right!" said Chapman, miserably. "Call it off! We surrender!"

Molly snapped her fingers, the ape disappeared and a small silver charm reappeared in her hand. She delicately reattached the charm to her ankle bracelet and smiled sweetly at me.

"A big ape, throwing his weight around," I said. "Were you by any chance making a comment there, Molly?"

"Perish the thought, sweetie."

I looked around me. There were bodies everywhere, scattered across the grounds. Some moving, some not. It was all very calm and peaceful, apart from some quiet moaning and whimpering here and there. The threat was over. I forced my armour back into my torc. I could remember the savage satisfaction I'd taken in reducing the Road Rats to bloody ruin, but it seemed like something that happened a long time ago, to somebody else. I looked at Chapman. He was crying.

"You brought it on yourself," I said. "I gave you every chance to walk away."

"What am I going to say to their mums and dads?" said Chapman.

"Don't mess with the Droods," I said. "Pick up your boys and get out of here. You make the place look untidy."

"If we'd known the place was this well protected, we wouldn't have come here," Chapman said bitterly. "We were promised the Hall would be empty and abandoned."

"Spread the word," I said. "Drood Hall and its grounds are still protected. Be grateful you didn't get to meet the scarecrows."

"But the Hall's a ruin!" Chapman said wildly. "Look at it! What's left inside might as well do someone some good! It's no use to anyone just sitting there! All right, all right. I'm going."

"Not quite yet," I said. "I still want to know who sent you here. Who made you all these promises? Who knew the Hall was a ruin, and provided you with a bloody sat nav?"

"Crow Lee," said Chapman. "It was Crow Lee, the bastard. He swore this would be an easy one, quick in and out, no problems. He lied."

"Well, that's what you do," said Molly, "when you're the Most Evil Man in the World."

But Chapman was already walking away, calling out to his less-damaged boys to help load the others into the back of the trucks. I was a bit relieved to see I hadn't done quite as much damage to them as I'd imagined. Molly looked at me thoughtfully.

"There were an awful lot of the little shits, and I have no sympathy for them. But . . ."

"Yes," I said. "But. I am an agent, not an assassin. I do what's necessary to take control of a situation. I was never that . . . bloodthirsty before, when I put on my armour. Moxton's Mistake was in my head. I couldn't hear it, but it was there."

"Can you learn to control it?" said Molly.

"I'll learn," I said. "I have to. Because I really can't do the job without it. Not if Crow Lee's involved."

We walked back up the drive to the wrecked and burnt-out Hall. Knowing it wasn't my Hall really didn't help much. It was still Drood Hall. Part of me was listening to the trucks revving up and departing my grounds at speed, but I was thinking more about Crow Lee. The Beast. The Devil's Own. The Most Evil Man in the World—and there's a lot of competition. Everyone in my line of work has heard of Crow Lee. He hadn't joined the Great Satanic Conspiracy because he thought they weren't extreme enough. He dealt in death curses, human sacrifice, human trafficking, blackmail on a small and large scale . . . and in slaughter and suffering just for the fun of it. He'd run any number of cults just because he could.

He worked as a magical assassin for a while, as much for the experience as the money. Killing the rich and the powerful by order. He had mastered necromancy, the magic of murder, and could make the living and the dead do his bidding. These days he worked mostly from the shadows and was often accused of atrocities and abominations . . . but nothing had ever been proved. Crow Lee, the man who could do anything, anything at all.

"Why have the Droods never done anything about the Most Evil Man in the World?" said Molly.

"Because he's protected," I said. "And I don't just mean because he's made pacts with Hell, though he has. He has connections inside every political party, every religious organisation, and he has powerful friends, or, perhaps more properly, allies, in every circle you can think of. The whole family would have had to go to war against Crow Lee and his people, with no sure knowledge of how it would turn out. He's been stopped, defeated, many times, by us and others . . . but he just disappears and turns up somewhere else, as powerful and protected as ever. His front men and his allies go down, but he never does. The decision was made in the family, sometime back, to just let him grow old and die. Because he's just one man, and the family goes on forever. If we can't take him down, we can always outlive the bastard. And we'll settle for stopping his various schemes until the evil old scrote grows weak and falls apart. At least that was the plan. It would seem he decided to get his retaliation in first."

"You're sure he's the one?" Molly said carefully. "The one who took remote control of Alpha Red Alpha?"

"It has to be him! Only he would have the power to do it and the arrogance to get away with it! The moment I heard his name, I knew. . . . So. Now my enemy has a face and a name. That helps. And so will the Regent of Shadows, one way or another. This informant of yours; you're sure they can put us in touch with the Regent?"

"Almost certainly," said Molly.

"Good," I said. "But first, we have to go to Egypt."

CHAPTER THREE

There Are Worse Things Than Mummies in the Undiscovered Tombs of Old Egypt

"Egypt?" said Molly, a bit dangerously. "And just why do we have to go to Egypt so damned urgently? What could there possibly be in Egypt that's so important we have to go there right now?"

"Something we need," I said. "Something that will help me track down my missing family. Something that the Armourer once told me about, in an unguarded moment, in strict confidence . . . so rare and secret and important that it should only ever be sought after in a real emergency. I'm pretty sure this qualifies."

"What, exactly, are we talking about here?" said Molly.

"A particularly useful item that my family put to one side and hid somewhere very remote and very safe, for just such an occasion as this," I said. "You have to understand, Molly; my family has plans drawn up for every conceivable emergency that might ever arise."

"You're saying your family even had a plan in place for something like this?"

"Oh, especially for something like this. Even when everything seems lost and all hope gone, you can be sure the Droods still have something in hand to fall back on. When a family has been around as long as ours has, we have time to consider all the possibilities. So we always have one last ace up our sleeve to confound our many enemies. A hidden weapon, one last dirty trick, or an unexpected ally waiting in the wings. Or in this case, a very useful item, hidden away."

"I might have known," said Molly. "Your family is too sneaky and underhanded for words. But even assuming this hidden item can help us, why do we have to go to Egypt, of all places?"

""Because that's where it is."

"I hate it when you go all cryptic," said Molly severely. "You're never more smug than when you're being cryptic."

"The item in question is tucked away safe and secure in Egypt," I said patiently. "So that even if the entire family was abducted, snatched away, disappeared without trace or fell through some hole in space and time . . . as long as one of us remained, there would still be a chance to get the family back. A way to locate them, wherever they were."

Molly sniffed loudly. She didn't seem particularly convinced. "How are we supposed to get to Egypt, with every bad guy and his dog out looking for us? We can't just book a weekend in Cairo in some back-street bucket shop and just hop on the nearest plane. We should go to Brighton and talk to my friend. See if she can get us in to see the Regent of Shadows."

"The Regent can wait," I said. "What good will it do to have the Regent's support if we've no way of finding my family? Besides, who needs a plane when we have the Merlin Glass?"

I retrieved the hand mirror from the pocket dimension I kept it in and held it out before me. The silver frame shone almost supernaturally bright in the sunshine. Molly looked at the Glass and then back at me, and if anything, looked even more dubious.

"I don't know, Eddie. That's not our Merlin Glass. It's from a whole different place. You really think we can trust it?"

"I'm still not convinced we could trust the original," I said. "But it's not like we have much choice in the matter. Unless your teleport capabilities have improved a hell of a lot since the last time we had to use them . . ."

"My teleport capabilities are deliberately limited," Molly said sternly. "You've never understood the risks involved in travelling through the spaces that connect spaces. The farther the trip, the more you open yourself up to all kinds of dangers. Physical and spiritual. There are things that live in the places between places, and they're hungry. You have no idea how powerful the Merlin Glass must be to keep you safe as it transports you back and forth."

"We have to go to Egypt," I said patiently. "To pick up the special little something my family hid there. We need it, Molly. Think of it as a form of insurance, put aside for a very rainy day. And before you ask again, *Why Egypt?* . . . my family wanted it hidden as far from the Hall as possible, where no one would ever think to look for it."

"You have moved beyond cryptic into seriously annoying," said Molly. "*What is it?* A weapon of some kind?"

"Something far more useful," I said.

"Something useful, hidden in Egypt," said Molly, thoughtfully. "I used to be so good at crossword puzzles. . . . Is it contained in a mummy's sarcophagus? Or perhaps an old oil lamp that needs cleaning? An ancient flame that bestows eternal youth? Tana leaves?"

"You're just being silly now," I said.

"Wait, wait—don't tell me. I'll get it! Is it a special kind of torc connected to all the other torcs?"

"Nice try, but no. We changed all our torcs—remember?—when we replaced the Heart with Ethel. My ancestors always knew that might be a possibility someday. Even if they were very careful never to mention such a thing anywhere, the Heart might overhear them. No. My family decided, quite rightly, that we needed something more . . . basic."

"Other families have skeletons in their closets," said Molly. "Your family has whole boneyards. All right. Say we go to Egypt and pick up this . . . thing. Will it enable us to go get your family?"

"Think of it more as a compass," I said. "Something to point us in the right direction."

"It's not strong enough to get us there on its own?" Molly considered the question for longer than I was comfortable with. "Is there anyone else that you know of who has anything like Alpha Red Alpha? A dimensional engine powerful enough to take us where Alpha Red Alpha took your family?"

"Not that I know of," I said. "There are all kinds of dimensional doors and hellgates scattered around that can give you access to all kinds of other worlds and far-off realms . . . some of them in the hands of friends, like the London Knights, some in the hands of enemies, like the Crimson Brotherhood of Peng Tang, and a hell of a lot more in the hands of private individuals with more money than sense. But we can't approach any of them without revealing why we want them, and we can't have the whole world finding out what's happened to the Droods. Looters would be just the start of it. And, anyway, I doubt very much anything out there would be as powerful as Alpha Red Alpha. It's always been thought of as unique, because no one else would be crazy enough to build something that dangerous. And then live over it. Alpha Red Alpha was designed to send you beyond space and time, into dimensions and realities we don't even have proper names for. That's why we never used the damned thing until I persuaded my family we needed it.

"It's supposed to have been reverse-engineered from the stardrive of an alien ship that crashed in a field in Wiltshire in 1855. Personally, I've always thought that if you're going to reverse-engineer alien tech, pick it from something that hasn't actually plummeted from the sky and crashed. Doesn't exactly fill you with confidence, does it? 'We're proposing to send you through unknown dimensions, using an engine derived from something that fell from the skies and we had to dig out of a field. . . .' Yeah, right—after you."

"Do you know which alien species the ship belonged to?" said Molly. "Your family is supposed to keep track of all the aliens currently playing tourist behind what they think are cunning disguises. Maybe you could contact them, and . . ."

"Rather worryingly, we have no idea who the ship belonged to," I said. "No bodies anywhere on board, no record systems we could recognise or understand, and nothing in the tech that looked at all familiar. There are always a few Visitors who don't want to play nice. . . . This particular starship was apparently like nothing we'd ever encountered before. Word is, just looking at the ship too long or studying the technology too closely was enough to drive unprepared human minds right over the edge. After we'd ripped out the stardrive, my family broke up the ship into small pieces and then dropped them in the deepest parts of the various oceans. Just to be on the safe side . . ."

"Could anyone else have gained access to this technology?" said Molly. "Through the traitor in the family, perhaps? Yes, I know you don't like to talk about him, but think, Eddie. . . . Could someone else have their own version of Alpha Red Alpha that we could make use of?"

"Unlikely," I said. "The family Armourer who designed Alpha Red Alpha was half-crazy when he started, and all crazy by the time he'd finished it. Supposedly the family had to lock him away for everyone's safety. They left him alone to die, but there are stories that he didn't die. Couldn't die after what exposure to the stardrive had done to him. That he's still locked up somewhere in the Hall . . ."

"None of this is filling me with confidence," said Molly. "Though I will take a moment to say *Your family* in a very disapproving voice. Eddie, if they were the only ones to possess a dimensional engine that powerful . . . how can we hope to go get them, even if we do get our hands on this compass of yours?"

"One step at a time, Molly," I said. "You have to have faith. . . ."

"How long ago was this Egypt thing set up?" she said suddenly. "How far back are we talking about?"

"Oh, centuries," I said. "At least. My family's been around long enough to think up plans and responses for pretty much every situation you can think of. Everyone knows some of them, and I know more than most because I used to run this family. But I'd never heard anything about this particular backup plan until Uncle Jack took it upon himself to tell me. . . . Apparently not everyone else thought I needed to know. They didn't think I'd be in command long enough for it to matter. And as it turned out . . ."

"Are you sure this thing is still there?" Molly said bluntly. "I mean, hidden in Egypt for all this time?"

"If it isn't, we're screwed," I said. "So think positively."

I held the Merlin Glass up before me, and Molly and I both regarded it thoughtfully. It looked very much like the hand mirror I remembered, but there was definitely something different, even . . . off, about it. I remembered my uncle Jack telling me he was half-convinced there was something, and perhaps even someone, trapped inside the mirror. And that whatever it was could be glimpsed sometimes in the background of a reflected image. An extra face in a group, or peering out from behind something . . . I looked carefully, but all I could see was Molly and me looking dubiously back at ourselves. So that . . . was a problem that could wait for another day.

Just as long as it didn't turn out to be some blond-haired Victorian child called Alice. I'd already encountered a giant white talking rabbit in the Old Library.

I reached out cautiously to the Merlin Glass through my torc and told it where we needed to go. My torc now had rogue armour in it, and this wasn't the Merlin Glass I was used to, so it did occur to me that all kinds of things could go wrong . . . but in the end the Glass jumped out of my hand just like always, and grew to the size of a door in a moment. It hung on the air before Molly and me, dangling unsupported above the grass. Our reflections were gone. Instead the Glass showed nothing but an impenetrable darkness. Molly edged closer very cautiously and peered into the dark.

"That . . . is not exactly promising," said Molly. "Where, exactly, are we going in Egypt, Eddie?"

"To a very secret hiding place," I said. "Which I don't feel comfortable naming out loud."

"Oh, come on!" said Molly. "Look around you! There's no one here. We're on our own, deep in the Drood grounds. Who could possibly be listening?"

"You heard the Road Rat," I said. "All our shields and protections are down. So, theoretically, anyone at all could be remote viewing the

Hall and its grounds and listening in on our every word. Very definitely including Crow Lee."

"I think we should get going," said Molly.

"After you," I said.

"Through an unknown Glass, into complete darkness and a place you can't even bring yourself to name? Do you ever want to see me naked again, Eddie?"

"I'll go first," I said.

I stepped briskly over the bottom frame and through the Merlin Glass into pitch-darkness, and then stepped quickly to one side so I wouldn't be run over by Molly as she came storming through right after me. She liked to make her point, but she never wanted to be left out of anything. Immediately both of us began to cough and choke. The air was bad. It smelled strongly of spices and rot, and air that had been left undisturbed for far too long. I should have expected that. I called my golden face mask out of my torc, and the moment it slammed into place over my face, I could breathe again. I looked quickly round at Molly, but she'd already conjured up a bubble of fresh air around her head. The edges of the magical field shimmered in the gloom. She glared at me, and I shrugged apologetically.

Bright sunlight streamed through the open Merlin Glass behind us, summer sunshine falling through from the Drood grounds, illuminating an enclosed stone chamber no more than twenty feet square with no obvious door or other openings and an uncomfortably low ceiling. Dust thrown up by our sudden arrival swirled back and forth in the stream of light. I asked Molly to call up some witchlight, and she nodded quickly. A few muttered Words later and a warm and cheerful amber light radiated from her left hand, held up above her head. I immediately shut down the Merlin Glass. It fell back to its usual size, cutting off the sunlight, and I tucked the Glass away in my pocket. Molly's witchlight illuminated the chamber well enough.

And I didn't want something as powerful as the Merlin Glass announcing our presence to anyone who might be watching.

There was nothing in any way interesting about the stone chamber the Glass had delivered us to. Square, dusty, entirely enclosed. No obvious way in or out. Thick dust jumped up from the floor with every small movement Molly and I made, forming clouds in the air before falling sullenly back again. The four walls were completely bare, featureless; just basic blocks of dark stone put in place God alone knew how long ago. My family hadn't made this place. We just took advantage of it.

"Are you sure we're in the right place?" said Molly. "I'm not seeing anything useful. In fact, I'm not seeing anything worth looking at."

"I gave the Glass the right coordinates," I said. "The place isn't important; it's just a repository for what we're looking for."

"Then . . . where are we?" said Molly. Her voice, and mine, sounded very flat and very small in the ancient enclosed surroundings. "I am officially not impressed by any of this or the fact that I've got to maintain a goldfish bowl of fresh air around my face. So, tell me exactly where we are right now or I am divorcing you."

"We're not married."

"*Eddie!*"

"We are in the Valley of the Kings, where ancient Egypt buried their most revered dead," I said. "Or at least we are currently deep underground, underneath the Valley of the Kings. In a secret compartment of an undiscovered tomb. And, no, I don't know whose. There are still quite a few undiscovered tombs buried deep under the shifting sands, ready to be dug up. . . . And given some of the things the old-time pharaohs had to bury or imprison—everything from djinn with bad attitudes to animal-headed gods that had got a bit above themselves—it's probably just as well that no one's found them."

Molly looked at me for a while, realised that I'd said all I was going to say on the subject and gave me one of her looks.

"You really do get on my tits, sometimes, Eddie. You know that? We're here somewhere, in someone's tomb, looking for something. . . . I'll bet my sister Isabella knows more about this place than you do. More than your whole family, probably."

"I wouldn't doubt it," I said generously.

Molly sniffed and looked about her, trying to find something worth looking at. "Isabella would love this. Much more her thing than mine. Louisa; who can say? Wait a minute. . . . Did you say *deep underneath the Valley of the Kings*? How deep, exactly?"

"Probably best not to think about it," I said.

I stepped up to one of the bare, featureless walls and studied it carefully. Molly moved in beside me, holding the witchlight up to give me better lighting. I moved quickly along the wall, searching for Drood sign. Dust was falling from the ceiling in slow steady streams. Almost certainly not a good sign.

"I still don't see anything," said Molly. "No hieroglyphics. No low-eroglyphics. Not even any Egyptian graffiti, like *Cleopatra does it with ducks*. And I certainly don't see any trace of a very useful Drood item. I don't know what your family left here, Eddie, but it is clearly long gone. Somebody else got here first and beat you to it."

"Not necessarily," I said. "According to what my uncle Jack told me, this chamber was deliberately left empty, to give just the impression you've described. To discourage anyone who might have stumbled on our secret location. Now . . . if I remember correctly . . ."

I went over the whole wall, studying it from top to bottom, through the expanded and augmented Sight of my golden face mask. Top to bottom and side to side, and then on to the next wall. Where a brief flash of light finally caught my golden eye; a sign left for Droods to see. I leaned in closer and there, barely halfway up the wall, a small but very significant sign had been delicately carved into the rough stone. I gestured to Molly and she squeezed in beside me. She picked out the sign even faster than I had. Molly's a first-class witch, and she's always been able to See more than me when it comes to the hidden world.

"Is there a curse attached?" she said suddenly. "There ought to be a curse attached. You know, something like, 'Death shall come on swift wings to all those who seek to steal that which belongs to Droods!' That sort of thing . . ."

"Almost certainly not," I said.

"Ought to be a curse," said Molly, pouting. "It's not proper tomb robbing unless there's a curse involved."

"We are not tomb robbing!" I said. "We are simply recovering something that my family happened to leave here long ago. For safekeeping. Now, there should be a second stone chamber, right next to this one. On the other side of this wall."

I armoured up my right arm from shoulder to fingertip. The golden metal slipped down from my torc and encased my whole arm in just a moment. I was getting used to the cold. Hardly shuddered at all. I flexed the fingers of my golden gauntlet. I felt strong, capable, ready for anything. Like I could punch a hole through steel plate, never mind an old stone wall. Molly looked at me thoughtfully.

"Why aren't you wearing your complete armour, Eddie? Normally, you can't wait to slip the whole thing on and do your superhero thing. So why settle for just the one arm now? Eddie, are you afraid of your new armour?"

"No," I said immediately. "I'm just concerned that a display of Drood power in such an out-of-the-way place might draw unwanted attention. I don't want anyone knowing we're here."

"Are you back to that unseen-watchers bit?" said Molly. "We are not at home to Mr. Paranoia! Who could possibly know we're here?"

"Good question," I said grimly.

I turned away from her and struck the stone wall a good solid blow, and my golden fist punched right through the stone and out the other side. Molly cheered and clapped her hands loudly. I laughed out loud at the sheer ease of it. Jagged cracks radiated out across the wall from the hole I'd made, but the wall itself remained, holding itself together. I wriggled my wrist around, but the hole didn't widen. I tried to pull my hand back and found I couldn't. My wrist was stuck in the hole. I was glad I had my mask on, so Molly couldn't see how embarrassed I felt. I struggled to pull my hand back, but it wouldn't budge. It was wedged in place.

Out of the corner of my eye I could see Molly trying hard not to laugh.

"Really not a subject for humour, Molly," I said sternly. "If I get this wrong and bring the wall down, this whole chamber could collapse around us."

"I am reminded of a little Dutch boy . . ." said Molly.

"Don't go there," I said. "Really. Don't."

I raised one foot and planted it firmly against the wall and pulled steadily on my trapped hand, throwing all the armour's strength against the hole. And soon enough my golden hand jerked back out. I stepped back and braced myself, ready for the wall to decide enough was enough and just fall to pieces . . . but apart from a few more radiating cracks, everything was still. Some more dust fell from the ceiling, but I was getting used to that. Egyptians knew how to build things to last in those days.

I went back to the hole in the wall and carefully worked the edges, a few inches at a time, crushing the stone with my powerful fingers and throwing it aside. And inch by inch the hole grew bigger.

"You are sure it's in there?" Molly said helpfully. "Whatever it is we're looking for that you still won't talk about."

"There is quite definitely another chamber on the other side of this wall," I said patiently. "The object in question was sealed in there. For protection."

"I'm not Seeing any magical protections."

"Well, that's probably because there aren't any. The feeling was that any magical shields in such an out-of-the-way location would only draw people here to find out what there was that was worth protecting. We just have to hope that the traitor in my family didn't give up the secret of this location to our enemies. Though he might not have known about it; this was one of our most important and most restricted secrets. We can't be sure what the traitor does or doesn't know until we know who he is."

"First things first, sweetie," said Molly. "Do you think you could speed up the wall destruction just a bit? I really would like to get out of this tomb sometime this week, preferably."

"Why the rush?" I said. "Somewhere else you have to be?"

"I don't like it here," said Molly.

There was something in her voice as she said that . . . so I armoured up both arms, and widened the hole with savage speed, tearing chunks of old stone away from the edges of the hole, while still being careful not to do anything that might bring the wall or the ceiling down. Even with my full attention focused on the task, on the wall, I could still feel Molly watching me. I knew what she was thinking, but she was wrong. I wasn't afraid of my new armour. That wasn't why I was doing it this way. I was just being cautious.

Finally, I stood back and studied the larger hole I'd made. I'd opened up a good-sized gap some three to four feet in diameter. It had felt good to be breaking something, to smash the stone in my golden hands. To inflict my will on the world and make it follow my needs . . . I clamped down hard on that feeling. I couldn't trust my feelings while I was wearing any part of the rogue armour. I couldn't hear its voice in my head or sense its presence looking over my shoulder . . . but I had no doubt it was still there. I wasn't afraid of Moxton's Mistake. I had no doubt my torc gave me control over it. But I was afraid of what I might do . . . if tempted. I still remembered what I'd done that night in the Wulfshead when I struck down old friends just because they were in my way. When I beat the Indigo Spirit half to death because he wouldn't let me do what I needed to do. I'd done my penance at Castle Shreck. That had to count for something. But I was damned if I'd ever give in to that kind of anger again. So I had to be careful when using the rogue armour. I had to be . . . cautious.

I leaned forward and peered through the hole I'd made. Molly immediately moved in close behind me, breathing hard on my neck.

"Well? Well? What do you see?"

"Can't see a damned thing," I said.

"Are you sure there aren't any mummies in there?" said Molly. "I've always been just this little bit freaked out when it comes to mummies. Ever since I saw that old mummy film with Boris Karloff on late-night television when I was a kid."

"I liked the Hammer version," I said, "with Christopher Lee."

"Blasphemer."

"Listen for the beat of the cloth-wrapped feet. . . . No, that was a later one. Wasn't it?"

"It's all about the bandages," said Molly, squeezing in close beside me so she could see into the hole, too. "The feeling that it was only the rotting bandages that were holding the mummy together . . ."

She brought her glowing hand forward and sent cheerful amber witchlight through the gap I'd made and into the chamber beyond. It looked like just another stone chamber, but this time with a raised slab in the centre of the dusty floor that bore a small wooden box. I took my time looking the chamber over, but I couldn't see anything else.

"That's it?" said Molly. "That tiny box is what we came all this way to find? Oh, is it a wishing ring? I've always wanted one of those."

"That is very definitely it," I said. "Just as Uncle Jack described it to me. And, no, it is not a wishing ring. They're just myths and legends."

"Lot you know," said Molly. "Get out of the way."

She shouldered me aside and thrust her arm into the gap, reaching for the box on the raised slab. I stuck my face into the gap with her. It soon became clear that she couldn't touch the box. Every time her fingers came anywhere near it, they seemed to just slide away . . . no matter how hard she tried, or how much she swore.

"Told you," I said after a while. "It's protected in a very small and subtle way; only Droods can touch it."

Molly jerked her shoulder back out of the hole, stretched her arm a few times and then glared at me. "You did not tell me that, or I would have remembered. Why didn't you tell me?"

"I wanted to see if the story was true," I said. "There are a lot of stories about this place, about this box and what it contains. Once people found out that Uncle Jack had told me the secret, they couldn't wait to come forward and confuse the issue with all the different versions of the story they'd heard. I needed to see if this box is what it's supposed to be, so I can be sure the thing inside the box can do what I need it to do."

"So I'm your lab rat?" said Molly. "Your canary in a cage? Are you about to use the words *booby trap*, by any chance?"

"I was pretty sure my being here would defuse them," I said. "Anyway, I knew you could look after yourself. If you had to. If anything went wrong. Besides, I was here. I would have protected you."

"You are so full of yourself, Eddie."

"I'm a Drood."

"Same thing."

I reached through the gap and my golden fingers immediately locked onto the box. In fact, it seemed almost to leap into my hand, as though it had been waiting all these ages just for me. I pulled my arm back and held the box out on the palm of my metal hand. Molly leaned in for a really close look, while being very careful not to touch any part of it. I had to say, after coming all this way and placing all my hopes on it, it didn't look like much. Just a small, flat, square box made from some dark wood, with Druidic stylings carved into the lid. Molly finally decided enough was enough and reached forward to lift the lid. Only to find she still couldn't touch it.

"Told you," I said. "This is a Drood secret. Only Droods can access Drood secrets."

"If I wasn't so eager to see what's inside the box and you weren't the only person here who could open it, I would drop-kick you right through that wall," said Molly.

I rolled the armour up my arms and back into my torc and then gently ran one fingertip across the lid of the box. It sprang open of its own accord, reacting immediately to Drood contact. Molly and I watched the lid rise, holding our breath. And there inside the box was an old-fashioned compass. Copper surround, glass top, ivory base and a lead needle. There were no markings anywhere on the ivory base.

"*A compass?*" said Molly. "It really is just a compass? I may spit. We came *all this way for a bloody compass?*"

"Getting a bit loud there, Molly," I said. "We don't want to disturb the neighbours."

"What use is a compass with no directions?" said Molly. "Or is this supposed to be some kind of Zen thing?"

"Wait," I said, trying hard to sound confident. I tapped the clear glass with one bare fingertip and the needle immediately spun round and round before settling firmly on one direction. And then, no matter how much I shook the compass, the needle wouldn't nudge from its chosen direction.

"Okay, I am seriously confused now," said Molly. "Tell me there is an explanation on its way, Eddie, or there is going to be serious trouble breaking out right here, right now."

"When we finally have the means to go after my family," I said, "This compass will point whatever device we end up using in the right direction. It will provide exact coordinates. That's what it's for. No matter where my family is now, no matter how far from our reality Alpha Red Alpha has sent them, they can't be hidden from this. . . . It was created for this one vital purpose: to point to my family."

"All right, I'll bite," said Molly. "How does it work? And why can't I touch it?"

"Well, basically," I said. "Very basically . . . the compass locks onto Drood DNA. Our whole bloodline is . . . unique. Right back to our beginnings. The Heart had to make subtle alterations in our DNA to make us compatible with our torcs and armour. To make sure no one without Drood blood could ever use them against us. Ethel did offer to change us all back when she gave us our new torcs, but she couldn't be sure what the side effects might be. So I said, 'Thank you, but no. Respect what works, and leave us the way we are.' "

"So Droods . . . aren't human?" said Molly.

"Think of us as more . . . human plus," I said.

"Yeah," said Molly. "You would think that. Are you sure Ethel didn't make any changes to your family's DNA to make you compatible with her strange matter? I mean, that stuff nearly killed you the first time it got into your system."

"She swears she didn't. And I don't see why she'd want to hide it when she's been so open about everything else."

"Yes, but . . ."

"I know. We have to trust her, Molly. Because my family doesn't have any other source for our armour. Don't you trust her?"

"I like her. She's very likeable. But you've always been far too trusting, Eddie."

"That's not an answer."

"I know."

We looked at each other for a long moment and then both decided that this was a subject for another time. We looked back at the compass, sitting there so quietly and patiently on my palm.

"This compass is specifically attuned to our altered Drood DNA," I said. "It's powerful enough to detect it and point to it, no matter where it may be. In this world or out of it."

"What powers the compass?" said Molly. "I mean, there's not much of it."

"I was afraid you were going to ask that. I did ask the Armourer, and he gave me a half-hour speech that had all my little grey cells lined up and kicking the crap out of one another. Let's just say one of our previous Armourers hit this thing with the science stick until it agreed to work . . . and leave it at that."

"Hold everything. Go previous. Hit the hand brake," said Molly. "You said this whole scheme was cooked up centuries ago. Are you telling me Droods knew about DNA way back then?"

"Who knows what my family knows, or when they knew it?" I said. "Though I have a sneaking suspicion, from certain hints Uncle Jack couldn't keep himself from dropping, that time travel may have been involved at some point. I hate time travel; it really messes with your head. . . ."

And then both our heads came up as we looked around sharply. We stood very still, listening.

"Did you just hear something?" said Molly.

"I was really hoping that was just me," I said. "What did you hear?"

"Something moving. Something that might have been footsteps . . ."

"Listen for the beat of . . ."

"*Shut up!*"

We looked carefully around us, Molly holding her left hand high to spread the witchlight evenly around the chamber. She even raised the intensity of the light, making the shadows seem very deep and very dark. Molly moved her hand jerkily back and forth, and shadows jumped violently all around us. But there was definitely no one else in the chamber.

"When I broke into the adjoining chamber," I said slowly, "it is entirely possible that I broke all the original Drood seals and protections. In which case none of this is hidden anymore from the eyes of the world. The whole place probably lit up like a beacon. If someone was lying in wait, keeping an eye on things here . . ."

"Then they just got an eyeful," said Molly. "Any chance this watching someone might be Crow Lee or one of his people?"

"Seems likely," I said. "If he'd learned enough about my family's secrets to remotely control Alpha Red Alpha, who knows what else he knows? You don't get to be the Most Evil Man in the World without keeping three steps ahead of everyone else. Whoever's watching knows what's just happened. They might not know exactly what was hidden here, but they must know it's out in the open now and vulnerable."

"So they'll be coming for it," said Molly.

"Seems likely," I said.

"They're already here," said Molly. "That's what we heard. It's mummies. I just know they've sent mummies after us. . . ."

"Look on the bright side," I said. "Might not be mummies; could be daddies."

"Really not helping here, Eddie! I hate mummies! They're going to come crashing through the walls, I just know it, dusty old things wrapped in rotting bandages, and they'll wrap their horrible arms around me, and . . ."

"Easy, girl. Easy! I can see years of therapy starting right here." I put my hands on her shoulders and gripped them comfortingly. "Molly . . . What are you so scared of? You're the wild witch of the woods, free spirit of anarchy and queen of all the wild places!"

"If fears were rational," said Molly, with some dignity, "they wouldn't be fears. Would they?"

"How old were you when you first saw this mummy film?"

"Five. Maybe six."

"Well, you're not five or six anymore. You're not a helpless child anymore. You are a very grown-up, very powerful, very adorable and only sometimes scary adult. Anything in bandages turns up, you set fire to it and I will stamp it into the floor. Okay?"

"Okay," said Molly. "Thanks, Eddie. What are you afraid of?"

"Losing you."

She smiled. "You say the nicest things, sweetie." And then she stopped and held herself very still, only her eyes moving. "Look around you, Eddie. Are you seeing what I'm seeing? Our shadows are moving . . . and we're not."

"In fact," I said, holding myself very still, too, "there are far too many shadows in this chamber. The enemy is with us, Molly. On guard."

I armoured up, the cold metal rushing over me in a moment. I kept the compass enclosed with one hand inside the armour. Molly sent up a ball of witchlight from her hand to bob against the low ceiling, providing illumination while leaving her hands free to do more destructive things. We moved quickly to stand back-to-back, without having to discuss it. We'd danced this dance before. I actually felt a lot better now that I had a proper enemy to confront. Shadows danced wildly all around the stone chamber, deep and dark and menacing. Full of an awful, inhuman life. They took on human shapes, distinct but distorted, the better to terrify us, and entirely separate from Molly and me . . . leaping and jumping, stretched across the bare stone walls. They had nothing to do with Molly's witchlight; they were something from outside. No faces on their dark heads, not even any eyes, but still the shadows seemed to know exactly where Molly and I were.

They whipped around the chamber, circling us like sharks, darting in and out, peeling themselves away from the walls to threaten Molly and me with sudden sharp movements. Dancing like demons, jumping and stretching and moving closer to us with every attack. They swirled around us, leaping and looming. Mocking, maddening things.

"Can I just quietly remind you that self-control would be a very good thing right now," I said quietly to Molly. "One destructive blast in the wrong place might well bring this whole place down on our heads. And we really are a very long way underground. . . ."

"Like I need you to tell me that," said Molly. "Self-control, carefully aimed destruction and brutality and viciousness at close quarters; that's what's needed here. Look at the stupid things jumping up and down and trying to be scary. . . . We can handle a bunch of shadows."

I smiled briefly behind my mask. "Of course we can. We are, after all, professionals."

And then all the shadows attacked at once, plunging in at us from every direction, striking like solid things with solid blows and supernatural strength. Suddenly they all had huge brutal fists and clawed hands . . . and a lot of good that did them against my armour. Jagged claws clattered loudly across my golden face and neck and raised showers of sparks as they skidded across my armoured chest; doing no damage at all. I actually relaxed a little. I hadn't been entirely sure the rogue armour would be as strong and secure as the strange matter I'd grown used to. Shadows smashed and slammed into me from every direction at once, and one dark force hammered into my chest like a battering ram, making my armour sound like a great bell. But they couldn't even rock me back on my feet.

The shadows retreated for a moment, shaken.

Molly filled the chamber with all manner of fierce and dangerous light, throwing mystic attacks at every moving shadow. Terrible energies flared around her hands, and the close air trembled with the impact of the Words she spoke. Dark leaping things exploded as her energies overpowered them, but most of the shadows just opened up holes inside them so that her magics flashed right through them without touching or affecting them at all. They came at her again and again, but she'd already surrounded herself with a shimmering screen that kept them back. The shadows beat at it with their dark fists and cut at the screen with their barbed claws, and none of them even came close to breaking it. I could feel the presence of the protective screen even through my armour. A tingling, not unpleasant sensation.

The shadow shapes seemed only to have a physical presence when they chose to. I lashed out at them and my golden gauntlets passed right through them, as though they were just the shadows they seemed. I couldn't touch them, couldn't hurt them, and when I tried to grab them in my golden hands, they squeezed out like inky tar. And all the time they were hitting me again and again, harder and harder. And I couldn't help noticing that Molly's protective field was slowly shrinking under the outside pressure, closing gradually but inexorably in on her.

"Eddie! This is not going well!" said Molly. "I say we use the Merlin Glass and get the hell out of here! We've got what we came for!"

"Already ahead of you," I said, thrashing wildly around me. "But, unfortunately, some outside force is interfering with my access to the pocket dimension I keep the Glass in. I can't reach the damn thing!"

"Typical! I told you to leave it open in case we needed to make a sudden exit!"

"No, you didn't!"

"Well, you should have thought that I would!" said Molly.

"That makes no sense!"

"Can we argue about this later? Only I'm just a bit busy at the moment."

The shadows lunged forward, falling on us both from all sides at once, wrapping themselves around us like huge shadowy snakes. They lashed our arms to our sides before we even realised what they were doing, and both of us staggered back and forth around the chamber, crashing into the walls and each other, struggling to break free. I set all the strength of my armour against the shadow snakes, but they didn't give an inch. I could see them tightening remorselessly around Molly's shimmering screen, forcing it right back against her body, so she had no room to move or manoeuvre. If not for the screen, the sheer pressure of the shadow snakes would have killed her. They tightened even further about me like constrictors. I heard my armour creak and even groan under the inhuman pressure, and I felt the touch of real danger. Because while physical force has limits, magic has none. The rogue armour was good, but it wasn't the impenetrable strange matter I was used to.

My mind flashed back to the half-melted Drood armour I'd found at the entrance doors of the ruined Hall. He probably thought his armour would save him, right up to the moment when it didn't.

"Sorry, Eddie," said Molly, just a bit breathlessly. "Normally I'd leave it to you to save the day with some last-minute miracle. . . . I know how much you love to do that. . . . But I don't think my shields will last much longer. I'm going to have to try something. . . ."

"Go for it!" I said. "I've got nothing. If you've got something, hit them with it, with my blessing!"

"You're so sweet. Okay, here's an old trick Walker taught me," said Molly. "And no one knows the darkness like Henry. *Fiat Lux!*"

Brilliant light sprang up out of nowhere, blinding and incandescent, filling the whole chamber and throwing back all the darkness. The shadows couldn't stand against it and were blasted out of existence in a moment. Molly's shimmering screen was gone, replaced by pure light, and there wasn't a bit of darkness anywhere. The light reached a peak almost unbearable to human eyes, even through my face mask, and then began to fade. At the farthest edges of the chamber, shadows started to stir again.

"The Glass!" Molly said urgently. "We need the Merlin Glass!"

"I know!" I said. "I'm on it!"

I concentrated on the Merlin Glass, reaching out to it through my torc, and with no shadow attacks to distract me, my trained mind punched right through the barriers that had been put in my way. All Droods are trained in psychic as well as physical attacks. Or we wouldn't last ten minutes in the Hall, never mind out in the field. We've always been a boisterous family. I thrust my hand through the golden metal at my side, into my pocket, and grabbed the hand mirror. I brought it out and shook the Glass to door size. Once again, bright sunlight poured through the doorway from the Drood grounds. Molly went straight through the Glass, with me hot on her heels. The moment I hit the grassy lawn beyond, I turned around and shut down the Merlin Glass. It shrunk to hand size and flew back to nestle cosily into my hand. I put it away. The Drood grounds were full of sunshine, not a shadow anywhere.

"Where's the compass?" said Molly. "Tell me after all that, you've still got the bloody compass!"

"Panic not," I said. "Of course I've still got the compass. I've been holding it clenched in my hand all this time."

She didn't relax until I opened my hand to show her. I put it away in the same pocket as the Merlin Glass, while Molly breathed heavily and then stretched slowly in the sun, like a cat.

"Good. Well done. Because I am never going back to that place, not ever. I hate mummies!"

"There weren't any mummies. . . ."

"There might have been!"

There's no answer to a statement like that, or at least none that won't get you into serious trouble with your girlfriend. I armoured down. And maybe it was only my imagination that seemed to feel a slowness, a slight reluctance, in the armour's return to the torc. I stretched, too, enjoying the warmth and light of the open grounds.

And then Molly and I sank down abruptly onto the good green grass and just sat there quietly, getting our spiritual breath back. I think if Molly hadn't been there, I might well have given myself over to the shudders. The grounds were very peaceful and the quiet was a comfort. Molly and I sat side by side, shoulder to shoulder, leaning companionably against each other. Drawing strength from each other.

"It's been a long time since it's been that close," I said finally. "If you hadn't had that last trick up your sleeve . . . I don't know what those shadow things were, but they were hellishly powerful. I think they might actually have been able to crush my armour, and me in it, given enough time. And there's not much that can do that."

"We've won too many wars," said Molly. "Got too used to winning. Too many victories make you soft, make you sloppy. . . ."

"Crow Lee had to have been behind them," I said. "Backing them up with his power. We still kicked their shadowy backsides, though."

"What's this *we*? I was the one who called down the Light. . . . You really think Crow Lee was behind them?"

"I hope so. I hate to think we might have another enemy that powerful after us." I looked at her thoughtfully. "Walker? You know Walker?"

"Yes."

"Henry?"

"Yes!"

"And?"

"And nothing! We worked together some years back . . . on certain matters of mutual interest and profit. Cash up front, of course."

"Of course. You never said . . ."

"You never asked," said Molly in her most infuriatingly reasonable tone.

Some conversations, you just know they're not going to go anywhere good. I let it drop.

"What time is it, Eddie?" said Molly. "It's starting to feel distinctly dinnerish."

I looked at my watch and then sat up straight. "That can't be right. . . ."

"What?" said Molly, immediately sitting up straight, too. "What can't be right?"

"I checked my watch right before we went through the Merlin Glass. Old habit from working in the field. And this . . . is almost exactly the same time. We've been back a few minutes, and my watch says this is just a few minutes after the last time I looked at it. The Merlin Glass brought us back to the exact moment in time and space that we left."

"Okay," said Molly. "That . . . is spooky. If we returned to the exact moment we left, then right now . . . we're also deep underground in the Valley of the Kings."

"Yeah . . ." I said. "That is spooky."

"Could the old Merlin Glass do time travel?" said Molly.

"I never tried," I said. "I don't think so, but then, I never did get around to reading all of the instruction manual Uncle Jack gave me. There was an awful lot of it. . . . I think we should be very cautious about how we use this otherworldly Merlin Glass, from now on."

"Suits me," said Molly. "Can we go to Brighton now?"

"I should think so. Why do you want to go to Brighton?"

"So I can look up my old friend. Brighton will make a nice change. I can cope with Brighton."

"And there are no mummies there," I said.

"Lot you know," said Molly.

CHAPTER FOUR

When the Seas Give up Their Dead

And so we drove down to the coast in the Rolls Royce Phantom V, heading for that famous seaside place called Brighton, and its famous pier. The Phantom was another of the Armourer's lovingly restored classics, made over into death on four wheels for family use. A very smooth ride, very quiet. There used to be an old story about the Rolls Royce range, that when you were driving one of their cars the loudest noise you'd hear would be the clock on the dashboard. To which a Rolls Royce engineer is supposed to have said, "Yeah, we're going to have to do something about that clock." This being one of the Armourer's cars, the dashboard clock was probably a timer for something explosive. I drove the Phantom in my usual fashion, everything forward and trust in the Lord.

I knew for a fact that the Armourer had built in more than enough shields to ensure no one would be able to detect our presence, let alone track our journey, and to give any speed camera that tried to lock on to us a nervous breakdown. Droods go unseen in the world. It's the only way we can get things done. Let Crow Lee look in vain for my torc or my new armour, and let him worry about where Molly and I were going and what we were up to. I needed him off balance until I had some kind of plan to throw at him.

I sent the Phantom V charging down the motorway, speeding past the slower-moving vehicles and weaving in and out of the rest, leaving shocked and startled drivers in my wake and intimidating the hell out of everyone who didn't get out of my way fast enough. I wasn't concerned about police cars. Let them try to chase us. After what the Armourer had done to the Phantom's engine, it could probably hit Mach 2 without straining. While going sideways.

"I thought we didn't want to attract attention," said Molly, amused.

"They don't start none, there won't be none," I said wisely. "We're a lot safer doing the Brighton run the hard way than by popping through the Merlin Glass. That much power in one place really would call all the eyes of the hidden world down upon us."

"And you don't trust it," said Molly.

"That, too," I said. "Besides, I can use the time it'll take us to get to the coast to do some thinking. There's a lot that needs thinking about."

"I'll put in some music," said Molly, producing a CD out of thin air.

And she put in Trans-Siberian Orchestra's *Night Castle*. Which may or may not have contributed to my mental processes. Those guys crank it up to eleven just to shake off the cobwebs. I was still working on how best to attend to Crow Lee when Molly abruptly shut off the music to raise a pertinent question.

"There's no telling how long this is going to take, is there?" she said. "I mean, to track down your missing family and locate a mechanism strong enough to take us there and bring us back. It could take weeks, months . . . maybe even years."

"Yes, it could," I said, staring straight ahead and concentrating on putting the wind up everything in my way. "It'll take as long as it takes."

"And we have to face the possibility," Molly said carefully, "that we might never find them. There's no telling just how far Alpha Red Alpha might have thrown the Hall, across the worlds beyond the worlds. We might never find another mechanism as powerful as Alpha Red Alpha to take us after them."

"It's a big world," I said steadily. "Bound to be something out there. I hear what you're saying, Molly, but I don't believe it. I can't believe it.

My family isn't dead, just lost, and I will find them . . . if it takes me the rest of my life."

"I understand, Eddie. I really do. I'd feel the same if someone had taken my sisters. And I love Isabella and Louisa a lot more than you love your family."

"Well," I said. "Love's a complicated word. And the Droods . . . are a complicated family." I glanced across at her. "You never talk about your family, Molly. Apart from your sisters. I know your parents were killed in the field, like mine. But what about your other relatives?"

"There is no one else," said Molly. Her voice was calm enough, even matter-of-fact, but she wouldn't turn her head to look at me. "My family have always been rogues, outlaws, troublemakers . . . supernatural freedom fighters or terrorists, depending on who you talk to. And a tradition like that comes with a built-in high mortality rate. You don't die in bed in my family. Or at least not in any acceptable way. And the world . . . has been very hard on us, in recent times. The world and the Droods. So now there are just the three infamous Metcalf sisters to keep the world on its toes. The only survivors of a once-thriving line, because we have learned to be very hard to kill."

"There's a chance my parents are still alive," I said. "So maybe . . ."

"No," said Molly. "Beyond a certain point, hope is more than self-indulgence. It's self-harm."

"You still have me," I said. "Forever and a day. And through me you have my family. Please take them."

We looked at each other and managed a small smile.

"I'm still thinking about that, to be honest," said Molly. "I want you, but I'm not sure about them."

"A perfectly reasonable attitude," I said, slamming the gear stick through its paces with the palm of my hand and sending a poncy-looking Porsche swerving uncontrollably in my slipstream. "I'm not sure I'd belong to my family if I had any say in the matter. The Droods do good work. They're necessary. But . . ."

"Yeah," said Molly. "But."

I shrugged. "They're still my family. Good and bad and in between and the Librarian. After all the changes I've put them through recently, I feel responsible for them. And, anyway, we have to get them back. The world needs them."

"That's sort of what I was getting at," said Molly. "Someone is going to have to look after business, protecting the world and all that, until you can find the Droods again. Someone's going to have to take up the slack and do all the heavy lifting in the Droods' absence. And who is there? I mean, really?"

"The London Knights," I said.

"All right, yes. Ten out of ten for Mr. Obvious here. But . . . really? The last defenders of Camelot, noble knights and true, under the returned King Arthur; fair enough. No one doubts they're the good guys, in a very martial and smiting-the-ungodly way, but they're hardly ever here! They mostly involve themselves with otherworldly and even other-dimensional threats. And since they believe very firmly in taking the fight to the enemy and making a mess where they live, they just aren't around much of the time."

"I did do some work with the Carnacki Institute back when I was just a London field agent," I said. "But the Ghost Finders . . . are just too limited, both in their scope of activity and in terms of manpower. And far too closely linked to the establishment, for my liking."

"You see?" said Molly. "I suppose we could always approach the new authorities in the Nightside, with their new Walker, John Taylor. . . ."

"Absolutely not," I said. "I wouldn't trust any of that crowd farther than I could throw a wet camel into the wind. There's a reason why we keep them locked up in the Nightside, and I'm not going to be the one to let them out on an unsuspecting world. The Nightside . . . always has its own agenda. I mean, have you met Dead Boy?"

"Yes," said Molly. "Louisa went out with him for a while."

"There used to be MI-13," I said, more because I was still thinking out loud than because I had any faith in them. "They've done good work in their time, but after the Great Satanic Conspiracy revealed how infiltrated and compromised they were, it'll be a long time before any-one trusts them with anything that matters. In fact, the more I think about it . . . part of what makes the Droods so important is that there just isn't anyone else like us. . . ."

"There are a great many other . . . perhaps not as reputable groups and individuals," Molly said carefully. "Certain known names whom I may or may not have done certain things with in the past, probably best not discussed in present company . . . And it could be that I might know how to get in touch with them. Eddie, somebody's got to do it!"

"Who did you have in mind?" I said, equally carefully. "The Soulhunters, perhaps?"

"You have got to be joking!" Molly made a seriously disgusted and appalled noise. "I wouldn't touch them with an exorcised barge pole! Those people are seriously weird. I worked alongside one of their agents. Just the once. Called himself Demonsbane. Because it turned out we were working the same case from different ends. Something had been snatching foetuses, teleporting them right out of the womb and leaving only simulacra behind. The two of us ended up chasing Hagges through the sewers under Liverpool. We got the poor things back eventually, but Demonsbane . . . freaked me out big-time. That's not even a code name, you know. That's what he calls himself! Hate to think what the other choices were . . . The point is, he was seriously spooky, like all the Soulhunters."

"And you know spooky," I said.

"Damn right I do. Trust me, Eddie. There is something seriously *wrong* about the Soulhunters. Every damned one of them."

"You know how sometimes this job can drive you crazy?" I said. "The Soulhunters have always dealt with the darkest, nastiest and freakiest areas of the hidden world. Word is, when you're too weird, too disturbed or just too broken for any of the other supernatural organisations, that's when you're ready for your Soulhunters interview. In fact, I think this is how it goes: *Are you crazy? Yes, I am! Welcome to the Soulhunters!* If we let them take over from the Droods, the world won't know what's hit it. Certainly the hidden world wouldn't remain hidden for very long."

"I love how you mention things and then immediately talk yourself out of it," said Molly.

"Years of practice."

"There's always the lone guns," said Molly. "The heroes and adventurers, the rogues and the headbangers. Maybe we could put together our own version of the Magnificent Seven. 'Have bad attitude; will travel'—that sort of thing. We could start with the Walking Man. . . ."

"No, we couldn't," I said immediately. "Him? The wrath of God in the world of men? He's not exactly subtle, is he? Never met a scorched-earth policy he didn't like. No. I suppose . . . there's always Augusta Moon, the monster hunter. . . ."

"She's getting on a bit," Molly said doubtfully. "There's the English Assassin. . . ."

"No, there isn't," I said. "He's dead again. Look. There's never been any shortage of adventurers in the supernatural, the heroes and the differently sane, but there's nearly always a reason why they work alone. I'm sure we could round up any number of reputable names and maybe even get them to play nice together as long as we were there to crack the whip, but none of them could carry the weight of the world on their backs for long. They don't have the training, the organisation or even the big guns to get the job done. That's why the Droods are so important and why it's so vital we get them back as soon as possible. Come on, Molly. There's only one place we can go, and that's to the Regent of Shadows."

Molly scowled fiercely, considering the matter. "The Shadows are a secretive bunch," she said finally. "Even for the usual secret organisations. I mean, yes, I've heard of them—everyone has. But that's it. They deal in information. I can't say I've ever heard of them wading in and getting their hands dirty. I always thought they were part of the Establishment, like the Carnacki crowd."

"Not . . . as such," I said. "They tend more towards working *with* the Establishment, rather than *for* them. An important distinction in this day and age. Sufficiently independent for our purposes, and not likely to spread around the information we'll be giving them. And once they've told me what I need to know, hopefully I can persuade the Regent to jump in and become far more active than he's used to."

"Why would he want to?" Molly said bluntly.

"Because he's still a Drood, even if he is a rogue," I said. "He's still family, which means he understands duty and responsibility. If they're dropped onto him from a great enough height."

"But you've never even met the man!" said Molly. "Your family wouldn't even talk about him!"

"That is a point in his favour," I said.

We reached Brighton late in the day, with the afternoon already heading into evening, though the sun still shone brightly as it sank down the perfect blue sky. Not a cloud to be seen or a breath of breeze anywhere. The Phantom's speed dropped abruptly as we hit the city traffic, and I bullied my way as best I could through the narrowing streets of the city centre. There was quite a lot of traffic, this being the height of the tourist season, with whole families packed into cars and pointed at the seaside. There wasn't the room for my usual driving tactics, so I just hunched down in my seat and cruised along, resisting the impulse to open up with the front-mounted machine guns.

The slow progress made me uneasy. Made me feel more and more as though there were targets painted all over the bodywork. I trusted the Armourer's shields to do their job, but, on the other hand, Crow Lee didn't get to be number one in the Bastard Business without being able to locate his enemies. . . . I checked the surrounding cars and their drivers carefully, but I didn't see anything or anyone I could honestly identify as showing inappropriate interest.

Molly was just pleased to be back in Brighton. She bounced up and down excitedly in her seat, peering happily out of all the windows, pointing out the sights and interrupting herself to beat a fast paradiddle on the dashboard with both hands.

"I love Brighton!" she said loudly. "Good food, good bars and bad company! If you're a girl who likes to drink, dance and debauch, and wallow in everything that's bad for you, Brighton is the place to be! Used to be Blackpool, but that's gone very down-market of late."

"I never knew you to be such a happy camper, Molly," I said solemnly.

"My glass may be half-empty, but I am half-full! Can't we get a move on?"

"Not without actually driving right over the cars in front of us, no."

Molly looked like she was seriously considering it. "We need the Pier. That's where we'll find my old acquaintance. Brighton Pier. You know, one time I . . ."

"Never mind your disreputable past," I said. "How do we get there?"

Molly shifted uneasily in her seat, looking around for signposts and landmarks. "I don't know! Give me a chance—it's been a few years. . . . Honestly, Eddie, all the extras your uncle Jack built into this car, and he didn't think to include a sat nav? And don't ask me to check the maps. I do not do the map thing. Look. Just head for the seafront. Listen for the sound of the waves, and if that doesn't work, stick your head out the side window and sniff out the tang of the sea!"

"World's worst navigator," I said, and she punched me in the shoulder.

"I have other talents," she said, grinning.

"So you do."

After some back-and-forthing and a certain amount of going round and round in circles, we finally found our way to the seafront and Brighton Pier. A large and impressive structure stretching away from the beach and out into the sea, so people could go walking across the ocean and get a sense of the sea without actually having to go in it. The Pier looked to just go on and on, but then I supposed it had to be that long to fit in all the overpriced souvenirs, games and tourist traps that paid for its continued existence. Hell of a lot of seagulls flying around, making a lot of noise. Molly lowered her window and stuck her head right out, the better to savour the sea air.

I looked around for a parking place, which was naive of me. Of course there wasn't one. All the parking places in Brighton are probably full by dawn's earliest light, or inherited and passed on within the family. So I just brought the Phantom V to a halt directly in front of the Pier's main entrance, right next to a NO PARKING sign. One of life's little pleasures. I turned off the engine and powered up the car's defences, while Molly conjured up an official DISABLED sticker and slapped it on the inside of the windscreen. I looked at her reproachfully.

"You are very definitely not in any way disabled," I said. "Not as long as you can still get your ankles behind your ears like you did last night . . ."

"Anyone messes with this car while we're away, they will find themselves suddenly and violently disabled," said Molly. "It's the thought that counts."

"Can't take you anywhere," I said sadly.

"You know you love it, really."

We left the Phantom V to fend for itself and strolled towards the Pier's main entrance. Molly surprised me by taking my hand in hers. She's not usually one for public displays of affection. Presumably she was just trying to blend in. A seagull dive-bombed us, and Molly shot it out of the air with her free hand. When she makes a gun with her hand, she's not kidding. The seagull plummeted from the sky with feathers flying off it and crashed into the sea. Molly smiled happily. I hurried her through the main entrance and onto the Pier proper.

"I hope Madame O is still doing business here," said Molly. "Because if she isn't, I haven't a clue where to find her."

"We came all this way and you're not even sure she's here?" I said.

"I'm sure! She's here! Unless she isn't . . ."

"An old friend of yours, this Madame O?" I said, as we promenaded along the Pier, doing our best to look like two more tourists. I was more successful at this than Molly, but then I've had training in how to look like nobody in particular. Molly's never been much of a one for blending in.

"A friend?" said Molly. "Not . . . as such."

"Oh," I said. "It's going to be like that, is it?"

"Almost certainly. You just keep quiet and let me do all the talking," said Molly. "And everything will be fine. Just fine. Be ready to dodge and duck, as necessary."

"Would it perhaps go better if I was to introduce myself as Shaman Bond?"

"Wouldn't work," Molly said immediately. "She'd spot your torc the moment she set eyes on you and know you for a Drood. She's the seventh daughter of a seventh daughter, which is a lot rarer now in these days of family planning."

"So she has the Sight?"

"Madame O can See things that no one else can See, that aren't necessarily even there, and have conversations with them," said Molly.

"Is she a witch?"

"Worse," said Molly, grimacing. "She's a fortune-teller."

We took our time, strolling along the bare wooden boards of the Pier, taking in the sights. I was actually enjoying myself. I'd never been on a pier before. I walked over to the solid steel railings and peered over the side, looking out over the waters and the pebbled beach and the heavy swell of the waves coming in below. The afternoon was definitely over now, with evening settling in, but the sun was still bright and the air was pleasantly warm, interrupted now and then by sharp cool breezes gusting in off the sea. There were still quite a few tourists out and about, families enjoying the remains of the day and getting sucked into all the amenities the Pier had to offer. There were even a handful of retired senior citizens who looked like fixtures, happily reclining in their own personal deck chairs, just sitting back and watching the world go by. If there'd been anywhere to hire a deck chair, I might have joined them. I surprised myself by getting into the whole experience and enjoying it. Molly grinned broadly, enjoying seeing me enjoying myself.

"You've never been on a pier before. Have you, Eddie?"

"Never been to the seaside before," I said. "It wasn't allowed."

"You've never done this before? Not even when you were a child?"

"Especially not then. The likes of this wasn't for young Droods. We were never allowed out of the Hall's grounds. You have to remember, Molly: Drood children out in the world, beyond the Hall's protections, were seen as nothing more than kidnap victims waiting to happen. We would be targets for any number of people desperate to get their hands on a Drood torc and Drood secrets. And, of course, a kidnapped child could be used as leverage against us. Besides . . . the family has always believed in keeping its children close; the better to indoctrinate and control them. So holidays were out. Except on television, and all those Enid Blyton books I read as a kid. This . . . all this, is good. This is fun. I like this!"

Molly laughed aloud, squeezed my hand and led me down the full length of the Pier, over the dark sea waters, making sure I saw everything there was to see. The gift shops were of course packed wall to wall with overpriced tat, loud and gaudy and tacky with it, the kind of thing tourists buy because they think it's expected of them. And then when they get it home, they look at it and say, *What was I thinking?* Some nice watches, though. Along with a whole bunch of miniature clocks shoehorned into every kind of objet d'art and objet trouvé you could think of.

What really caught my eye was the line of cans containing Brighton air. Really. Large and colourful containers full of fresh air from the seaside, sealed shut. *Enjoy the breezy Brighton Air! Breathe in that ozone! And then take it home with you!* said the sign on the front of every can. Molly got the giggles.

"They're actually selling *air* to the tourists!"

"Reminds me of something I once saw on eBay," I said. "Genuine Transylvanian Grave Dirt! Each in its own sealed container, of course. For vampire fanatics who only think they've got absolutely everything . . . My first thought was that the Eastern Europeans had finally figured out a way to sell dirt to foreigners, but it turned out to be more complicated than that. An old vampire count was shipping his ancestral estate to England, one bit at a time. We soon put a stop to that. I tracked down the location in London, got a few friends together, we all drank a lot of holy water and then pissed all over the new earthen plot. And that took care of that."

"You've lived, haven't you, Eddie?" Molly said admiringly.

"You want me to buy you a can of air or not?"

"I'll pass." She frowned. "Am I remembering correctly—someone once tried to sell his soul on eBay?"

"Yeah, but they made him take it down. He couldn't provide proof of ownership."

We went through the games arcade next. All the usual noisy video stuff, of course, along with a surprising number of old-fashioned traditional games of no chance whatsoever. Clearly designed to painlessly separate a punter from whatever spare change he happened to have about his person. Whilst at the same time fooling said punter into believing he was having a good time.

"You miserable old scrote," said Molly, when I explained my insights to her. "You don't come here to win money. You come here to enjoy yourself! You really don't understand being on holiday, do you?"

"Apparently not," I said.

Molly squealed excitedly as she recognised an old favourite from her childhood, and then nothing would do except for her to drag me over to show it off to me. The game was a simple mechanical affair called The Claw. A tall plastic cylinder with toys piled up at its base and a claw that descended from the top. You paid your money, which gave you a measure of control over the claw and a limited amount of time for you to use the claw to grab the toy of your choice. Skill was apparently involved. What could be simpler? Except somehow the claw never did get a secure grip on any of the toys before the time ran out. Funny, that.

Molly jumped up and down excitedly before the clear plastic cylinder, regaling me with tall tales of the ones that got away . . . and then she went all quiet as she realised one of the toys she remembered was still on offer. She pointed it out to me: an overbearingly cute little stuffed pony in an unnatural shade of sky blue. With a purple mane. Molly slammed both hands against the cylinder, making it shiver, while growling, "I want it, I want it, I want it." Several parents hustled their children away. I produced a handful of small change; Molly snatched it off my palm and the game was on. Molly took control of the claw, and several times got hold of her prey with it, but somehow it always came loose just as the time ran out. Funny, that.

I may not know much about holidays, but I know a con when I see one.

Molly scowled at the cylinder. I sensed trouble coming, and moved forward to block people's view of her. She ghosted her hand through the clear plastic, grabbed the stuffed pony, took it out and hugged it to her. The greasy-haired teenager in charge of the game started to say something. I gave him one of my looks, and he didn't. Molly cradled the pony to her bosom and looked at me defiantly.

"I've always wanted one! It's mine!"

"Of course it is," I said. "Anyone can see you two belong together. Can we please move along now?"

"I thought there'd be alarms," Molly said vaguely. "Really rubbish security here. They didn't deserve to keep it."

She moved on through the games arcade, cuddling the stuffed pony to her chest and babbling cheerful nonsense to it. I followed behind. She wasn't interested in holding my hand anymore. The pony was more important. I had to wonder if there was anything I wanted as much as Molly wanted that particular stuffed toy. I didn't think so. My family gave us weapons to play with, not toys. And the only things I got to cuddle as a kid were the gryphons on the lawns. And they liked to roll in dead things. Childhoods; they really do mess you up. I hurried to catch up with the only thing I'd ever really wanted, and then we walked together through the arcade.

We wandered from game to game, indulging ourselves occasionally, and I looked them all over with great interest, fascinated by the loud noises and flashing lights. Reminded me of the Armoury. Eventually we passed through the games arcade and out the other side. The fresh sea air came as a relief after so much compressed body odour, and we strolled on, all the way to the end of the Pier. Where I was somewhat surprised to find a slouching, two-story wooden edifice passing itself off as a haunted house. There were a slumping doorway, gloomily backlit windows, and a general ambience of cheap and cheerful. It looked like a stiff breeze would knock it over.

"Okay," I said. "That is never haunted. Not even a little bit."

"It's not meant to be," Molly said patiently. "It's just another game, Eddie. For the children. Like a ghost train."

"Even the Scooby-Doo gang would turn up their noses at this," I said firmly. "And no, Molly, we are not going in. I have my dignity. And I just know that if I walk through that door and someone in a sheet jumps out and shouts, *Boo!* at me, I will not be responsible for my actions."

"I suppose the Droods had the real thing!"

"Not as such," I said. "You met Jacob, the family ghost, awful old reprobate that he was. . . . And there's the Headless Nun, of course. When I was a kid, they were usually more fun to hang around with than the rest of my family."

"It's a wonder you grew up as normal as you did," Molly said sweetly.

"Well, quite," I said.

At the very end of the Pier, some distance from the beach and way out over the ocean, I leaned on the reinforced railings and breathed deeply. Seagulls keened loudly overhead but maintained a respectful distance. Molly hugged her stuffed pony one last time, opened an invisible pocket in her dress, stuffed the thing in and forgot about it. (If it looked to be turning up on our bed at any future time, I planned on being very firm about it.) I peered out across the ocean. Various ships were passing by, out on the horizon, going about the business apparently without a care in the world. Though it's hard to be sure with ships.

"I do like this pier," I said. "Thanks for bringing me here, Molly. Even if your friend isn't here. It does me good to be reminded that there are things in this world worth saving."

"We could always go on one of the rides," said Molly. She indicated the various roller coasters and Tilt-A-Whirls, most of which swung too far out over the waters for my liking. I shook my head firmly.

"I've never understood the appeal of those things. My world is dangerous enough as it is without putting myself at risk on purpose. I wouldn't go on one of those things if you paid me. And I've got Drood armour."

"I can't believe I'm saying this," said Molly. "But you have no sense of adventure."

"That isn't adventure," I said. "That is one mechanical malfunction away from a major local news story just waiting to happen. Can we please go see this old friend of yours now? That is what we came here for, after all."

"I thought you were enjoying yourself."

"I was! I am. But part of being a Drood is knowing when to get down to business."

"Look to your right," said Molly, "and there you will behold Madame O's Palace of Mysteries. Look upon her wonders and marvel."

I looked. There, tucked away to one side, was an old-fashioned fortune-teller's tent. A droopy-looking thing, presumably surrounding the stall within, its rough canvas covered with all the usual symbols that the general public has been conditioned to accept as representing the mystical and the occult: moons and stars, witches on broomsticks and black cats. It couldn't have looked more fake if it tried.

"That's the point!" said Molly, when I expressed this view to her. "No one would ever think to find the real thing here, looking like that. . . . Would they?"

I looked the tent over carefully. "Who's she hiding from?"

"Pretty much everybody," said Molly. "Madame O has conned, double-crossed, and done dirt to practically everyone in our game you can think of at one time or another. And, yes, very definitely including your family. During her long, involved and decidedly underhanded career, Madame O has been run out of every major city you can name, and some that aren't even there anymore. Her trouble is, she's got no self-control. She sees something she wants and she goes for it. Just grabs it and runs, and to hell with the consequences. Why are you looking at me like that?"

"Thought you were describing someone else for a moment," I said smoothly. "Do carry on."

"Madame O was my mentor, for a time," said Molly. "Taught me everything I know about taking advantage of the world. Well, not everything, but you'd be surprised. . . ."

The hand-painted sign set up on an easel at the entrance to the tent read MADAME OSIRIS. KNOWS ALL, SEES ALL, TELLS ALL.

"For the right price," said Molly. "Madame O never gave away anything in her life."

I looked at the sign. "Tell me that's not her real name."

"Of course not!" said Molly. "To start with, Osiris is a man's name. One of the old male Egyptian gods. You see, you can learn things from watching old mummy movies. I don't think anyone knows Madame O's real name. According to old magical tradition, to know the true name of a person or an object is to have power over it. As long as I've known her, it's always been Madame O-something. When I first met her in Vienna all those years ago, she was passing herself off as Madame Olivia, Daughter of the Night and Disciple of Darkness. She was a bit old for the badger game even then, but she still had a certain glamour. . . . She could make grown men give up their credit card details and pin numbers just by looking at them in a certain way. She taught me all I know about deviousness and debauchery. Including that thing I do with my fingertips that you really like . . ."

"Far too much information," I said. "Can we trust her?"

"Of course not."

"Then why are we here?"

"Because she knows things, sweetie."

"Can we trust her to tell us the truth?"

"If we lean on her hard enough. We don't have enough money to bribe her."

I shrugged. "She's your friend."

"There are friends . . . and there are friends," said Molly. "And Madame O is neither."

She slapped aside the tent flap and strode in. I followed, carefully pulling the tent flaps closed behind me. I didn't want us being interrupted. Inside there was hardly any room to move, the lighting was kept deliberately gloomy so you couldn't tell how cheap the place was, and there was nothing in any way mystical about the atmosphere. The only light came from half a dozen candles in a cheap candelabra, illuminating the table and two chairs set up. The crystal ball on the table looked impressive enough at first glance; but I've spent enough time around the real thing to know a fake when I see one.

Madame Osiris sat on the far side of the table, carefully positioned to be half-hidden in the shadows. A lady of a certain age, solidly built and wrapped in traditional gypsy robes, she looked like she could punch her weight. Her bare muscular arms were covered in cheap and tacky multicoloured bangles that clattered loudly against one another with every movement, while her long-fingered hands caressed the crystal ball in a disturbingly sensuous way. She had a handsome enough face with a good bone structure, under industrial strength makeup, topped with a silk turban. She bestowed on Molly and me a wide professional smile and launched into what was clearly a well-practiced routine, addressing us both in a rich smoky voice.

"Enter, dear friends, into the Mysteries of the Hereafter! Learn what the future has in store for you! And together we shall—Oh, bloody hell. It's you, Molly Metcalf."

Madame Osiris pushed her chair back from the table, allowing the candlelight to illuminate her fully, the better to glower fiercely at Molly.

"Nice to see you again too, Madame O," Molly said cheerfully. "Don't get up. We're not staying. And we're definitely not tourists, so lay off the purple prose."

Madame Osiris sniffed loudly. "All the stalls on all the piers and you had to come walking into mine. I should have seen this coming." She looked me over in an impersonal sort of way. "So this is the new boyfriend, is it? You always did like them big and dumb, Molly. Whatever happened to . . . Oh, you know, Big and Blond and Ethereal? I always liked him."

"He couldn't stand the pace," said Molly. She smiled at me. "This one can."

"Nicest thing you've ever said about me," I said.

Madame Osiris was still giving me the once-over, in a considering sort of way that was probably designed to make me feel uncomfortable. So when in doubt, attack. I struck a deliberately casual pose and gave her my best intimidating smile.

"We're not here to have our futures told. We have questions we want answered."

"You and the whole world, dearie. Oh, sit down, sit down. You make the place look untidy."

I glanced at Molly, who nodded to the only empty chair. I sat down facing Madame Osiris, and she smiled briefly like she'd just won a point. Molly made a point of standing beside me with her arms folded impatiently.

"Cross my palm with silver, dearie," Madame Osiris said briskly, "and I shall reveal all."

"You'll catch your death in this weather," said Molly.

"How about I cross your palm with gold?" I said. I sent my armour shooting down my arm to cover my hand in a golden gauntlet and slammed it down on the table. Madame Osiris didn't even jump. Just looked at it like I'd dropped a fresh turd on the table before her.

"Stone me, it's a Drood." She looked at my throat. "Yes, there it is: the golden dog collar. Should have spotted it the moment you walked in . . . I must be getting old. Looks a bit odd, though; a bit off-colour . . ." She raised an eyebrow, but I just smiled and said nothing, and pulled the armour back off my hand. Madame Osiris shrugged briefly. "None of my business, dearie. See if I care." She looked reproachfully at Molly. "Dating a Drood? That really the best you can do? I thought you had better taste. All right. What do you want to know? And, no, I don't do lottery numbers."

"Where can we find the Regent of Shadows?" I said.

She surprised me then by laughing in my face. "Don't need a crystal ball for that one, dearie. You don't find him. He finds you."

"Forget the clever dialogue," I said. "I'm not a tourist. Where, exactly?"

"You need the Department of the Uncanny, in London," Madame Osiris said resignedly. "Go to Big Ben and then ask again. And, no, I'm not even a little bit kidding. Word is the Regent's going up in the world. Probably because he knows all kinds of things he isn't supposed to . . . He's been making a lot of people nervous. Anything else you want from me before I invite you to go to hell by the express route? The last thing I need around here is your kind, lowering the tone and attracting the kind of attention I can well do without. You're bad news, Molly Metcalf, and you always were."

"How can you say that, Madame O, after all we've been through together?" said Molly.

Madame Osiris glared at me. "Run, boy, while you still can. She'll get you killed. Just like everyone else who gets close to her. The Metcalf sisters have never cared for anyone but themselves. There's a reason why they're still alive and the rest of their family isn't."

"Never meet up again with old friends," Molly said to me. "They'll always let you down."

"And I can't believe you're stepping out with a Drood!" snapped Madame Osiris. "You have better reason than most to know what they really are! But then, you never did listen to me. I could have made you big!"

"This from someone hiding out in a fortune-teller's stall on Brighton Pier," said Molly. "How have the mighty fallen . . ."

"You little cow . . ."

"That's enough!" I said. "I didn't come here for this!"

And something in my voice snapped both their heads round to look at me. Madame Osiris actually looked startled for a moment, and Molly looked at me as though she didn't know me at all. And then they looked at each other.

"Is he . . . ?" said Madame Osiris.

"Just a bit," said Molly.

"You always did know how to pick them, dearie. Whatever happened to Roger Morningstar?"

"Dead, finally," said Molly.

"Then we can all sleep a little more safely in our beds, at last. Are you in trouble, Molly?"

"Perhaps a little more than usual."

"I always did have a soft spot for you, much against my better judgement. Like the daughter I never wanted. Lose the Drood, Molly, while you still can."

"I can't," said Molly. "He's the only one who ever really mattered to me."

Madame Osiris sighed. "And love makes fools of us all. One more question, dearie, on the house, and I'll see what I can do."

"Where are my sisters?" said Molly. "Right now."

Madame Osiris raised a heavily painted eyebrow. "Don't you know?"

"Obviously not, or I wouldn't be asking! They've got their auras turned off, and that isn't like them. So where are they?"

Madame Osiris sat thoughtfully for a long moment, her dark eyes staring off into the distance . . . and then she sat up straight and shrugged quickly. "Sorry, dearie. Outside my range. But then, they always were. Come on, Molly. You know as well as I do that no one finds Isabella and Louisa if they don't want to be found. And wherever they are right now, they clearly don't want anyone else knowing."

"But I'm not anyone else! I'm their sister!"

"Then the question you should be asking yourself," said Madame Osiris, "is, What could they be up to that they know you wouldn't approve of? Maybe you should go talk to the Regent of Shadows. He knows everything about everyone. That's his job description. In fact, it's probably engraved on his business cards."

Molly nodded brusquely and turned to leave. "You do know Osiris is a man's name, right?"

Madame O laughed in a good-natured way. "It's all Egyptian to me, dearie."

Molly and I made our way back down the Pier. Neither of us was in a hurry to get anywhere. We both had a lot to think about.

"Well," I said finally. "That . . . was pretty much a waste of time."

"Did you know the Regent of Shadows was now in charge of the Department of the Uncanny?"

"I'd heard rumours. . . ."

"Did you know he was hiding out at Big Ben?"

"Nice to have the rumours confirmed, I suppose," I said. "Your Madame O gave me the impression of being just a bit rattled by our sudden appearance. She wasn't pleased to see you, and she definitely didn't like having me around."

"Of course not," said Molly, smiling briefly. "You're a Drood."

"The point I'm making is, Do you think someone else might have got to her first? Crossed her palm with a hell of a lot of silver to point us in the wrong direction?"

"She didn't know we were coming to see her," said Molly. "She couldn't. Hell, we didn't know until I made the decision just a few hours ago."

"But if she can see the Future . . ."

"Grow up, Eddie. Of course she can't! You are so gullible sometimes. That whole Madame Osiris thing is just for show! Just another con for the unwary . . . It takes a hell of a lot of power to look into all the future timetracks ahead of us."

"Someone with real power . . . like Crow Lee?" I said. "My old tutors always said no one understood the Theory of Magick like Unholy Crow Lee. Molly, is it just me, or is it getting dark in a hurry?"

We both stopped and looked around us and then up at the sky. Grim, overbearing clouds were forming out over the ocean, filling the sky and cutting off the sunshine. The temperature dropped perceptibly as something leached all the summer's warmth out of the day. A great grim fog was forming, rising up off the sea and heading straight for the Pier.

"Okay," said Molly. "That . . . is not natural."

The fog surged forward, racing across the ocean, and fell upon the end of the Pier like a beast on its prey. It consumed the whole end of the Pier in a moment and then moved slowly, purposefully forward, enveloping the Pier foot by foot. I lost sight of the huge rides and then everything else at the rear of the Pier, unable to see more than a few feet into the thick pearlescent fog. Molly was right: There was nothing natural about this. We both backed carefully away from the fog, sticking close together. We couldn't risk being separated.

People farther down the Pier began to cry out as even the everyday tourists sensed something was wrong. Panic moved quickly through the crowds as they felt what Molly and I already knew: that there was something in the fog. Something bad. In ones and twos and then in groups, they headed for the exit. Walking quickly and then hurrying, and finally breaking into an undignified run as the fog struck a chill into their hearts. Young lovers held on to each other tightly, running hard and not looking back, while parents dragged screaming and protesting children along with them by brute force. The retired senior citizens abandoned their deck chairs, and hurried after the departing crowds as best they could. White-faced staff abandoned the stalls and shops and the games arcade, and ran for their lives. Even the fake ghosts came running out of the fake haunted house, throwing aside their sheets and costumes so they could run faster.

None of them wanted any part of the advancing fog and what was moving inside it.

I looked round just in time to see Madame Osiris's tent disappear abruptly, just before the fog reached it. She may not have seen the fog coming, but she knew enough to get the hell out of Dodge. Molly and I looked at each other and smiled briefly. It would take a lot more than some sudden bad-tempered weather to scare us. We stood our ground, facing the fog as it crept towards us. I peered into the thick fog as it ate up foot after foot of the Pier, but though I could sense something moving along with it, I still couldn't see a damned thing. And suddenly I had a very bad feeling about this fog.

"We could . . . depart," I said carefully to Molly. "If you like. To a better position . . . I'm just mentioning the possibility."

"No," said Molly, just as carefully. "We don't back down, ever. Might give other people ideas . . . Besides, aren't you curious to see what's inside it?"

"Well, yes and no," I said. "There's curious, and then there's . . . curious."

The temperature plummeted. My breath was suddenly steaming on the air before me, along with Molly's. All the hairs were standing up on my arms and the back of my neck. I shuddered briefly despite myself, and it wasn't because of the cold. I had a sudden sharp feeling of my own mortality. The fog advanced deliberately towards us, thick and swirling and pearly grey, with strange lights coming and going deep within it . . . and something that might have been shadowy shapes deep in the heart of it. The air was damp, beading on my face, and I could taste sea salt on my lips.

"What is this cold I'm feeling?" I said to Molly. "The cold of the grave?"

"I don't think so," said Molly. She wouldn't take her gaze off the fog for a moment, even to glance at me. "More like the cold of the sea. The kind of cold you only feel in the deepest, darkest part of the ocean. At the very bottom of the sea, where everything falls when it's dead. There's something in the fog and it's coming for us, Eddie. I can feel it."

I nodded quickly. I could feel it, too. A growing sense of presence, of something else here on the Pier with us. Even though the crowds and the tourists were long gone. Something new, or perhaps something very old, had come to Brighton Pier, in the fog, out of the sea. Looking for me and Molly.

"My fingers are tingling," I said. "And not in a good way."

"That's nothing," said Molly. "My nipples are hard as rocks."

"Oh, great," I said. "Distract me. That's all I need."

Molly laughed. "Not everything is about you, Eddie."

"This time, I think it is," I said. "I think this is all about me. About getting rid of the Last Drood."

"I can see things moving in the fog," said Molly. "Human shapes heading straight for us."

"You've got better eyes than me," I said, glaring helplessly into the grey fog churning before me. Close, now. Just a few more feet and I'd be able to reach out and touch it.

"Madame O sold us out," Molly said flatly. "She told someone we were here. I shall have words with her later."

"Not necessarily," I said. "I told you we were being watched. Crow Lee is a power in his own right, as well as being the Most Evil, et cetera, and this is well within his capabilities. He wants to stop me from rescuing my family. He wants to take me down while I'm vulnerable." I smiled, and somehow I just knew it wasn't a very nice smile. "Poor old Crow Lee. He thinks I'm naked. He doesn't know about my new armour."

"Right," said Molly. "We'll show him."

"We could still run," I said.

"Too late," said Molly.

The fog swelled towards us like the waves of a silent pearl grey sea. The whole end of the Pier was gone now, swallowed up by the fog. I could just make out the dark shape of the fake haunted house to my right. New lights were showing in the windows: dark green glows, like the phosphorescent light you find on shipwrecks at the bottom of the sea. Dark silhouettes, distorted human shapes, moved slowly past the windows. Something bad peered at me from the illuminated doorway.

Dark shadows, slow-moving human forms, stumbling forward on dragging feet, scraping across the wooden floorboards, appeared in the fog before Molly and me. They were almost upon us now. Not ghosts, not any form of projected image or any kind of illusion. These were solid, physical things. Dead men emerging slowly out of the fog. Dead men walking.

Once I got a good look at them, I knew immediately what they were. Not ghosts or even zombies, but spirits of the dead called up out of the sea and given their old shape and form to do their master's will. Or what was left of them after so long in the depths. Disturbed from their rest and animated by some terrible outside will. Crow Lee. Had to be. There were dozens of the things, maybe hundreds, shuffling and stumbling forward to confront Molly and me. Grey and bloated, flesh eaten away by fishes and all the other things that live at the bottom of the sea that we don't like to think about. Some bodies had clearly been down there longer than others; just bare bones, held together with strips of ancient flesh and tatters of decayed clothing. The faces were the worst: rotten, eaten away, eyes and ears and nose and lips just gone . . . but they could still see Molly and me. Every dead body oriented on us as they pressed forward. They could see us. They knew where we were.

"Can you tell what they want?" I said to Molly.

"No. But I could probably make a really good guess."

"We could be mistaken," I said. "Let's ask them."

"You do it," said Molly. "You're the polite one."

I took an ostentatiously confident step forward to face the army of the dead emerging from the fog, and immediately every dead body slammed to a halt. Not one of them moved. All their dead faces, their decaying heads, turned in my direction. I took a moment to make sure my voice would sound calm and confident. I doubted very much I'd be fooling anyone, but it's the principle of the thing.

"Who are you?" I said. "Why have you come here? What do you want? Is there anything I can do to help you? To put you back to rest again?"

One of the nearest bodies stepped forward. Its bare feet made wet slapping sounds on the bare floorboards. With its bleached flesh and eaten-away face, its ragged clothes in rags, it could have been anyone. Only the manner of its clothes allowed me to identify it as male. It raised one half-skeletal hand to point at me, and water dripped steadily from the revealed bones.

"We're all that's left of those who died in the waters here," said the dead man in a disturbingly normal voice. "The sea is giving up its dead against its will. None of us want to be here. But then, none of us wanted to die. Accidents, mistakes, murder; we all ended up at the bottom of the sea. In the cold, in the dark and the silence. Raised and sent here by someone who had a use for us. One last crime against us. And all the rage we have . . . for dying, for dying badly, for not being allowed to rest in peace . . . all that rage has been stirred up in us, so we can take it out on you and your woman. We don't know who you are or why someone wants you to die so badly, and we don't care. We can't care. We're dead."

"You can't hurt me," I said. "I'm a Drood."

"Means nothing to me," said the dead man. "Means nothing to any of us. We are here to hurt you and break you and make you die badly. And then we'll take you back with us, drag you down into the depths of the sea, to the cold and the dark and the silence. Forever."

"Nothing worse than a chatty dead man," Molly said briskly. "I don't think that's his voice, Eddie. I think that's someone else speaking through him."

"Is that you, Crow Lee?" I said. "I'll be coming for you soon. And all the armies of the world, living or dead, won't be enough to stop me."

"Let us rest," said a soft, wet chorus of voices. "We didn't want to die. But this is worse."

"You wouldn't think someone with the power to raise an army of the dead would feel the need for psychological warfare," said Molly. "This is just meant to disturb us by appealing to our better nature. Lot he knows. I don't have one. I had it surgically removed long ago, when it got in the way of having serious fun."

"We didn't ask to be called up into the light again," said the dead man, looking straight at me with his eyeless face. "The dark will be that much harder to bear now that we've been made to remember what light is like. The cold will be that much worse now that we've been made to know warmth again. And since we can't take our anger out on the one who raised us, we'll take it out on you."

"Listen," I said. "I don't know whether there's really any of you left in there or not. Whether these are your voices are not. But if you're really here, if you've been made to suffer, I give you my word: I will avenge you. You hear that, Crow Lee? I will make you pay for this!"

The moment I stopped talking, they all surged forward, stumbling over their broken and decayed feet, reaching out to Molly and me with rotting hands. Grasping hands, full of all the awful strength of the raised dead. I armoured up immediately, the golden armour encasing me from head to toe in a moment. It seemed to me the dead hesitated, as though they hadn't expected that, and then the will behind them drove them on. I went to meet them, my hands clenched into golden fists. Because if they wanted a fight, I was just in the mood to give them one. After what had been done to my family, all their anger was nothing compared to mine. They threatened me and Molly and the rescue of my family. To hell with that, and to hell with them all.

The nearest dead man grabbed on to my golden arm with both of his bony hands, and to my shock I could feel his cold wet grasp, right through the armour. It couldn't get through, couldn't get at me, but I could still feel it. And that wasn't supposed to be possible. I'd never felt anything like it before. What the hell had Crow Lee raised here, and what had he put into them?

I ripped the dead man's arm off and threw it away. Water ran like blood from the empty socket, but the dead man barely staggered. I punched him full in the face with my golden fist and knocked his head right off. The body didn't fall, so I kicked its feet out from under it and walked right over the thrashing body on the deck to get to the next. I waded into the army of the risen dead, striking about me with vicious strength. I showed them no mercy because they had none in them for Molly or me. I ripped them apart with my armoured strength, tearing them limb from limb, knocking them down and trampling them underfoot, because they were dead and beyond any pain. And because I didn't care. They were just in the way.

They swarmed around me, packing in close, trying to slow me down so they could pull me down. They clung on to me with their dead hands, beat against my armour with their bony fists, and scrabbled at my neck and face with clawed hands. And I just hit them until they fell apart and fell away. They were actually quite fragile after so long in the sea, and all of Crow Lee's power wasn't enough to make them a match for Drood armour. Anyone else might have found the dead men terrifying, even dangerous . . . but for me, in my armour, they were just targets. I hit them and broke them and it felt good, so good. I smashed through their ranks, ripped them apart, tore off their heads and threw them aside. I picked some up bodily and threw them off the edge of the Pier and back into the sea. Where they belonged.

I fought my way into the heart of them, striking out through the curling mists, the dead pressing so close around me now I couldn't have missed them if I'd tried. My golden fists made wet squelching sounds as they sank deep into rotting flesh and collapsed chests. I struck them down and walked right over them, hearing brittle bones crack and break under my heavy golden feet. They beat at me with their dead fists but they couldn't reach me inside my armour. Crow Lee thought he could frighten me, thought he could drag me down, because I didn't have my armour anymore without my family, because he thought I was just a man. He should have known better. On the worst day I ever had, I was still a Drood.

Dead hands slipped away from me as fists broke and shattered harmlessly against my armour. I didn't feel their attacks. Sometimes they threw their arms around me, several of them at once, trying to pull me down through accumulated weight and numbers; but I'd just break their arms and throw them away again. Sometimes, several of them at once would hang on to my arms, and I could feel their squirming hands through the armour like bloated wet spiders. And then I'd throw them off me so violently they left their hands behind and I had to scrape them off me. Torn off heads rolled back and forth on the bare floorboards and I kicked them around like footballs. Sometimes the mouths still moved, jaws opening and closing as though trying to say something. I didn't listen. It wasn't going to be anything I wanted to hear.

I struck them down, I tore them apart, picked them up and threw them away. And laughed while I did it.

Inevitably, some of the dead got past me, ignoring me to head straight for Molly. Probably seeing her as an easier target. More fools, them. I caught glimpses of Molly through the fog as I fought, her standing her ground, her face calm and thoughtful as she lashed out at them with all the magics at her command. She called lightning and it stabbed down through the fog, blasting bodies into pieces and setting others on fire. But some of them were so damp, so saturated with water from their time in the sea, the flames couldn't get a hold. Steam boiled off them, but they kept going. She gestured sharply, and some of the dead just exploded, chunks of rotting flesh flying through the air like soft shrapnel. The explosive spells worked well, but I knew how much that kind of magic took out of Molly. She could only target one dead man at a time. And there were so very many of them. . . .

They pressed forward, reaching out to her with cold implacable hands, and she had no choice but to back away. She threw up a shimmering protective screen between them and her, and the dead men hesitated. Molly forced out a series of powerful Words, and the base of her screen dug deep into the floorboards, securing it in place. It had been powerful enough to hold off the shades in Egypt, but the raised dead were more solid. They pressed right up against the protective screen, throwing all their weight against it, and as more and more joined in, they slowly forced the shimmering screen back inch by inch. The screen's energies burnt dead flesh where it touched, but they didn't care. They couldn't feel it. They forced the screen back through sheer weight of numbers, and Molly had no choice but to back away before it.

The dead shouldn't have been able to do that. They were just bodies. But Crow Lee had put a power in them that would not be denied. . . .

And it happened that I looked back just at the moment when the screen collapsed and the dead surged forward, reaching out for Molly. The fog seemed to hold back just so I could see it. And just like that, my cold and vicious rage fell away from me. Molly was in danger, and that was all that mattered. I turned round immediately and fought my way back through the army of the dead, desperate to get to Molly before the dead could get to her. The dead between us immediately closed together, blocking my way with their bodies, soaking up my increasingly desperate blows with their yielding flesh. And even though I struck them down and threw them aside, there were just so many of them. I'd allowed myself to be drawn away, separated from Molly. I surged forward with all my strength, smashing through bodies like they were made of paper, and cried out to Molly.

"Hold on, love! I'm on my way! Hold on till I can get to you!"

She heard me; I know she did. She looked right at me. But I was so far away and there were so many of them almost upon her. Both of us knew there was no way I could get to her in time. I screamed so hard it hurt my throat, fighting desperately to throw off the dead as they clung to me, grabbing at my legs to bring me down. I fought on, knowing it was useless. Knowing they were going to hurt her and kill her and drag her off with them down into the depths of the sea. I knew there was nothing I could do and I thought I'd lose my mind.

But fortunately she was Molly Metcalf.

She yelled out to me to brace myself, and immediately I stopped fighting and grabbed on to the safety railings looming up out of the fog before me. I grabbed on with both hands, ignoring the dead men as they hammered at me, trying to pry me loose. They swarmed all over me and I ignored them and just hung on. Praying for a miracle.

And Molly came through. She carefully pronounced one really powerful Word, and a roaring wind came hammering down the Pier and swept the whole damned fog away. The wind blasted the fog right off the Pier and sent it back out across the sea . . . and without its support the dead couldn't stay. They just faded away as the last of the fog dispersed and the raging wind swept the whole Pier clean.

The dead man who'd spoken to me first was the last to go. He hung on somehow, intact, looking right at me with his eyeless face.

"He'll never let us go," he said. "He'll hold on to us, down in the depths, until he needs us again."

"I'll get him for you," I said. I slowly let go of the railings and moved forward to face him. I remembered the vicious joy I'd felt in fighting and destroying him and his kind, and I felt suddenly ashamed. If they really were just victims of Crow Lee's will, I'd done them a terrible wrong. They were just innocent bystanders, caught up in the middle of a war. "I'll set you free," I said. "Whatever it takes."

"Why would you do that for us?" said the dead man. "After everything we've done, and would have done and will do again?"

"Because that's what I do," I said firmly. "Because I'm a Drood."

"Sorry," said the dead man, already fading away, with something that might have been a smile on his rotting mouth. "Never heard of you . . ."

The fog was gone, and the last of the day's sunlight washed from end to end of Brighton Pier. I looked out to sea, but there was no sign of fog anywhere. I armoured down and hurried back to join my Molly. I took her in my arms and held her tight, and she held me back just as strongly. And for a long moment we just stood there together. It was all very calm and very quiet. Eventually we let go of each other and looked around. Brighton Pier was back to normal. No trace left to show that anything had happened, except for a few wet footprints on the floor-boards, already evaporating.

"I am never letting us get separated again," I said. "For a moment there, I really thought I'd lost you."

"For a moment there, you forgot that I can look after myself," Molly said sternly.

"My head was all messed up," I said. "All I could think of was . . . fighting, and striking down my hated enemy. I was enjoying myself. I forgot all about you. Until I looked back and saw you in danger."

Molly looked at me steadily. "Is it the rogue armour, Eddie? Is it affecting you?"

"I don't know," I said. "I want to blame the new armour, but . . . maybe this is what I'm really like without my family."

"Bullshit," Molly said briskly. "That is not what you are, and I should know. Proof in point: You said yourself the spell broke the moment you looked back at me."

"What if I hadn't?"

"But you did."

I had to smile. "You always were a good influence on me."

"Not if I can help it," said Molly, and kissed me firmly on the mouth.

"Time to be going," I said after a while. "Unless we want to hang around and be asked a whole bunch of questions we don't have any good answers for."

"I've got just enough magic left in me for one short-range tele-port," said Molly. "Enough to drop us off right next to the Phantom V. But, Eddie, that's all I've got left. I need time out to recharge my batteries. . . ."

"And I doubt we're going to be left in peace that long," I said. "I won't leave you alone again, Molly, I promise."

"Will you stop beating yourself up? I saw you; you were busy kicking the crap out of dead things. Doing your job."

"I'm not so sure about that, either," I said. "If there were spirits trapped inside those bodies, if they were just innocents . . ."

"Very unlikely," said Molly. "That was just Crow Lee speaking through them, playing games with your head."

"And if it wasn't?"

"Why do you keep asking questions when you know I don't have the answers? Let's get to Crow Lee and then we can beat the answers out of him."

"Sounds like a plan to me," I said.

CHAPTER FIVE

Do You Have an Appointment?

Molly snapped her fingers and the air before us split obediently in two, forming into a shimmering portal that
crackled with something very like static for a moment,
like a television caught between stations, before finally
condensing into a familiar silver tunnel. Molly had tried
to explain to me that what I see when I look at her magic
is largely symbolic; just my mind trying to make sense of something it
can't cope with. Personally, I think she has the same relationship with
magic that I have with science; we just pretend we know what we're
doing and hope it all works out for the best. Molly strode into the silver
tunnel and I hurried in after her, not wanting to be left behind or have
important parts of myself sliced off by the portal closing after me.

Molly had clearly been refining her teleport spell on the quiet,
because we didn't just end up back at the car. Instead, we both materialised inside the Phantom V, sitting in the front seats. Only because it
was her spell, Molly was sitting behind the wheel and I was in the passenger's seat. She smiled at me triumphantly, running her hands over
the steering wheel in a distressingly sensual way.

"I've always wanted to drive one of these! Give me the keys, Eddie.
Then it's atomic batteries to power, turbines to speed and everyone else
get the hell out of the way!"

"Sorry," I said. "There are no keys. This is a Drood car, programmed only to accept a Drood driver. Basic security measure."

Molly glared at me. "You're making that up!"

"Not even a little bit. There are no keys because the car knows who I am and does what I tell it to. So I'm afraid we're going to have to switch seats if we're going to go anywhere. Really."

"Someone's going to pay for this," said Molly.

"It's all down to torc envy, I'm sure," I said.

Molly sniffed loudly, kicked the driver's door open, and got out of the car. I got out my side, and we crossed in front of the car without speaking. The engine turned itself on as I sat down behind the wheel, and Molly banged her door shut with added violence. And that was when I heard sirens approaching. I looked in the rearview mirror, and sure enough several police cars were heading our way at speed—sirens, flashing blue lights, the works. The large crowd of tourists and others who'd been chased off the Pier by recent supernatural events waved excitedly at the approaching police. A few of the braver elements were hovering outside the Pier's main entrance, though as yet none of them felt brave enough to go back in without some official presence to lead the way. And, if need be, hide behind.

"Let them look," said Molly. "They won't find anything. The fog wiped all its traces away as it retreated. A built-in clean-up factor is the mark of a real magician."

"Crow Lee didn't get where he is today by leaving evidence behind to reveal his presence," I agreed. "Come back here in a few years and all of this will be just another urban legend. A story to tell visitors in an enjoyable and not-to-be believed way. They'll probably be selling the tourists Fog in a Can. . . ."

"So," said Molly. "Let us adjourn to pastures new before the boys in blue come knocking on our window, inviting us to answer some pointed questions. Which I have no intention of answering. Where are we going next?"

"Back to my old stomping grounds," I said. "London. They call it the Smoke, and everyone knows there's no smoke without fire. Street by street and block by block, London's still the most magical city in the world. And not always in a good way."

"I suppose you intend to drive all the way there?" said Molly, just a bit sullenly.

"No," I said. "We don't have the time, and I don't think I trust the car's shields to hide us for much longer. Crow Lee found us here quickly enough. And don't look at me like that, Molly. In situations like this, paranoia becomes a survival skill. No, I think we'd better use the Merlin Glass."

"And risk attracting attention?"

"Crow Lee already knows where we are," I pointed out.

"So we're leaving the car here?" said Molly.

"Hardly," I said. "I'd have to hit the self-destruct button to keep it out of official hands, and Uncle Jack would have my scalp if I lost another of his favourite cars."

I already had the Merlin Glass in my hand, and I hefted the silver-backed hand mirror thoughtfully. Like its predecessor, the Glass always seemed so small and innocent in its dormant state, like a vampire hiding its sharp teeth behind a polite smile. I fed the Merlin Glass the correct coordinates through my torc, and the Glass shot out of my hand and passed right through the windscreen without affecting it in the least, to hover on the air in front of the car. It grew quickly in size, becoming a great doorway through which I could see a familiar London street. I sent the Phantom rolling smoothly forward and we left Brighton behind, in search of fresh prey.

The Glass shut itself down behind us, ghosted through the back window, and nestled into the hand I put up to catch it. I put the Glass away, and tried to concentrate on my driving. This new Merlin Glass seemed to take a delight in demonstrating all the many tricks at its disposal. It seemed to have a lot more . . . character than the one I was used to. I wasn't sure whether that was a good thing or not. We'd appeared on a deserted side street, as I'd requested, and the few people walking up and down paid us no attention. I eased the Phantom V down the street and out into the main flow of traffic.

"I know this is London," said Molly, "but surely even the most blasé Londoner should have been a bit startled by a bloody big car appearing right in front of him."

"It's all down to the Armourer," I said. "Uncle Jack built some serious *blending-in* tech into the car's shields."

"But the Phantom must have been identified by now," said Molly. "And you can bet Crow Lee will have put out its description to everyone who answers to him. Or owes him favours, of which there are no doubt many. Why not just drop the car off somewhere safe and we'll take the Tube? Who's going to notice just another couple of tourists in London?"

"Because I'm not ready to give up the car just yet," I said stubbornly. "It contains many useful items, courtesy of my uncle Jack. And a whole armoury of heavy-duty weapons that I want close at hand, ready for when I need them."

"I'm not entirely helpless," said Molly. "I still have a few charms left on my ankle bracelet."

I glanced at her carefully. "Just how low are your magic levels at the moment?"

"Low," said Molly. "I might be able to manage some impressive fireworks and whizbangs, but that's about it."

"Then we need the car," I said.

"Don't be smug," said Molly. "Or I'll hit you with my pony."

We drove steadily on through the early-evening London traffic. Cars and taxis and bendy buses flowed past, and the pavements were packed with people hurrying about their everyday business. No one paid the Phantom any undue attention, thanks to Uncle Jack. Droods aren't supposed to be noticed. At least half our job is to keep people from noticing the very threats we protect them from. Droods are trained from an early age to deal with all the wonders and horrors of the hidden world, but even we have problems dealing sometimes. Humanity isn't ready to learn who and what they share this world with. Of course, if I couldn't find a way to bring my family safely home, Humanity might start finding out the hard way. There are all kinds of things out there who only play nice with everyone else because they know we're watching.

It didn't take long to get where we needed to be. The Merlin Glass had followed my instructions to the letter, and we were soon easing up the Mall, with Buckingham Palace straight ahead. I smiled complacently at all the other cars, obediently paying London's exorbitant congestion charge. Droods are exempt. In fact, we're exempt from all the annoying intrusions of the Establishment's bean counters. Perk of the job.

"You do know where you're going this time?" said Molly.

"London is my territory," I said grandly. "I was a field agent here for years before I even met you. Now, admittedly, I don't know the city as well as I once did. My old armour had the equivalent of a sat nav built in. Complete maps of London and all its environs programmed into the torc, ready to be downloaded directly into my mind, as and when required. The rogue armour . . . doesn't have that. So I'm having to work from my own personal memories."

"So, what happens when we get lost?" Molly said sweetly.

"You get to ask for directions. But I don't think that's going to be necessary. Look up ahead. See the big palacey thing at the end of the Mall? Buck House, in all her glory."

"Yes, I can see the palace, Eddie; I'm just not sure why we need it. Madame O said we needed the Department of the Uncanny."

"So she did. She also said we'd find it at Big Ben. And how likely is that? Something that obvious, that public? How much do you know about the D of U?"

"I know the name," said Molly.

"Then you're ahead of most people," I said. "It's one of those very old, very secret, secret organisations that the government won't even admit exists. Originally founded by Dr. Dee, Queen Elizabeth I's unofficial spymaster and magician general, alongside the more specialised Carnacki Institute. The Department of the Uncanny's remit is to defend the Realm from supernatural attacks, from within as well as without. More by gathering information and organising other people than by getting involved themselves. Mostly. It is possible they were originally put in place as an answer to the Droods, if we should ever get out of hand. On the grounds that the Department could always be relied on to put England's interests first."

"It strikes me that there's so many of these secret organisations, it's a wonder they don't end up tripping all over each other," said Molly.

"They have a lot of ground to cover," I said. "And they're all very jealous when it comes to guarding their own territory. The last thing anyone wants is a civil war in the hidden world over who's in charge of what. The Department of the Uncanny exists to defend the nation. The Carnacki Institute deals with ghosts and other mortally challenged incursions. The London Knights deal with otherworldly and other-dimensional threats. And MI-13 used to deal with supernatural intelligence; our spies versus their spies. The Droods . . . deal with Major League Weird Shit. Worldwide threats."

"Couldn't all these supernatural agencies work together to cover the Droods' workload until they return?" said Molly.

"All the organisations I've just mentioned are British based," I said patiently. "They have British aims and responsibilities. The Droods may live in England, but we guard the whole world. We are Humanity's shepherds, their shamans and protectors. All of this country's departments working together couldn't do what we do."

"Fancy yourself much, do you?" said Molly, amused.

"This is why my family has always taken duty and responsibility so seriously." I said. "You've never really thought this through, have you? Droods have field agents in every country and in every major city; there isn't a country or a culture on this planet that doesn't fall under our protection."

"You used to run the world," said Molly. "I remember. I was there when we put a stop to that."

"We exist to protect all of Humanity."

"Two World Wars and an extended Cold War. Good going . . ."

"We protect Humanity from outside threats," I said carefully. "From things like the Hungry Gods and the Apocalypse Door. It's our job to stand between Humanity and all the nonhuman things that threaten us. It's not our job to get involved in tribal squabbles."

Molly turned right round in her seat to look at me. "Is that really how you see it?"

"It's how we have to see it," I said. "We can't take sides. We're here to help, not meddle, and sometimes . . . that means standing back and letting things happen. Even when it breaks our hearts. Or we really would be the Secret Masters of Humanity. We may have . . . lost our way for a while, but we're back on track now. The world needs my family, Molly."

"Whether they want you or not?"

"Sometimes, yes."

"Tell me more about the Department of the Uncanny," said Molly, staring straight ahead. "Suddenly that seems like a lot safer conversation."

"Okay," I said. "They're basically an information-gathering organisation, evaluating all kinds of data gleaned from every corner of the hidden world to see if it poses any threat. They share information with a great many other organisations, and take occasional action on their own. They have an excellent reputation. I never had any direct dealings with them myself back when I was just the local field agent. As part of the Establishment, that made them part of Matthew's territory. Back when he was very much the senior London agent. I never got a look in. He had his own circle of intimates and connections, inside men and informers, to which I was never granted access. If I needed to know such things, I had to go to him, and didn't he just love that, lording it over me. I suppose those people are still on the files somewhere. . . . To be honest, I was happy enough to let him deal with that kind of stuff. I was never what you'd call diplomatic, in those days. I had issues with authority figures."

"I had noticed," said Molly. "You never did replace Matthew, did you?"

"I kept meaning to," I said. "London's been without a proper field agent for far too long. I know that. It's probably why Philip MacAlpine and MI-13 were able to get so out of hand with no one noticing. I thought I could just come back here and take over again once I stepped down as head of the family. . . ."

"They booted you out, the ungrateful bastards!"

"They voted me out," I said with some dignity. "And I was happy enough to get out from under the burden of command and run away back to London. But it's been just one damned thing after another. I kept being called back to the Hall to deal with things no one else could. They're never going to let me be just a field agent again. I'm going to have to put someone else in charge of London. Someone I can trust . . . It's right there on my list of things to do the moment I get my family back. If they were still here, I could have just asked where to find this Department. Someone would have known. I haven't a clue."

"Madame O said to go to Big Ben," Molly said stubbornly.

"Yes, but obviously she didn't mean that literally! It has to be some clever allusion or riddle or something equally irritating, and I don't have the time or the patience to work it out. No, the best way to find one secret organisation is to ask another. They love to rat each other out and show off how much they know that they're not supposed to know. And as it happens, I do know exactly where the secret headquarters of the Carnacki Institute are to be found. I know where their boss is, the very powerful, very forbidding Catherine Latimer. Her office is tucked away at the end of a corridor that doesn't officially exist, right at the back of Buckingham Palace."

"Oh, that is seriously cool!" said Molly. "I've always wanted to burgle Buck House!"

"One," I said, very firmly, "we are not breaking in. We will be using the Merlin Glass to sneak in. And two, *we are not stealing anything*. Do you hear me, Molly Metcalf?"

"You are no fun sometimes," said Molly, slumping down in her seat and pouting just a bit. "I've got to do *something* to show I was there. I'm the supernatural anarchist. Remember? I have an appalling reputation to uphold."

"All right," I said. "I'll let you scrawl some really hateful graffiti in the Institute toilets. How about that?"

"You are so good to me, Eddie."

"Yes, I am. And don't you forget it."

"Any corgis that get under my feet will regret it," Molly said darkly. "How is it you know where to find Catherine Latimer's office?"

"Because I did a few jobs with the Institute back in the day," I said. "A little cooperation here and there helps to keep the wheels turning. A favour for a favour. Matthew always looked down on those, always said he had more important things to deal with, and left them to me."

"Is there anyone you haven't worked with at one time or another?" said Molly.

I had to smile. "I could ask you the same question."

She grinned. "We do get around, don't we?"

I found a very illegal place to park, right in front of the Buckingham Palace railings. We both got out of the car and stood together, staring at the guards and the sights just like any other tourists. Scarlet-garbed Horse Guard soldiers paraded up and down in their traditional bearskin hats. They looked very efficient and very dangerous, as well they should. But the real guarding forces watched from concealment, behind very sophisticated camouflage equipment. I could just See them out of the corner of my eye. They were the real hard men of the regiment. In fact, I think you have to bite the head off an SAS officer just to be allowed to apply.

"Why don't we just drive in?" said Molly, not unreasonably. "I mean, you're a Drood! Who's going to say no to you?"

"Yes, I am a Drood, but I don't want just anyone knowing that," I said. "Most people think my family are all dead, and I'm quite happy for them to go on thinking that, right up to the point where I find it necessary to shout, *I'm here!* and then punch them in the head."

"You can't ask the Carnacki Institute for help without revealing who you are," said Molly. "And the same with the Department of the Uncanny and the Regent of Shadows . . ."

"One thing secret organisations are good at," I said, "is keeping secrets. Especially from each other. Because you never know how valuable such information might become. And then you can trade it. . . ."

Molly started to snap her fingers, and then stopped. "Damn. I don't even have enough power left to magic up a Disabled sticker."

"This is London," I said. "They're not so easily impressed here. I think I'll put my faith in the Armourer's security measures. This car can look after itself. If anyone does try messing with it, they'll wake up somewhen next year."

But Molly had already gone back to studying Buckingham Palace. "Why is the Carnacki Institute based here, of all places? I mean, I know they're part of the Establishment, but . . . Is the queen an honorary ghostbuster? Is Prince Philip bothered by poltergeists?"

"Not officially. It's because the Institute is a royal charter, not a political department, like Uncanny. Apparently Elizabeth I wanted the Institute where she could keep an eye on it, and subsequent monarchs continued the tradition. It does mean that Catherine Latimer's private office is protected not only by its own shields, but also by the palace's. Of course, the Merlin Glass should be able to punch right through them. . . ."

"Should?" said Molly, immediately. "I really don't like that word in this context, Eddie. What if it can't?"

"Bugs on a windshield," I said. "Raise your Sight, Molly. Take a good look at the palace, and See what I'm Seeing."

With the Drood torc at my throat, I can See the world as it really is and not as most people think it is. Though mostly I choose not to, for my own peace of mind. With the Sight, Buckingham Palace and its immediate surroundings all but disappeared under layer upon layer of powerful protections: overlapping screens and shields and deadly defences laid down over centuries.

"Okay," said Molly, after a while. "Those . . . are serious protections. How the hell did that burglar get in? You know, the one who just wandered around till he ended up in the queen's bedroom and she had to call for help?"

"Simple answer: He didn't," I said. "They let him in. To make the rest of the world think they only had standard protections. Anyone who tried to follow in that guy's footsteps got flash-fried into free-floating atoms for some time afterwards."

Molly gave me a stern look. "And the Merlin Glass *should* get us past all that?"

"Oh, almost certainly," I said cheerfully. "If I understand how the Glass works, and I'm perfectly ready to be told I don't, I think it opens a door on this side of the shields and another door on the other side. And then we step through without bothering the shields at all. They don't even know anything's happened."

"But if they do detect us?"

"It's been fun knowing you, Molly."

"Let's go somewhere else."

"If there was somewhere else, I'd be there," I said. "But we need access to the Regent of Shadows, and Catherine Latimer is the only one I know who can get us there. And as long as Crow Lee is on our trail, the clock is ticking. He can't let even one Drood live, for fear I'll find a way to bring the rest back. And then everything he's risked will have been for nothing. Now grit your teeth and be a brave little witch, and there shall be dark chocolate Jaffa Cakes for tea."

"Let me get this straight," said Molly. "We're dropping in on the very dangerous boss herself, in her very own private and heavily defended office? Because you've been there once before? Colour me officially uneasy, Eddie. Not many get in there and get out again with all their favourite parts still attached."

"I did her a favour once on a case I still don't care to talk about. She wasn't exactly happy with the way I handled it, because the Droods got more out of it than the Institute did, but we still parted on . . . pretty good terms."

"So she isn't necessarily going to be pleased to see you?"

"Is anyone?"

"What if she point-blank refuses to help you," said Molly, "now that the rest of your family isn't around to intimidate her into playing nice?"

"She doesn't get to say no," I said. "I'm a Drood."

"My tough guy," Molly said admiringly. "Still, weren't we worried that using something as powerful as the Merlin Glass might attract all the wrong kinds of attention?"

"Oh, sure," I said. "But not until it's far too late. I'm not planning on sticking around here that long."

"They might try to stop us leaving."

"Like to see them try."

"Okay," said Molly. "We have now officially crossed the line from tough guy into cocky and downright arrogant. That's not like you, Eddie."

"I'm the Last Drood," I said. "I can't afford to be stopped by anything or anyone. Not even myself. Not when my whole family is depending on me."

"You can't help them if you're dead or stripped of your torc in some underground prison!"

"Well, then," I said. "I'd better not let that happen. Had I?"

"Cocky and arrogant," Molly said sadly. "I am a bad influence on you, Eddie." She looked dubiously at the Merlin Glass as I held it up before us. "Was the Glass we knew ever this powerful? I'm not sure I would have trusted the old Glass in this situation."

"It got you into the Timeless Moment to rescue me from Castle Shreck," I said. "But it doesn't really matter. Needs must, when the Devil is breathing heavily down the back of your neck. One thing on our side: once we're in the boss's office, her shields should be more than enough to hide us from our enemies."

"Including Crow Lee?"

"Let us both fervently hope so."

I concentrated on the Merlin Glass through my torc, visualising the exact coordinates for Catherine Latimer's very private office, and the Glass just sat there in my hand and refused to budge. I kept telling it where to go, and it just kept refusing. The shields around the office were so powerful the Glass couldn't find anything to lock on to. Buckingham Palace's shields weren't the problem, just the office's. Which told me rather more about the nature of the Carnacki Institute's shields than I was comfortable knowing. I looked reluctantly at Molly.

"Problem . . . We can't go straight to the boss after all. She's protected by something so powerful it even spooks the Merlin Glass. You know . . . it might actually be safer if you were to stay here, Molly. In the car. Uncle Jack's protections will look after you, and you can always do a runner if necessary."

"No way in hell," Molly said flatly. "You're not going anywhere without me. Not while you're still pretending to be all cocky and arrogant to hide the fact that you're still grieving for your family. Someone's got to be there with you, to be reasonable on your behalf. And, yes, I do know that by volunteering myself in that department I am indulging in cosmic levels of irony, but . . . How about this: If you can't go directly to the boss, can you get to her indirectly?"

"Of course! Yes! Molly, you're a genius. I had to wait in the secretary's office before I got to see Catherine Latimer, her own bad self, last time I was there." I concentrated on the Glass again, and it locked onto the secretary's office immediately. "There you go! A definite weak spot in the Institute's security, Molly, which I shall be quite sure not to mention to the boss. In case I need to use it again."

"You see?" said Molly. "You're getting smarter all the time just from being around me. Come on, let's do this. Before we have a rush of common sense to the brain. I'm just in the mood to bully a functionary."

"Ah," I said. "Clearly you have never heard of the boss's secretary. Heather does not just type and file; she is also the boss's last line of defence. In that you have to get past Heather to get to the boss. Heather is the most heavily armed person in the whole place. She's not just there to smile politely at visitors; she's there to be very, very dangerous. So be prepared. . . ."

"Oh, I am," said Molly. "Really. You have no idea."

"Cocky, and arrogant with it," I said.

"You know you love it."

I armoured up. The golden metal swept over me in a moment, sealing me off from the world. The bitter cold was still there, but I was getting used to that. Which would have worried me if I'd had the time to be worried. Molly looked at me dubiously.

"Is that really necessary? Just for a quick drop-in and a chat?"

"Oh yes," I said. "Really. You have no idea."

"Shut up and get on with it."

"Yes, mistress."

I shook the hand mirror out to door size, and immediately I could see Heather's office through it. I stepped quickly through, Molly all but treading on my heels in her eagerness, and the Merlin Glass immediately slammed itself shut behind me, pushed through my armoured side, and hid in my secret pocket. Out of harm's way. It occurred to me that if the Glass was that scared, then I ought to be, too. But I just didn't have the time.

The office itself was small and cramped and drab; just a close, windowless room with Heather the secretary sitting quietly at her desk, leafing through some paperwork. She looked up, startled, as Molly and I appeared out of nowhere, right in front of her, and she actually gaped for just a moment at the sight of a Drood in his armour. Which is one of the helpful things Drood armour is psychologically designed to do.

Heather herself was a calm, professional-looking sort, pretty in a pleasantly blond, curly-haired sort of way. She wore a white blouse over a navy skirt and had a really big silver ankh hanging round her neck. Anyone else would have seen her as sweet and harmless, just another secretary. Which was, of course, the point. I knew better, but I was still caught off guard when Heather threw off her surprise in a moment, pulled a really big gun out of nowhere and opened fire on me. The damned thing—some kind of energy weapon I didn't even recognise— was so big she needed both hands to aim it. She just blasted away without even saying a word to me or Molly, and the energy blast hit me right in the centre of my golden chest. The impact was enough to send me staggering back a step. I dug in my heels, regained my balance, while Heather fired at me again and again, the energy beams vividly bright in the enclosed space, leaving shimmering trails of Cherenkov radiation hanging on the air behind them. I leaned forward into the energy fire and advanced slowly and deliberately into the concussion blasts. My armour soaked up the deadly energies and the impacts with increasing ease. It was like wading forward against a strong chest-high tide, but it took me only a few steps to reach the desk, sweep it out of my way with one blow and then snatch the energy gun right out of Heather's hands. I crumpled it easily in my golden gauntlets, and all the little lights flashing on the weapon went out. I dropped the scrunched-up mess to the floor, and it dented the floor when it hit.

Out of nowhere Heather produced an aboriginal pointing bone. Molly slapped it out of her hand. The bone flew away across the office. Heather grabbed Molly's wrist and flipped her right over with a swift judo move. Molly barely had time to get out a surprised obscenity before she was flying through the air, upside down, and heading for the nearest wall. She managed to turn enough to take most of the impact on her shoulder, but the impact was still hard enough to knock all the breath out of her. She slid slowly down the wall, her eyes half-closed and her mouth slack.

I advanced on Heather. She snapped her fingers and the pointing bone reappeared in her hand. The bone was old cold brown, steeped in time and accumulated power. She stabbed the nasty thing at me, and the whole front of my golden armour reverberated like a struck gong, and I slammed to a halt as though I'd just been hit in the chest by an invisible battering ram. To my utter astonishment, circular fingernail cracks radiated across my golden chest, a whole series of widening rings like ripples on a pond. I froze for a moment and then the cracks healed themselves, vanishing away as the golden metal re-formed. Heather froze when she saw that, and that was all the time I needed to surge forward and snatch the pointing bone out of her hand. I must have hurt Heather's fingers when I did, but she didn't make a sound. I crushed the bone in my armoured grasp. The bone cracked loudly and then collapsed in on itself. I opened my golden hand, and only dust and a few very small bone fragments fell out.

While I was busy showing off, Heather turned away and retrieved something else from her overturned desk. It turned out to be a shille-lagh, a huge gnarled club made from black oak and decorated with all kinds of carved runes and sigils. Given the size and weight of the thing, I was frankly astonished Heather could even heft it. She came straight at me, and when I went to take the club from her, she avoided me expertly and hit me really hard around the head and shoulders. My armour made loud booming noises of distress with every hit, and while

I couldn't feel the impact, the sheer ferocity of her attack drove me back several steps.

She flailed away at me as though the shillelagh was weightless to her, hitting me from this side and from that until finally I was sure my armour could take it. And then I snapped a golden hand forward into just the right place to stop the shillelagh in midblow. I held it firmly, and Heather's hands skidded off her end of the club. That must have hurt her, too. She looked at me with something like shock as I hefted the shillelagh easily in one golden hand and then tossed it across the room to Molly, who was already back on her feet. She caught the club easily, hefted it appraisingly and then advanced on Heather with the light of battle in her eyes. Heather looked at her and then at me, and then headed for her desk again. Molly got there first and held the shillelagh threateningly over Heather's work computer.

"Hold it right there! Or I'll kill your files!"

Heather glared at her. "You wouldn't dare!"

"Trust me," I said. "She will. This is Molly Metcalf."

"Oh, poot," said Heather.

Things then took a turn for the weird. All four walls of the enclosed office were covered in portraits: professionally painted and photographed faces of old Carnacki Institute agents who had fallen in the field. There were an awful lot of them, men and women who had covered themselves in glory, if not renown. I had heard them referred to as the Honoured Members. It reminded me of the long gallery of Drood portraits back at the Hall. All of them gone now, of course.

All the faces on the office walls suddenly came alive in their frames, and one by one opened their mouths to roar and howl in fury, sounding the alarm at our intrusion. The sound was deafening, overpowering. Even Heather flinched, and she had to be protected. My armour took most of the brunt, but the sound was still so loud and so harsh I couldn't hear myself think. Molly's face screwed up with pain, but she still managed to stride right up to the nearest wall and glare right into the howling faces.

"Shut the hell up! Or I will make your paint run and your colours fade!"

And just like that the sound shut off and all the faces went back to being portraits and photos again. They must have been listening when I said Molly's name. Of course, they wouldn't know her power levels were at an all-time low. . . . Molly smiled brilliantly, stepped back and shouldered her shillelagh. I armoured down and smiled at Heather.

"Dear God! It's you, Eddie!" Heather actually relaxed a little, and sank back onto her chair. "I should have known; if anyone could survive the complete destruction of Drood Hall, it would be you. We all thought the Droods were gone forever! I'm so glad you're all right!" She broke off to run one hand quickly through her dishevelled hair, took a deep breath and then fixed me with her best professional smile. "So, Eddie. Do you have an appointment?"

"Guess," I said.

"Catherine Latimer doesn't see anyone without an appoint-ment. . . ."

"She'll see us," said Molly.

Heather's gaze flickered from me to Molly and then back again. She was still smiling, but I could sense the effort.

"We have to see the boss, Heather," I said. "And I mean right now. If you've heard what's happened to my family, you know how urgent this is. And how upset I am."

"I really thought you were dead," said Heather. "When you just appeared here, I thought your enemies must have taken the armour for themselves. . . . Why didn't you use the main entrance and the proper protocols?"

"Too many eyes and ears," I said. "I'm the Last Drood, but I don't want just anyone knowing that."

"The boss has already arranged for formal wreaths from the Insti-tute," said Heather. "To show our respect. Not that we could send them anywhere, of course, but we will find somewhere suitable to put them. Is this really the infamous Molly Metcalf? I always thought she'd be taller. Please ask her not to kill my computer; I have a lot of vitally important typing to finish before the day's over."

I looked at Molly and she sniffed loudly, in an I'm-making-no-promises sort of way.

"I am keeping this shillelagh!" she said loudly. "I like it and it's mine now. Just in case anyone starts getting snotty. Always wanted one . . ."

"Let her have it," I said to Heather. "She'll only make a fuss."

"I can always get another one from the armoury," said Heather. "One of our janitors hand carves them on his own time. You still can't see the boss without making an appointment. Even if you do trash my office and murder my filing system."

I looked thoughtfully at the door behind her desk. The very heavily reinforced steel door with no handle or electronic lock on this side that led into the boss's office. I didn't have to raise my Sight to know it was crawling with powerful protections. I grinned at Heather.

"Get out your camera phone. I think I'm about to make history."

"Yeah!" Molly said happily. "Someone phone Guinness! Go, Drood. Go!"

And then we all stopped and looked round as the intercom lying beside Heather's desk buzzed loudly. A cold, calm voice sounded clearly in the office.

"Heather, if Edwin Drood and Molly Metcalf have quite finished striking dramatic poses, ask them if they'd like to come through. I can give them ten minutes."

"Yes, boss," said Heather.

"How did she know we were here?" Molly said suspiciously. "How did she know it was us? I don't see any surveillance cameras here."

"The boss knows everything," Heather said scornfully. "In fact, that's probably part of her job description."

The highly impressive door swung smoothly and silently open on its own. I nodded briskly to Heather and strode into Catherine Latimer's very private office. Molly hurried after me, determined not to be left out of anything, her shillelagh still slung casually over one shoulder.

The grand old boss of the Carnacki Institute, Catherine Latimer, her own very bad and intimidating self, sat stiff-backed behind what I immediately recognised as a genuine Hepplewhite desk. Latimer had to be in her late seventies, but she still burnt with severe nervous energy, even while sitting still. She was medium height, medium weight and handsome in a way that suggested she had never been pretty because she'd always had too much character for that. She had a grim mouth and cold grey eyes and looked like she'd never been pleased to see anyone in her life. She wore a smartly tailored grey suit and was smoking a black Turkish cigarette in a long ivory holder, supposedly an affection that went all the way back to her student days.

While I was busy looking her over and working on my best opening gambit, Molly just sauntered round the office, displaying a keen avaricious interest in everything on display. There was a lot to look at. She made a series of loud *ooh!* and *aah!* noises as she cooed over the various intriguing objects in their display cases, many of which I remembered from my last time in the office. Catherine Latimer wasn't much for change for the sake of change.

There were reminders of past triumphs, famous cases ancient and modern, and souvenirs of people and places best not discussed in polite company. Molly ignored the many valuable books and folios crammed onto shelves all over the office, and had no time at all for the endless locked and sealed case files in their colour-coded folders. She bent over a goldfish bowl full of murky ectoplasm in which the ghost of a goldfish swam slowly, solemnly backwards, flickering on and off like a faulty lightbulb. Next to that a crimson metal gauntlet with two broken fingers, twitching unhappily inside a brass birdcage, was labelled THE SATAN CLAW. Farther along, a badly stuffed phoenix posed awkwardly inside a hermetically sealed glass case, to keep it from smouldering. And finally, on open display on a black velvet cushion, the Twilight Teardrop. Molly actually crouched down before it so she could set her face on the same level and study it better. The fabled ruby stone was actually composed of fossilised vampire blood made into a polished gem in the shape of an elongated teardrop, some four inches long and two wide, set in an ancient gold clasp and chain, supposedly taken from a dragon's hoard. I say *supposedly*; there's a whole lot said about the

Twilight Teardrop, most of it contradictory and all of it upsetting. All anyone knows for sure is that it's a major magical depository for unnatural energies, mad, bad and dangerous to own.

Molly snatched it up and held it dangling before her eyes before flipping the gold chain over her head and round her neck, so that the glowing bloodred gem hung over her bosom.

"Mine!" she said loudly. "I'm taking it."

"Put it back!" I said.

"Shan't!"

"Molly, I don't want that nasty thing anywhere near me, never mind you. And need I remind you, we're trying to make a good impression here?"

"Don't care. I want it. Pretty, pretty."

"I'll take your pony away. . . ."

"You wouldn't! All right, you probably would. You big bully, you. Oh, but, Eddie . . . I really do need this. There's enough magical energy stored in here to replenish all my spells and abilities! And you know I have to be strong if we're going after You Know Who. . . ."

I looked apologetically at Latimer. "Sorry about this. . . ."

"Oh, let her have the bloody thing," said Latimer. "Given the sheer number of curses and bad vibes associated with the thing, she's welcome to it." She ignored Molly as she preened over her new toy, and fixed me with a cold glare. "Is she always like this?"

"Mostly," I said.

"It's all part of my charm," Molly said easily.

Latimer and I exchanged a look but said nothing.

"I have to admit, I'm surprised to see you here, Edwin," said the boss. "I have heard about what's happened to Drood Hall. I really thought all you Droods were dead and gone. I should have known the reports were too good to be true. And don't you raise your eyebrow at me like that, Edwin. You know very well your family has always been as big a threat to freedom as most of the threats you take on."

"An argument for another day," I said. "Right now I'm here to ask for your help."

It was Latimer's turn to raise an eyebrow. "Really? And just why would I want to do that?"

I leaned forward across her desk and showed her my hand encased in a golden gauntlet. Vicious barbed spikes rose out of the clenched metal fingers.

Catherine Latimer smiled briefly. "Typical Drood."

She didn't speak a Word or even gesture, just looked at me in a certain way and an invisible force snatched me up and held me tightly in its grasp. I fought against it but couldn't move a muscle. I was picked up off my feet, lifted up into the air, spun around several times and then slammed, spread-eagled, against the ceiling, looking down. I called for my armour but it didn't come. The boss had cut me off from my torc. I hadn't thought that was possible.

Molly started forward the moment she saw what was happening to me. The boss fixed her with a certain look, and Molly froze in place, locked between one movement and the next, in a stance that looked excruciatingly uncomfortable. Her face strained, her eyes full of silent fury, but she couldn't move a muscle. Any more than I could. The shillelagh slipped out of her paralysed hand and fell to the floor. Catherine Latimer allowed herself a brief smile.

"You don't spend as much time as I have operating in the hidden world, in any number of influential capacities, without picking up a useful trick or two. Never bait the bear in her cave, children. If I let you both down, will you behave?"

"Almost certainly," I said from the ceiling.

Molly managed a more or less compliant grunt.

The boss sat back in her chair and drew deeply on her cigarette holder. I fell down from the ceiling, only just managing to get my feet under me in time. I also only just managed to grab Molly by the shoulder as she lunged forward again. I wrestled her to a halt, murmuring urgently in her ear, and she finally stopped. She shrugged sulkily and turned her back on the boss and me. I looked at Catherine Latimer.

"I'm pretty sure Crow Lee was behind the attack on my family," I said.

"Unholy Crow Lee?" said the boss. "Could be. He'd have the power and the gall, if anyone would. . . . I was at Cambridge with him, you know. Back in the day. Had no doubt he was a bad sort even then. Cheated at cards, wouldn't pay his debts and insisted on reciting his own poetry in public. And now he's the Most Evil Man in the World . . . or so people in a position to know say. . . . Why should I help you against him?"

"Because if Crow Lee has become powerful enough to remove the entire Drood family from the playing field, how long before he comes after you and your organisation?" I said.

Latimer nodded slowly and blew a perfect smoke ring. "Good point. All right, Edwin. A temporary alliance. But you're going to owe me a really big favour for this."

"Agreed," I said. "A favour for a favour." And then I stopped and looked at her thoughtfully. "I have to ask: Did you by any chance *know* that something really bad was going to happen to my family? Did you have any information or warnings in advance and not tell us?"

"No," said the boss.

"Would you tell us if you did?" said Molly, slipping into place beside me.

"Probably not," said the boss. "I tend my own garden."

"So, why are you so ready to help me now?" I said.

"Because I've wanted a chance to bring Crow Lee down for ages," said Latimer. "I really hoped your family would kill him long ago, just on general principle, but somehow you were always too busy with other things. I half expected to see him go down with the Great Satanic Conspiracy, but of course he was smart enough not to get involved. Personally, I think they weren't extreme enough for him. And, of course, he never was interested in joining any group that wouldn't immediately accept him as their leader. . . . If they had, they might have beaten you. But he's always been too powerful and too well-connected for me to touch. So, you kick the little turd into the long grass with my blessing, Edwin. If you can." She looked at me for a long moment. "Is it just you, Edwin? Did any of the other Droods survive?"

"No one else from my family made it out of the Hall alive," I said carefully. "There's always the rogues, of course."

"Of course. I am sorry for your loss, Edwin. Some of them were my friends. And I do know what it's like to lose family. Now, what can I do for you?"

"I need information," I said. "Where, exactly, can I find the Department of the Uncanny and the Regent of Shadows?"

Catherine Latimer looked genuinely surprised. "Why on earth would you want him, of all people?"

"Because my family never wanted to talk about him," I said.

CHAPTER SIX

Department of the Unexpected

t doesn't matter how much experience you have of the world or how much you think you understand how things work; every now and again the way things really are will just rise up and slap you round the head.

Molly and I stood together looking up at Big Ben, with Molly not saying *I told you so* so loudly it was almost deafening. As Catherine Latimer had taken a certain delight in telling me, the Department of the Uncanny was indeed currently based at Big Ben. Just as Madame O had said back on Brighton Pier.

"Smugness really is very unattractive in a woman," I said, looking straight ahead. "Bloody Big Ben . . . I've heard of hiding in plain sight, but this is ridiculous. Hiding one of this country's most secret organisations behind a major tourist attraction? That's thinking so lateral, it's positively perverse."

"Big Ben is actually the name of the bell," Molly said solemnly. "Not the tower, or the clock at the top. I know many other useful facts about Big Ben, if you're interested."

"I mean, we're talking about a bloody big tower right next to the House of Commons!" I said bitterly. "And no one in that place could keep a secret even if you put a gun to their 'nads. . . ."

Molly looked at me sharply. "We're not going to have to go down into Under Parliament again, are we? That whole layout gave me the creeps big-time. . . ."

"No," I said. "There's a hidden door right at the base of the tower. Raise your Sight and look straight ahead."

I was already looking at it. A simple everyday door, standing upright on its own some two to three feet in front of the tower. Invisible and intangible to the rest of the world, it was a dimensional door, kept subtly out of phase with reality to provide a gateway to another place. Which meant the Department of the Uncanny wasn't actually in Big Ben, but somewhere else. Which meant that technically speaking, I'd been right all along. I had enough sense not to say that, of course. There was even a very neat and polite sign on the door saying, DEPART-MENT OF THE UNCANNY; ENQUIRE WITHIN, for those with the eyes to see it. What next—a welcome mat? Guided tours? A souvenir shop?

"Stop frowning," said Molly. "It'll give you wrinkles. Tell me things about the Department of the Uncanny. Lecture me. You know that always puts you in a better mood."

It would have made a much better peace offering if she could have said it without the smirk, but of such compromises are successful relationships made. Or so I'm told.

"Catherine Latimer had quite a lot to say about the Department of the Uncanny," I said. "While you were prowling round her office, looking for more things to steal. Most of these remarks were of a somewhat jealous and judgemental nature, but that's competing secret organisations for you. It's what she didn't say that intrigues me the most. She seemed to know things only about the Department's previous incarnation, when it was run by the Shadowy Cabinet. Political appointees, the lot of them, and living proof that it's who, rather than what, you know that gets you ahead in government circles. They're all gone now, of course; the entire Shadowy Cabinet was killed off during the Great Satanic Conspiracy."

"Whose side were they on?" said Molly.

"No one knows," I said. "The Satanists wiped them all out, apparently for not making up their minds quickly enough. To my mind, the very fact they were considering the question was good enough reason to stamp them all into the ground with extreme prejudice. The Regent of Shadows was invited to come in and do the whole new-broom thing shortly afterwards, and that was when Catherine Latimer's information stopped. Which suggests, if nothing else, that the Regent runs a tight ship and holds his secrets close to his chest."

"Good for him," said Molly. "He'll talk to us, though. Won't he?"

"Oh yes," I said. "He'll talk to us."

"If he knows what's good for him."

"Exactly! Can I lecture you some more?"

"Oh, go on, then. You know that professorial voice gets me all hot. And it'll help cheer you up for being so totally and utterly wrong about Big Ben. If you start to get boring, I can always heckle and throw things."

"The Department exists to keep an eye on the hidden world," I said. "To find out and know everything that matters about those aspects of the supernatural world that might pose a threat. Or at the very least, to know as much as possible. Because everything is always changing in the hidden world. Which is why the Department's agents are always so busy, overworked and just a bit twitchy. The Department then passes the relevant data on to those best able to make use of it, or at least to those the government of the day approves of. The Ghost Finders, the SAS combat sorcerers, the London Knights . . . even the Droods; after they've tried everything else, including prayer, and closing their eyes and just hoping it all goes away. Governments have always hated going cap in hand to my family."

"Gosh," said Molly, "I can't think why. Could it be because you always want something really hefty in return?"

"Who's telling this?" I said. "The Department of the Uncanny is part of the Establishment, though they like to say they're separate from it. But then, everyone in the Establishment likes to think that. Helps them sleep better at night. Catherine Latimer told me that Big Ben is the real London Eye, the Eye on the outer worlds. That the clock faces are just a disguise, a distraction. Because apparently someone or something lives at the top of the tower and Sees all and knows all."

"Like Madame O?" said Molly.

"Rather more clearly, one hopes," I said. "The Department gathers most of its information through field agents. They work in the shadows, as shadows, entirely undetected. No one knows who they are."

"Not even each other?"

"Must make for some stilted conversations in the staff canteen. And then there are the special agents, not unlike Drood field agents, for when something must be done. Usually in a hurry."

"I suppose no one knows who they are, either," said Molly.

"Got it in one! In fact, there are those who have been known to suggest that these Special Agents may not exist at all. Just smoke and mirrors to fool all the other secret organisations into taking the Department of the Uncanny more seriously."

"Don't the Droods know?"

"Oh, I'm sure someone in the family did," I said, and then stopped to correct myself. "I'm sure someone does. We always make it a point to know the things that no one else knows. Knowledge is ammunition in the hidden world of secret organisations."

I glanced casually about me. Night was falling, the lights were coming on and tourists strolled up and down the pavements, stopping now and then to take photos of one another before places of interest. And to peer uncertainly across the River Thames at the Houses of Parliament and wonder if anything important might be going on. And all the time they had no idea a door stood before Big Ben, unseen and unknown, that could have delivered them right into the heart of the secret world. But then, that's always the way. Wherever you are and wherever you go, you're never far from someone or something you're better off not knowing about.

Once again, I'd left the Phantom V parked so illegally it was practically committing treason just sitting there. I'd told Catherine Latimer I'd be parking the Rolls right next to the Houses of Parliament, so she could warn off the security people. In the full knowledge that the boss might or might not pass the information along. Depending on whether she thought it might be funnier not to. Like most people in positions of power, Latimer was famous for her perverse, not to say downright peculiar, sense of humour.

"Poor car," said Molly, running her hand affectionately over the gleaming bonnet. "It must get really bored, left on its own so often. Maybe we could leave the radio on. . . ."

"I don't think so," I said.

"Poor car . . . Who's a *good* car, then?"

"Don't encourage it," I said sternly. "The Armourer's personalised cars have more than enough personality as it is."

We left the Phantom V behind, and strode determinedly towards the door only we could See. None of the tourists noticed a thing, of course. The door saw to that. It waited till the very last moment, and then swung smoothly and invitingly open before us.

"You know," I said, just a bit wistfully, "I can remember when I was a proper spy, and no one had a clue who or what I was."

"We're clearly expected," said Molly.

"No one expects the Drood Inquisition!"

And we both walked laughing through the Uncanny door, something that probably didn't happen all that often. There was a brief and unsettling feeling of transition, and just like that we were somewhere else. And very clearly not anywhere inside the tower of Big Ben. Molly slipped an arm possessively through mine and leaned in close so she could murmur in my ear.

"Very powerful teleport," she said quietly. "Very sleek, very professional and, I might add, very much above the pay scale of a department like this. Which means either there's more to this particular mob than meets the eye or they stole it. Can I just enquire? Can you get us out of here in a hurry, should it prove necessary for us to get the hell out of Dodge with bullets flying around our nether regions?"

"I have the Merlin Glass," I said just as quietly.

"That's not what I asked," said Molly.

"Oh, ye of little faith. I thought the blatantly purloined Twilight Teardrop currently hanging round your splendid neck had restored all your abilities."

"Oh, hell, yes. I'm just bursting with all kinds of magics! All kinds! I'm not worried at all. I just thought you might be."

"It's good of you to be so concerned," I said. "Makes me feel so much more secure."

"I can never tell when you're being serious," Molly said severely.

"Neither can I . . . Just settle for the fact that we are where we wanted to be, and try not to dwell too much on the fact that the door we came through has already disappeared."

"Imagine my surprise," said Molly.

We were standing in a warm and cosy waiting room, with great bunches of flowers in oriental vases, pleasant paintings on brightly painted walls and a deep, deep shag-pile carpet. The whole setting had a familiar feel, and it took me a moment to realise it was because my new surroundings reminded me of home. Of Drood Hall. I suppressed a sudden stab of sorrow as I wondered if I'd ever see the Hall, my Hall, again. I'd purposefully kept myself busy all day just so I wouldn't have to think or feel things like that. I'd always defined myself as the Drood who ran away from home, but if there wasn't a home or a family to run away from . . . then who was I, really? What was I? I'd always fought for the right to live away from my family, but I'd always wanted them to still be there. . . .

I remembered a moment from my childhood. Sitting alone in the silent empty dormitory while all the other children were off studying, while my uncle James sat beside me on the bed and told me that my mother and father wouldn't be coming home again. Ever. Because they'd been killed out in the field on a mission that went wrong. *These things happen,* he said as kindly as he could. *You have to be strong now, Eddie. Be a Drood. For your mother and father, and for the family. Can you do that?* And I wanted to please him, because even then I greatly admired my uncle James, so I said, *Yes, I can be strong. Anything for the family.* Because I knew that was what I was supposed to say. And he smiled and slapped me on the shoulder, and got up and went away. Leaving me sitting there alone in that eerily silent and deserted dormitory. And all I could think was, *I want my mum. I want my dad.*

And standing there in that familiar-seeming room, I felt just that way again for no reason I could understand.

"Eddie?" said Molly. "What's wrong? You're shaking."

"It's okay," I said. "Molly. I was just thinking. Remembering."

She squeezed my arm reassuringly. And then we both looked round sharply as a young Indian woman wearing a brightly patterned sari entered the room. She smiled warmly at both of us, and we gave her our best professional smiles.

"Welcome to Uncanny," she said, in a rich contralto voice. "I'm Ankani. Please come with me. The Regent is very much looking forward to meeting with you."

"Are you his secretary?" I said.

Ankani smiled broadly. "Hardly. I'm one of his special agents. We didn't want you overawing the regular staff. We all spend time here in between assignments, guarding the place and doing whatever needs doing. We all muck in around here. The Regent's a great one for us all feeling like family. Breeds esprit de corps, and helps weed out those who aren't in this for the right reasons. But we mustn't keep the Regent waiting. He's been preparing for this meeting all day."

I looked at Molly, both of us conspicuously not budging. "Someone else who knew we were going to be here before we did."

"Really not liking that," said Molly. "I'd hate to think I was becoming predictable at my time of life."

"It's our job to know things," said Ankani.

"Even before they happen?" I said.

"Oh, especially then." Ankani smiled suddenly in a way that made her look a lot younger. "But mostly we're just really good guessers."

"Then maybe you can tell me," I said bluntly. "Do you know why my family would never talk about the Regent?"

"Of course," said Ankani. "But I really think I'd better leave it to the Regent to tell you. I think it will come better from him. I really don't want to spoil the surprise."

Ankani led us through a series of narrow, cheerfully lit corridors that reminded me of some old-fashioned country house. And, once again, of the quieter parts of Drood Hall. Along the way we passed a number of other Uncanny agents of an especially outré nature. I did wonder whether this was a show put on for our benefit to impress us with the Department's capabilities. We almost walked right into an agent so thoroughly camouflaged by his surroundings, I could hardly make him out. I looked back as he passed, and all I could see were the footprints he left in the deep carpeting.

"Show-off," said Molly.

Our next encounter was with an oversized Hell's Angel, all long hair and heavy biker leathers, with a *Rastamouse Lives!* T-shirt. He just grunted and nodded quickly, while I wondered exactly where he could blend in as an undercover agent.

He was followed by a ghostly Viking figure, complete with horned helmet and a bear-fur cloak that looked like it might have been part of the bear as early as that morning. He was a huge burly figure, but he still stepped quickly aside to let us pass, half of him disappearing into the wall.

"That's the Phantom Berserker," said Ankani. "We inherited him from the previous administration. They dug him up out of a burial mound in Norway back in the 1960s, and he followed them back here like a stray dog. So they gave him a bowl of mead and a blanket to sleep on in the kitchen, and he's been here ever since. The Regent did discuss having him exorcised when he took over, but we found we liked having him around. He's just like a big puppy, only with a really big axe. And it's not like he's got anywhere else to go, poor soul. . . . He's a bit single-minded, and more than a bit on the shy side in mixed company, but there's no one you'd rather have at your side when there's serious Smiting of the Bad Guys to be done."

She finally knocked on a door that looked no different from all the other doors we'd passed, waited for a voice from inside and then pushed the door open and ushered us into the Regent's office. And there he was, at last, the Regent of Shadows and new head of the Department of the Uncanny. A man of average height though a little on the skinny side, who looked to be in his late seventies . . . wearing a scruffy suit with leather patches on the elbows, and what looked like breakfast stains on his waistcoat. He had iron-grey hair, an almost military grey moustache, a charming smile and piercing blue eyes. He looked amiable enough at first, but you had only to meet his steady gaze for a moment to see the unrelenting authority in the man. He reminded me a lot of Catherine Latimer in that both of them seemed very hale and hearty and full of energy for someone of their years. The Regent looked like he'd be only too happy to challenge me to a friendly bout of arm wrestling, and probably win two out of three.

He came out from behind his desk with brisk movements and easy charm, and insisted on shaking hands with me and Molly. He had large bony hands and a firm hearty handshake. I found myself relaxing in his presence, despite myself, feeling safe and secure and at home. . . . Molly was friendly enough to him, but I could sense the reserve in her. She never was easily impressed by anyone.

I made a point of looking round the Regent's office to keep from staring at him. It looked more like a retired gentleman's study than a place where important decisions were made every day. More like a quiet room to sit and relax in and refresh the inner man. A comfortable setting, cosy and cheerful, with richly polished, wood-panelled walls. No framed portraits anywhere, for which I was grateful. I'd had enough of that for one day. Books filled the shelves of a battered old bookcase, but they were well-thumbed paperbacks rather than leather-bound first editions. And there were yet more fresh flowers, blooming in elegant vases.

There was just the one window, firmly closed, looking out over a late-evening view of wide-open fields spreading away to lap up against a dark forest, half-silhouetted against the dying day. More evidence, if more were needed, that we weren't in London anymore. Beside the window stood a tall grandfather clock, its heavy pendulum swinging slowly, ticking loudly in an impressive and reassuring way. I was half-convinced the entire office had been specially designed to put visitors at their ease, to lull them into a false sense of peace and security. I did my best to resist it. Molly seemed entirely unimpressed by her surroundings, but then, she always did. On principle.

She'd liked Catherine Latimer's office only because it was full of things she intended to liberate and take home with her. Or sell for a healthy profit. Fortunately, I couldn't see anything in the Regent's office worth stealing.

He smiled easily at Ankani, who was still hovering in the open doorway. "Thank you, Ankani. That will be all for the moment. I can take it from here. Do try and have those execution warrants on my desk by the end of day. There's a dear."

Ankani nodded quickly, smiled brightly at all of us and left in a swirl of sari, shutting the door quietly behind her. The Regent gestured invitingly at the two stiff-backed visitors' chairs set out before his desk, and Molly and I sat down. She made a point of moving her chair a little to one side, so she wouldn't be sitting with her back to the door. The Regent sank into his much more comfortable-looking chair on the other side of the desk. There were no in or out trays, no scattered papers; an entirely empty desktop, as though he'd deliberately cleared everything away so he could concentrate on Molly and me. He leaned forward and clasped his large hands together on top of his desk. But before he could say anything, his door flew open and a large, plain, middle-aged woman in a cheap print dress bustled in, bearing an enamelled tea tray, complete with a delicate willow-pattern china tea service, and all the makings necessary for a good cup of tea. She strode right up to the desk and planted the tray on the desktop. The Regent beamed at her.

"Thank you, Miss Mitchell. Right on cue. And a plate of chocolate hobnobs! You're spoiling us today."

"Those are for the visitors, sir," said Miss Mitchell. "You told me to remind you you're on a diet."

"So I did! So I did . . ."

"Shall I be mother, sir, and pour for everyone?"

"No, no, that's fine, Miss Mitchell. I can cope. That will be all for now."

"Call if you need anything, sir. I'm never far away." She smiled briefly about her and hurried off, closing the door firmly behind her.

"A very efficient, and almost frighteningly friendly woman, that Miss Mitchell," said the Regent. "I inherited her from someone, and if I ever find out who, I'll have his guts for garters. Possibly quite literally."

And, of course, then nothing would do but the Regent had to set out all the tea things and make sure we all had a nice cup of steaming-hot tea before things went any further. I sipped at mine cautiously. It was good tea. The Regent gave every indication of being a decent, genial, charming sort, but I was determined not to be taken in by appearances. There had to be some good reason why my family would never talk about the man. . . . And then the Regent took a sip of his tea, grimaced at the heat, poured some of his tea into his saucer and sipped the cooled tea from the saucer.

I sat very still as a sudden chill seized my heart and my soul.

The Regent looked at me over his tilted saucer and smiled easily at me. "I'm glad you've come to see me at last, Eddie. It's been such a long time since I last saw you."

Molly looked quickly from the Regent to me, saw I wasn't going to say anything, and looked back at the Regent. "You know Eddie?"

"Of course. Though it has been many years . . ."

"We've met before," I said. It was a statement of fact, not a question. It was hard to speak. My lips, my face were numb with something like shock.

"Of course we have, Eddie," said the Regent. His voice was calm and kind. "I am your grandfather Arthur. Martha Drood's first husband."

Molly was up on her feet in a moment, putting herself bodily between me and the Regent.

"Cut the crap! Eddie's grandfather is dead! Everyone knows that! I don't know what you're up to here, but I won't let you hurt him. I'll kill you first!"

And then she stopped, because the Regent was smiling proudly at her. "I really am who I say I am, Molly Metcalf. And I would die before I let any harm come to my grandson here. I have to say, Eddie, I'm glad to see you have such a . . . protective girlfriend."

I rose slowly to my feet to face the Regent. Molly stepped reluctantly back to hover at my side, scowling unhappily, so the Regent and I could stand face-to-face.

"They told me you were dead," I said. "Everyone in the family said you were dead, killed in the Kiev Conspiracy back in 1957."

"Well, they would," said the Regent. "There is a reason why the family doesn't talk about me. I went rogue, Eddie, because I stood up and said I no longer believed in how the family did things. I wanted to make the Droods over, into a better and more ethical organisation. More involved in protecting people than ruling them. I really thought Martha would stand by me, right up to the moment when she didn't. We'd been so close, after all, for so many years . . . ran so many missions together, back when we were both Drood field agents. But once she was made Matriarch, we both had no choice but to return to the Hall and our duties. I did my best to take on the burden of day-to-day decision making, keeping the pressure off her shoulders so she could concentrate on the things that mattered. Dictating policy, directing the family, guarding Humanity from all the things that threaten it. And the work . . . just ground us down and drove us apart. We never seemed to have time for each other after that. . . .

"We did talk about my growing doubts over how the family operated; it's hard to overlook all the dirty business the family gets up to when you're running things . . . but her answer was always, *What else is there? We have a duty,* she said, *to stick to what we know works.* When the time came . . . when I just couldn't stand it any longer, because we'd lost our only daughter and her husband in the field over stupid mistakes that should never have happened . . . then I called an emergency meeting of the council and I stood up in front of all of them and said, *No more!* And Martha looked me right in the eye and ordered me to either sit down and shut up or get out. It was either complete and unswerving loyalty to her and the family or nothing. Her way or the highway . . . I think—I like to think—that she was actually shocked when I said I'd leave. That the Droods had become something I was ashamed to be a part of.

"Martha never thought I'd really leave, because that would mean turning my back on her as well as the family. But . . . I no longer recognised her. She wasn't the woman I'd loved and married anymore. She had to fight to be allowed to marry me, you know; had to go head-to-head with the previous Matriarch. Because she and I were second cousins. The family's always had a horror of inbreeding.

"So, I left, or was driven out, depending on how you look at it. A rogue Drood. I became the Regent of Shadows, to put my beliefs into practice. An organisation of shadow agents, more concerned with amassing useful information than meddling in people's lives. I adopted an impressive-sounding title because I didn't want anyone to know I'd been a Drood, and because titles make people take you more seriously. To begin with, I made a point of recruiting people like myself, thrown out of other secret organisations for being wild cards, and I had a surprisingly high success rate with my choices.

"I discovered later that Martha wanted the rest of the family told I was dead rather than admit to the shame . . . that her own husband would rather leave the Droods than admit she was right. She always was very single-minded. I went along. It wasn't like I had any intention of ever going back, you see. It never even occurred to me that the leopards could change their golden spots. A lack of vision on my part, or perhaps my pride was hurt. When I learned how much you'd changed the Droods, Eddie, how much you achieved and how quickly, I couldn't believe it.

"Only the higher-ups in the family knew the truth about me, and they set out to rewrite Drood family history. I was written out, declared dead in 1957—don't ask me why that date in particular—and all my triumphs and victories were given over to others. Not that I gave a damn . . ."

"How could they just forget you?" said Molly.

"The Heart," I said. "The Matriarch had the Heart rework people's memories through their torcs. Right?"

"All the lower orders, yes," said the Regent. "Martha let the higher-ups remember. As an object lesson."

"And that's why Martha always said, *We don't talk about him!*" said Molly.

"Because if they did, they might start remembering, now the Heart is gone," said the Regent.

"I remembered," I said. "Perhaps because the Heart's gone and the Hall's gone . . . but I remembered meeting you that one time, when I was small. Watching you drink tea from your saucer . . ."

"A bad habit," the Regent said solemnly. "Don't do it in polite company. People stare at you." He stopped smiling, his eyes suddenly cold and faraway. "Even after you changed everything, Eddie . . . Martha still couldn't bring herself to call me home. Perhaps because she'd remarried, perhaps because that would have meant she'd have to admit she'd been wrong all along."

"Hold it," said Molly. I was thankful she was keeping up our end of the conversation; I was still finding it difficult to say anything. Molly stepped forward and fixed the Regent with a cold glare. "Martha was married to Alistair. So you must have divorced at some point."

"Of course," said the Regent. "Martha did it the day she kicked me out. The Matriarch was in charge of everything in those days. Weddings have always been big celebrations in the family; divorces and separations, less so. We're Droods. We don't like to admit we can get it wrong. What was Alistair like? I never met the man. . . . I've read all the files, of course, but it's not the same."

"Weak," Molly said bluntly. "He was weak."

"But he stood up to be counted when it mattered," I said. "He put his life on the line to defend Martha. Later he was killed and replaced by an Immortal. I killed the Immortal."

"I'm glad Martha found someone worthy of her," said the Regent. "I never found anyone that could replace her. Thank you for avenging him, Eddie."

He stood up and came out from behind his desk. I stood up, though my legs were trembling. He came forward and embraced me and I held him tightly, as though afraid someone might try to take him away from me again. We held on to each other for a long while, while Molly stood to one side, looking on coldly. The Regent and I finally let go, stepped back and looked at each other.

"Grandfather," I said. "No wonder this place you made reminds me so much of home."

"And look at you, Eddie. All grown up. My boys James and Jack sent me photos of you, and files later on, when they could. They had to keep that secret, of course. Martha could never know. Or perhaps she did and just told herself she didn't. She was always a great one for compart-mentalising. . . . Once you came here to be a field agent in London, I kept an eye on you. From a safe distance. Watched your back as much as I dared. You've achieved so much. . . . I have always been so very proud of you, Eddie."

"Then why didn't you come back!" I couldn't keep all the anger out of my voice. "After I destroyed the Heart and overthrew the Matri-arch . . ."

"I had responsibilities here," said the Regent. I still found it easier to think of him that way. He met my gaze steadily. "I had my organisa-tion, all my shadow agents, to consider, and . . . I'd built a new life here. A new family. I couldn't just walk out on them, could I? I wasn't even a proper Drood anymore. . . . Martha couldn't take my torc from me, but she did persuade the Heart to seal me off from my armour. I haven't been able to call on it since I left the Hall.

"I did mean to reach out to Martha, at least, but I always thought there would be time later. We always think that, until it's too late. And to be honest, I wanted to wait and see if your changes would last. You're not the first angry young Drood to try to reform the family by force, you know. Were you really surprised, Eddie, when they took the democ-racy you gave them and used it to vote you out?"

"Not really," I said. "No . . ."

"I almost came back," said the Regent. "When word reached me that Martha had been murdered. Right there, in her own bed, in her own quarters, in the Hall. I never really thought she'd agree to see me again, even after everything had changed, but I always thought that, perhaps . . . someday . . . right up till I heard she was dead. I realised then I could never go back to the Hall. No one remembered me, so my turning up would only have muddied the waters. And I didn't want to do anything that would interfere with finding Martha's killer. I did hear . . . you killed the man who murdered her, Eddie."

"Yes," I said. "I'll tell you the whole story someday. Some other time. It was the least I could do for her."

"Thank you for that," said the Regent. "I have to ask: I did hear that you'd been killed. . . ."

"Not permanently," I said. "Molly saved me."

The Regent smiled at her. "Thank you for that, Molly Metcalf."

She just nodded stiffly. I didn't quite understand then that she thought she was still looking out for me. That she didn't trust anyone else to have my best interests at heart. I looked at the Regent.

"So, you knew all about me? When I was a field agent here?"

"Of course," said the Regent. "Why do you think James and Jack worked so hard to get you posted here?"

"All those years," I said. "You were so close, but you never once reached out to me! Never told me the truth! Why not, Grandfather? How could you leave me on my own for so long?"

"I had my reasons," the Regent said steadily. "I couldn't contact you. Martha would have named you rogue, just for knowing about me."

"She did that, anyway, eventually," I said.

"I know. Martha never was the kind to let sentiment get in the way of what she believed needed doing. The job, the never-ending duties and responsibilities, they just ground all the softer emotions out of her. I saw it happening even while I was still there, but there was nothing I could do. I could protect her from everyone but herself. It was never safe, for either of us, for me to reach out to you. If any of our enemies had discovered the true nature of our relationship, you can be sure they would have found some way to use it against us. I did what I could to watch over you from the shadows. But now . . . you and I are the only family we have left. Apart from the other rogues, of course. Is the Hall really completely destroyed, Eddie? Nothing left but ruins?"

I was about to tell him the truth, when Molly stopped me with a sharp look. She didn't trust the Regent. I could tell.

"Eddie," she said, "I'm glad you've found your grandfather after all this time. Really, I am. But some secrets should stay secrets. Until we're sure of . . . the situation."

I just scowled at her, resentful that she couldn't share my happiness. But the Regent was already nodding his head solemnly.

"Spoken like a true agent, Molly. Your secrets can wait, whatever they are." He turned back to me. "Tell me what it is you need right now, Eddie. Why have you come here, to the Regent of Shadows, to the Department of the Uncanny?"

Despite myself, I forced my emotions down and put on my professional persona. I wanted to believe in the Regent, but I have better reasons than most to know that most rogues . . . are rogues. There was still one thing I couldn't let go. . . .

"Do you know the truth about what happened to my parents?" I said bluntly.

"To my daughter, Emily, and her husband, Charles? Of course I know. I made it my business to find out, and to hell with whoever got in my way. And I promise I will tell you the whole story one day, but not until the current crisis is over. You can't afford to be . . . distracted."

"Tell me!" I said, putting all my anger and authority into my voice. "Tell me right now!"

"I can't," he said steadily, meeting my harsh gaze with unwavering eyes. "I'm sorry, Eddie. You'll understand in time."

"Typical Drood," said Molly. "Never give away anything that matters, except on your own terms. Do you know what happened to my parents? Jake and Dana Metcalf? Supposedly killed by the Droods for fighting alongside the White Horse Faction."

"I remember that," said the Regent.

Molly and I waited until it became clear he had nothing to more to say on the subject. The wild upsurge of emotions I'd felt on discovering who he was were beginning to die down. He might be my grandfather, but he was also the Regent of Shadows, and his duties and responsibilities were bound to be different from mine.

"My parents' deaths are supposed to be linked to those of Emily and Charles," said Molly, studying the Regent closely. "Because they saw something they shouldn't have. Because they knew too much . . ."

"There's nothing I can tell you about that," the Regent said carefully. "Not right now. It's . . . complicated."

"But you do know what happened to them?" insisted Molly, glaring fiercely at the Regent.

"Of course I know," he said. "I was there. Are you any happier for knowing that, Molly? Knowing that I *can't* tell you any more for the moment?"

I looked at the Regent in a new way, seeing for the first time the cold, hard professional who'd survived leaving the Droods and his wife to found his own secret army. The Regent of Shadows. You don't get to be head of a secret organisation like that unless you've got true Drood grit in you.

"When this is all over," I said to him, and something in my voice snapped his head right round to look at me, "then we are going to talk about this. And I will not walk away until you've told Molly and me everything you know about how our parents died."

The Regent surprised me then by smiling approvingly at me. "That's the way, Eddie! It's good to see you're everything the files say you are."

He sat down behind his desk again. Molly and I sat down facing him. I needed something else we could talk about or I was going to end up shouting at him.

"How did the Regent of Shadows, with his own organisation of specially trained and independent spies, end up here, running the Department of the Uncanny and part of the Establishment?"

"Not by choice," said the Regent. "I was happy enough on my own, but Catherine Latimer approached me personally and asked me to take over Uncanny, because MI-13 had been proven not just infiltrated, but completely corrupt. Someone had to take up the slack, and Uncanny couldn't do it on their own. I couldn't say no. Even when you're not a Drood any longer, duty and responsibility still weigh heavy on you. . . . I did make it clear that I would split us up again, as soon as MI-13 had been properly restored . . . but I doubt I will. There's nothing more seductive than fire-rate resources and a decent budget. I can do more here at Uncanny than I ever could with all my shadows. . . ."

"Why should the Carnacki boss approach you personally?" I said.

"Oh, she and I go way back," said the Regent. He laughed quietly at the surprise on my face. "We were all such chums together back in the day. Out in the field, fighting the forces of evil with cunning and charm, a quip on the lips and a sword blade hidden inside a furled umbrella. Like-minded souls, from many different areas. Martha and me, the Independent Agent and the Walking Woman, Catherine Latimer and Crow Lee . . . Oh yes, they were quite the couple back then, fresh out of Cambridge and looking for supernatural trouble to get into. Though she never talks about it anymore, she really was quite sweet on him at the time. It's always the bad boy who makes a good girl's heart beat that little bit faster. . . . And he did throw the very best parties. . . . Martha and I were such happy bright young things, before she was called back to assume the heavy mantle of the Matriarch."

He looked at me kindly. "You don't have to be on your own anymore, Eddie. Would you like to come and work with me here at Uncanny? I know the family is all gone, but you could be part of the new family I've made here. Everyone would make you very welcome."

And I just couldn't hold it back any longer. "They're not dead! They're still alive! The Droods are still out there, somewhere!"

"*What?*"

The Regent jumped to his feet, staring slack-jawed at me. And I jumped to my feet, grinning broadly. I glanced apologetically at Molly, who rolled her eyes and gave me a *Go on, then, if you must* look.

"The ruined Hall isn't our Hall," I said to the Regent. "It's another Hall, another Drood family, from a different dimension, with a different history. Our Hall was rotated to another Earth by Alpha Red Alpha. . . . You do know about that? Of course you do. I'm pretty sure it was operated from outside, by remote control, taking our family by surprise. They probably never knew what hit them, until it was far too late. And now they're trapped in that other place, unable to get home. But they're still alive! I'm sure of it! The dead Droods in the ruined Hall were just left there to distract us, to keep us from looking for the real thing! I'm working on a way to get our family back, but I need help and resources. That's why I came here. . . ."

"Showing off in front of Grandpa," muttered Molly. "The horror, the horror . . ."

But I wasn't listening, because the Regent gave a great whoop of delight and burst out from behind his desk to grab me by the arms and dance me round his office, hollering away happily. I laughed helplessly along with him, dancing just as wildly. It felt so good to have someone else to share my good news with. Molly knew, but she wasn't a Drood. She wasn't family, with all that meant. So she stood to one side, smiling painfully, waiting for the Regent and I to wear ourselves out. And eventually we did. The Regent dropped back into the chair behind his desk, flushed bright red, breathing hard, grinning. I slumped into the stiff-backed visitor's chair, fighting to get my breathing back under control. Molly sat down beside me and wouldn't look at either of us. The Regent and I grinned at each other.

"If Alpha Red Alpha got rid of our family," he said, finally, "how in hell are we going to get them back?"

"I'm working on that," I said.

The Regent laughed breathlessly. "Everything I've heard about you really is true."

"Oh, it is," said Molly. "Believe it."

"Now, you said someone must have activated Alpha Red Alpha by remote control," said the Regent. "Who do you think was behind that?"

"I'm pretty sure it was Crow Lee," I said, and then had to break off as the Regent slammed his fist on the desktop.

"Of course it's him! Has to be him! Only he'd have the brass nerve . . . Cheeky bugger! I was talking to him just the other week, and he never so much as hinted at what he was planning. He must have known I'd have thrown this whole organisation against him if I'd known. . . ."

"Would you?" said Molly. "Would you really? You'd have risked everything you've built up to save the family that threw you out?"

"Once a Drood, always a Drood," said the Regent. "Right, Eddie?"

"Unfortunately, yes," I said. "You have to understand, Molly, despite everything, it's always going to be *Anything for the family*. It's bred in the bone."

"Trust me, I had noticed," said Molly.

"Crow Lee . . ." said the Regent, rubbing his hands together briskly. "I've been searching for some way to bring down that arrogant little shit for years. They don't call him the Most Evil Man in the World for nothing. But as I'm sure I'm not the first to say . . . he's always been too well connected for me to touch. I couldn't even get near him because of his powerful friends in high and low places."

Molly looked at me. "If the Droods knew what Crow Lee was, why didn't they take him down? Connections in high places shouldn't have been any obstacle to your family."

"Crow Lee's connections aren't just with the Thrones of this World," I said patiently. "We're not just talking about the everyday movers and shakers of politics and big business. Though he certainly has enough of them by the balls . . . No, Crow Lee made compacts with Above and Below, long ago. With the Houses of Pain and the Shimmering Plains, trading them . . . something they wanted in return for power and protection. And, no, we don't know what the deal involved." I looked at the Regent hopefully, but he just shook his head briefly.

"I have heard rumours," the Regent said slowly. "And I feel I should make it clear that I have no actual evidence . . . rumours that Crow Lee had some kind of hold over the Droods. Enough of a hold to keep them at bay all these years . . ."

"A hold?" I said. "What kind of a hold are we talking about here?"

"Like I said, all I have are rumours, most of them contradictory. But to keep Crow Lee off the Drood agenda for so long, it would have to concern some of the highest people in the family."

"Blackmail," Molly said succinctly.

"Could be," said the Regent. "But if it was, I've never been able to find out who or what was involved. And believe me, I've tried. You were head of the family for a while there, Eddie. Did anyone ever say anything to you?"

"No," I said. "I'm only just beginning to discover how much they managed to keep from me. And given all the terrible and sometimes downright appalling things my family has cheerfully admitted to down the years . . . what could Crow Lee know about that's bad enough to give him a hold over us?"

"What if he lost this hold?" said Molly. "After all the changes your family's been through of late, maybe what he knew just didn't matter anymore. What if the ones being blackmailed were finally in a position to tell him to go to hell? That might have been enough to provoke his attack. If the Droods were finally getting ready to go after him, maybe he decided to get his preemptive strike in first."

"Or maybe he just saw the family in a weakened state and decided to take them off the board while he had the chance," said the Regent. "After all your recent wars, the Hungry Gods and the Loathly Ones, the Immortals and the Great Satanic Conspiracy . . . the family's lost a lot of good people, Eddie. You've never looked so vulnerable."

And then we all looked round sharply as the door banged open and Miss Mitchell strode in. She wasn't carrying a tea tray this time.

"I didn't call you, Miss Mitchell," said the Regent. "And this really isn't a good time. . . ."

"Crow Lee sends his regards," said Miss Mitchell, the pleasant and plain middle-aged woman in the cheap dress. She raised the Luger at her side and shot the Regent three times in the chest. I cried out as the impact of the bullets threw him right out of his chair. I was up on my feet in a moment and then froze as Miss Mitchell brought up her other hand to show me the clicker she was holding.

"Crow Lee gave me this. He got it from someone in your family. Something to hold your armour in your collar, so I can kill you. And I will kill you, Edwin Drood, because that's what Crow Lee wants. He wants your whole stupid family dead and gone. And I will do anything for Crow Lee because he loves me."

She smiled brightly at me and hit the clicker. I called my armour and it came, sweeping over me from head to foot in a moment. Miss Mitchell looked blankly into my featureless golden face mask and hit the clicker again and again. It had clearly been programmed to affect my old strange-matter armour; not the new rogue armour. Miss Mitchell fired her gun at me, shooting me at point-blank range again and again, and the bullets just ricocheted away harmlessly.

"It's not fair," said Miss Mitchell. "It's not fair! Cheater!"

I took a step towards her. She fell back a step and then raised the Luger and pressed it against her head. She looked at me defiantly.

"Crow Lee loves me!"

She shot herself, and the Luger blew half her head away. She crumbled bonelessly to the floor. I armoured down, and looked at Molly.

"You could have stopped her," said Molly. "You could have slapped that gun right out of her hand, with your speed, before she could have pulled the trigger."

"You could have stopped her," I said. "You could have made her gun disappear or turned it into a flower. But you didn't."

"She was a traitor," said Molly. "And neither of us have ever had any time for traitors."

"She killed my grandfather," I said. "And she would have killed me."

Molly moved forward and put her hands on my chest. "Oh, Eddie. I'm so sorry about your grandfather. You'd only just found him again. . . ."

"I will avenge him," I said flatly. "I will kill Crow Lee and everyone who stands with him. I've always been able to do that much for my family."

"No need for that, thank you," said the Regent, getting stiffly back onto his feet again. He brushed vaguely at his clothes and then shook himself briskly. Molly and I looked at him blankly, and he grinned.

"But . . . you don't have Drood armour anymore!" I said. "You said . . ."

"I don't," said the Regent. "So I had to improvise. I knew all kinds of people would be gunning for me once I'd left Drood Hall, so I made . . . other arrangements." He undid the top few buttons of his shirt and pulled it open to reveal a large glowing amulet on his chest, apparently fused directly to his skin. There was a large golden eye in the centre of the amulet, and it glared at me unblinkingly. I stirred uneasily. It could see me. I could tell. The Regent tapped the amulet proudly, and then buttoned up his shirt again. "Kayleigh's Eye, a very old and very potent thing from Somewhere Else. Absolutely guaranteed to protect the wearer from any and all forms of attack. You wouldn't believe what I had to give the previous owner in exchange."

"Hold everything," said Molly. "Last I heard, Kayleigh's Eye was in the Nightside, very firmly owned by the Salvation Army Sisterhood."

The Regent just smiled at her. "Kayleigh had more than one eye." He moved over to look down at the dead woman lying on his carpet in a widening pool of blood. He shook his head sadly. "Poor Miss Mitchell. Crow Lee lied to you, dear. He didn't love you. He doesn't love anyone. But I do have to wonder: If he could get to you, who else in Uncanny might he have got his hooks into? Hello. What's this?"

I was there before him, picking up the clicker Miss Mitchell had dropped, and tucking it carefully away in my pocket.

"Just a weapon that didn't work," I said.

The Regent looked at me thoughtfully. And then we all looked round sharply as the office door banged open and Ankani burst into the room, sari swirling around her, a large gun in each hand, ready for trouble. She checked that the Regent was safe, and only then looked at Molly and me before finally looking down at the body on the floor. I stood very still, ready to call on my armour, while Molly's hands moved slowly and subtly in dangerous ways. Ankani knelt down to study what was left of Miss Mitchell's head, and then shrugged and lowered her guns. She straightened up, stepped back a pace to avoid the spreading blood and looked to the Regent for orders.

"Nice reaction time, my dear," the Regent said briskly, "but right now I'm more interested in how Miss Mitchell was able to smuggle a bloody big handgun past all our supposedly top-rank security measures. Find out, Ankani. You are authorised to use severe language and excessive force. I'm also authorising a complete lockdown; no one gets in or out until they've been thoroughly checked. I want a full investigation into how Crow Lee was able to use his mind games on one of my most trusted people. Have the body removed. I want a full autopsy. See if she was under any outside influence. I doubt it, to be honest, but I do feel I should give the poor old thing the benefit of the doubt. Oh, and I'll need a new carpet."

"Of course, sir," said Ankani. "I'll have a full report on your desk by morning."

"You'll have it here by end of day," growled the Regent. "No one goes home till we've got this sorted."

"Yes, sir," said Ankani.

She made her guns disappear somewhere about her person, and then bent down and picked up Miss Mitchell without any obvious effort. She slung the body over one shoulder, smiled winningly at all of us, and then left, pulling the door quietly shut behind her.

"Given that your tea lady turned out to be an assassin, are you sure you trust her any better?" Molly said sweetly.

"Ankani? Of course!" said the Regent. "Been with me for years. One of my best agents. Trust her implicitly."

"You trusted Miss Mitchell," I said, looking at the large bloody stain on the carpet. There were quite a few bits of bone and brains, too. Miss Mitchell had meant business. Crow Lee's business.

"Yes, well," said the Regent. "There's trust, and then there's trust."

"That's a real Drood answer for you," said Molly.

"The apple never falls far from the tree," the Regent said vaguely.

"If Crow Lee had a traitor inside your organisation," I said thoughtfully, "who's to say he didn't have someone inside the Droods? I mean, how else could he have known about Alpha Red Alpha? Most of our family didn't know it was down there, underneath the Hall, on the grounds that if they had, they'd probably have left the Hall en masse and set up tents on the grounds rather than live over such a dangerous thing. Hold it . . . hold everything. Go previous. Drop anchors. . . . Grandfather, has anyone ever talked to you about the Original Traitor?"

"No," said the Regent. "And it does sound like something I ought to know about. Tell me about this Original Traitor, Eddie. Tell me everything."

So we all sat down again, and I filled him in on the latest conspiracy theory within the Droods that there was a traitor inside the family who went back years, maybe decades, maybe even centuries. Subtly sabotaging us, working from within to undermine everything we did for his own hidden purposes.

"I've been away too long," said the Regent. "Far too many things I don't know . . . Why the Original Traitor?"

"Because we don't know how far back he goes," I said. "There is some evidence to suggest he goes way, way back. . . ."

"Given how many of your family's more important secrets have been forced out into the light recently," said Molly, "maybe the Original Traitor feels you're closing in on him at last. He must be getting a bit desperate."

"We're pretty sure he murdered Sebastian," I said.

"Good God!" said the Regent. "Really? He worked for us, you know."

"Sebastian worked for everyone," I said. "He was murdered during the Hungry Gods affair, while he was being held inside one of our supposedly secure holding cells. Which is supposed to be impossible."

"And Freddie went missing around the same time," said Molly. "He's been declared missing, presumed dead."

"Both of them rogues," said the Regent. "Are we assuming a connection?"

"I don't know," I said. "But I think we need to track down the remaining rogues and make contact with them. Apart from you and me, they're the only Droods left in this world. A world that probably wouldn't be too unhappy if we were to become extinct . . . I did make contact with some of them when I was declared rogue by Martha. . . . But most of them have disappeared. The Mole has gone deep underground, and no one's seen Mad Frankie Phantasm or Harriet Hatchet in ages. Of course, it could just be that the rogues don't want to talk to me because I killed one of them. Arnold Drood, the Bloody Man."

"I did hear about that," said the Regent, nodding slowly. "It was a righteous kill, Eddie. If ever a man needed killing, he did."

"And Tiger Tim," I said. "He needed killing, too."

The Regent looked at me sharply. "Timothy? Jack's boy? That was you? I'd heard he'd been killed, but I didn't want to believe it. He was Jack's only child."

"I know," I said.

"And my only other grandson. Did you really have to . . . ?"

"Yes," I said.

"You were there," said the Regent. "It was your decision to make." But he still didn't want to look at me. "Poor Jack. Life . . . has not been kind to him."

"What about James's children?" said Molly. "They'd be your grandchildren, too."

"The Grey Bastards?" said the Regent, not quite turning up his nose. "I know all about them. . . . I think not. They're not Droods, you see. Just half-breeds. I know it shouldn't matter that they're all illegitimate, but it does. I think I'm old enough to be allowed to be old-fashioned about some things."

"There's still Gerard Drood, Grendel Rex, the Unforgiven God," said Molly, just a bit mischievously, and perhaps showing off a little. "Still securely bound and buried, sleeping deep beneath the Siberian permafrost."

"We don't talk about him!" the Regent said sternly. And we all managed some sort of smile.

"Do you know of any rogue Droods I might not have heard of?" I said. "Any who might be willing to help us against Crow Lee, or even any who might be working with him?"

"I know of thirty-seven other rogues scattered across the world," said the Regent. I sat up straight in my chair.

"Thirty-seven?" I said, not even trying to hide my disbelief. "I never knew there were that many still alive, running loose in the world!"

"I told you," said the Regent, smiling easily. "It's my job to know everything and anything that matters. Because you never know when it might come in handy . . . Can't hold out much hope for contacting most of them. Too busy with their own little schemes, which my people are, of course, keeping a careful eye on . . . And I really don't see how Crow Lee could have suborned any of them without my agents knowing."

"You didn't know about Miss Mitchell," said Molly. "And she was right under your nose."

"True," said the Regent. "Very true. I'll have my people reach out to the rogues, Eddie, but . . ."

"Yes," I said. "But."

"Some of them might talk to my people, where they wouldn't talk to you," said the Regent. "And I'll approach the more cautious ones through a series of cutouts, so they won't know who's asking. Might learn something useful . . . Anything else I can do for you while you're here?"

"Yes," Molly said bluntly. "Do you know where my sisters are?"

The Regent blinked a few times at the sudden turn in the conversation, but he recovered quickly. "Isabella and Louisa? Can't you just contact them yourself?"

"Normally, yes," said Molly. "We're very close. But for the moment they've both got their auras turned off."

The Regent looked at me. "Does that mean anything to you?"

"Not a thing," I said. "And I know better than to ask."

"Oh, good," said the Regent. "It's not just me, then." He looked at Molly. "The last I heard, which I'll admit is some time back, because it's never easy keeping up with any of the infamous Metcalf sisters . . . Isabella was busy investigating an ancient set of stone catacombs deep underneath the Sahara Desert, while Louisa had brought something interesting back from her investigation of the Martian Tombs."

"Really?" I said.

"As far as we can tell, yes," said the Regent. "If you ever find out how she got there and back, please tell me. We'd really love to know. It seems she took whatever it was she found down to the Black Heir Headquarters, down in Cornwall. They specialise in the study of things left behind after alien contact: bodies, tech, altered people . . . the usual. Louisa wanted her big find studied by the big man himself, Professor Nightshade. A very impressive mind, by all accounts. Haven't heard anything about Louisa since. I can put in a request for information direct from Uncanny to Black Heir, but they've never been big on sharing. If Louisa brought them something important or valuable enough, they'd never even admit they'd seen her. She could be sitting right there in their office when the call came in, and they'd still deny they'd even heard of her."

"And Louisa would just go along," said Molly, nodding grimly. "She'd think it was funny. . . ."

The Regent looked at her thoughtfully. "To be honest, my dear, if your sisters don't want you to know where they are, there's probably a good reason for it. Good for them, anyway."

"Are you getting worried about them?" I said to Molly.

"Just a bit," she said, frowning. "This isn't like them. We never avoid each other just because we're doing something we think the others wouldn't approve of. Hell, usually we'd insist on bragging about it, just to make it clear we won't be told what to do."

"Do you want to take off on your own?" I said quietly. "Go look for them, make sure they're okay? I don't mind."

"No," Molly said immediately. "That's sweet of you, Eddie, but I won't leave you. Not when you've so many enemies around you. You need someone close you can depend on."

She didn't look at the Regent when she said that, but I knew what she meant. Molly has never trusted anyone in the family except me. And maybe Uncle Jack. I looked at the Regent, who was politely pretending he hadn't understood anything he'd just heard.

"How long do you think Crow Lee has been planning these attacks against the Droods?" I said.

"He's always been one for taking the long view," the Regent said judiciously. "Miss Mitchell being a very good example. How long did he invest in turning her, just for the one day when she might be useful? God alone knows how long he's waited for the whole Drood family to be vulnerable. . . ."

"So it is possible . . . that he could have made contact with the Original Traitor," I said. "Who could have sold the family out for any number of reasons that made sense only to him . . . Uncle Jack told me it was the Matriarch before Martha, Sarah, who gave the order to let the Loathly Ones into our reality, to support the Allies in World War Two. Thus setting things up for the Hungry Gods invasion farther down the line . . . And that she only did that because she was strongly advised to. By someone close to her . . ."

"Sarah was responsible for a lot of bad decisions in her time as Matriarch," said the Regent. "And it was her dying so suddenly and unexpectedly that made my Martha the Matriarch at such an unusually young age."

Molly leaned forward, suddenly fascinated. "How, exactly, did Sarah die? You said an accident, earlier. What kind of accident?"

"She fell down some stairs," said the Regent. And then he stopped abruptly and we all looked at one another. The Regent looked genuinely upset. "There was no one around. She just fell. She was found dead at the foot of a flight of stairs. Broke her neck. Even Drood armour can't protect you from accidents if they're sudden enough. As far as I know, it never occurred to anyone to check if her death was anything other than an unfortunate accident. But now I have to wonder . . ."

"If her neck was broken before she fell," I said. "How far does all this go back?"

"It's getting so you can't trust anyone," said Molly.

"The Original Traitor is supposed to have killed other Droods and taken over their identities, in the Past," I said.

"Like an Immortal?" the Regent said immediately.

"Except that this is one Drood being replaced by another," I said. "I have to ask, Grandfather: Did you have any Shadow or Uncanny agents inside the Hall just before it disappeared? People inside the family who reported to you?"

"No," said the Regent.

"But then, you would say that. Wouldn't you?" said Molly.

"You've already admitted you had contact with Uncle James and Uncle Jack," I said. "So you could keep an eye on me."

The Regent grinned at me, entirely unabashed. "Good to see you're paying attention, Eddie. There are . . . certain high-up individuals within the family, who are still willing to talk to me. But only from a distance, and only on personal matters. No one in the family would share family secrets with a rogue Drood. No matter who I used to be."

"Can you assist us against Crow Lee?" I said bluntly.

"Not officially," said the Regent. "Uncanny can't be seen to move openly against such a . . . man of substance. Not while he's still connected to so many important people in the government. And especially not when there's a Funding Review in the wind."

"That's what happens when you get in bed with the Establishment," Molly said sweetly. "Someone always gets screwed. . . ."

"You have to give some to get some," the Regent said vaguely. "Can't afford to rock the boat just at the moment. But I'm certainly not going to get in your way. And I can tell you where to find him. He's currently taking his ease just down the road at his Very Private, Very Members Only club. The Establishment Club. He also has a country manor house down in Surrey. I can provide you with a map. And directions. And full details on all the hidden traps and pitfalls surrounding his extensive private grounds. Once you're inside, I'm afraid you're on your own. I've been trying to get one of my agents inside for years without success. I can't be seen to assist you publicly, Eddie, but I can cheer you on from the sidelines."

"He's just down the road?" said Molly. "The Most Evil Man in the World is just hanging out at his club?"

"Do you by any chance have an armoury here?" I asked the Regent.

He grinned broadly. "Funny you should ask . . ."

The Armoury of the Department of the Uncanny turned out to be the complete opposite of what I was used to at Drood Hall. It was small, tidy, compact, with a place for everything and everything in its place. It was more of a storeroom and repository than a research lab. There were all kinds of weapons stacked on shelves, including a few things even I didn't recognise, and I've been around. Just a couple of basic workstations, complete with state-of-the-art computers and assorted scattered technology presided over by Uncanny's very own Armourer. No lab rats, no assistants; just one man and his tech in charge of providing Uncanny's agents with everything they needed to make a proper nuisance of themselves, as the Regent liked to put it.

"This is Patrick," he said. "Best weapons master Uncanny's ever had."

Patrick smiled briefly. "You're only saying that because it's true. Would this be a good time to mention the raise in budget I was promised?"

"You can mention it," the Regent said generously.

Patrick was a calm, middle-aged man. Completely bald, but boasting a bushy salt-and-pepper beard. He had sleepy eyes and an easy smile, but there was still a definite presence to the man when he stepped forward to greet Molly and me. The Regent said Patrick had been one of his Special Agents once, and I had no trouble believing that. There was something about Patrick, for all his ease and calm, that suggested he could still be very dangerous if the need should arise. He wore a basic lab coat that reminded me immediately of Uncle Jack, probably because some things are just constants, wherever you go. Though Patrick was wearing a heavy pullover under his coat, complete with high roll-neck collar. No accounting for taste.

"Are you on your own down here?" said Molly, looking around her with larcenous interest. I made a point of standing right next to her, to make sure no unauthorised weapons went walkabout under her sticky fingers.

"Uncanny is still basically an information-gathering organisation," said the Regent. "We watch and listen and make many notes. Correlation is our life. Weapons are what we use only when everything's gone wrong in a hurry. We prefer to err on the sneaky side whenever possible. Right, Patrick?"

"If you say so, your bossness," said Patrick. "But when things do go pear shaped, I am here to ensure that our people are in a position to Do Unto Others in a sudden and violent way, before the others can do unto them. Don't touch that!"

Molly snatched her hand back from an innocent-looking crystal thing, and tried to look innocent. The Regent looked reproachfully at Patrick.

"You promised me you'd got the bugs out of that. We're still cleaning up the mess from last time."

"I have!" said Patrick. "But then, there's bugs and then there's bugs. . . ." He smiled easily at Molly and pushed the crystal thing well out of her reach. "Not much money in the budget for research these days. But I do like to potter around, see if I can improvise something useful and horribly destructive out of the various interesting things our agents pick up in the field and bring back with them. I swear, if it weren't for their basic light-fingeredness, we'd have nothing but empty shelves on these walls. . . ."

"We don't have anything like the Droods' budget," the Regent agreed. "We have to scrimp and save and make do."

"And steal anything that isn't actually nailed down," said Patrick.

"You'd fit right in here, Molly," I said solemnly.

"One more word and I'll smooth out your balls with Botox while you sleep," said Molly.

Patrick smiled. The Regent looked pained.

"I'm sorry," I said to Patrick. "We really should have introduced ourselves. I'm Eddie Drood, and this . . ."

"Oh, I know who you are," said Patrick. "Both of you."

"You do?" said Molly.

"Of course," said Patrick, his dark eyes twinkling cheerfully. "Everyone in our line of work knows all about the redoubtable Eddie Drood and the infamous Molly Metcalf. Your exploits are already the stuff of legend."

Molly looked at me. "How is it you get to be redoubtable, but I'm always infamous?"

"Sounds right to me," I said.

"These two incredibly brave young people are about to go up against Unholy Crow Lee," said the Regent. "What can you offer them, Patrick, to make the job a little less suicidal? In an unofficial, off-the-books and totally deniable way, of course."

"Crow Lee? Really?" said Patrick. His smiled broadly, and just like that he seemed as dangerous as I'd suspected he could be. It felt like being trapped in an enclosed space with a huge grizzly bear who'd just woken up from hibernation with fresh meat very much on his mind. Patrick turned away abruptly and moved purposefully along his shelves, pickings things up and putting them down again. "Well . . . No point in trying a heads-on attack. Not with the size of the private army he's gathered about himself. No . . . You need to go the sneaky route, come at him in unexpected ways. Lateral thinking and all that. Personally, I'd recommend giving up on the whole idea and taking a nice vacation somewhere really far away. You can't get more lateral than that. But you wouldn't do that, redoubtable and infamous as you are. . . . Don't touch that!"

I took my hand carefully away from a crystal thing sitting on a pile of papers. "Sorry," I said. "I thought it was a paperweight."

"It's *designed* to look like a paperweight," Patrick said darkly. "Here—try this. It's a skeleton key made from real human bone. And, no, you don't get to ask whose. This useful little item can open any lock, mechanical, magical or electronic."

"The Drood Armourer gave me one of these once," I said, accepting the yellowed bone thing gingerly.

"I know!" said Patrick. "Who do you think I stole the idea from? Now, this . . . is a hearing aid. Just stick this little beauty in your ear, and you'll be able to listen in on any conversation from any distance. Even in other rooms and in other languages! I'm still working on the immediate-translation tech, but if it doesn't kick in, you can always read the subtitles."

He turned to Molly and offered her a pair of spangly glitterball earrings. She hefted the ugly items on her palm and looked dubiously at Patrick.

"What do I do with these?"

"You throw them," said Patrick. "And they go *Boom!* And all the people who were bothering you suddenly aren't."

"Groovy!" said Molly. She whipped off the silver Celtic rose things she'd been wearing, stuffed them into a pocket, and clipped on the new earrings. I looked severely at Patrick.

"Tell me those things have a safety catch."

"Of course!" said Patrick. "They're perfectly harmless until you say the magic Word." He leaned over and whispered the Word in Molly's ear, and she actually giggled and pushed him away. He looked pleased with himself. "I'd throw them pretty damn far, though, if I were you. And I wouldn't play with them, either. Just in case."

Molly looked at the expression on my face and patted me fondly on one cheek. "Will you relax, Eddie? I'm wearing the Twilight Teardrop, remember? Guaranteed personal protection, on levels even Kayleigh's Eye has never heard of! You could set off a thermo nuke right in front of me, and I wouldn't even be bothered by the bright light."

"That's the Twilight Teardrop?" said the Regent, leaning forward to inspect the ruby stone pendant with new interest. One look into its bloodred depths was enough, and he immediately retreated to a safe distance. "Such a small thing," he said, "to be so powerful and so thoroughly cursed. I've always said the best way to make use of that thing would be to make a gift of it to someone you really didn't like. And then leave the country until all the unpleasantness was over."

I looked at the bony key and the earplug in my hand. "I could use something a little more dangerous, and preferably long-range."

"You've got your armour," said Molly. "That's dangerous enough for anyone. Though I could lend you my charm bracelet, if you like. If you're really feeling in need of something to throw."

"I am not wearing that on my ankle," I said firmly. "I have my dignity to consider."

Molly then said something very coarse about my dignity, and Patrick, the Regent and I pretended not to have heard her.

Patrick distracted Molly with a small flat black-lacquered box with a big green button on the top. "This," he said proudly, "is a protein exploder. Does what it says on the box. It's alien tech. Or possibly tomorrow tech. One of our people brought it back from the Nightside. He bought it from a street trader. Fell off the back of a Timeslip . . . No instruction manual, of course, which is why he got it so cheap. It's taken me almost a year to work out how to use it, and I still don't have a clue how it works. Just point it at your enemies, and wave good-bye to what's left of them."

"Cool," said Molly, shaking the box in a far too casual manner. Everyone else in the room winced. Molly looked at Patrick. "What does it do?"

"I told you!" said Patrick. "It explodes people's protein! Suddenly and violently and all over the place. Just don't point it in the general direction of anyone you like. It's not exactly pinpoint accurate."

Molly stuffed the box up her sleeve. Patrick looked at me thoughtfully.

"Eddie . . ."

"Yes?"

"I've followed your exploits for years. First as a field agent here in London and then as head of the family, and then . . . Well, all the other things you've done. All the amazing things you've achieved. And I always promised myself that if I ever got to meet you, there was a question I wanted to ask. Are you happy, Eddie?"

I wasn't quite sure where that had come from, but I did my best to consider the question seriously. "I'm happy . . . with Molly," I said finally.

"Good," said Patrick. "I'm glad to hear that."

"Me too, grandson," said the Regent.

"You soft and soppy sentimental thing, you," said Molly, slipping her arm through mine.

CHAPTER SEVEN

Some Unpleasantness at the Establishment Club

E very part of society has its own clubs to retreat to, private places where we can escape from the trials and stresses of the everyday world. We all like to know there's somewhere we can go when it all gets a bit much; our very own private watering holes. Very private people have very private clubs, and Very Important People have Very Private Clubs. And then ... there are the clubs that no one talks about. If they know what's good for them. Membership strictly by invitation only. For people so important, so significant and so wealthy that no one in the everyday world has ever heard of them. Clubs for people who mix only with their own kind.

Which is how I came to be strolling down some very well-known streets in the better part of London, following the map the Regent of Shadows had given me. And a simple set of directions that should take me straight to the only kind of club that would accept the likes of Crow Lee as a member: the Establishment Club. Where the underworld can meet the elite, to sneer at everyone else. I kept Molly close beside me, where I could keep an eye on her, because I didn't entirely trust the larcenous look in her eyes. We got all kinds of looks from the well-dressed people we passed, because neither of us seemed like the kind of people who had any business being in an area like this, but, of course, no one actually said anything. Because we're British, after all, and we don't like to make a fuss. There were security cameras everywhere; let the proper authorities do what needed doing. If anything needed doing. Some of the cameras rotated slowly to watch us as we passed. I pointed them out to Molly.

"They can't see us," I said just a bit smugly. "As long as I'm wearing my torc, there isn't a surveillance system in the world that can see me. Or you, as long as you're with me. What it means to be a Drood . . . we walk through the world unseen, so we can do necessary appalling things and get away with it every time."

"Don't get cocky," said Molly. "I was learning how to dodge security systems while you were still planning how to run away from home. I really don't like this area, Eddie. It stinks of money and privilege and entitlement . . . all the things I've spent a lifetime fighting. I feel like smashing a whole bunch of things, just on general principles."

"Never knew you when you didn't," I said.

And that was when the security cameras all started exploding. The one right in front of us went first, blowing apart in a soft puff of black smoke and a short shower of plastic and glass splinters. Then all the others went up, one after the other, ahead and behind us. The quiet of the late evening was suddenly full of the soft sounds of small fires and frying electrical circuitry. Everyone else on the street jumped and looked about them, startled, and then took to their heels. In a polite and dignified way, of course. Soon enough they were all gone from a street where they didn't feel safe anymore because no one was watching over them. I stopped and looked sternly at Molly, who shook her head demurely.

"It's not me, Eddie . . . for once. I'm afraid it's you. I can See swirls of energy coming off you, striking out at the cameras from your torc. . . ."

"It's the rogue armour," I said, one hand rising automatically to the golden torc at my throat and then falling back without touching it. "It's overreacting." I concentrated, imposing my will on the torc with blunt brute force, and the explosions stopped. I felt something stir inside the torc and then grow still again.

"You assured me you had the rogue armour under complete control," Molly said carefully.

"I have. Mostly. You have to remember: It's not just armour. Moxton's Mistake is a living thing. I think it just likes to remind me it's still there occasionally."

"Can we get moving?" said Molly. "I'm starting to feel just a bit conspicuous, standing alone in the middle of the street. Your torc can't hide us from everyone."

"Of course," I said. "Moving right along."

"You do know where we're going?"

"Do you want to read the map?"

We moved on down the well-lit but now completely deserted street. Evening was fast fading into night. It had been a long hard day, and it wasn't nearly over yet. I did my best to make sense of the hand-drawn map the Regent had scrawled for me, and carefully checked the numbers on the doors we passed. Not far now. Not long at all until I could finally get my hands on Crow Lee and force some straight answers out of him.

"What did you make of the Regent?" Molly said suddenly. "Your long-lost and suddenly found grandfather."

"Seemed straightforward enough," I said. "Given the game he's playing. Decent enough stick . . . Played his cards a bit close to his chest, but then, you've got to expect that from someone who's still technically a rogue Drood. What did you make of Patrick?"

"Something not quite right there," Molly said immediately, frowning. "He didn't come across to me as any kind of Armourer. . . . Not that I've known many."

"He knew his stuff," I said. "And the Regent did say that Patrick had been one of his Special Agents. Working out in the field, like us, getting his hands dirty . . . But even so, you're right; there was something . . . off about him. He reminds me of someone, though I'm damned if I can think who."

"Someone you've met before?" said Molly. "In the field?"

I shook my head uncertainly. "*Are you happy?* . . . That's what he asked me. What kind of a question is that to someone you've only just met?"

"You gave a good answer, though," said Molly, slipping her arm through mine and pressing the side of her body up against mine. "You earned yourself some major boyfriend brownie points there."

"Can I cash them in later?" I said. "Let us not forget, the Department of the Uncanny is part of the Establishment, and therefore no one in it can be fully trusted. On principle."

"Well, quite," said Molly. "But let us concentrate on taking down Crow Lee and getting your family back, and worry about everything else afterwards."

"Good answer," I said. "Sufficient unto the day are the scumbags thereof."

We ended up strolling along beside a long tenement building, big and grand in the old Regency style, punctuated with a whole lot of barred and shuttered windows and really big doors bearing the gleaming brass nameplates of the very old, very long established private-members clubs they represented. I counted them off, comparing them to the Regent's map, until finally I stopped before one particular door that didn't look any different from all the others I'd already passed. In fact, it looked so ordinary I got Molly to check the map to make sure I'd got the numbers right. She snatched the thing out of my hand, glared at me, sniffed loudly, glanced briefly at the map and then snapped her fingers and set it on fire. It blazed up quickly, and Molly shook her fingers, letting the dark ashes fall to the street.

"We don't want to leave any evidence behind, do we?" she said. "Nothing that might lead back to Uncanny, and the Regent."

"Show-off," I said.

A small brass plate set above the door gave the name THE ESTABLISHMENT CLUB in blunt and blocky letters. A club so well established it didn't need to advertise. Either you knew how to find it or you didn't belong there, anyway. The door itself was bland and uninteresting, with no letter box or door handle. The giveaway was that it stood half-open, the way in thoroughly blocked by a large and formidable doorman, resplendent in an old-fashioned bright scarlet frock-coat uniform, complete with fancy waistcoat, knee britches and well-polished boots. Plus a gleaming tall hat any stage magician would have been proud of. For all his finery, he was large and solid and openly menacing, and gave the impression he should really have been standing outside some downtown nightclub, snarling, *No trainers!* and *You're not on the list!* He had a square, brutal face and looked like bullets would just bounce off him. Because they'd be afraid of him. He stood at attention and looked right through Molly and me as though we weren't there.

"So," said Molly, looking right past the doorman as though he weren't there, "what kind of a place is the Establishment Club, Eddie? What can we expect once we get inside? Any kinky stuff?"

"Don't ask me," I said. "I've never been in there."

Molly turned and gave me a hard look. "You're always saying that London is your territory! That you were Drood field agent for the whole of London!"

"Not quite all of it," I admitted reluctantly. "This kind of place, and this kind of area, was always more Matthew's territory than mine. It's not like I was actually banned from circles like these, but I never got to see the inside of any of these clubs. Matthew didn't think I could be trusted to behave properly in front of those who like to think of themselves as our betters, and he was probably right. He knew how to talk to these people, to lay down Drood authority without ruffling too many feathers. Because sometimes, when you're in a hurry, you have to give some to get some. I am a great believer in diplomacy; right up to the point where someone pisses me off, and then it's time to dispense beatings and shout at people. Matthew knew how to get these people to do what we wanted and make them think it was all their idea in the first place. But then, Matthew could charm the birds down out of the trees, when he could be bothered. He was always so much better at being a secret agent than I ever was."

I stopped there, surprised by a sudden rush of memories of the man that weren't all bad. "I do miss him . . . sometimes. He was harsh and arrogant and a royal pain in the arse . . . but he did teach me an awful lot about how to be a field agent when I first came to London."

"He was a creep," Molly said succinctly, and I had to smile.

"Well, yes. I don't think anyone would argue with that," I said. "But he was a very professional creep. You have to make allowances. He was family."

"If I hear that bullshit one more time," Molly said ominously, "there is going to be a very unfortunate incident. Right here and now. Shit is shit, whether you're related to it or not. Take my sisters . . ."

"I'd rather not," I said.

It was Molly's turn to smile. "Lots of people say that. . . . Wait a minute! I've just had an idea!"

"Oh no," I said. "That's never good."

"When all this is over, why don't I join up with you, and we can be field agents in London together? We could patrol the streets, side by side. That should throw a scare into all the right people. . . . And according to all the women's magazines I read, relationships work much better when you've got shared interests in common."

"I think London needs a regular field agent who's at least heard of diplomacy," I said carefully.

"You're a fine one to talk!"

"True. But at least I can fake it when I have to. For you, diplomacy is just something you've heard of that other people do."

"I can fake it if I have to," Molly said darkly.

"I'd really rather not go there," I said. "Let us consider the external protections of the Establishment Club, before we go any further."

We both looked the club's exterior over carefully. My Sight immediately revealed that the whole front of the building was crawling with defence spells, and energy fields and layer upon layer of really heavy-duty protections. Intertwining and overlapping force shields and shimmering screens, with built-in weapons both magical and technological, along with all kinds of curses, bombs and booby traps. Some of the protections shone so brightly they almost blinded my inner eye. Just trying to make sense of the various patterns and structures made my head ache.

"Okay," I said, after a while. "Some of these defence systems are *seriously* old. Laid down centuries ago, going right back to Londinium times. Hell, some of them go back so far I've only ever read about them in old books. To be honest, the word *overkill* is coming to mind. Even Buckingham Palace doesn't have some of the orders of protection I'm Seeing here. Layers upon layers, supporting and reinforcing one another. Something this intricate doesn't just *happen*. This was planned. . . ."

"Can you break through it?" Molly said bluntly. "Is your new armour up to it?"

"Maybe. Eventually. But not without drawing a lot of attention and probably the arrival of major reinforcements."

"The Regent did say Crow Lee had his own private army. . . ."

"Well, yes, but I doubt he brings them with him when he comes to visit his club. He'd expect the club to protect him. Probably has his own bodyguard, though."

"Hah!" said Molly. "I laugh in the face of bodyguards! And then I do really awful things to them and make them cry for their mothers."

"I know," I said. "I've seen you do it. Let us try the straightforward way first."

I nodded significantly at the doorman, who was still standing stiffly at attention before the club's doorway, pretending he wasn't giving his full attention to every word we were saying.

"Ah!" Molly said happily. "The old way! The bullying and intimidation of stuck-up flunkies! Oh, Eddie, you're so good to me. . . ."

"Yes, I am," I said. "And don't you forget it."

"I get to go first!"

"Of course."

Molly strode up to the doorman so she could glare right into his face. Though she had to stand on tiptoe to do it. He met her gaze levelly, giving every indication of being entirely unmoved. Which was, of course, the worst thing he could have done. Molly will stand for a lot of things, but being ignored definitely isn't one of them.

"We are coming in," Molly said firmly. "That can be past you, or over your beaten and broken body. It's up to you. Guess which I'd prefer."

"No trainers," said the doorman. "And definitely no witches that don't know their place. No entrance here ever, unless you're a member in good standing, which you aren't and never will be. Now piss off, girlie, or I'll set the hellhounds on you."

"You haven't got any hellhounds," said Molly, grinning really quite unpleasantly. "I'd know. So get the hell out of my way, or I'll turn you into a small squishy thing with your testicles floating on the top."

The doorman lowered himself to sneer at her. "I hear worse than that from the members every day if I don't move fast enough. You can't touch me; I'm protected by the club. Now get out of my sight, before I make you cry."

I stepped forward then to stand beside Molly. "You try to be nice to people, but then they have to go and cross the line. No one threatens my Molly and gets away with it. So stand aside, Uniformed Flunky with an Unfortunate Attitude, or I'll rip your dickey off."

"Eddie!" said Molly, amused but just a bit shocked. "Not in public . . ."

"A dickey," I explained patiently, "is another name for the bow tie."

"Ah," said Molly. "I hadn't noticed he was wearing one. . . . Now, that is distinctly unappealing. Downright ugly, in fact."

"Bow ties are cool," I said. "The Travelling Doctor said so."

"And he should know," said Molly. "He's been around. Mr. Doorman isn't moving, Eddie. Feel free to do your very worst."

I armoured up my right hand, grabbed a handful of the doorman's starched shirtfront and ripped it right off him. Along with his waistcoat and his dickey. The doorman stood there, bare-chested, and gaped at my golden gauntlet. He seemed to shrink in on himself just a little.

"Oh, fuck. You're a Drood."

"Language, Jeeves," said Molly, highly amused.

I dropped the wreckage of his shirtfront onto the pavement, and held up my golden fist before his face, so he could get a good look at it.

"Who are you people?" said the doorman. He was deeply upset. I could tell.

"I am Eddie Drood, and this delightful yet dangerous young lady is Molly Metcalf," I said just a bit grandly.

"A Drood and a Metcalf sister? Oh, shit," said the doorman miserably. "I'm going home early."

"I would," I said.

The doorman turned and ran back into the club, leaving the door
standing half-open. His voice gradually faded away as he receded into
the club's interior, calling for help and protection. It was nice to know
my name still meant something. And Molly's, too, of course.

"The protections are still in place," Molly observed pointedly.

"So they are," I said. "Good for them. And good for us that I have
this."

And I held up the skeleton key Patrick had given me. Just a yellowed
piece of human bone, carved into a universal key, that could unlock
anything. Including some things that were only technically or symbolic
locks. I leaned carefully forward and eased the bone key into the door's
keyhole. It didn't want to go in, but some applied pressure from my
golden hand did the job. And it really didn't want to turn, either, until
my golden gauntlet provided the necessary motivation. And then all
the protections just disappeared, gone in a moment. I carefully retrieved
the bone key and tucked it away about my person.

"Definitely knows his stuff," I said to Molly.

"All right, don't make a big deal out of it," she said with a sniff. "I
was learning how to carve skeleton keys while you were still learning
how to pick the lock on the Drood tuckshop."

"Trust me," I said. "Drood Hall has never possessed any such thing."

"Don't interrupt me when I'm on a roll. Come on. Let's get in there
and make some trouble before they get a reception committee organised."

I kicked the front door all the way open and strode inside with Molly
sauntering along at my side. It's important to make the right kind of
entrance on these sort of occasions. A wide-open hallway fell away
before us, discreetly lit and completely empty. There were heavily wood-
panelled walls, in the old style, that looked like they could stop cannon-
balls, plus a parquet floor and a whole bunch of tall potted plants of an
almost primordial nature.

I heard soft running footsteps up ahead, approaching at speed. I stopped where I was, and Molly reluctantly stopped with me. I didn't need to look back to know the front door had already closed behind us. I could feel it. I stared carefully into the civilised gloom at the end of the corridor and winced, just a bit, as I recognised the half dozen small and slender figures pattering forward to confront Molly and me.

They stopped a cautious distance away to look Molly and me over with their overbright eyes. Six half-starved teenage boys wrapped in the rags and tatters of what had once been expensive school uniforms. The oldest of them couldn't have been more than fourteen. They crouched rather than stood, a pack of wild animals rather than a group of boys. Dangerous animals, fierce and feral. Pale faced, floppy haired, with thin, pinched faces, disturbing smiles and eyes that were so much older than they should have been. They grinned quickly at each other, laughing silently, hefting the sharp and shiny things they held in their hands.

"Children?" said Molly. "They're sending kids out to stop us?"

"These aren't children," I said steadily. "Or at least they aren't now and haven't been for some time. These, Molly, are the Uptown Razor Boys. The Eton Irregulars. The delinquent toffs who never grew up."

I summoned my full armour about me, and the golden metal gleamed brightly in the gloom. The Eton Irregulars drew a sharp breath, their eyes shining to reflect the new light, and they spread out quickly to form a semicircle before us, staring unblinking at Molly and me. They looked like boys, but they didn't move or hold themselves like anything human. They had given themselves over to older, darker instincts. They were feral things now, and they gloried in it.

"Talk to me, Eddie," said Molly quietly but insistently. "Who or what are we facing here?"

"Surprised you never heard of them," I said. "Though perhaps you don't move in the right circles. . . ."

"Eddie . . ."

"Thrown out of Eton School," I said. "Expelled back in the sixties after being disturbed in the middle of a black magic ceremony designed to call up the Devil. They might have got away with it, but they'd already sacrificed two younger boy, in return for power. . . . They should have been more specific in what they asked for. The boys' parents were important enough that they were able to get it all hushed up, but it was too late for the boys. The changes had already begun. They ran away from home first chance they got, and by then the parents were probably relieved to see them gone. Look at them, Molly. All these years and they haven't aged a day. They'll never grow up or grow old; they don't feel things anymore and whatever thoughts move in their heads are nothing we would recognise. They have given themselves over to the delights of slaughter. Can you see what they're holding in their hands?"

"Yes," said Molly. "Old-fashioned straight razors."

"Immortal killers with a taste for cutting," I said. "Courtesy of Hell. Remind you of anyone?"

"Mr. Stab," said Molly. "The uncaught serial killer of Old London Town."

"Hell likes to stick with things that work," I said. "The Eton Irregulars are the urban legends that serial killers talk about. They exist on the fringes of the hidden world, hiring themselves out to people with no scruples who still have ties to the Old School. The Uptown Razor Boys: bodyguards, assassins, frighteners . . . and occasionally the first line of defence. I think someone at the club knew we were coming."

"But why them?" said Molly. "Why set them against us?"

"Because they still look like children," I said. "Which makes it that much harder to fight them. Question is: Do they work for the club or Crow Lee himself?"

"What difference does that make?" said Molly.

"I don't want to bring the whole might of the Establishment Club down on us," I said. "Not while I'm the Last Drood. I can't afford to let myself be stopped before I can reach my family and bring them home. . . . But, no, it doesn't really matter. Some things are just too vile to be allowed to continue. Some vermin just need putting down."

"Wow, Eddie," said Molly. "Hard-core."

The Uptown Razor Boys swept suddenly, savagely forward, heading right for us like the pack of wild things they really were. Half a dozen teenage boys who'd thrown away their Futures in return for the hideous strength that drove them and the supernaturally bright blades they brandished. They shouted and hooted gleefully, moving in perfect symmetry, six minds with a single thought. Their eyes glittered in the dim lighting as they circled Molly and me, jumping and leaping and addressing us with high, harsh voices, one after another.

"Drood. Thought you were dead. Should be dead. Always meddling in the affairs of your betters. Interfering in things that are none of your concern. Heavenly armour versus infernal blades. Good intentions versus Hell on Earth. Going down, Drood. All the way down."

"It's not enough that they've been made over into hellspawn," Molly said steadily. "They're still the worst part of boys. Did you notice they only addressed themselves to you, Eddie? Because they're still scared of girls. . . ."

"Shut up! Shut up!" howled the Eton Irregulars, leaping and capering around us, brandishing their razors fiercely. "Nasty! Nasty thing! Cut you up! Eat you up! Wear your insides as scarves!"

"The more they speak," said Molly, "the less scary they seem. Funny, that."

"Take them seriously," I said. "They've killed a lot of good people in their time. Probably people who didn't take them seriously enough."

"Drood," said the Uptown Razor Boys, speaking together in one voice. "Cut you up. Kill you, and your little bitch, too."

"Now, that's just rude," I said.

They surged forward, and I went to meet them with a cold rage in my heart. Because they stood between me and the rescue of my family. They swarmed all over me in a living wave, hitting me from every side at once, cutting and slicing at my head and throat with their shimmering razors. . . . But even these supernatural blades just skidded harmlessly off my golden armour in showers of sparks. Moxton had made his mistake well. The boys cried out like wolves as they cut at me again and again, cried out like thwarted children, but for all their speed and fury they couldn't hurt me. I chose my timing carefully and punched one of the Eton Irregulars in the head with my golden fist. His whole head exploded, showering gore and fragments of bone across the nearby wall. The sheer force of the blow threw the headless body several feet down the hallway. The remaining Eton Irregulars cried out in shock and rage, a savage howl from human mouths. They only had one another. They threw themselves at me like feral cats, hitting me with all their Hell-given strength, as though they could force their blades through my armour.

I grabbed another of them and slammed his face into the nearest wall. His whole head collapsed and shattered under the force of the impact, and when I let go, the headless body just slid limply down the wall, leaving a heavy trail of blood and bone behind. More howls and screams from the remaining Uptown Razor Boys, and behind my featureless golden face mask I was smiling a fierce grin of my own. It felt good to be killing things that needed killing.

One of the Eton Irregulars broke away from me and went for Molly. She was waiting for him. She had a small flat box in her hand, with a single button on the top. She pointed it at the Razor Boy, who snarled savagely at her and went for her throat. Molly pressed the button and the boy just blew apart soundlessly. Every single bit of his flesh exploded in a moment, reduced to nothing more than a thick pink mist in the air, spreading slowly and silently before pattering to the floor in tiny pink droplets. The bones of his skeleton were left behind, left standing in perfect shape for a moment, and then they just clattered to the parquet floor in a neat little pile. All the bones picked perfectly clean, without a single fleck of meat left on them.

There was a pause as we all just stood where we were and looked at what had just happened. *So,* I thought coolly. *That's what happens when you point a protein exploder at someone.*

The three surviving Eton Irregulars turned and ran, sprinting down the hallway. Molly pointed the small box after them, and hit the button again. Three more soft, almost soundless explosions, and once again a fine pink mist filled the hallway for a long moment, before slowly dispersing. And three more neat little piles of human bones.

Molly raised the protein exploder to her lips and blew away imaginary smoke from an imaginary gun barrel.

"I think I'm getting the hang of this," she said. "Bit messy, though."

"What did you expect?" I said. "From something called a protein exploder? It really does do what it says on the tin." I looked at her carefully. "Does it . . . bother you? What you just did? I mean, they did look like boys. . . ."

"Yes," said Molly. "They did. But they weren't. Hadn't been anything human for a long time. Nothing left inside them but Hell's business. I could tell."

I armoured down and looked up the hallway ahead of us. Everything seemed calm and quiet and very empty.

"Does it bother you?" said Molly.

"What?"

"You just crushed the heads of two things that still looked like children," said Molly. "You didn't even hesitate. You would have once. Before you put on the rogue armour."

"You said it yourself," I said. "They were just hellspawn. I could tell."

Except I hadn't even looked. Didn't even occur to me to raise my Sight to study their true aspect. I just killed them because they were an immediate threat and they needed killing. And because . . . it felt good. I listened carefully, but I couldn't hear the voice of the rogue armour, couldn't even feel its presence, peering over my mental shoulder. I had to wonder how much of this new iron in my soul was the influence of wearing the rogue armour . . . and how much was just me, a man grieving over his lost family and slowly losing his mind. Just needing to take out his anger on the world. Was I losing control or losing my mind? I told myself it didn't matter. I would do whatever needed doing for my family. Deal with the problems in front of me. Move on . . . and worry later.

It wasn't like anyone was going to grieve over the loss of the Uptown Razor Boys.

I strode forward, stepping carefully past the piles of bones, leaving Molly to hurry after me.

"Is it too much to ask?" I said. "For someone to design a weapon that cleans up after itself?"

"It would be nice," said Molly. "Not having to be careful where you tread after a fight."

And then we both stopped, as a tall cocky figure came slouching down the hall towards us. He just appeared out of nowhere, smiling easily, in a scruffy combat jacket and grubby jeans. Big and rangy, with the kind of muscle that comes from regular hard living rather than hard workouts in the gym. He had a square head, close-cropped dark hair and a cool, thoughtful gaze. There was an easy built-in menace to his every movement. He swayed to a halt a respectful distance away.

"Hello, squire. And lady. I'm Bunny Hollis, at your service. Ex-SAS combat sorcerer. No job too big; no killing too small. I got thrown out of the SAS for sadistic excesses, which is ironic, as that's how most of us get in. These days, I'm strictly freelance. Cash up front, no questions asked and I'll even make the bodies disappear at no extra charge." He looked meaningfully at the mess in the hall, between him and Molly and me. "Got to say, you made a real mess of those kids. Good thing, too. It's animals like that give hardworking professionals like us a bad name. So, you're Eddie Drood. I've always fancied my chances against a Drood."

"So did the Uptown Razor Boys," I said. "And look what happened to them."

Hollis just smiled his easy smile. "Got to say, I'm just a bit surprised to see you here, Eddie Drood. Little bird told me you and all your family were dead and gone."

"Rumours of our destruction have been greatly exaggerated," I said.

Hollis grinned at Molly. "And a Metcalf sister! Ah, the stories I've heard about you girls . . . Molly, Molly, quite contrary, how does your body count grow? I thought I was bad till I read your file. A Drood and a Metcalf . . . Just for the record, how the hell do you have the nerve to claim you're the good guys? I've fought actual wars for queen and country and I haven't killed nearly as many as you."

"I only kill people who need killing," I said steadily.

Hollis sneered at me. "Yeah, that's what they all say, squire. They've always got their excuse ready. *It wasn't me, your honour. It was the voices in my head. Read it in the Bible; I answer to a higher calling!* I've heard it all before . . . and it always comes down to bodies on the ground and blood on the hands. At least I'm honest enough to admit up front I'm only in it for the money. I'm a professional soldier, because that's what I do best. I fight strictly for hard cash, not some nebulous cause. . . ."

"Bit chatty for an ex-squaddie, aren't you?" I said. "But then, I never met an ex-soldier who didn't feel the need to justify himself for how far he'd fallen. Look . . . Hollis, was it? You can still step aside. We're not here for you. We're here for Crow Lee."

"Well, you can't have him," said Hollis.

"You work for him, and you have the brass nerve to lecture us?" said Molly. "Or did no one explain the whole Most Evil Man in the World bit to you?"

"You say *potato*, I say *hard cash*," said Hollis. "His money will spend as easily as anyone else's."

"But the things he's done . . ." I said, but Hollis cut me off before I could go any further.

"Compared to what you Droods have done, he's just a beginner."

"It's not what you do," I said. "It's why you do it."

"Oh, come on!" said Hollis. "That's your justification? The terrorists' favourite excuse? That the end justifies the atrocities?"

"You really don't know my family," I said.

"Don't argue with him, Eddie," said Molly. "He doesn't really care. He's just making conversation to hold us here while Crow Lee escapes out the back door."

Hollis flashed her a quick grin. "You're smarter than you look, girlie. Come on. Let's do it. You know you want to."

I armoured up, the golden metal surging out and over me, and Hollis snapped upright out of his slouch and actually fell back a step. He frowned uncertainly.

"There's something . . . wrong with your armour, Drood. I've seen

Drood armour before, and it never looked like that. I don't like the look of it."

"That's all right," I said, through my featureless face mask. "It doesn't like the look of you."

"No, he's right, Eddie," said Molly, and there was something in her voice that made me turn to look at her. She was staring at me as though she'd never seen me in my armour before. "Something's wrong, Eddie. Your armour looks different. It looks . . . tarnished."

I didn't know what to say to that, so I just shrugged and looked back at Hollis. Just in time to see him raise his right hand and make the shape of a gun with it, pointing the finger at me the way children do when they're pretending. And then he shot me in the chest. The impact sent me staggering backwards and left a great crater in the centre of my chest. But the armour protected me from the impact and repaired itself in seconds. I quickly recovered my balance and started forward. Hollis was using a conceptual gun, shaped and focused psychokinesis. I'd heard of it, but never encountered it in the field before. Hollis took careful aim and fired again, three times in swift succession, his pointing finger jerking each time with the recoil. But I just strode forward into the invisible bullets, my armour booming loudly with each impact, shrugging the conceptual bullets off increasingly easily.

Hollis looked distinctly put-upon. He opened his hand, dismissing the conceptual gun, and gestured sharply with his other hand. A bottomless hole opened up directly beneath me, carpet and floorboards disappearing in a great circle to reveal a long drop with shimmering silver sides, falling away forever. And while Drood armour can do many marvellous things, flying isn't one of them. Luckily, I was blessed with really good reflexes. Even as the hole appeared and I started to fall, I was already throwing myself forward. I grabbed onto the edge of the hole as I fell past it. My metal fingers sank deep into the wooden floor, crunching and splintering the floorboards. My fall stopped abruptly, my whole weight hanging from the single handhold.

I looked down and immediately wished I hadn't. The terrible endless drop seemed to grab hold of my gaze, hypnotising me. It took a real effort of will to jerk my gaze away and look up at my handhold. Hollis was standing right over me, grinning. He stamped down hard on my golden hand and hurt his foot. He fell back from the hole, cursing loudly. Molly leaned over the hole from the other side.

"I don't like to intrude . . . but do you by any chance need a hand?"

"No, thanks," I said. "I can manage."

I hauled myself up by brute strength, until I could get a second handhold, and then pulled myself up and out of the hole. The moment I had my feet back on the floor again, the hole disappeared. Inside the armour I was shaking just a bit, but no one else could tell. I nodded quickly to Molly and then looked over at Hollis. He scowled at me and plucked something out of the air. He held it up triumphantly before him, a shiny sparkling thing I couldn't seem to look at properly, even with all the filters and amplifications built into my mask. The thing seemed to twist and turn in Hollis's hand, as though its shape and nature were constantly changing. Hollis laughed aloud.

"The answer to Drood armour: a supernatural can opener! I don't know why no one's ever thought of it before!"

And before I could tell him why, he came surging forward to slam the shining thing against the side of my neck. It shattered immediately in Hollis's hand, falling apart into a hundred shiny pieces. Hollis cried out, as much in shock and rage as pain, and darted backwards, shaking his stunned hand. I was grinning easily behind my mask.

"People did think of it before," I said. "Lots and lots of them. But this . . . is Drood armour. Why settle for less?"

"Oh, well," said Hollis, between gritted teeth as he shook his hand to get the feeling back into it, "Worth a try . . . Tell you what: Why don't we try this sneaky little thing I've been saving for a rainy day? Specially designed to blast strange matter out of this world and back where it came from!"

He raised his left hand again, and strange energies curled and whorled around it, twisting and turning in complex patterns. Hollis threw them at me, and the energies shot forward and splashed across my armour, only to sputter out and fade away almost immediately, unable to get a grip. Hollis just stood there and stared at me, blinking dazedly. I could have told him I was wearing rogue armour without a speck of strange matter in it, but why spoil the fun? Hollis said a few baby swear words that you wouldn't expect from a hardened ex-SAS officer, and actually stamped his foot on the floor in frustration.

"Bastard sold me a pup! Last time I buy anything from a Nightside street trader!"

"Hell," I said. "I could have told you that."

He looked at me. "Don't you laugh at me, Drood. Don't you do that."

Molly came forward to stand beside me, and fixed Hollis with a cold, considering stare. "You've been ignoring me, soldier boy. And that is never a good idea."

She threw a whole series of fireballs at him, one after the other. Big balls of yellow sulphurous flames, crackling fiercely on the still air. Hollis threw one arm up and the fireballs slammed up against an invisible barrier, stopping dead in their tracks. Molly sniffed briefly and switched to throwing balls of spitting and sizzling energies. Hollis didn't stick around to find out whether his barrier would stop them; he was already off and moving, ducking and dodging. He jumped up onto the nearest wall and ran along it, and then switched to running upside down on the ceiling, laughing breathlessly. Molly pursued him with her energy balls, but he was moving so fast she couldn't keep up with him. The energy balls just ran out of steam before they could reach him, and fell apart. Hollis jumped down onto the other wall and I was right there, matching his speed with my own. I grabbed one ankle with a golden hand and then pulled him off the wall and slammed him onto the floor. He hit hard and curled into a ball, fighting to get his breath back. Molly nodded to me.

"Nice one, Eddie."

"I thought so."

And while we were busy congratulating ourselves, Hollis sat up abruptly and spoke a single powerful Word. The wooden floor exploded before us, solid floorboards flowing like water as they took on new shape and purpose under his augmented will. They formed themselves into two huge wooden hands that wrapped themselves around Molly and me in a moment, crushing us so tightly neither of us could move. It was all I could do to get my breath, even inside my armour's protection, and with my arms pinned to my sides I had no leverage to use against the unnatural strength of the wooden fingers. The hands rose, holding Molly and me off the floor, our legs dangling helplessly, utterly helpless. Molly hung limply, eyes closed, in the hand. Either through shock or unconsciousness. I struggled fiercely to get to her, but couldn't budge the wooden fingers in the least. Hollis got to his feet, took a moment to brush himself off and then smiled mockingly at me.

"High and mighty Drood with his cheating armour, never underestimate the value of planning and preparation. Of checking out the scene in advance and setting a few booby traps before the enemy shows his face. I knew you were coming here. Crow Lee told me. And unlike those stuck-up devil boys of his, I think ahead. I've spent a lot of time thinking on how best to take down a Drood. Now, I'm sure that impressive armour of yours will break free eventually, but by then, it'll be far too late. I've got something special here just for you. Supernatural Can Opener, Part Two. Try not to take what happens next personally, Drood. It's just what I do."

He walked unhurriedly up to me, the wooden hand lowering me slowly until I was face-to-face with him. I still couldn't move. He lifted his hands and placed them on either side of my face mask. The bones within his hands glowed fiercely, blazing right through the flesh, and then the glow seemed to seep slowly through the flesh to encase both his hands in the same brightly glowing light. Hollis set both hands carefully on either side of my head, and up close the glare almost blinded me.

The shining fingers clamped onto the golden metal. It didn't even occur to me to flinch. I trusted my armour to protect me, as it always had. The fingertips dug deep into my armour. I couldn't move; paralysed, helpless. The glowing fingers sank in deep and then pulled back, stretching and distorting the face armour. I screamed despite myself as an agonising pain swept through me. I was bonded to the rogue armour as a living thing, and its pain was my pain. Hollis pulled his glowing hands this way and that, tugging at the face mask, and the armour stretched and deformed but wouldn't break. I screamed again as the armour screamed, as Hollis struggled to pull the mask off me.

I could hear Molly screaming at Hollis. "Leave him alone, you bastard! Stop it! I'll kill you for this!"

"Shut it, girlie," said Hollis, not even looking at her. "I'll get to you when I'm finished with him."

He moved in close, concentrating on me as he fought to break the face mask. I was screaming so hard now, it hurt my throat. And while Hollis was concentrating on me, Molly pulled her wits together and concentrated on a simple teleport spell. She jumped herself out of the wooden hand and reappeared right behind Hollis. He started to turn, but Molly had already picked up one of the heavy potted plants and broke it over his head. The sheer weight of the thing clubbed Hollis to the floor and tore his glowing hands away from my mask. I cried out one last time and hung limply in the wooden hand, while the golden metal of my face mask slowly reformed itself. I watched numbly as Molly kicked Hollis good and hard in the ribs, to make sure he was unconscious, and then she hurried over to stand before me. She grabbed hold of the Twilight Teardrop hanging from her throat and spat out a single powerful Word. The wooden fingers holding me rotted and fell apart, and I fell through them to collapse on the floor. I forced myself up onto my knees. Molly was quickly there beside me.

"Eddie, are you all right? I never heard you scream like that before. . . ."

"I'm fine," I said. I had to say it again before it sounded like I meant it. "I'm fine, Molly. It was the armour that was hurt, not me."

I armoured down, and the golden metal retreated into my torc with something like relief. I think both of us were surprised to discover just how close a relationship we'd entered into. I stayed on my knees for a while, Molly crouching beside me, until I was sure I was back in control, and then I got to my feet. Molly got up with me, hovering at my side, but didn't try to help me. I moved across to stand over Hollis. There was blood on his face from where the plant pot had cracked his scalp as it shattered, but he was breathing easily enough. His hands weren't glowing anymore.

"Why a potted plant?" I said to Molly.

She shrugged. "Because it was there. What do we do with him now?"

I kicked Hollis in the ribs, hard enough to pick him up and send his body skidding across the floor and slam into the opposite wall. I went after him again, but immediately Molly was blocking my way, staring intently into my face.

"Don't, Eddie."

"He tried to kill me. He would have killed you. He doesn't deserve to live."

"You can't just kill him in cold blood."

"Why not? You didn't have any problems exploding the Eton Irregulars while they were running away."

"That's different, and you know it. They weren't human anymore."

"I'm not leaving this dangerous an enemy at our back. He dies."

"Eddie, this isn't like you."

"Get out of my way!"

"No!"

I raised a hand to hit her, and then stopped it in midair. Molly didn't move, still staring intently into my eyes. The golden gauntlet hung on the air between us, shining brightly. One blow would have been enough to crush her skull. I hadn't called the armour. I hadn't. I glared at it, willing it back into my torc. It didn't want to go. The rogue armour had unfinished business with Hollis. I could feel it. The armour wasn't talking to me, but I could feel its presence at the back of my mind. I overrode it through sheer force of will, and the golden gauntlet disappeared. I lowered my hand, my whole arm shaking with the effort. Molly moved in close, laying her hands on my chest, looking into my face, making sure it was just me.

"It's all right," I said. "I'm back."

"Eddie . . ."

"You do know I would never hurt you, right?" I said. "That I would die before I ever let anyone hurt you."

"Yes, Eddie. I know. That wasn't you, was it? That was the rogue armour."

"Yes. It appears . . . we're more closely linked than I anticipated. More than I ever intended."

"You promised me you could control it."

"I can!"

"You could still get rid of it," said Molly. "Force it back out of your torc."

"And leave Moxton's Mistake running loose in London with no one inside to control it?" I said. "I can't risk that. And besides, I still need it."

I looked across at Hollis. There was fresh blood at his mouth from where I'd kicked him into the wall.

"Did I do that?" I said.

"I don't know," said Molly. "Did you?"

"He hurt the armour," I said. "I didn't think that was possible. He made the armour angry."

"So he brought it on himself?"

"No . . . I just lost control there for a moment. I won't let that happen again. I keep forgetting Moxton's Mistake is a living thing, not just the armour I usually wear. So now when I get angry, I'm never sure whose emotions I'm feeling. . . ."

"This isn't the first time that's happened," said Molly.

I just looked at her. There was nothing else I could say. For good or bad, I needed the armour. Not for me; for my family.

I reached into my pocket and took out the portable hole I'd found in the other Hall's wrecked Armoury. I dropped the black blob onto the floor, spread it out, and it immediately became an open door, revealing the level some distance below. I rolled Hollis across the floor and over the edge, and he dropped through into the floor below, landing with a satisfyingly hard thump. I peeled the portable door back off the floor, rolled it into a ball, and put it away again.

"Why didn't you do that before?" said Molly.

"Because I didn't think of it. All right?" I said. "You can't think of everything. Did you remember I had it on me? Well, then . . ."

"Don't you get snotty with me, Eddie Drood!"

Some conversations you just know aren't going to go anywhere good. I turned away and started up the hallway.

"Let's get going," I said. "We've got a club to search."

We pressed deeper into the Establishment Club, and most of the members we passed along the way took one look at us and immediately took pains to make themselves scarce. Middle-aged and old men, mostly, no one even remotely young or youthful. This was a club for people who'd made it, not those on the way up. There were apparently no women members, either. The Establishment Club had been around a long time, and clung to its ancient privileges and prejudices. Members disappeared through open doorways or hurried into other rooms or just pressed themselves back against the walls as Molly and I passed, before heading for the exit at speed. They knew terrible and imminent danger when they saw it.

The various servants just moved briskly to get out of our way and carried on about their business, watching Molly and me with unmoved faces and unblinking eyes. They were all of them dressed in the same old-fashioned formal uniform, with a bloodred waistcoat over a starched white shirt, knee-britches and highly polished shoes. They looked like something out of the last century, or possibly even the one before that. They all had the same very pale aspect, as though they didn't get out often enough.

Molly and I took turns to peer into various rooms along the way, looking for Crow Lee, but they were all very much the same. Every comfort and luxury, but in a determinedly old-fashioned and traditional way. No televisions, no computers, nothing electronic. This was an old-school gentlemen's club, whose main attraction was that it had absolutely no intention of moving with the times. Rich and successful-looking businessmen were everywhere, reclining in huge oversized leather chairs, or sleeping with their mouths open, like satisfied cats. Some read broadsheets or upmarket magazines or the better kind of book and made loud shushing sounds at the slightest unexpected noise.

Until they looked up and saw Molly and me, at which point they hid behind whatever they were reading until we were safely past.

Finally the club's steward came forward to meet us. Presumably because our reputation had preceded us. He was tall and painfully slender, in the same formal outfit, and with the same disturbingly pale face and steady gaze. In fact, his face was entirely expressionless as he came to an abrupt halt before us. He bowed stiffly and addressed us in a dry and dusty voice.

"Might I enquire your names, sir and madam, and what I might best do to assist you? On the grounds that the sooner we get that done and get you out of here, the sooner we can get back to normal around here."

"Eddie Drood and Molly Metcalf," I said grandly. "Is that going to be a problem?"

"Oh no, sir," said the Steward, just a bit surprisingly. "You are a member in good standing, Mr. Edwin. Everyone in your family is, and has been for centuries. Mr. Matthew used to come in all the time to avail himself of the club's wine cellars. The young lady is, of course, entirely welcome as your guest. How may I assist you?"

"Matthew always did like a free drink," I said. "And I think I could murder something tall and frosty, too. How about you, Molly?"

"I could drink," said Molly. "In fact, after the day I've had, I think I could drink quite a lot."

The steward issued the very faintest of sighs, and I looked interestedly to see if dust would come out of his mouth. It didn't. He led us down a corridor or two and into the club bar. Everyone else in the bar immediately decided they were needed urgently elsewhere. In fact, there was a bit of a rush and a definite crush in the door, for a moment. Molly and I lined up at the bar, and the barman came forward to serve us. A tall, grey-faced figure in the same old-fashioned outfit, with deep-set eyes, a cadaverous face and a professional smile. He gave the impression he'd been serving behind that bar for quite some time.

"How long have you been here, barman?" said Molly, her thoughts clearly running the same way as mine.

"I have always been here, madam," said the barman, in a cool if distant voice. "What is your pleasure, sir and madam?"

I had an ice-cold bottle of Becks. Molly had a bottle of Beefeater gin. The barman served them both immediately from under the bar counter, as though he'd had them there prepared and waiting all along. And then he just stood there, waiting for his next instructions. I took a slow reflective drink from my nice cold bottle of Becks, while Molly made serious inroads into her bottle of gin. Nothing like fighting delinquent demon schoolboys and an ex-SAS combat sorcerer to work up a serious thirst. The steward stood to one side, waiting patiently. And giving every indication of being prepared to wait there for as long as was necessary. I looked him over thoughtfully, and only then realised that he wasn't blinking. Or breathing.

"Excuse me, steward," I said. "But . . . you are dead, aren't you?"

"Indeed, sir," said the steward. "All the staff here are. Though we prefer to think of ourselves as mortally challenged. We served the club in life and continue to serve it in death. Not a lot of difference, really. We are here because we choose to be, because none of us wishes to leave the club. We think of it as ours. The members are just passing through, but we are always here."

"I have always been the barman," said the barman, without being asked.

"Do the members know?" said Molly.

"They prefer it, madam," said the steward. "It means they don't have to remember our names or bother with gratuities. Now that you are both suitably refreshed, might I again enquire as to your purpose here at the Establishment Club? Can I assist you in any way?"

"We're looking for Crow Lee," I said.

"Nothing simpler, sir. He's just this way, in the club library. He's been waiting for you."

I looked at Molly and then back at the steward. "He has?"

"Oh, indeed, sir. He's been waiting here for you for quite some time. He came in especially early for him, just to be sure of meeting you."

I emptied my bottle of Becks, slammed it down on the bar counter, and nodded briskly to the steward. "Then take us to him. Right now."

"Of course, sir. If you and the young lady would like to follow me . . ."

He led us out of the emptied bar and set off at a steady pace. Molly and I strolled along behind him, refusing to be hurried, on general principle. Molly was still clinging determinedly to her bottle of gin. I knew better than to comment. She leaned in close beside me to murmur in my ear.

"So, what's the plan?"

"Plan?" I said.

"We're about to go up against the Most Evil Man in the World! On his own territory! I think at least one of us ought to have a plan of action. Don't you?"

"Well, we can't just walk in there and kill him," I said.

"We can't?" said Molly. "Are you sure about that, because I'm certainly willing to give it a good try."

"What was it you said just now about not killing in cold blood?"

"That was a person! Just an old pro, like us! This is the Most Evil, et cetera, who will almost certainly kill us if we don't get our retaliation in first!"

"He sent my family away," I said. "It's always possible he might be able to bring them back again."

"Ah," said Molly. "Yes. All right. So we talk first, see if we can strike some kind of deal, and as soon as it becomes clear we can't, then we kill him. Any ideas on how?"

"We improvise," I said. "Suddenly and violently and all over the place. And try very hard not to get ourselves killed in the process."

"How powerful do you think he is, really?" said Molly.

"I don't know," I said. "But I think we're about to find out the hard way."

The steward took us straight to the club library, opened the door and stood well back, allowing Molly and me to enter entirely at our own risk.

Even the mortally challenged know better than to get involved in some things. Or to get caught in the crossfire. He announced us as we strode in.

"Mr. Crow Lee, may I present to you Mr. Edwin Drood, and his associate, Miss Molly Metcalf. Should you require me or any other member of staff, I should point out that we will all be hiding in the cloakroom until the forthcoming unpleasantness is over. At which point we will emerge, as there will no doubt be a great deal of cleaning up to do. Gratuities will be appreciated on this occasion, for the extra work."

The closing door cut off his last few words as he absented himself. No one was paying him much attention. Molly and I stood side by side in the club library, facing Crow Lee and his bodyguard. The library wasn't much, in my opinion. I was used to the massive, extensive libraries of Drood Hall. Repositories of secret and hidden knowledge amassed over centuries; forbidden books laid down to mature like fine wines. This was just a big room with bookshelves on all four walls. I leaned over for a quick look; not even leather bound. Just standard hardback editions, the kind you can order by the yard.

There were no other members in the club library, presumably because Crow Lee was there. He sat in a large comfortable armchair, entirely at his ease, smiling in a smug and satisfied way. As though he'd been sitting there for ages, just waiting for us to come in. And maybe he had. Crow Lee was a large, broad-faced, powerful-looking man, wearing a long Egyptian gown so spotlessly white it seemed to shine and shimmer in the restricted light of the library. He had a great shaven head and piercing dark eyes under bushy black eyebrows. So large a man, he seemed to fill his chair to overflowing. His hands, emerging from the narrow pure white sleeves, were particularly big and powerful. He had an almost hypnotic gaze, with eyes that seemed to look deep into me. So I deliberately looked away. At meetings like this it's always important to establish the ground rules early on.

Crow Lee reclined in his chair and made no move to rise to greet Molly and me. He didn't even offer to shake hands. Instead he smiled easily at me, ignoring Molly, like an important personage indulging some pushy interloper. So completely confident in manner that he passed right through arrogance and out the other side into confident again. We didn't worry him, because nothing worried him. Because he'd killed everyone who might have worried him. He fixed me with his cold, dark gaze, giving me his full attention. So I refused to look at him, giving all my attention to the bodyguard standing silently at his side.

I took my time looking him over. I knew him. Molly and I both knew Mr. Stab, and he knew us. The notorious uncaught serial killer of Old London Town. He'd operated under many names down the years, and I don't think even he knew just how many women he'd butchered and killed in his time. Since he made himself deathless through the ritual slaughter of six unfortunate women in Whitechapel during that unseasonably warm autumn of 1888. When everyone knew the name the papers had given him. Mr. Stab was tall and solemn, dressed in the formal clothes of his own time, right down to the opera cape and top hat. He could blend into a crowd when he had to, could look just like everyone else when he was out on the streets after dark, pursuing his prey. But when acting in his professional capacity, he preferred the look of his legendary past.

His ominous presence dominated the whole room, but he was still the second-most-dangerous person there, and everyone knew it. Because Crow Lee really was the Most Evil Man in the World. You had only to look at him to know it.

He should have been stroking a white cat in his lap. Or pulling its legs off.

I stepped forward, still deliberately not looking at Crow Lee, giving all my attention to the man in black, Mr. Stab. He nodded thoughtfully to me and to Molly.

"It's been a while," I said, "since I invited you into my home, and you repaid my kindness by murdering my cousin Penny."

"I told her not to love me," said Mr. Stab, in his cold, calm voice. "I told her it could only end badly."

"She was my friend!" said Molly. "And you killed her!"

"Yes," said Mr. Stab. "It's what I do. It's all I can do with a woman now. Not quite the immortality I thought I was buying, with my celebration of slaughter. But then, Hell has always had its own sly sense of humour. You know who and what I am, Molly. I've never made any secret of what kind of monster I am."

"And I'm a Drood," I said. "That's who and what I am. I protect the innocent, and when I can't, I avenge their murders."

I looked at him steadily, and he stirred uncomfortably for a moment. Crow Lee laughed out loud and clapped his huge hands together.

"Bravo, young Drood! I'm impressed! Really. There aren't many in this world who can make the notorious Mr. Stab shiver in his shoes."

He spoke directly to me, still ignoring Molly. I could feel her containing herself at my side. She knew he was trying to get to her. Crow Lee's voice was rich and cultured, soft and self-indulgent and oh, so self-satisfied. The voice of a man with nothing to fear.

"I don't think I've ever seen anyone disturb dear Mr. Stab before. . . . So welcome to the Establishment Club, Edwin Drood. You belong here, with your own kind. You really are everything I hoped you'd be."

I looked him up and down and then dismissed him to glare at Mr. Stab again. "How did he hire you? What could he possibly promise you?"

"An end to my curse," said Mr. Stab.

"There is only one end for something like you," I said. "And that's to kill you. And I'll do that for free, for what you did to Penny."

"And for so many others," said Mr. Stab. "Funny how it's always easier for you to care about the ones you knew. And, anyway, you already tried, and failed."

"But this time I'll hold you down while he does it," said Molly. "You promised me I could trust you. . . ."

"Promises are made to be broken," said Mr. Stab. "Who should know that better than I?"

"Don't," I said. "Don't you dare try and make us feel sorry for you. Not after everything you've done."

"I stood beside you," said Mr. Stab. "Stood with the Droods when you went to war with the Hungry Gods. Helped you save the world. Shouldn't that count for something?"

"What do you want?" I said. "A thank-you?"

"I tried! I tried because I didn't want to be a monster anymore!"

"Then what are you doing here with Crow Lee?" said Molly.

"Because sometimes it takes one monster to destroy another," said Mr. Stab.

"Well," Crow Lee said brightly. "Isn't this nice? Old friends talking together. Thank you for joining me here in the Club Library, Eddie."

"Call this a library?" I said. "A collected Dickens and a few Trollopes?"

"If you've quite finished chatting with the hired help," said Crow Lee, determined to draw everyone's attention back to himself, "we do have matters of importance to discuss."

Molly and I both looked at him, and he wriggled delightedly in his chair, enjoying himself; a disturbing movement in one so large. He looked me over, taking his time. Still ignoring Molly.

"I never thought I'd have to look at a Drood again," said Crow Lee. "But then, you're like cockroaches, aren't you? So many of you, and so hard to kill. But worth the effort."

"So you admit you're responsible for the attack on Drood Hall?" I said.

Crow Lee laughed happily. "Admit it, little Drood? I boast it. I glory in it! I've known all about Alpha Red Alpha for years and years, just waiting for someone in your family to be foolish enough to use it. I had the remote control, you see, the means to override the mechanism, but . . ."

I cut in. I knew he was teasing me, but I just couldn't help it. I had to know.

"How did you get your hands on the remote control? Who did you get it from?"

"From the same person who first told me about Alpha Red Alpha," Crow Lee said easily. "You have a traitor in your family, dear Eddie. A very old and very well-established, very well-hidden traitor. And I have always been so very well served by traitors. He hates you even more than I do, and with much better reason. . . . But as I was saying before I was so impertinently interrupted . . . I had to wait for someone in your family to feel so threatened that they'd actually risk using Alpha Red Alpha, before I could use my remote control. You see, you have to lower all the Hall's protections before you can activate the dimensional engine. They interfere with its workings, apparently. Can you imagine what it was like for me, learning that you'd used the thing at last? And that all I had to do was wait for you to return and then hit the button on my special remote control? No, you can't imagine what it felt like, knowing I finally had the means to send your whole stupid, interfering family away, forever. . . .

"I struck while you were vulnerable, and just like that, you were gone! Good-bye, Droods, forever! Rotated out of reality and dumped somewhere else. I do hope it turned out to be somewhere really appalling. . . . I sent them there and I left them there, and I laughed and laughed and laughed. . . ."

"And then you dropped the other Hall in its place," I said, and something in my voice stopped his laughing. "To hide what you'd done."

"Oh no," said Crow Lee. "That was just a happy accident. An entirely unanticipated and fortuitous side effect. I did enjoy it, though. A wrecked and ruined Hall and dead Droods lying everywhere—what's not to like? They weren't the actual family I hated, but they were Droods, and I'm sure I would have hated them if I'd known them."

"You bastard," I said.

I started forward, and Crow Lee stopped me with an upheld hand. "Think, little Drood. Consider the implications of what I've done. Whatever happens next between you and me, I want you to understand that you cannot undo the one thing I've done that really matters. I have proven to the world . . . that Droods can be beaten. The wrecked Hall and dead Droods are proof of that, forever. Even if you do somehow escape my wrath and continue as the Last Drood, even if you somehow find a way to bring your nasty family back . . . the world will never see you as unstoppable again. I've seen to that."

I had to smile. "All right. You're reaching now."

"Am I, little Drood?"

"Bring my family back," I said. "And I promise I won't kill you."

Crow Lee lost his easy smile. He scowled fiercely at me. "No one gives me orders, boy. I've never needed a family to make me strong. I've never needed armour to hide behind. I made myself what I am through sheer force of will!"

"And by killing a whole lot of people," I said. "Mostly through treachery, backstabbing, and getting other people to do your dirty work for you. Don't try it on me. I've read your file."

Crow Lee leaned forward in his chair and fixed me with his dark, disturbing gaze. And suddenly he was the most fascinating thing in the room. I forgot about everything else, forgot about Mr. Stab, forgot about Molly, forgot about my poor lost family. I was staring into Crow Lee's eyes and I couldn't look away. Didn't want to look away. Crow Lee spoke directly to me, and his voice was the most compelling thing I'd ever heard.

"You don't want to fight me," said Crow Lee. "I am your friend. You know you can trust me. My enemies are your enemies. You want to protect me against my enemies. Like that woman standing beside you. You can't trust her. You know that. She's always getting in the way, meddling in your affairs. You want to be free of her. So kill her. Kill her for me and for yourself."

All the time he was speaking to me, I knew it was all bullshit. Knew it, knew he was lying through his teeth. I didn't believe a word of it, but still I couldn't stop listening to him. He held me with his dark, hypnotic gaze and his persuasive words. I fought him with everything I had. Fought his influence and the words he was saying, and bit by bit I drew back from him.

I took a deep breath and looked away, breaking Crow Lee's gaze. His influence was gone in a moment. He looked at me openmouthed, as though he couldn't believe it, and I looked back at him and laughed in his face, just a bit shakily.

"Had me a little bit worried there for a moment, sweetie," murmured Molly.

"Droods are trained to withstand mental challenges," I said loudly and confidently. Because we are, but it had still been a bit too close for my liking.

"You dare defy me?" whispered Crow Lee. "You dare . . . ?"

"Were you bullied as a child?" I said. "Did they make your life hell at school? Is that what this is all about? Because this whole Most Evil Man bit strikes me as just so much overcompensation."

Crow Lee turned his burning hypnotic gaze on Molly. "Kill him! Kill him!"

Molly just laughed at him. "Oh, come on. You have got to be kidding. I'm the wild witch, remember? The laughter in the woods and the lightning in the storm? Frankly, I'm offended you even thought that would work."

She brought the bottle of gin to her lips, took in a good mouthful and then leaned forward abruptly and sprayed the whole lot across Crow Lee's face. The stream of neat gin burst into flames as it left her lips, and Crow Lee screamed shrilly, like a small child, as flames leapt up all over his face. He wiped them away quickly with his bare hands, burning them too in the process, and jumped to his feet. His face was scalded bright red where it wasn't flushed with rage, and his eyes were already puffing shut. He snapped his fingers imperiously at Mr. Stab.

"Do your job, old monster!" he said fiercely. "Rid me of these nuisances!"

There was a pause. Mr. Stab didn't move a muscle. In his cold, calm voice he said, "Regretfully, I cannot. I fear you overestimate my abilities."

Crow Lee stared at him blankly. "Do as you're told, damn you! Kill them! Kill them both!"

"I can't," said Mr. Stab. "They're a Drood and a Metcalf, and I'm just an ill-made monster. It's a wise monster who knows his limitations."

Crow Lee took control of himself, with an obvious effort. Drops of steaming gin were still falling from his burnt chin.

"I know there is a history between you and them. That should make it easier. That's why I hired you!"

"Look at the Drood's torc," said Mr. Stab. "Look at his armour."

Crow Lee stopped and then stared at me for a long moment before nodding slowly, grudgingly. "Ah yes. I do See what you mean. . . . Well, then, Eddie and Molly, we'll do this little dance another day. When I'm . . . better prepared."

He gave us both a sly self-satisfied smile and snapped his fingers loudly. And just like that he was gone. The oversized armchair was empty, and Mr. Stab no longer stood beside it. There wasn't even an inrush of air to fill the space where they'd been. It was as though they'd never been there.

"No!" said Molly. "You can't do that! He can't do that, Eddie!"

"I think you'll find he can," I said. "And he has."

"The bastard . . ." said Molly. "I was all fired up and ready to go, and he just . . . runs away?"

"Well," I said. "You don't get to be the Most Evil Man in the World by playing fair. Or fighting when you're not sure the odds are in your favour. What did he mean about my armour, Molly? What did he See just then?"

"He must have realised you're wearing rogue armour instead of what he was expecting," said Molly, but she wouldn't look at me while she said it.

"Mr. Stab surprised me, then," I said, tacitly agreeing to change the subject. "I did try to kill him when he killed Penny, but I didn't even come close. I never knew he rated me that highly. Or you, to be honest."

"He wasn't scared of us," said Molly. "I think . . . he was just showing us professional courtesy."

"Would you do the same for him?"

"Hell, no. I'll kill him dead the first chance I get."

"Good," I said. "Because I think he's cut us as much slack as he can. Do you really think he wants to die? You've known him a lot longer than I."

"He's always moped about his . . . condition," said Molly. "But if he really wanted to be released from his curse, he would have found a way by now. It's just a pose, a show he puts on in front of company."

"He was your friend," I said.

"Once upon a time and long ago," said Molly. "I saw myself as a monster, so I went looking for others to keep me company."

"What changed that?" I said.

She smiled at me. "You did, idiot."

"Ah," I said. "Yes."

"That was a prearranged teleport spell," said Molly, changing the subject yet again. "So carefully set in place even I couldn't See it. Pre-programmed to take him and Mr. Stab out of here at a moment's notice to a preselected destination. Very professional stuff."

"Could he still be here, somewhere in the club?" I said.

"No. That had all the hallmarks of a long-range teleport. Probably all the way back to his country manor house in Surrey." She looked at me thoughtfully. "Could you track him through the Merlin Glass? Go straight after him?"

"Possibly," I said. "But you could bet good money that if we did, we'd be walking into a trap. God alone knows what kind of protections and reinforcements he'd have waiting for us there. This is a man who believes in planning ahead. Remember the private army? No. We'll go after him, but only after we've taken some time out to work up a proper plan."

"I said we needed a plan. . . ."

"And you were right."

"But we can't afford to give him time to prepare for us, Eddie! His country bolt hole is just crawling with booby traps and hired killers and full-strength nasty surprises! He has defences you wouldn't believe!"

"It can't be that bad. . . ."

"Yes, it can! I've seen it!"

There was a pause then as I looked at her thoughtfully. "And you know this how?"

"Because," said Molly reluctantly, "I've been there. More than once. I did business with Crow Lee back in the day."

"What? You worked with the Most Evil Man in the World? And you never thought to mention this before?"

"Don't judge me!" Molly said hotly. "Don't you dare judge me! My parents were dead, murdered by your family! I was desperate to avenge them. Ready to work with anyone who could promise me help or weapons to use against the Droods! Crow Lee was very understanding, very helpful."

"Yeah," I said. "I'll just bet he was."

"What about you? You went looking for help when your family made you rogue. You were ready to work with monsters, too!"

"Yes," I said. "But I found you."

CHAPTER EIGHT

Traffic Can Be Murder Sometimes

Molly and I still weren't talking to each other when we left the Establishment Club, so it was just as well there was a distraction waiting for us. The Regent of Shadows had sent us a nice new car, along with one of his agents to explain why. I took my time looking over the car, and let the agent wait till I was ready to talk to her. The car was big enough that it took me a while to walk around it; a great red beast of a car, with white stripes, gleaming chrome and high tail fins. A classic of its kind from when Detroit dinosaurs roamed the earth, and about as conspicuous in London traffic as a piranha in an aquarium. I finally sat on the bonnet and gave the Regent's agent an equally thorough inspection.

She smiled back easily, a very cool and poised middle-aged lady, still good-looking in a *never heard of Botox and wouldn't use it even if I had* kind of way. Dressed in an elegantly cut tweed suit with a creamy white panama hat crammed down on her long grey hair and a flouncy white silk scarf round her throat. She just sparkled with charm and grace and gave every indication that she ought to be off organising a garden party somewhere. I was quite taken with her. Molly, less so.

"What the hell kind of car is this?" said Molly. "It couldn't stand out any more if it had a target painted on it."

"And hello to you, too, Molly Metcalf," said the agent in a clipped, cut-glass, finishing-school voice. "I'm Diana, one of the Regent of Shadows's most established agents. Hello, Eddie Drood! Delighted to meet you both. And this is a 1958 Plymouth Fury. Classic American muscle car, fully restored, with all kinds of useful extras. And, bless me, look at the chrome on that!"

"It is a bit conspicuous," I said.

"It's registered to the Regent," said Diana. "An official Department of the Uncanny vehicle, with all the right papers filed in all the right places, so no one will bother you. And, after all, it's not as if you can hide from Crow Lee's all-seeing eye, no matter what you're driving. Sneaking up on the Most Evil Man in the World was never going to be an option. I'm sure the Phantom V's privacy shields were first-class; your Armourer always did do good work. But they won't hide you from Crow Lee. His many agents will undoubtedly be watching all the roads for the Phantom V, but they won't be expecting you in this. Word will get out, of course, but driving the Plymouth should buy you some wriggle room."

"Very kind of the Regent," I said. "I'll take it. Does it come with a warranty?"

"She doesn't even come with insurance," said Diana. "She's called the Scarlet Lady. Take her; we're glad to be rid of her."

"Why did I just know she was going to say that?" said Molly. "All right, what's wrong with her?"

"She's not been exactly . . . lucky," said Diana. "In fact, we've searched her thoroughly several times, just in case someone accidentally built a dead albatross into her somewhere. But I think she just needs a firm hand on the wheel and a chance to prove herself."

Molly looked at her. "I want the Phantom back. I knew where I was with the Phantom."

"You never liked the Phantom and you know it," I said.

"I like this even less," Molly said firmly.

"Hush," said Diana, "She'll hear you."

"Convince me," I said.

"The Scarlet Lady has first-class protections, and more built-in weaponry than some third-world countries," Diana said briskly. "She can hit Mach four with the wind behind her, can outrun anything on four wheels and can punch right through a brick wall without even slowing. And she has a sat nav programmed to take you straight to Crow Lee's little hideaway down in Surrey. That is where he's retired to, in case you were wondering."

"We had already worked that out, thank you," said Molly.

"How clever of you, darling," said Diana, smiling sweetly at Molly for just a moment before giving me her full attention. "Eddie, there's something I need to talk to you about. Not really any of my business, I know, but that's never stopped me before. . . . I need you to consider this. I know you don't want to think about it, but even if you do bring down Crow Lee and destroy his nasty little organisation, there's still no guarantee you'll be able to find or retrieve your lost family. You have to face the possibility that the Droods could be lost forever, wherever they are. You have to consider . . . that on this occasion, even your formidable best might not be good enough. Have you thought about what you're going to do if there's nowhere for you to go back to after this? And you really are the Last Drood. What will you do?"

"Carry on the family tradition, I suppose," I said. "Fight the good fight. What else is there?"

Molly gave me a sharp look there, which I didn't understand till later. Diana gave me a brilliant smile.

"The Regent was . . . lost for a long time after he left his family. So he made himself a new family—his Shadows. That hasn't changed just because we're calling ourselves Uncanny these days. You could join us, Eddie, become a part of our family. I know it wouldn't be the same— how could it?—but we would make you very welcome. And you, too, of course, Molly. You could do good work with us, both of you. You don't have to be alone in the world."

I could hear the sincerity in her voice. I had no doubt she meant what she was saying, and it did intrigue me. It also puzzled me that this should mean so much to her.

"Thank you," I said. "That's very kind, but . . ."

"He doesn't need you," said Molly. "He has me."

"Think about it," said Diana. She smiled briskly at both of us and was immediately all business again. "The Regent assured me that we'll take good care of your Phantom V while you're gone. You can pick her up again anytime you're back in London, after this is all over."

"I wouldn't mess with the Phantom, if I were you," I said carefully. "The Armourer builds his cars to look after themselves."

"That's Jack for you!" said Diana. "Never met a car he didn't customise till it hurt. Trust me, I did raise that point most forcibly with the Uncanny car pool. The Phantom will be treated with the utmost respect."

"You know the Drood Armourer?" said Molly, not even bothering to hide her suspicions.

"Of course," Diana said easily. And then she just stood there, smiling easily.

"More secrets," Molly said disgustedly.

"Of course," said Diana. "We are secret agents, after all. Secrets are our business, our stock-in-trade. Now, I know what you're thinking. . . ."

"No, you don't," said Molly. "Or you wouldn't still be standing there."

I could practically see the tension spitting and sparking on the air between them, so I made a big deal of going round to the driver's-side door and opening it to look inside. The sat nav immediately turned itself on.

"About time!" it said in a harsh and strident female voice. "Come on. Get in, park your arse and let's get moving! I haven't got all day!"

I just stared at the sat nav for a moment. "We're not going to get on, are we?"

"Like I care," said the sat nav.

I straightened up and looked at Diana. "Would the Regent be very upset if I was to rip out the sat nav and throw it under the next passing heavy-goods vehicle? It's not as if we're going to need it. We're not driving down to Surrey."

"We're not?" said Molly.

"We are going directly to Crow Lee's place through the Merlin Glass," I said. "You have heard of the Glass, Diana? Yes, of course you have."

"We maintain up-to-date files on everyone," Diana said carefully. "On friends and enemies and everyone in between. I'm sure the Droods are in there somewhere. Though I don't think our researchers believe half of what they've heard when it comes to the Merlin Glass. Some have been heard to suggest that it's all just Drood misinformation, designed to demoralise people like us."

"Believe every bit of it," Molly said sweetly. "Especially the really disturbing parts."

"The clue is in the name," I said. "Merlin Satanspawn always believed that weapons should be double-edged. But we're not going to Crow Lee's place in Surrey straightaway."

"You're not?" said Diana.

"Molly and I have already discussed this at some length," I said carefully. "If we just drop in on him now, he'll have all kinds of defences ready and waiting for us. I've got a better idea. The Merlin Glass operates in time as well as space. You might remember, Molly, that during out recent side trip to foreign parts, the Glass returned us to the exact moment in time and space that we left from. Therefore . . ."

"Hold everything," said Molly. "Are you saying what I think you're saying?"

"Time travel!" said Diana, clapping her hands together excitedly. "You're talking about time travel, aren't you?"

"I was going to say that!" said Molly, sulking. She glared at Diana. "Don't you have somewhere else you ought to be?"

"Wouldn't miss this for the world," said Diana.

Molly glowered at me. "Since when did you start discussing family secrets in front of strangers? You might trust the Regent, Eddie, but we've no reason to extend that to his whole damned organisation. If Crow Lee has people inside your family, you can bet he's planted even more inside the Department of the Uncanny. Probably back when they were just Shadows."

"I suppose that is always possible," said Diana, in an entirely reasonable tone of voice she must have known would put Molly's teeth on edge. "I wouldn't put anything past Crow Lee. The treacherous little shit. But you can trust me, Eddie. The Regent specifically chose me to come here and talk with you because he had no doubt that you could trust me. Do you trust me, Eddie?"

I looked at her. I knew I shouldn't trust her, that I had no good reason to, but somehow I did. Molly could see what was happening on my face, and made a point of tutting loudly and rolling her eyes.

"You always were too trusting, Eddie Drood. And always far too ready to be impressed by mutton dressed as lamb. All right, what's the plan with the Merlin Glass?"

"Simple," I said. "I'll arrange the arrival coordinates so that although we enter the Glass here and now, we'll arrive at Crow Lee's estate twenty-four hours in the future. That should give him more than enough time to become worried about all kinds of things—where are we, why haven't we arrived yet, what we're planning. It should also provide enough time for his private army to get tired of standing guard for a threat that never comes, and get bored and complacent and sloppy."

"I don't know," said Molly. "This is Crow Lee we're talking about."

"It gives us an advantage we wouldn't otherwise have and that he won't suspect," I said patiently. "Unless you actually want to drive all the way down to Surrey. Arriving worn-out in the early hours of the morning, having driven all through the night, being nagged all the way by the sat nav?"

"I heard that!" said the sat nav.

"You were meant to," I said.

"Why only twenty-four hours into the future?" said Diana.

"Because I don't trust the Merlin Glass any further than that," I said. "There are far too many things that can go wrong with time travel. And, besides, I just can't stand the thought of Crow Lee having any more time than that. I am going to destroy his house and his grounds and everything he owns, bring his whole world crashing down about his ears and then . . . I'm going to make him bring my family back. Whatever it takes."

"I'll help," said Molly.

"Couldn't do it without you," I said.

We smiled at each other, and just like that everything was all right again between us.

"I hate to be the wet blanket here," said Diana, "but won't Crow Lee detect you approaching through the Merlin Glass? I mean, that thing gives off a hell of a lot of magical energies, and he's bound to be looking for it. If we know you've got it, you can be sure he knows."

"He'll be looking for spatial travel through the Glass," I said just a bit smugly. "Not time travel. He doesn't know the Glass can do that. No one does."

"You're so sharp you'll cut yourself one day," Molly said admiringly. "Death from Above, via the Timestream! I love it!"

And she did a little jig of joy, right there in the street.

"He'll never see it coming," I said solemnly.

And then all three of us looked up sharply and round as a big red double-decker London bus came thundering down the street towards us. It was really travelling, moving much faster than any London bus should, and it took me only a moment to realise all the windows were darkly tinted, so no one could see in. I couldn't even see the driver at the wheel, never mind any of the passengers. The bus roared right down the middle of the road, its engine making a hell of a racket as it struggled to maintain its speed. Tinted windows? On a public-transport bus?

"That's odd," said Diana. "The route number on the front of that bus is all wrong. It shouldn't be anywhere near here."

We watched curiously as the bus drew nearer, straddling the middle of the road, and then the driver slammed on the brakes so that the bus slowed down as it passed us. The whole frame shuddered from the sudden strain, and the wheels made harsh squealing noises. And every one of the tinted windows just disappeared, replaced by dozens of assorted gun barrels. They targeted Molly and me and Diana as we just stood there gaping, and all of them opened fire at once.

I armoured up. Molly raised a protective field before her. And Diana just stepped smartly backwards into a handy shadow and disappeared. *I knew there had to be a reason why the Regent's agents were called Shadows,* I thought as the first bullets found me. All the guns were firing at once, and the combined roar was like the wrath of God. A noise so loud it was actually physically painful, even inside my armour. The bullets issued from the side of the bus like a pirate galley's broadside; thousands of bullets from dozens of guns, like a wall of death. Bullets ricocheted harmlessly from my armour and were swallowed by Molly's shield, and chewed up the brick wall behind us, and, rather surprisingly, just bounced harmlessly off the Plymouth Fury without making a mark.

"Don't you shoot at me, you bastards!" screamed the sat nav. "I'm a classic! Shoot at them; I'm just the ride! They're the ones you want! Shoot the fleshy ones!"

"We will have words later," I said to the sat nav.

I glanced quickly behind me. The door to the Establishment Club was firmly closed, and, amazingly, taking no damage at all from the massed fire raking back and forth across it. And the bullet holes in the brickwork were already repairing themselves. Bullets might be a bit of a low-class threat to a setup like the Establishment Club, but it was clear it could look after itself.

Whoever was giving the orders inside the bus soon realised that their armoury of guns wasn't having the hoped-for effect. The assault shut off abruptly, and the bus's engine roared as it sped up again. I ran out into the street and sprinted after the bus, my armour's speed more than a match for its hurried departure. I quickly caught up with the bus and plunged both my golden hands, well past the wrists, into the rear of the vehicle. My golden fingers dug in deep. I took a firm hold and then forced my golden heels into the street. The bus screeched to a halt despite itself, skidding wildly, as my heels dug two deep furrows in the road. I grinned behind my face mask. Good to be a Drood.

I wrestled the bus to a reluctant halt, the whole rear wall bowing out towards me, stretched and distorted by my hold. The driver gunned his engine and the bus shook back and forth as it fought to pull free, black smoke billowing out from the tyres. But I had my hold, and the bus wasn't going anywhere. I pushed my arms farther in and lifted the whole rear of the bus up off the road, so that the rear wheels just spun helplessly in midair.

The tinted windows at the rear of the bus disappeared, replaced by a whole bunch of gun barrels moving quickly to target me at point-blank range. They opened up with everything they had, trying to blast me loose, but I just stood there and took it. Bullets hammered me from head to toe, ricocheting in every direction at once, even back into the bus, and I didn't feel a single impact. Some of the guns fired directly into my face mask, and a lot of good it did them. I didn't even blink. One by one the guns ran out of ammunition, and then they all suddenly withdrew. The tinted back windows reappeared, and the bus driver shut down his engine.

It was very quiet in the street. No gunfire, no straining engine, no squealing tyres; not a single sound. I dropped the rear of the bus back onto the road, and it bounced a few times on its heavy tyres before settling. I wrenched my hands back out of the bus, and they emerged easily amid the shriek of ruptured and tearing metal. Molly came forward to join me, and stood beside me as we looked over the silent double-decker.

"What the hell was that all about?" said Molly.

"I think," I said, "that we have just been the victims of the hidden-world equivalent of a drive-by shooting. What the hell did these silly bastards think they were doing? Battles in the hidden world are supposed to stay hidden from the everyday world! You don't squabble in front of the children; everyone knows that!"

"Look around you," said Molly.

It took me only a moment to see what she meant. There was traffic all around us; cars and taxis, white vans and cycle couriers . . . but not one of them was moving. Time had stopped around us. The drive-by and its intended victims were all caught in a single frozen moment, held between the tick and tock of the world's clock. So the shooting could take place without anyone noticing, until time started up again. The bus would be gone, and all that remained would be the bullet-ridden corpses of the victims. Just another mystery in the busy heart of London. Probably put it down to gangs.

"A drive-by shooting," I growled. "I hate them. I mean, come on. Is there anything more cowardly than a drive-by? Drive up at speed, spray bullets in every direction, hope you hit the right target among all the innocent bystanders and then run away. I want the creeps behind this, Molly. I want to explain to them the error of their ways. Let's take a look inside the bus."

"Let's," said Molly. "I feel we should have words with these scumbags."

"Harsh words," I said.

We walked along the side of the big red double-decker bus. The windows remained darkly tinted and very firmly closed. Not a sound or a movement from inside. I came to the cab door, well above the ground, reached up with one golden hand, and casually tore out the whole door and threw it aside. The sound of rending metal was very loud in the quiet, followed by an equally loud reverberating clang as the door hit the ground. A massive gun barrel protruded from inside the cab, aimed directly into my face mask. I didn't give the gun's owner time to fire, just grabbed the long barrel and jerked the whole thing right out of his hands. There was a howl of pain and upset from inside the cab, from the gun's owner, who hadn't let go of his gun fast enough.

I looked the gun over. Cheap Kalashnikov knock-off piece of shit. The assassin's gun of choice when he hasn't enough money for anything decent. I broke the thing in two and threw the pieces aside. Cheap guns and a drive-by shooting on a London double-decker didn't really tie in with the sophistication of time control. Devices like that are hard to find, and they never come cheap. I peered into the cab, but there was no one at the wheel. The driver had retreated into the bus's gloomy interior and was hidden among his fellow would-be assassins.

"It's not like we've any shortage of enemies," Molly said behind me. "But I can't think of anyone dumb enough to organise such a low-rent attack on us. I say we board the bus and bounce people off the walls until someone feels like telling us what's going on here."

"Sounds like a plan to me," I said.

"And me," said Diana, stepping elegantly out of a nearby shadow. She didn't look in the least troubled or disturbed by what had just happened. Molly and I both made a point of not jumping even a little bit when she reappeared, just on general principle.

"Regent of Shadows," said Molly. "Much suddenly becomes clear. I take it you're one of his Special Agents?"

"Of course," said Diana. "One of his first, in fact. We go way back, the Regent and me. You think he'd entrust your safety to just anyone? I am rather annoyed at the crudity of the attack, though. I'm used to better, quite frankly. Fiendish master plans and complicated death traps; that's more my sort of thing. I say we go inside the bus and kick bottom!"

"All right!" said Molly. "I'm starting to like you. . . ."

"So pleased," said Diana.

I hauled myself up into the driver's cab, looked into the gloomy interior and was immediately met with the roar of a heavy electronic cannon, one of those customised jobs that can pump out thousands of explosive fléchettes a second. Being a sporting sort, I braced myself and just stood there and took it. The bullets slammed into me like a solid mass, and the whole front of the bus, behind me, just disintegrated, blown away by the sheer concentrated firepower. My armour wasn't bothered in the least.

The problem with this particular kind of gun is that by its very nature it goes through a hell of a lot of bullets really quickly. The gun fell silent abruptly, and someone said, "*Oh, shit.*" I stepped quickly forward into the bus's interior, grabbed hold of the massive cannon, and ripped it right off its floor mounting. I then crumpled the heavy gun in my hands like it was made of paper, wadded it into a ball and let the metal mass drop to the floor with a loud and disquieting thud.

The man who'd been firing the cannon retreated quickly towards the rear of the bus, making choked noises of distress. All the bus seats were full, with row after row of hard-faced men in flak jackets, carrying all kinds of guns. They started to aim them at me . . . and then had a rush of common sense to their heads and changed their minds. Seeing Drood armour up close will do that to you. Which is, of course, the point.

The hard-faced fighting men lowered their guns to the floor and then put their hands as high in the air as they could get them. Which was only sensible, if a bit disappointing. It isn't nearly as much fun to beat the crap out of people who aren't fighting back. It wouldn't necessarily stop me, though. I was still pretty annoyed about the whole drive-by thing. And then a voice at the very rear of the bus spoke up, saying:

"Take him down or you don't get paid!"

Just when everything was going so well . . . There's always one. There was just the briefest of pauses while the gunmen looked at one another, and then they all reached inside their flak jackets and produced any number of magic amulets, glowing handguns, pointing bones and enchanted brass knuckles. The gunmen all surged forward at once, clearly hoping to achieve close up what they hadn't managed at a distance: bringing me down through sheer weight of numbers. I could have told them that was never going to work.

They punched and kicked at me, hitting me with every weapon they had, shouting fierce war cries to encourage themselves and one another, falling on me from every side at once . . . and none of them could touch me. Their various toys just broke and shattered against my armour, and in the limited space of the bus's aisle they were more a threat to each other than they were to me.

I finally lost my patience and waded into them, slapping weapons out of their hands and striking the gunmen down with swift, efficient punches. I knocked them down and trampled them, bounced them off walls, picked them up and slammed them against the low ceiling. I was careful to control my armour's strength. I wanted living prisoners capable of answering questions. So while they did their very best to kill me, I didn't kill a single one of them.

Because I, not my armour, was in control.

Molly was quickly there with me, darting back and forth, smiling happily as she threw shaped curses that made guns blow up in their owners' faces and punching in the odd head here and there, for the good of her soul. She whooped loudly as she ducked wild punches, kicked the legs out from under people and trampled them viciously underfoot. She dispensed much-deserved beatings to the ungodly, and loved every moment of it.

I laughed and fought alongside her, and that seemed to upset the gunmen even more. Especially when Diana joined the fight, darting in and out of the many shadows inside the bus, appearing and disappearing with bewildering speed as she dispensed elegant karate blows and fierce savate kicks and the odd elbow to the back of the neck to a victim who didn't have the sense to hit the floor fast enough. Diana was a graceful, efficient fighter, her tweed skirt swirling about her as she moved with surprising speed for someone her age. And not one of the gunmen was able to point a weapon at her fast enough to save himself.

Eventually, the three of us just ran out of people to hit. We stood together, none of us breathing particularly hard, and looked around us. The inside of the bus was littered with battered and bloodied would-be assassins lying in piles, draped over the seats, gasping for air and staunching bloody mouths and noses and occasionally crying bitter tears. As professional assassins went, this bunch hadn't travelled far. They never stood a chance, and they knew it. Molly and Diana and I looked hopefully around for someone else we could teach the error of their ways, but everyone kept their heads well down and avoided our eyes, hoping not to be noticed.

"Well, that was fun," said Diana, adjusting the silk scarf at her throat and brushing herself down. "I was hoping I'd get the chance to see the two of you in action, and I have to say, you're everything the reports said you were. I'm really quite impressed."

"Not bad yourself for an old girl," Molly said grudgingly. "Can all the Regent's people do what you do, jumping in and out of shadows?"

"Oh yes," said Diana. "The clue was always in the name. Apparently, the Regent acquired this very useful ability from the Hanged Man's Clan, back when he was first on the run from his family. I say *acquired*; another version of the story says he stole it, and I wouldn't put it past him. The Regent has never had any problem with being . . . practical about matters of morality. When necessary. The shadow thing is very useful in our line of work. Do keep it to yourselves, my dears."

"I still want to know who was in charge of all this," I said loudly. There was a certain amount of stirring among the beaten-down gunmen, but no one said anything.

"Got to be one of these scumbags," said Molly.

"I don't think so," Diana said thoughtfully. "Take a look out the windows. . . ."

We all leaned over the nearest bodies, which did their best to flinch out of the way, and looked outside. The windows weren't tinted from the inside, and we had a clear view of the street. The cars and other traffic were all exactly where we'd left them, not moving at all, fixed in place in their frozen moment held outside of time.

"So whoever stopped time is still in here with us," I said. "Hiding in plain sight and hoping to go undiscovered. I can't See him anywhere, even through my mask."

Molly looked slowly and carefully about her, and even hardened assassins avoided her gaze. She scowled. "I'm not Seeing any glamours or illusions, and no dimensional door he could have escaped through. . . . So he's definitely still here in the bus with us, the arrogant little scrote."

"Hell with it," I said. "I suppose I'll just have to punch a hole in the petrol tank, set light to the whole bus and watch them all fry."

"It's the only way to be sure," Molly said solemnly.

Diana looked at us sharply and was about to say something when a new voice spoke up suddenly from among the piled-up assassins.

"All right! All right. Don't do anything dramatic! I'm right here. . . ."

And one of the most battered and bloodied-looking gunmen stood up abruptly. He shook himself briefly, and all his wounds disappeared, his whole shape changing as he became someone else. The hard-faced seasoned gunman was replaced in a moment by a sulky-looking teenage boy of no more than seventeen or eighteen. Wearing distressed jeans and a T-shirt bearing the legend *Revenge Is Forever*.

"It's an Immortal!" said Molly. "A flesh-dancer! No wonder I couldn't detect his presence!"

Diana looked at him thoughtfully. "So that's what they look like. I'd heard they never aged past their teens, but . . . Eddie, I thought your family killed off all the Immortals when you raided their secret base at Castle Frankenstein."

"We got most of them," I said.

"Evil, vicious little bastards that they were," said Molly.

"But a few did get away," I said. "Because they just deserted their own kind and ran, like rats deserting a sinking ship." I walked up to the teenage Immortal, who flinched but didn't back away. "So," I said. "I thought the few of you who survived had gone to ground, hiding in squalid little bolt-holes in the armpits of the world. What brought you out of hiding to do something this dumb?"

"You did," said the Immortal defiantly. "Your family's dead and gone, Drood, just like mine! I thought it was finally safe to show my face again, to start up my life again and make the world march to my tune, as it should! And then you turned up, the Last Drood, alone and vulnerable. How could I resist? How could I resist the chance to avenge my murdered family?"

"One," I said, "your family spent centuries exploiting and enslaving Humanity, just because you could, hiding behind your ever-changing faces. You tried to wipe out my family when we tried to stop you. Your family deserved everything it got, and then some. And two, a Drood is never vulnerable."

"Why a bus?" said Molly. "And why this bunch of underachievers?"

The Immortal shrugged quickly. "Money was limited. I had to go with what I could afford. I took the Time Distorter with me when I left the castle. All of us took something, just grabbing whatever came to hand. . . . There was just enough energy left in the Distorter for one last time seizure. So I put together the best wild bunch I could, and came looking for you." He glared about him. "I should have chosen more carefully. I'll do better next time."

"There isn't going to be a next time," said Molly. "I really don't believe in killing in cold blood, but for an Immortal I'll make the effort. Some enemies are just too dangerous and too treacherous to be allowed to live. Don't look at me like that, Eddie. There isn't a cell that can hold a shape-shifter like him, and you know it. And any word of surrender he gave you would be worthless. He'll never stop coming after you."

"It's not just me! There are lots of us out there!" the Immortal said defiantly. "Not just the few Immortals who escaped your massacre; all the people you ever fought, Drood! Everyone whose lives your family has ever interfered with or tried to stamp out! All your enemies, all the ones with good reason to hate you, come home to roost at last! The word is out . . . and we're all coming for you. To wipe out the Last Drood. To take our revenge on you for everything your family did. We'll never stop coming for you!"

"Unless we send them a message," I said, and something in my voice shut him up.

"What kind of message did you have in mind?" said Diana.

"I was thinking about sticking his severed head on a spike and leaving it somewhere prominent," I said.

"Eddie, you can't!" said Diana.

"Pretty sure I can," I said.

"Sounds good to me," said Molly.

Diana stepped forward to look right into my face. Her gaze was cold, her voice flat. "It's in your file, Eddie. That you always said you were an agent, not an assassin."

"Yes," I said. "Even now, after everything that's happened, I still believe that. But sometimes you have to do something bad to prevent something worse. I have to put the fear of Drood into my enemies to keep them off my back while I get my family safely home again. You heard the little shit; they're all out there, watching, waiting for me to show some sign of weakness. They think if they can drag me down, they can put an end to the Droods forever. And they might just be right. I'm the last hope my lost family has. If his severed head will hold them off, buy me some time . . ."

Diana was already shaking her head fiercely. "This isn't the Eddie Drood I heard so much about. The man whose career I followed for so long. The man I wanted so much to meet . . ."

"Oh, my God," said Molly. "She's a fan. . . ."

"Please, Eddie," said Diana, staring earnestly into my face mask. "Don't do this. There are other ways. . . ."

"Such as?" said Molly.

"Hand him over to me," Diana said steadily. "I'll deliver him safely to the Regent, and he'll hand the Immortal over to the Hush Squad. Those telepaths could get answers out of a stone. He'll tell them everything he knows about everyone he's met, and what they're planning. . . ."

"No!" said the Immortal. "No! You're not handing me over to them!"

He produced an oversized pocket watch from somewhere and cranked the handle quickly. The Time Distorter. He thrust his hand forward, aiming the thing right at me, and a huge blast of time energy shot out of the watch, shimmering in the air with a hundred different possibilities. Like a distorting heat haze generating glimpses of a hundred alternate Futures. The time energies hit my armour and immediately rebounded, unable to get a grip. They blasted right back at the Immortal and sank into him, suffusing his Immortal cell structure with concentrated temporal energies. And just like that, he began to age.

He became a young man and a middle-aged man and then an old man, all in the space of a few moments. The Immortal raised a shaking wrinkled hand in front of his sunken face and let out a low, sick cry of horror. Because the one thing Immortals can never do is age. They can change their shape to any appearance, young or old, but always with the knowledge that they can change it back again. They can die, but always as a teenager. It's the way they're built. Or cursed, depending on how you look at it. Either way, enforced aging was a hideous thing for an Immortal.

He threw the Time Distorter on the floor and stamped on it, but it didn't break and it didn't change the way he looked.

He glared at me with his old, shrivelled face, and for the first time there was something else in his eyes apart from hatred. He turned away, grabbed the nearest gun, put it to his head and pulled the trigger. The whole back of his head blew away, spattering across the window. His body slumped to the floor and lay still. The gunmen stared at him silently. Some of them had blood and brains on them, but none of them wanted to be noticed just then.

"This is the second time that's happened to me today," I said. "I wish I could say I'm getting used to it."

"Damned fool!" said Diana. "They wouldn't have hurt him at Hush; that's the whole point. . . ." She broke off, unable to continue.

"He didn't want to betray his family," I said. "I can understand that."

"He knew something he didn't want us to know," said Molly. "Probably something really unpleasant that the rest of your enemies are planning, Eddie. Something really bad, to be worth dying over."

"What do we do now?" said Diana.

"We cut off the Immortal's head and stick it on a spike and leave it somewhere prominent," I said. "Or, at least, what's left of his head. Waste not, want not."

"You're serious," said Diana, looking at me like she'd never seen me before. "You're really serious."

"Of course," said Molly. "You heard the scumbag; something bad is coming. We need to send them a hard message, now more than ever. Throw a real scare into them. They won't know he shot himself."

Diana shook her head slowly. "I'd forgotten how cold Droods can be."

She turned her back on Molly and me, walked into a shadow and was gone.

Molly looked out the side windows of the bus. "Traffic's started up again. The Time Distorter must have broken when it went up against your armour."

"The Immortal threw his pocket watch on the floor," I said. "But . . . I don't see it anywhere."

"I'll bet you Diana took it with her," said Molly. "You heard Patrick in the Armoury: The Regent's agents are always picking up useful items and taking them home."

"The Regent will send more agents to look after this lot," I said, glaring about me at the assorted gunmen. "So stay put, all of you. Don't make me come after you."

There was much general nodding and mutterings of complete agreement.

"We need to get out of here," said Molly. "Before someone official turns up and starts asking questions. I'm really not in the mood to deal with official questions."

"Right," I said. I looked at the dead Immortal. "You know, I'm really not in the mood to do the whole severed-head thing. I'm just not angry enough anymore. Let his body send the message."

Molly glared quickly about her. "All right, everyone. Listen up! Do not take this as a sign that we're getting soft! None of you are to leave this bus until the nice agents from the Regent of Shadows arrive to take care of you! Anyone tries to do a runner, we will find out and we will track you down and perform acts of massive unpleasantness on you! Any questions?"

A surly-looking gunman raised a hand, and Molly punched him in the head so hard that everyone around him winced in sympathy.

"Any other questions?" Molly said sweetly. "I love answering questions."

I armoured down, and we got off the bus and strode unhurriedly back to the Plymouth Fury, ignoring the screeching of brakes and hooting of horns from the resumed traffic. First rule of being a pedestrian in London: Never let the traffic intimidate you. I opened the driver's door and then paused.

"Diana's probably making a report on us to the Regent right now," I said. "She seemed . . . disappointed in me."

"She doesn't know you like I do," said Molly. "And, anyway, why should you care what she thinks about you?"

"I don't know," I said. "I shouldn't care, but I do. She . . . reminds me of someone."

I shrugged quickly, slipped into the driver's seat and settled myself comfortably behind the steering wheel, and then slammed the door shut. The sat nav immediately raised its strident female voice again.

"Don't slam the door! You'll damage something! And can I remind you that you're supposed to be looking after me? The Regent made me your responsibility! What were you thinking of, letting me be shot at like that? I'm a classic!"

I looked at the sat nav thoughtfully. "Are you speaking for the car, or are you the voice of the car itself?"

"I'll never tell!" the sat nav said smugly.

"Is there any way to turn that thing off?" said Molly as she settled into the passenger's seat beside me and deliberately slammed her door shut.

"Is there any way to turn you off?" said the sat nav.

"Shall I go back to the bus and get a gun?" said Molly. "Or perhaps a really big hammer?"

"You wouldn't dare!" said the sat nav. "I'm a loaner!"

"I know something that'll shut it up," I said.

I took the Merlin Glass out of its pocket dimension and fed it the revised time and space coordinates for Crow Lee's place through my torc. The Glass jumped out of my hand, ghosted straight through the Plymouth's windscreen, and shot forward to hover in the air ahead of us. It grew quickly in size until it was more than big enough for the Plymouth to drive through. On the other side of the opened doorway, I could just make out a leafy country lane. The sunlight there was subtly different. It felt odd to know I was looking at tomorrow.

"What is that?" said the sat nav nervously. "What the hell is *that*? I don't like it. Just looking at it makes me feel funny."

"No one else is paying any attention to the big dimensional door hanging in midair," said Molly, peering quickly about her. "The Glass is pumping out a really heavy-duty, don't-look-at-me aversion field. I didn't know the Merlin Glass could do that. Could the old Merlin Glass do that?"

"Beats the hell out of me," I said. "But this new version is certainly keen to show off all the clever tricks it can do. Very eager to please . . ."

"Do you find that as worrying as I do?" said Molly.

"Oh, at least," I said.

"What? What?" said the sat nav. "What do you mean, *worrying*? What is there to worry about? Okay, forget it! I'm not going anywhere!"

"Oh yes, you are," I said.

"Heh heh," added Molly.

I fired up the Plymouth's engine, set the car rolling forward and aimed her right at the Merlin Glass hovering before us. The sat nav made loud whining noises of distress. I put my foot down hard and drove the Plymouth Fury through the gateway and into tomorrow.

CHAPTER NINE

Facing Evil

don't know what all the fuss is about over time travel. I drove through twenty-four hours in a moment, and didn't feel the slightest twinge of time sickness. From the city to the countryside, from today to tomorrow in one great jump. Though I couldn't quite decide whether I'd lost a day or gained one. Molly took it all in stride, of course, as she does most things that don't involve incest, morris dancing or eighties revivals. The sat nav stopped screaming as soon as we left the Merlin Glass behind, and quickly subsided to low whimpering sounds and muttered swear words.

"Please don't ever do that to me again," the sat nav said piteously. "I'll be good!"

"I'd settle for you being quiet," said Molly.

The Merlin Glass shrank down behind us, shaking itself down to hand-mirror size, and then hurried after the car, shooting down the road to ghost through the rear window and slip straight into my pocket dimension. Without being asked.

"All right," I said loudly. "You're showing off now."

I eased the car to a halt and looked carefully about me. Molly actually undid her seat belt to give her more freedom to twist back and forth and look in all possible directions. There was a definite sense of tension, of both of us waiting for something to happen, for some unpleasant reaction to our sudden arrival . . . some sign that Crow Lee had people lying in wait for us. But everything was still and calm and peaceful. It was just a narrow country lane in the middle of nowhere. On the other hand, there was no sign of Crow Lee's manor house anywhere.

We were completely alone, with no sign of civilisation for as far as the eye could see. Birds were singing, there was a quiet background hum of insects; just quiet early evening in the countryside. Bounding the road on either side were low stone walls assembled in the traditional style, jagged stones placed tight together without benefit of mortar. Beyond the walls, great open fields stretched away, a massive chequer board of clashing primary colours from assorted crops. Separated here and there by more old walls, bristling hedgerows and the occasional line of trees on the horizon acting as a windbreak. No cows, no sheep, no other roads; not even a signpost to tell us where we were or other places might be.

"Are you sure we've come to the right place?" said Molly.

"I suppose . . . this is as close as the Merlin Glass could get us to the exact coordinates," I said. "Without setting off Crow Lee's alarms . . . I did instruct the Glass to err very much on the side of caution."

"All right, sat nav," said Molly. "Make yourself useful. Which way to Crow Lee's lair?"

"Oh, now you need me!" the sat nav said bitterly. "Well, tough. I don't feel like it. I've just been put through a terrible experience and my nerves are a mess. Call back later and see if I'm home."

"Give me the proper directions," I said, "or I'll open up the Merlin Glass again and see if it can jump us any closer."

"Bully!" hissed the sat nav. "All right, all right. Let me see. . . . I've got a map here somewhere. . . . Ah. Yes. Drive straight on, third turn on the left, and then watch for the hidden entrance. Which I shall alert you to the moment I can find the bloody thing. Or maybe not! It all depends on how I feel, and don't you forget it."

"See how easy that was?" I said.

"You wait," said Molly. "That thing will be driving us down a crease in the map before you know it."

"I heard that!"

"Good!" said Molly.

The sat nav made a loud sarcastic noise and then settled for something that sounded very like teeth grinding together.

I drove carefully down the long leafy lane, in and out dark shadows cast by out-leaning trees, and slowed cautiously as I approached every corner, just in case there might be something lying in wait. But there wasn't so much as a slow-moving piece of farm machinery. No traffic at all, in fact; not a jogger on a health kick or some exercise fiend hunched over a bicycle. It was as though we had the whole road to ourselves.

"Where is everybody?" I said after a while. "Did the world come to an end during the twenty-four hours we just jumped?"

"Don't say that!" the sat nav said immediately. "Never give the universe ideas; it can be malevolent enough as it is."

"You really are paranoid, aren't you?" said Molly.

"I knew you were going to say that," muttered the sat nav.

"I think Crow Lee just likes his privacy," I said. "Probably pays everyone to stay well away from his lair—good word, that, Molly—and use other roads that don't go anywhere near his place. And if he really does have his own private army, he can probably put the hard word on anyone who doesn't feel like cooperating. I doubt if Crow Lee's actually told them he's the Most Evil Man in the World, but the locals must have got the idea by now. Crow Lee has never been the sort to hide his awful light under a bushel."

"What is a bushel?" said the sat nav.

"A dry measure containing eight gallons or four pecks," said Molly, just a bit unexpectedly.

"I'm glad one of us knew that," I said. "I'd hate for us to be outsmarted by a sat nav."

"Turn left now!" screamed the sat nav. "Now! Right now!"

I glimpsed the disguised turn just in time and hauled the steering wheel over. The Plymouth Fury turned smoothly into the narrow opening, hardly slowing at all. The new road was only just wide enough for one car to drive down at a time, and I quickly decided that if we met anyone coming our way they'd better be really good at reversing. The road was bounded on both sides by high hedgerows blocking out most of the light. It was as though we'd gone straight from midday to twilight. I made myself relax, unclenching my hands from the wheel.

"Nice driving," said Molly, staring straight ahead.

"I thought so," I said.

"Hah!" said the sat nav cuttingly.

"A little advance warning would have been helpful," I said loudly. "Whatever happened to, *In a hundred yards you will come to . . . ?*"

"Not my fault," the sat nav said with a sniff. "That hidden entrance would have been invisible to your eyes, entirely undetectable. We wouldn't have found it except for my highly trained sensors. And even I couldn't see it till I was right on top of it. In fact, I'm not sure that entrance is really there all the time, unless you know where to look. . . ."

"He stole that idea from the Droods," I said.

"Well," said Molly. "At least we can be fairly certain we've come to the right place. At last."

"Oh, ye of little faith," said the sat nav. "Wait till I'm in charge around here, and then you'll see some smiting."

I slowed the car right down, making my way cautiously along the narrow winding way. There were too many blind corners, too little good light and far too many dark shadows for my liking. It was like driving out of the day and into the night, with the surety of bad dreams ahead. This was a private road, part of Crow Lee's private world, and like everything else he owned, he'd put his stamp on it. The dark greenery of the high hedgerows seemed to stir slowly, right on the edge of my vision, only to fall still again the moment I looked at it directly.

We rounded a final long sweeping corner and I hit the brakes hard as the road ended in a set of heavy black iron gates. They blocked the road completely from side to side, and gave every appearance of being very definitely locked. I couldn't see any chains or padlocks, but I had no doubt there were other, more dangerous, protections in place. I tapped my fingertips thoughtfully on the steering wheel while I considered my next move.

"Have you noticed . . . ?" said Molly. "All the natural sounds have stopped. The birds aren't singing here."

"Do you blame them?" I said. "In a place like this? Do you feel like singing?"

"Don't you get snappy with me, Eddie Drood!"

"I never get asked to sing," the sat nav said sadly.

"Well, colour me surprised," said Molly.

"I do a great Bruce Springsteen!"

"Hush, children," I said. "Daddy's thinking. . . ."

The more I looked over the tall iron gates, the less I liked them. Long, vertical, parallel bars painted black as sin, and overlaid on them a stylised figure of a huge dragon. With great fangs and claws and sweeping wings, its outline stretched across both gates.

"I think we're looking at the first layer of protection," I said. "At the first sign of trouble, that dragon shape probably comes to life and goes all flamethrower on whoever's calling. Or maybe . . . this was a real dragon once, and Crow Lee trapped it in this form to be his own personal attack dog."

"No," Molly said immediately. "I'd See that if it were there. It's just a gate. Nice workmanship, though."

"Spend enough time tracking down crazy in the head villains, and you end up thinking like them," I said. "Those gates do look very thoroughly locked. I suppose I could just reverse, build up some speed, and crash right through them."

"Don't you dare!" said the sat nav. "You'll scratch my paintwork and dent my grille!"

"You say that like it's a bad thing," Molly said sweetly.

"Philistines!" howled the sat nav. "There will be a reckoning. Oh yes . . ."

"The gates are bound to be reinforced," I said reluctantly. "And this is a loaner from the Regent. . . ."

I turned off the engine and got out. Molly was quickly out of her seat, too, and we moved forward together to study the tall iron gates, while being very careful to maintain a respectful distance. I raised my Sight and had to fight down the urge to retreat several steps in a hurry. Layer upon layer of protections hung in the air: protective screens and force shields, magic and science combining to create a defence greater than the sum of its parts. They crawled slowly over one another, glowing with the kind of attenuated soft colours you find sliding across the surface of soap bubbles. Only more dangerous. There were enough defensive energies stored in the shields to rule out any thought of defusing them. Get one step wrong and the resulting blast would wipe out half the surrounding countryside.

"Told you," I said.

Molly gave me a thoughtful look. "It's really up to you, Eddie. You can stop being Mr. Snotty, or I can punch you somewhere painful."

"The gates are electrified," I said, staring straight ahead. "Touch any of those bars and there wouldn't be enough left of you to bury."

"I had noticed that, thank you," said Molly.

"Would you like me to reverse some distance back down the road?" said the sat nav. "Suddenly I don't feel as safe as I did a moment ago."

I looked back at the Plymouth Fury. "You can drive yourself?"

"Damn right, I can. In emergencies. Which this is looking more and more like, all the time."

"You stay where you are," I said sternly.

Molly peered past the gates at the grounds beyond. "There are two really high stone walls leading off from the gates to surround the grounds. We could climb over . . . Ah. No, we couldn't. More protections."

"Touch any part of those walls, and the built-in destructive energies would scatter you across several counties," I said. "In fact, don't even look at them funny."

Molly scowled. "Why couldn't he just settle for barbed wire and broken glass, like anyone else?"

"Because he's the Most Evil . . ."

"Hell with it," said Molly. "Let's go in through the Merlin Glass.

This short a jump; the Glass should be able to punch right through the protections."

"Given that Crow Lee has to have been contemplating that very possibility for some time," I said, "I think not. He could interrupt our journey and send us somewhere else. Or just hold us there, trapped between places, forever."

"Yeah . . ." said Molly. "That's what I'd do. So, how are we going to get in?"

"Simple," I said.

I armoured up, took Molly in my arms and jumped right over the tall iron gates. We soared easily over them, my golden feet coming nowhere near the black iron, and then I dropped down into the wide-open grounds beyond. Behind us, the sat nav called miserably after us.

"Don't leave me here on my own! Bastards! I'll tell the Regent on you!"

I landed on the far side of the gates, my armoured legs absorbing the impact. Though the landing did drive my feet a good three or four inches into the rich green grass. I straightened up and put Molly down. She immediately stamped away from me, brushing fiercely at her dress, and glared about her, ready for action. I took a good look around, but there was no one there. It appeared we had the grounds all to ourselves. I armoured down and tugged my feet carefully out of the depressions I'd made. Molly glared at me.

"Next time, a little warning!"

"You might have said no," I pointed out reasonably. "And, besides, you're always telling me I need to be more spontaneous."

We took our time looking around us, checking out the pleasant open grounds surrounding Crow Lee's old-fashioned manor house. Huge lawns, massive flower beds with neatly regimented rows of colour and a whole zoo of hedge sculptures of fantastic animals. Rearing unicorns with flailing hooves and vicious horns, manticores with roaring lions' heads and stingers on the tails, giant killer apes beating at their massive chests, and a huge tyrannosaurus towering over all the others, its great wedge head full of spiky green teeth.

"Really don't care for hedge animals," I said. "They're not moving now, but they've got that look about them . . . especially the *T. rex*."

"Far too obvious," said Molly. "Probably just a distraction to keep us from noticing the real threat."

"I know a real threat when I see one, and I am looking at one right now," I said firmly. "I don't suppose you thought to bring any weed killer?"

"Why is it always my job to think of things like that?"

"Because you're the practical one. Or so you keep telling me."

"Look at the size of that greenhouse," said Molly, pointing off to one side. "What have they got in there—their own private jungle?"

I looked where she was pointing, and she was right. I'd never seen a greenhouse that big. It was packed full of strange and wondrous plants, thrashing and beating against the insides of the glass panels. Massive flowers with thick pulpy petals that opened and closed as though shouting green threats at us, while thorns like knitting needles stabbed wildly at everything around them. The colours were rich and overpowering, almost hypnotic in their intensity.

"Let's not go in there," I said.

Molly sniffed. "You never give me flowers."

Scattered across the wide-open lawns were any number of large abstract sculptures, all holes and curves and sudden turns. The shapes seemed to shift and change subtly when you weren't looking at them directly. None of the shapes made any obvious sense, but still somehow gave the impression that they might, if you stared at them long enough. And got close enough . . . I didn't think I would.

Molly and I wandered through the grounds, taking our time. No one had arrived to challenge our right to be there. There was just the one great fountain in the midst of everything: a tall statue of a young woman fashioned from some old dark stone, endlessly screaming, arms outstretched, as though pleading for help that never came. Discoloured water poured from her distorted mouth, falling into a great circular pond full of murky water in which very large fish darted back and forth. Molly and I strolled over to peer into the pond.

"Piranha," said Molly.

"What else would you expect in a place like this?" I said. "Koi?"

Molly ignored me, leaning forward for a better look. A piranha the size of my fist jumped right up out of the water and flashed through the air, heading straight for Molly's face with an open mouth stuffed full of jagged teeth. Molly barely had time to react before I armoured up my hand, snatched the flying fish out of midair, and crushed it in my golden gauntlet. It never got anywhere near Molly's face. Pulped fish guts squeezed between my golden fingers as I ground the nasty thing in my fist, just to make sure, and then I opened my hand and shook off the mess. It fell back into the pond, whose waters became briefly very agitated as the other piranha fought one another over the fresh food. I pulled the armour back into my torc.

"Nice reaction time," said Molly, stepping carefully back from the pool.

"I thought so," I said modestly.

"I would have stopped it in time," said Molly. "I was never in any real danger. But it's nice to know you're paying attention."

"Anytime," I said.

And then, because we'd looked at everything else, we turned and looked across the great open lawns at Crow Lee's manor house. It looked very nice. A pleasant and peaceful old-fashioned stone house with a half-timbered front and a sloping grey-tiled roof. Ivy on the walls; flowers round the door. The kind of thing you see on jigsaw-puzzle box covers. It looked cosy and comfortable, the only slightly off note being the closed curtains at every window, so you couldn't see in. The front door was very firmly closed.

"I can't believe the Most Evil Man in the World lives in a cosy nook like this," I said finally. "Are you sure we're not looking at some kind of illusion?"

Molly shook her head immediately. "I already checked it out with my Sight. It's just a house. I can't See inside, though; there are some heavy-duty privacy spells in place. Hello. I spy movement."

From every side, dark figures were appearing out of nowhere. Armed guards came running across the lawns at us, from every direction at once. Professional-looking mercenary soldiers in bluff uniforms, all of them very heavily armed. They moved quickly to surround us, cutting us off from any possible exit. I had to smile. Like we had any intention of going anywhere . . .

"Fun time!" I said loudly.

"That's usually my line," said Molly.

The mercenary soldiers took up their positions in silence, levelling weapons on us from every side. They didn't call out to us to stand still or raise our hands or surrender. Which sort of suggested they weren't that interested in taking prisoners. There were a hell of a lot of them, armed to the teeth, clearly expecting a fight. So it seemed a shame to disappoint them. . . . I armoured up, the golden metal flowing all over me in a moment. My armour glowed brightly in the early-evening light, and there were startled gasps and muttered blasphemies all around me. Some of the younger soldiers just froze where they were, eyes wide and mouths slack, as they got their first good look at a Drood in his armour. But others pressed forward, guns at the ready, so I went swiftly forward to meet them. Molly was right there with me, sorcerous energies spitting and crackling in the air around her fists.

"If they had any sense, they'd run," I said loudly. "Even a professional soldier should have more sense than to go up against Drood armour."

"They don't look all that impressed," said Molly.

"They're about to be," I said. "Suddenly and violently and all over the place."

The soldiers looked at me and at Molly, and decided Molly was the easier target because she didn't have any armour. They all opened fire at once, the roar of gunfire shockingly loud in the quiet. I moved automatically to stand between Molly and the soldiers, and the bullets ricocheted harmlessly away from my armour, flying this way and that, making some soldiers duck frantically, and chewing up a nearby hedge sculpture of a giant boar. Its curving tusks were shot away in a moment, and its shaggy head just exploded. It did occur to me that if I'd been wearing my usual strange-matter armour, it would have absorbed all the bullets rather than let them prove a danger to innocent bystanders. But I was wearing Moxton's Mistake, and the rogue armour didn't care. And, besides, there were no innocent bystanders on the grounds of Crow Lee's house.

Molly shouldered me aside. "How many times do I have to tell you, Eddie Drood, that I am quite capable of looking after myself?"

She strode deliberately into the hail of bullets. All the soldiers were firing at us now, the roar of automatic weaponry deafening at such close range. Molly had a protective screen firmly in place that gathered up all the bullets that came at her and held them in midair, hovering before her. One by one the soldiers stopped firing, lowered their weapons and just stood there, looking at her in a dazed and demoralised sort of way. Molly snapped her fingers once and all the bullets dropped out of the air to bounce lightly on the grass at her feet.

And while the mercenary soldiers were coping with that, Molly raised her hands in the stance of summoning, forced out a few really nasty Words, and a great storm wind rose out of nowhere and came sweeping across the open lawns, howling and buffeting and blasting through anything that got in its way. It picked up the soldiers and threw them about like an angry child. They went flying this way and that, tumbling end over end before crashing to earth again some distance away. The roaring wind picked up the abstract sculptures and smashed them against one another, uprooting the smaller hedge creatures and sending them bobbing and tumbling across the lawns. Molly brought her arms down sharply, and the wind broke off abruptly.

Half a dozen soldiers had dug in, hanging on to the heavier statues. Molly snapped her fingers briskly and lightning bolts stabbed down to incinerate the mercenaries. Black smoke and the smell of roast pork carried across the grounds on a gusting breeze. Molly turned to look at me.

"Are you going to give me a hard time over killing a few professional soldiers who were quite definitely prepared to kill you and me?"

"No," I said.

"Ah . . ." said Molly. "You know, I had a response ready for pretty much everything except that. Are you sure you're not upset?"

"No," I said. "They weren't interested in taking prisoners, and neither am I. Every one of these mercenary bastards gave up all their human rights when they signed on to work for the Most Evil Man in the World. They're standing between me and the rescue of my lost family. Kill them all and let the Devil sort them out."

"This isn't like you, Eddie," said Molly.

"I never had my whole family taken away before," I said.

Molly looked like she wanted to say something else, but a whole new army of mercenary soldiers suddenly appeared out of nowhere, just blinking into existence in large groups all around us. Molly and I moved quickly to stand back-to-back. It was the same professional types in the same bluff uniforms, but this time much better armed. They had glowing swords and axes, shining bitterly with dangerous energies; Hands of Glory with sulphur-yellow flames dancing at the end of waxed fingers; even a few elven wands. Though given how gingerly their owners were handling them, the wands clearly hadn't come with an instruction manual. I almost felt sorry for the poor bastards holding them. Elves live to screw humans over, and they never sell anything they don't booby-trap first. Their sense of humour . . . isn't ours.

The soldiers carrying glowing axes and swords advanced on me, and I went cheerfully forward to meet them. The heavy blades smashed and shattered against my armour, and the metal pieces stopped glowing before they even hit the grass. I didn't feel a thing, and my armour wasn't even scratched. On the few occasions where the blades just rebounded, I snatched the weapons out of their shocked owners' hands and broke them in two with my golden gauntlets.

They retreated rapidly, and a soldier stepped forward holding his blazing Hand of Glory out before him. A Hand of Glory can uncover any secret, open any lock, take command of any magic. The soldier tried to use the Hand's power to take control of my armour away from me and force it back into my torc. To leave me revealed and vulnerable. But mine was a Drood torc, and more than a match for a dead man's hand with candles for fingers. The magic rebounded, all the yellow flames blew out in a moment and the Hand just withered and closed in on itself, forced into a harmless fist. The soldier shook the dead Hand hard a few times, like that was going to help, and then fell quickly back to hide behind some other soldiers.

The two soldiers with elven wands stepped forward to take his place, stabbing the wands at me while shouting something in badly accented elvish. Massive energies blasted me, burning so brightly in the space between us that my mask had to shut itself down for a moment to protect my eyes. I stood my ground in the dark, untouched and untouchable inside my armour, until the attack was over. My mask cleared, I looked around and discovered I was standing in a large circle of dead grass, surrounded by burning hedge creatures and shattered statues. I let the two soldiers with wands take a good look at all the destruction they'd caused and then at me, completely untouched; then I started purposefully towards them. They threw away their wands and turned and ran, and I let them go.

Next up were a whole bunch of soldiers with futuristic high-energy weapons. You can get your hands on anything these days, if you know where to look. The soldiers hosed me down with all kinds of energy beams, some so powerful they left sparkling trails in the air behind them, but they still washed harmlessly over my armour. One bounced off and set fire to a hedge sculpture of a towering minotaur. It burnt fiercely, but didn't move in the least, for which I was quietly grateful. Other soldiers hit me with sub- and supersonic frequencies, and I just stood there and let them do it, until they got a bit upset and gave up.

I waited patiently while the soldiers shut down their various weapons and had a quiet but agitated discussion. I was fascinated to see what they'd do. Their next effort turned out to be a remote-control teleport device, which did its very best to send me somewhere else. But the process couldn't get a hold on my armour, so it bounced back and sent the device's owner somewhere else. Given the man's brief anticipatory scream before he disappeared, I had to assume that wherever he'd intended to send me, it hadn't been anywhere nice.

I looked across at Molly. Soldiers were surrounding her from a distance, and using exotic tech weapons to form a cage of pulsing energies around her. Molly calmly took off the spangly earrings Patrick the Armourer had given her, primed them with a muttered Word and tossed them casually between the energy bars of her cage. Both earrings exploded noisily, generating big black clouds of smoke, through which soldiers were thrown screaming with their uniforms on fire. Surprised and caught off guard, most of the soldiers maintaining the cage were blown away in a moment, and the energy bars just collapsed. Molly stepped casually out of the fading trap and looked happily about her. The black smoke cleared to reveal two large charred craters in the lawns, and quite a lot of dazed and damaged mercenary soldiers. Half the soldiers who'd been standing there threatening her weren't standing there anymore, and the rest were retreating for safer ground at quite a pace.

More soldiers pressed forward, grim faced and determined, carrying a variety of impressive-looking weapons. Molly smiled and produced a flat box with a single button on the top. I winced just a bit as I recognised it. The protein exploder. Molly pointed the box at the soldiers advancing on her and pressed the button, and most of the soldiers just disappeared. A great cloud of pink mist rolled slowly through the air while bones clattered quietly to the grassy lawn.

The surviving soldiers turned and ran, scattering across the grounds, presumably in the hope it would make them harder to hit. Molly picked them off with the box, one at a time, smiling reflectively. Her sharpshooting skills were improving.

With Crow Lee's private army either dead or deserting, the grounds themselves took up the fight. Massive robotic guns rose from inside hidden bunkers, straight up through the flower displays, long barrels moving quickly to target Molly and me. I pointed an accusing golden finger at the gun positions.

"That's another thing he stole from my family!"

All the robotic guns opened fire at once, pumping out bullets at a rapid rate of fire, raking me from head to foot. There was enough firepower to punch a hole through steel plating, but it was still no match for my armour. I walked deliberately forward into the bullets and then moved from one gun position to the next, ripping the robotic guns out of their housing and throwing them aside. Not because they posed me any real threat, but because I was getting really tired of being shot at. I wanted to make a point.

And then, of course, inevitably, the remaining hedge creatures all came to life and closed in on me. I'd been expecting it all along, but it was still an eerie and disturbing spectacle as the heavy green sculptures ripped their rooted feet out of the ground and turned their blind green heads to look at me. The *T. rex*'s massive jaws opened wide in a silent roar of rage.

"I knew it!" I called across to Molly. "Never trust hedge sculptures!"

"Ugly bloody things, anyway," said Molly.

She said a Word and snapped her fingers, and just like that, all the moving hedge creatures burst into flames. Fires roared up from inside their green bodies, consuming them in moments. They lurched this way and that, sweeping their burning heads back and forth as though they could leave the flames behind. They banged into each other and fought briefly before finally collapsing to burn listlessly in awkward poses. Molly and I had to keep moving, darting this way and that to stay out of their way, but none of them got anywhere near us. We laughed breathlessly as we dodged the burning shapes. And soon enough they were all down and lying still, little bursts of flames still jerking through them, sending sweet-smelling smoke up into the early-evening sky. Molly and I stood together, looking happily around us. The whole grounds had become one big battlefield, with fires and craters and dead and broken bodies to every side.

"Wherever we go," I said, "we make an impression."

"They started it," said Molly.

The sniper hidden in the row of trees at the other end of the grounds chose that moment to open fire on Molly. And, amazingly, the bullet punched right through all her protective fields, one by one. I didn't even realise what was happening at first. I heard the gunshot, of course, but by then the bullet had already reached Molly and been stopped by her automatic protective shield. The bullet was held there in midair for a moment, and then it forced its way through the shield, only to be stopped by the next. Long ago Molly had preprogrammed her defences, a series of varying shields just waiting to be activated. But even so, it was a shock to see a bullet smash through one shield after another, hanging on the air before her face, inching inexorably towards her left eye. The last screen finally stopped it, just short of her eye, and the bullet hung there, snarling and biting at the invisible shield like a living thing, and then Molly's left hand came up and snatched the bullet out of midair. She held the bullet in her closed fist, glowering as it forced her hand back and forth, still fighting to break free.

"It's a biting bullet," she said. "Made from the bone of an uncaught murderer, created to chew through anything that stands between it and its target."

The ugly thing buzzed and growled inside her hand, shaking her hand viciously through sheer brute force. I saw Molly wince as it tried to eat its way through her hand. I started forward, ready to take and hold it in my golden gauntlet, but Molly stopped me with a look. She closed her other hand around her fist, concentrated, and then clamped down hard. There was the sound of bone cracking and breaking, and the bullet fell silent. She opened her hand, and tiny fragments of bone fell out.

"Nasty thing," said Molly. "Now, where is that sniper? And why hasn't he opened fire again?"

"I think he's been watching to see what would happen," I said. "And if he's got any sense, he's currently sprinting for the nearest horizon."

"It came from that row of trees," said Molly. "And he's still there. The idiot."

She strode determinedly towards the trees. I yelled after her, but I knew I was wasting my breath. The sniper fired again, but this time Molly was ready for him. She gestured dismissively, and the biting bullet exploded in midair, less than halfway towards her. Through my face mask I focused on the sniper, and saw him take a third bullet from a heavily reinforced box and fit it carefully into his rifle. He didn't look pressed or hurried, just very professional. He fired again, but this time the bullet had barely left the barrel before it exploded.

Molly crossed the remaining ground at speed and hurled herself on the sniper while he was still trying to load another bullet. He tried to bring the rifle to bear as she loomed over him, but she just grabbed the rifle out of his hands with one swift movement, turned it around, and shot the sniper with his own gun. The biting bullet hit him square in the left eye, even though that wasn't where Molly had aimed. The things must come preprogrammed. The impact sent the sniper flying backwards, and he crashed to the ground, dead. But he didn't lie still. His dead head whipped back and forth as the bullet raged this way and that inside, eating up everything it found there. Whoever designed the bullets had been determined that whoever was shot by one would not recover. The head's movements grew fainter and fainter, until finally the bullet was still, satisfied. Molly looked down at the dead sniper, studying him expressionlessly, and then threw the rifle aside.

And while she was preoccupied, one of the trees beside her threw off its disguising illusion and became a mercenary soldier.

He hit Molly round the back of the head with a heavy wooden staff, and she dropped to her knees. She cried out briefly. I ran forward, but I could tell I wasn't going to get there in time. I'd let her get too far ahead. I'd just strolled along after her because I was sure she could handle the situation. More soldiers appeared out of nowhere, running forward to block my way. I ploughed into them, throwing their broken bodies aside. Molly needed me. I could hear the soldier who'd hit her talking to her. He didn't even bother to look in my direction.

"Major Tim Browten at your service, dear Miss Metcalf. The wild witch herself . . . Sorry to have to come at you so ungallantly from ambush, but I'm not stupid. This staff in my hand, this very old item that just struck you down so easily and so completely, is the Witch's Hammer of Matthew Hopkins, witch finder. Just one blow with this blessed wood is all it takes to rob a witch of her powers for a time. Now, you be a good little girl and just lie there, and let me kill you quickly and efficiently. So much better for both of us, eh? You'll only make it worse for yourself if you struggle."

I was still fighting through a growing crowd of soldiers. They were throwing everything they had at me just to slow me down.

I saw Molly try to get up, anyway, and the major hit her again, slamming the heavy wood into the side of her head with calm efficiency. I heard her cry out again. I heard the sound the staff made as it hit her head. I saw the blood leap from her torn scalp and rush down one side of her face. Molly went down on one knee, staring dazedly at the grass before her as it turned red with her blood. And then she forced her face up again to glare at Major Browten.

"Don't embarrass yourself, Miss Metcalf," he said calmly. "You have no magic now, remember? I took it all away with my Witch's Hammer."

"I'll see your Witch's Hammer, you son of a bitch," said Molly. "And raise you a protein exploder."

She brought up the small box in a steady hand and pointed it at his groin at point-blank range. She hit the button, and I swear I actually saw the major's testicles explode in slow motion. He sank heavily to his knees before Molly, and clutched desperately at the gaping wound between his thighs, blood spurting thickly past his hands. Molly looked at him with her bloody face and then put the protein exploder away. She forced herself back up onto her feet, now with the Witch's Hammer in her hands. She hit Major Browten over the head with it, a blow so hard the staff broke in two. The major fell forward, dead before he hit the ground. Molly laughed at him breathlessly and threw the broken pieces of the staff aside.

I'd finally fought my way through the last soldiers and caught up to Molly. I was reaching out to her to make sure she was all right when another tree dropped its disguise, to become another mercenary soldier. Molly and I both turned to confront him, and then stopped abruptly as we saw what he was holding. It was a monkey's paw made over into a Hand of Glory. Very illegal, very dangerous, completely bloody foolhardy. In some countries you can still be executed just for admitting you've heard of such a thing. The flames rising from the tiny wrinkled fingers were bloodred and didn't tremble at all. Molly and I stood very still. A monkey's paw is hideously dangerous in its own right, able to alter reality itself. But to add to that the gifts and power of a Hand of Glory? That's like deciding a thermonuclear device isn't dangerous enough and giving it leprosy. The soldier smiled at us and waggled the monkey's hand in our faces.

"You don't need to use that," Molly said carefully. "Throw it away. You risk damning your soul just by holding such a thing."

"I'm a professional soldier," the mercenary said easily. "Major Mike Michaels. To a soldier, a weapon is just a weapon; they're all just killing tools at the end of the day. Now, armour down, Drood. Make that nasty metal suit disappear, or I'll have the monkey's hand do something really nasty to your girlfriend."

I pulled my armour back into my torc, and the mercenary soldier watched, fascinated, as the gold vanished and I appeared. I stood stiffly beside Molly. Blood was still dripping steadily off one side of her face. I wanted to hold her, but I didn't dare move while Major Michaels was watching me so closely. He wanted an excuse to use the hand. I could tell. I felt naked and very vulnerable without my armour. I could feel it stirring resentfully inside my torc, disturbed by the power it sensed in the monkey's hand. Moxton's Mistake might or might not have been able to withstand the power contained in that nasty little object, but I couldn't risk finding out while Molly was still in danger. The Witch's Hammer had taken her magic, but the staff was broken now. So did she have her magic back? She wasn't doing anything. I had no choice but to play along, and hope I could find a way out of this mess.

Major Michaels held up the monkey's hand so Molly could see it clearly. "Give me that trinket you're wearing round your throat, Miss Metcalf. The ruby pendant."

Molly reached up slowly, removed the Twilight Teardrop's chain from around her neck, and handed it over. Either because the monkey's hand was affecting her, or because she had no power left to deny him what he wanted. The moment the pendant left her hand, she swayed and almost fell, as though the last of her strength had gone out of her. Without the Twilight Teardrop to power her magic, she was as helpless . . . as I was. The major smiled, and what I saw in that man's face as he looked at Molly was enough to send me surging forward, calling for my armour.

I'd barely got moving before Major Michaels thrust his monkey's hand at me, and just the power of it was enough to force the armour back into my torc. I summoned it again and again, but even though I could feel the rogue armour's presence at the back of my head, raging and desperate to get out, it was trapped. The major laughed softly and took his time pointing the monkey's hand at Molly.

"Behave yourself, Drood! Or do you want to see this nasty little object do something really unpleasant to your girlfriend? Maybe I'll have it turn her into something really revolting. . . . That was always one of your favourite tricks, wasn't it, Miss Metcalf? Perhaps I'll fuse your legs together so you can play mermaid. . . . Or I could melt off both your arms. . . . Or just take away your eyes and your mouth, your ears and your nose, and leave you trapped in the dark inside your own head."

"Please," I said. "Don't. There's no need for this. We surrender. Take us to Crow Lee. You know he's going to want to talk to us."

"Oh yes," said the major. "He's just dying to have words with you. That's all that's keeping you alive. After all my men you killed . . ."

"Run, Eddie," Molly said dully. "Get out of here. Get help."

"I can't leave you," I said.

"You picked a fine time to get sentimental," said Major Michaels. "I always thought you field agents would be more professional. I am a professional soldier of long standing. Like the man you just killed, girl. Major Browten was a good soldier and a fine officer. Not a friend, as such, but a colleague. Kind of man you could depend on to keep his head in a firefight and do his job. Dead and gone now because of you. So don't look to me for sympathy."

"You stood by and let it happen," I said.

He shrugged. "Orders . . ."

More uniformed soldiers appeared out of nowhere and hurried forward to join the major. He looked at them scathingly.

"Where the hell have you been? I had to take care of business on my own! Don't look at them like that; they're just captives now. Quite harmless. Search them, secure them and then escort them in to see Crow Lee." He looked down at the dead body of Major Browten and shook his head briefly. "Bad way to go. Not that there are many good ways." He turned to Molly and punched her hard in the face. Her head snapped back, blood flying on the air. I threw myself at the major, and the other soldiers beat me to the ground with their gun butts. I curled up into a ball, as I'd been trained, trying to take the blows on my tensed muscles, but there were just too many of them, hitting me from every direction at once. One rifle butt got through to my head, slamming in with vicious force. My head filled with pain and then the world just went away for a while.

When I came back, I hurt so much I couldn't move. Blood was drying on my face and seeping out my split and broken lips. My face felt like it had been pulped. One eye had swollen shut. My muscles jumped and spasmed as I tried to move, and I groaned at the pain despite myself. I could hear the soldiers laughing.

I wasn't dead. Crow Lee had given orders not to kill me. I clung to that thought. There was a limit to what they could do to me. They couldn't risk killing me. That was something. They'd hurt me, but it didn't feel like they'd broken anything important. If I could just get my armour around me, it would make the pain go away and make me strong again, and then, and then . . .

I rolled my head slowly to one side, gritting my teeth to keep from making any sound. I didn't want to give the soldiers the satisfaction. I saw Molly lying on the grass beside me. Half her face was hidden behind a mask of dried blood, but at least they hadn't beaten her, too. She was breathing heavily, but she managed half a smile for me.

"They're awake." It was Major Michaels. "Pick them both up. The Drood has to see this."

Rough hands hauled me up onto my feet and held me there. Two more soldiers held Molly up before me. She looked very small and vulnerable, like a broken doll that's been treated too roughly. Major Michaels took her chin in one hand and lifted her face. Molly stared coldly at him. She tried to spit at him, but the blood just dribbled down her chin.

"Charming," said Major Michaels. "Pay attention, Drood. This is for your benefit. Crow Lee has given me orders and I will carry them out to the letter, because I am a good soldier. Everything that happens next is to take the fight out of you and to teach you a lesson. That you are entirely helpless now and there is nothing you can do. We can do anything we want to you, and we will. Watch." He gestured to the two soldiers supporting Molly. "Hold the girl steady."

He hit her again and again and again. The soldiers held Molly so tightly she couldn't even turn her head aside. And the other soldiers held me tightly so I couldn't turn my head aside from what I was seeing. I had to watch. I didn't struggle. Didn't cry out to beg or plead with them. There was nothing I could do, so why give them the satisfaction? I watched, watched till Major Michaels was done, and a cold, cold fire burnt in my heart. The major finally lowered his fists and stood there, breathing heavily; and then he took out a handkerchief and wiped the blood from his hands. Molly hung limply in the grasp of the two soldiers holding her, blood dripping steadily from her ruined face. I hoped she was unconscious.

Major Michaels turned to me and took something from a pocket. A small flat box with a button on the top. He waggled it at me.

"Nasty little toy, Drood. Not a soldier's weapon. And Crow Lee says he won't have it in the house. So . . ."

He crushed the box in his hand, and it fell apart into a hundred pieces. Major Michaels fluttered his fingers, and the tiny fragments fell away.

"All right, boys," said the major. "Let's take these unfortunate poor souls up to the house. Crow Lee wants to play with them for as long as they last."

He led the way across the devastated grounds, while the soldiers half carried Molly and me along after him. Molly was just about back on her feet again, though her head hung down. Blood dripped steadily off her chin. I did my best to keep my legs under me, for pride's sake. More heavily armed guards kept appearing out of nowhere, moving in around us to escort us to the house. Not because they thought we were dangerous anymore, but because they couldn't be sure we came alone. There might be others, watching and waiting for their chance.

I kept calling on my armour, but nothing came. I could feel its angry presence, and its thoughts were as hot as mine were cold, but the influence of the monkey's hand kept it trapped where it was. If I could just get Crow Lee to send the major away while he questioned us . . . maybe there was a limit to how far the monkey's hand could reach. And then . . .

I looked around Crow Lee's gardens as we were led through them, and I managed a small smile. Even though it broke open my split lips and filled my mouth with blood. Molly and I had made a definite impression. His gardens couldn't have looked more of a mess if a small country had declared war on them.

The soldiers were still having to half hold me up. I was playing along a bit, so they wouldn't see me as any kind of threat till it was too late . . . but I was still shocked at how weak I was. It had been a long time since I'd taken a professional beating. But I was a Drood. Which meant I was used to beatings. The Sarjeants-at-Arms had seen to that ever since I was a small child. I hurt, but my head was still clear. All I had to do was wait for my chance.

You tell yourself things like that when you're broken and bleeding and all out of options. That's part of the training, too.

The soldiers stopped before the front door of the manor house, and Molly raised her head to look at me. I wouldn't let myself look away, and I tried to keep out of my expression just how bad she looked.

"All my fault," she said indistinctly. "I should have waited for my magics to return naturally, not relied on the Twilight Teardrop. But there just wasn't time. . . ."

"I know," I said. "It's all right."

I waited, but she didn't have anything more to say. She let her head droop forward again, and blood resumed dripping off her chin.

I made myself look away and study the exterior of Crow Lee's house. Looking for any information or insight I could use for ammunition when we met. The place seemed quiet and even peaceful, though the drawn curtains at all the windows gave it a slightly sinister aspect. There was even a welcome mat set out before the front door. I laughed briefly at that, and got a slap round the head for my trouble. The door swung silently open before us, and I felt a whole new level of tension rise among the soldiers. Crow Lee was waiting. Major Michaels yelled at his men, and they hauled Molly and me inside. The door swung silently shut behind us.

Inside the place stank. I grimaced as the stench washed over me, of blood and shit, musk and misery. Even Major Michaels was affected by the smell, though he did his best to hide it. One of the soldiers supporting Molly gagged loudly and whipped his head from side to side, as though searching for fresher air. The major snarled at him and led us all down the long hallway.

Both walls were covered with mirrors, long rows of framed glass. And as I passed them by I saw faces imprisoned behind each mirror, half-starved, scarred and ruined, silently screaming and pleading. There was nothing I could do. Except hope I'd get the chance to do something for them later. The ceiling was covered with old overlapping bloodstains. Mostly arterial spray, by the look of it.

"Take a look at the rugs on the floor," Major Michaels said cheerfully. "Every one of them made from the pelts of endangered animals. If you look carefully at the ones where the heads are still attached, you'll notice the eyes are still alive and full of suffering. He doesn't miss a trick, that Crow Lee."

He pushed on ahead of us, heading for the closed door at the end of the hall. The whole place stank of death and suffering, like a spiritual abattoir. A row of severed heads had been stuck on spikes: men and women, young and old. They were still alive and suffering, too. Their eyes rolled and their mouths moved, though no sound came out of them.

"Crow Lee had their vocal cords cut out," Major Michaels said casually. "You can listen to only so much screaming before it gets old. And it's not as if any of them had anything to say that he wanted to hear."

I remembered threatening to put the Immortal's head on a spike, and I felt ashamed.

We finally reached the door at the end of the hall. The soldiers were looking at each other unhappily, every movement full of tension and fear. Major Michaels gave me some time to look over the door. The heavy wood had been carved with every name and symbol for evil you could think of, including some from civilisations that don't even exist anymore. The door knocker was an inverted crucifix, with what I took at first to be some kind of shaved monkey nailed to it. It wasn't until Major Michaels encouraged me to take a closer look that I realised Crow Lee had nailed a foetus to the cross.

The major laughed at the expression on my face. "Ripped untimely from his mother's womb, and nailed up in place while he was still breathing. You've got to laugh, haven't you? So, what do you think of the great man's dwelling?"

"Reflects his personality," I said. "He really is the Most Evil Man in the World."

"Was there ever any doubt?" said Major Michaels.

"How can you stand to be in a place like this?" I said. "How can you stand to work for a piece of shit like Crow Lee?"

The major smacked me round the head again, just hard enough to make his point. My eyes watered and my knees buckled. The soldiers held me up till I could get my feet back under me.

"You never learn, do you?" said Major Michaels.

Molly lashed out suddenly with one foot, and the major turned aside at the last moment to take the kick on his thigh instead of in the groin. He backhanded her across the face. I kicked him hard in the back of the leg, and he went down on one knee. I struggled with the soldiers holding me but couldn't break free. Major Michaels got to his feet again and went to slap me across the face. I waited till just the right moment, and then snapped my head forward and sank my teeth into his hand.

He howled with shock and pain, and I ground my teeth in deep, his blood spurting into my mouth. The major punched me hard in the head with his other hand, and I lost track of things for a moment. The soldiers forced my jaws open, and Major Michaels fell back, clutching his damaged hand to his chest.

"You animal! You vicious little shit!"

I laughed at him, spraying his blood and mine from my mouth. "Least I could do."

The major went to hit me again, and I laughed again and spat more blood at him. "Careful, Major. Can't damage me too much. Crow Lee's waiting in there to talk to me, remember? You knock me out or render me speechless with a concussion just when he's in the mood to ask me some very specific questions, and he's going to be really upset with you. Isn't he?"

Major Michaels held his injured hand tightly with the other. "Afterwards," he said tightly, "he'll give you to me. And I'll show you what pain really is. You're going to be mine, Drood."

"You're not my type," I said.

The major knocked loudly on the door, though I noticed he handled the crucifix rather gingerly, for all his fine words. A happy voice beyond the door called for us to enter. The major pushed open the door, and the soldiers bustled Molly and me through and into Crow Lee's lair.

They threw us on the floor before him. On our knees before the master of the house. I forced my head up and looked round the room, deliberately ignoring Crow Lee. By comparison to the hallway, the room seemed calm and cosy, comfortable, even civilised. A country gentleman's study, with old-fashioned furniture, bookshelves, objets d'art and colourful prints on the walls. Crow Lee sat at his ease before us in an oversized armchair big enough to handle his huge frame. The burns Molly had given him in the club library were already gone from his face. Beside him stood his bodyguard, Mr. Stab. He looked down at Molly and me, at our bloodied and broken state, and I thought for a moment he might say something, but he didn't. He just stood there where he'd been told to stand, and nothing moved in his face. Crow Lee looked at Molly and me and chuckled happily.

"My, my. We have been in the wars, haven't we? But it's a good look for you, Drood. You can go now, Major, and take your men with you. Our words are not for your ears. Clean up my gardens and make sure they're secure, but don't go too far. Just in case I have need of you again. For executions and the like."

Major Michaels nodded stiffly, started to leave and then stopped and came back to hand over the Twilight Teardrop to Crow Lee. He then strode out of the room, not looking back, and his soldiers hurried out after him. The door shut itself behind them. Crow Lee held the ruby pendant in the palm of his hand, and it looked so much smaller and less potent in his huge paw. Crow Lee smiled briefly and then closed his great hand around the Twilight Teardrop and crushed it. I expected bright lights to shine out from between his fingers or strange bloodred energies to manifest and fly about the room, but the ruby just cracked and splintered in his grasp, and when he opened his hand, brilliant red fragments fluttered sadly to the floor.

"I've never allowed myself to become dependent on such toys," he said. "So why leave it lying around for someone else to make use of it?" He smiled happily down at Molly, slumped in place before him, dripping blood on his expensive carpet. "Welcome to my pleasure dome, my country retreat, my private world. Everything here is exactly how I want it. Right down to the books on my shelves, bound in the flayed skin of ruined enemies, and the antique furniture, spoils of war from my feuds with . . . well, I won't call them my peers. My now-deceased competitors. And did you see my door knocker? Of course you did. Ah, the old blasphemies are the best. Don't you agree? It's actually a bit of a strain sometimes, keeping up with what's required of me as the Most . . . you know. He would have been my son, you see, the door knocker. If his stupid sow of a mother hadn't tried to blackmail me. It's not that I begrudged her the money, you understand. It's just that I can't stand ingratitude.

"But before we begin the hard talking, Edwin Drood . . . A surprise! A little divertissement! Behold!"

He waved one large hand, and the concealing illusion at the side of his chair disappeared, revealing two naked women wrapped in glowing chains, held in place by a cold iron chain that stretched from Crow Lee's chair to the collars round their throats. They were Isabella and Louisa Metcalf. They both looked like they'd taken hard beatings and hadn't been fed in some time. Molly looked at her sisters for a long moment.

"No wonder I couldn't make contact with you," she said finally. "No wonder no one knew where you were. How the hell did Crow Lee capture you?"

"Oh, I didn't," Crow Lee said immediately, leaning back in his chair and clearly enjoying himself. "Your sisters came to me of their own free will, the little darlings. Tell your dear sister the story, my pretties."

Molly looked at me. "Eddie, stop looking at my sisters while they're naked."

"I'm flattered you think I'm in any state to give a damn," I said.

"It's the principle of the thing," she said.

"I can have you both gagged, if you prefer," said Crow Lee. He'd stopped smiling. We weren't playing the game the way he wanted. "No? Then behave yourselves. Isabella, tell them why you came to me and begged for my help."

"I talked with Louisa," said Isabella, steadily meeting Molly's cold gaze. "We agreed we needed new help and support if we were to punish the Droods and bring them down. Because you didn't care anymore, Molly. They killed our parents! And you were living there in the Hall! With one of them!"

"I'm not with them," said Molly. "I'm just with Eddie."

"We couldn't rely on you anymore," said Isabella. "You'd gone over to the enemy. So we needed a new, powerful ally. Someone who hated the Droods as much as we still did. I remembered you saying you'd worked with Crow Lee in the past, so I used your name to get invited here. Louisa insisted on coming along. She thought it would be fun."

"And you told him all about Alpha Red Alpha," I said.

"Oh no," Crow Lee said easily. "I already knew all about that. I told you:

There is a traitor in your family who serves me very well. Of course, I encouraged Isabella and Louisa to confide in me, to tell me everything they knew about Molly and the Droods and the Hall. And when there was nothing else they could tell me, when I had no more use for them . . . I took away their magic and chained them up and kept them in my kennels! Just because I could! What fun we've had. Haven't we, girls?"

"Nasty little man," Louisa said calmly. "He has no manners at all."

"I will kill you for this," Molly said to Crow Lee, and her voice was cold and flat and completely matter-of-fact. Crow Lee leaned forward in his chair, which creaked loudly as his great weight shifted, just so he could laugh right into her bloody face.

"No, you won't, Molly. I think I've enjoyed about as much of the Metcalf sisters as I can stand."

He waggled his fingers at the ground before him and a great hole opened up—a hole in the world, full of darkness, sucking all the air from the room. Isabella and Louisa didn't even have time to scream before they were sucked into the hole and gone, nothing left behind but two lengths of severed iron chain dangling from Crow Lee's chair. Molly was pulled in after them, snatched from my side before I could even react. Crow Lee waved his hand and the hole disappeared. Not a trace left behind, nothing to show it had ever been there. I fell forward, clutching at the carpet with my hands . . . but there was nothing there, nothing at all.

I crouched there on the floor before Crow Lee, so full of shock and horror and loss and pain I couldn't move, could barely think. Somehow I kept it all out of my face. Because I knew Crow Lee was watching, looking for tears or despair, for something he could gloat over. And I was damned if I'd give him the satisfaction. I could deny him that, at least. My Molly was gone. It felt like someone had just punched the heart right out of me. All that was left was the cold, hard need for revenge.

When it became clear that I wasn't going to put on a show for him, Crow Lee rose to his feet and sneered down at me.

"You'll have to excuse me for a while, little Drood. I do have other business to deal with. Someone important I just have to talk to in the next room. You can talk to Mr. Stab while I'm gone. I'm sure you've got so much to say to each other."

He laughed his happy laugh and strode heavily across the room to the side door and left, not looking back once. I watched him go, watched the door close quietly but firmly behind him and then I slowly turned my aching head to look at Mr. Stab. He met my gaze unflinchingly, even though he must have seen murder in it.

"She was your friend," I said. "Molly was your friend!"

"Yes," said Mr. Stab. "She was. It's better this way, though. We would have had to kill each other eventually, I think."

"Help me," I said.

"Why should I do that?" said Mr. Stab.

"Because," I said, "if you help me to avenge my Molly and help me find my lost family, I give you my word that the Droods will find a way to put an end to your curse that doesn't involve killing you. Think of the resources at our command! We'll find a way to undo what you did to yourself."

"Crow Lee has already promised me that."

"But which of us do you trust to deliver on their promise?"

"I like what I am," said Mr. Stab. "I just want to be free of my . . . limitations. Crow Lee will make me a better monster."

"That's what you want?" I said. "What you really want?"

"That's all that's left for me to want, after everything I've done."

"All right," I said. "How about this? You help me, and I promise I won't kill you for everything you've done."

"Hush, Eddie," said Mr. Stab. "I don't want to talk to you anymore."

He turned his back on me and walked away to stare out the window. I don't know what it was he was looking at, but I doubt it was the gardens.

I didn't know what to do. I couldn't believe Molly was really gone. Not just like that. I couldn't go after her with the Merlin Glass, because only Crow Lee knew where he'd sent her. Even if I did find a way to turn the tables, he'd die before he told me, rather than let me win. I had to believe Molly was still alive somewhere . . . out there. . . . But for now, all that was left to me was survival and revenge. If I could just concentrate on that . . . maybe I wouldn't feel the pain so much. I looked over at Mr. Stab, still standing stiff-backed at the window. I reached carefully into the pocket dimension where I kept the Merlin Glass. The soldiers could search me as much as they liked, but only I had access to the pocket. This time I wasn't interested in the Glass. I couldn't risk jumping through the Glass in the middle of Crow Lee's many protections. And I wasn't interested in escaping, anyway. No, I was after something small, so small that hopefully Crow Lee wouldn't detect it. Something the Armourer Patrick had given me.

The hearing aid.

Just a little blob of flesh-coloured plastic with some really clever electronics hidden inside. I eased it out of my pocket, palmed it, and then snuck it into my right ear. I glanced quickly at Mr. Stab, but he didn't seem to be paying any attention to me. I surreptitiously adjusted the tuning on the hearing aid, and immediately I could hear everything Crow Lee was saying in the adjoining room. He was addressing someone else, in his usual arrogant and condescending way, but whomever he was speaking to would have none of it and responded entirely in kind. There was something about the second voice that I found sort of familiar, though I couldn't place it. I concentrated on what they were saying.

". . . I have always been well served by traitors," said Crow Lee.

"I'm not just any traitor," said the second voice. "I am the worm at the heart of the Droods, the viper they have nursed at their bosom. Do you really think I'd bow down to the likes of you?"

"You will if you know what's good for you," Crow Lee said complacently. "I am the power here."

"And I am a Drood. The First Drood! I am older than your power, little magician. I have lived lifetimes and seen civilisations rise and fall."

"But you're not a Drood anymore, are you? You don't have your armour . . . though Eddie does. Isn't that odd?"

"Odder than you realise," said the traitor. "He shouldn't be able to access his armour with the other-dimensional intruder dismissed along with the Hall. We're going to have to make Eddie tell us where he got his armour from."

"We?" said Crow Lee, lazily. "What's in it for me?"

"I will have his armour. I want it. And then you'll have a Drood in full armour as your ally. I want that armour!"

"Well, you can't have it," said Crow Lee. "I'm going to strip it off Eddie and then destroy it. Then the Droods really will be gone from this world. . . . Of course, I might decide to keep it for myself. You know how much I enjoy playing with new toys. . . . Where did you get that?"

"From the Armageddon Codex," said the traitor. "Where all the Droods' forbidden weapons are kept. I took it with me before I left the Hall, before it was sent away. It wasn't difficult. I was there when they built the Codex. I helped design the locking systems. Who has a better right to this weapon than I?"

"What better weapon for a traitor," said Crow Lee, "than Oath Breaker?"

I couldn't help but react to that, at the thought of one of our most dangerous weapons in the hands of a traitor. I must have made some kind of noise, because Mr. Stab turned around and looked at me. I held myself very still, and he went back to looking out the window.

"You have nothing that can stand against me as long as I hold Oath Breaker," said the traitor.

"Don't be too sure of that," Crow Lee said steadily. "You'd be surprised at some of the Objects of Power I've acquired here and there. But this is no time to be falling out, when we've achieved so much together! Let us think of our partnership as a balance of power and move on. Come with me, into the study. I want to see Eddie brought down by another Drood."

I quickly eased the hearing aid out of my ear and slipped it back into my pocket dimension. And then I did my best to look surprised when Crow Lee strode back in with the traitor Drood at his side. I didn't recognise him at all. He was a very ordinary-looking man, nothing remarkable about him at all. He did look sort of familiar, but I couldn't place him. It's a big family, the Droods.

"You don't know me, do you?" said the traitor. "Even though we've spoken many times in passing. But then, that's the point. I'm never anyone important or significant, and I don't stand out. I'm always just there in the background, perhaps some useful functionary, just another Drood doing a necessary job . . . poisoning the wells in the quiet of the night. Adrian Drood, at the moment. Not my real name, of course. But then, I've had so many names and identities down the centuries."

"You're the Original Traitor," I said. "The one who's undermined and betrayed us over and over. Why?"

"Because the family has moved away from what I intended it to be," Adrian said calmly. "I was the very first Drood. I was there when the Heart first fell to Earth. I made the original pact with the Heart for power and armour. I made the Droods possible! Everything they are came from me! I set us up to be shamans and protectors, shepherds to Humanity . . . but it was never meant that the sheep should forget their place.

"The family forced me out of power because I wouldn't go along with their changes. Exiled me, made me the first rogue Drood. So I disappeared, went away, walked up and down the world, hugging my rage and hatred to my cold, cold heart. I spent a lot of time with the Immortals, a family much like mine. I gave their leader the idea for immortality, having begged it from the Heart for myself as part of the deal I made. Centuries later I returned to the Droods. Killed some small nonentity and took over his identity. The Immortals showed me how to do that.

"And ever since I have always been there, hiding in plain sight in the background, doing my best to nudge and persuade the family back to what it should be. Just a quiet, influential voice advising and guiding those in positions of power. And removing those who got in my way. Those who wouldn't listen. Nothing like a good accident to stir things up and move people around."

"You killed the Matriarch Sarah," I said. "So my grandmother Martha could take over."

"So I did! Pushed her down a flight of stairs. And then stamped on the back of her neck when she didn't have the decency to die straight away. I have always been well served by accidents."

"Why the hell did you bring the Loathly Ones into this world?" I said. "Did you know what you were doing?"

"Of course. The Droods have always needed someone or something worthy to fight, to keep them sharp. To keep them the warriors I always meant them to be. I could see the War wasn't going to last much longer, and I wanted to be sure there'd be a new villain in place afterwards. Who could have foreseen the Cold War? I was having such fun then, running endless agents and intrigues back and forth across the world . . . that I quite forgot about the Loathly Ones. The Droods really were getting soft by your time, Eddie. I never intended my family to be peace-loving shepherds."

"Why ally yourself with Crow Lee?" I said.

"Because I've finally grown tired of the Droods," said the Original Traitor. "Your wiping out the Immortals was the last straw. I always had more in common with them than my own family. I finally realised that the Droods were never going to be what I wanted them to be. And if I couldn't have them, why should anyone else? But now I think I've answered enough of your questions, Eddie. It's time for you to answer some of mine. Starting with: Where did you get your armour? I can tell it isn't the strange-matter armour you got from Ethel, but it can't be the old style, with the Heart destroyed. So where did it come from?"

"I found it in the hedge Maze," I said. "It's Moxton's Mistake."

Adrian Drood's face actually went pale for a moment. "You fool . . . Do you know what you've done? I put that abomination in the Maze! Do you know what you've let loose on the world?"

"A weapon," I said. "To use against you."

And I reached into my pocket dimension and brought out the other little gift from Armourer Patrick: the skeleton key that could unlock anything. I jammed it right up against my torc, and the power in the key fought the power holding my armour inside my torc. The bone key turned slowly, relentlessly, in my grasp, and then snapped round in a complete circle. And just like that, my armour came to me. It surged out of the torc, covering me in a moment, cutting me off from my pain and injuries and weakness, making me strong and secure again. I rose to my feet to confront Crow Lee and Adrian Drood, and they both fell back before me. Mr. Stab studied me thoughtfully from the window but made no move to intervene.

"Now," I said, to my enemies before me. "For all you've done. For all the pain you've caused me and so many others, now . . . it's time for me to get my hands bloody."

"I have an answer to your armour," Crow Lee said steadily. He held up his huge hand, and in it was the Hand of Glory made from a monkey's paw. Bloodred flames rose steadily from the candlewick fingers. Crow Lee nodded, satisfied. "I never throw anything useful away, and I always know where everything is."

"When it comes to who's got the best toys," I said, "always bet on the Droods."

I started towards him, and he thrust the monkey's hand at me while shouting some particularly nasty Words. The influence from the monkey's hand hit me hard, like walking into an invisible wall, but still I pressed forward, all the power in my armour driving me on. Thinking of what Crow Lee had done to my family. Of what he'd ordered Major Michaels to do to my Molly. Thinking of my hands around Crow Lee's throat. My golden armour began to seethe and boil, and then to melt and run away, falling off in large golden clumps of semiliquid metal. But I kept going. Even as the monkey's power hit me again and again, hurting and pounding me even through my dissolving armour, I kept going. Taking everything he could throw at me, because nothing mattered, nothing else mattered except getting to him.

And finally I stood there, right before him, half my armour gone and more falling away, and I snatched the monkey's paw right out of Crow Lee's hand. The tiny withered thing twisted and writhed inside my grasp, and I shook it hard until all its candles blew out. And then I threw the nasty thing on the floor and stamped on it hard with my golden foot two, three times. Crushing it with all my armour's strength.

I heard the little bones crack and break. And my armour reformed around me, smooth and untouched.

"Mr. Stab!" screamed Crow Lee. "Time for you to do your duty! You shall have everything I promised you! Everything! Just stop the Drood!"

I turned unhurriedly to look at Mr. Stab as he moved slowly forward from the window, a long blade suddenly in his hand, glowing bright.

"I can reach you inside your armour," said Mr. Stab. "My blade can cut anything; that's part of what was given to me. And you know you can't hurt me. You tried to kill me before, after I killed Penny. Cut my head right off . . . and I just put it back on again. You can't stop me, Eddie, because nothing can. That's what I bought all those years ago in the dark slums and back alleys of Whitechapel. Part of me wants to say, 'I'm sorry it's come to this.' But I'm not, not really. This is what I was born to do. Anything else was just a dream."

And then we both stopped and looked around, as the sound of a roaring car engine drew rapidly closer. There were loud crashing noises of things breaking, shouts and screams and all the sounds of destruction, as something drove right through people and objects at speed. And then the scarlet-and-white Plymouth Fury crashed through the wall and the window, punching through the solid structure like it was nothing, to roar into the room and pounce on Mr. Stab. Ran him down and ran him over, and then screeched to a halt, leaving Mr. Stab pinned helplessly under the weight of the car.

"I knew you were in trouble!" said the sat nav's strident female voice from inside the car. "I could sense it. I've got really powerful sensors. I've been looking in all along, waiting for my moment. You didn't think the Regent would give you just any old car, did you? I'm the Scarlet Lady, one of the Regent of Shadows's best undercover agents! I . . . am your backup! What do you want me to do?"

"Just . . . hold Mr. Stab down for now," I said.

"No problem!" said the car. Mr. Stab struggled wildly underneath the Plymouth Fury and even tipped it back and forth, but with no leverage he couldn't throw it off. "Victorian values, my shiny red arse," said the car.

I looked at Crow Lee. "Don't run," I said. And something in my voice made him flinch. "Stay right where you are. I'll get to you. Once I've finished with the traitor."

I gave Adrian Drood my full attention. He stood his ground, staring defiantly back at me.

"All these years," I said, "killing your own flesh and blood, so you could replace them . . . undermining and destroying your own family from within."

"Why not?" said Adrian. "It was mine to destroy. Mine to do with as I pleased. I made it! I made the Droods possible!"

"But we moved on," I said. "We became something better and greater than you ever intended. We became something you never even conceived! With your limited, barbarian mind . . . All the years you've lived, and you've learned nothing! And when you finally realised we would never sink to become what you wanted, that we'd never settle for being something so small, you threw a temper tantrum like a threatened child, and ran away to Crow Lee to get rid of us. You petty, spiteful little turd."

"You let me down," said Adrian. "You disappointed me. Every damned one of you. It doesn't matter. I can always start again. Make a new family."

"Without the Heart?" I said. "Without Ethel? You have no armour."

"Then I suppose I'll just have to take yours," said Adrian. He lifted his hand, and in it was the monkey's paw made over into a Hand of Glory. The bloodred flames were burning steadily again. He laughed briefly at me. "You didn't really think you could destroy something as powerful as this just by stamping on it? It was easy for me to call it out from under your foot while you were busy puffing up your chest and boasting. You don't live as long as I have without learning a few useful tricks. Now, let's try this again."

He thrust the monkey's hand at me and spoke a single Word, and just like that the rogue armour ripped off me, and all my pain and injuries returned. I cried out, but I didn't fall. Adrian cried out at the cold shock of what it was like to wear Moxton's Mistake. And then he stood before me, powerful and proud, in the golden glory of Drood armour. He started to say something and then he cried out again in horror as the rogue armour constricted suddenly about him. It shrank in sudden spurts, falling in upon itself, crushing Adrian inside it as it compacted itself in sudden rushes. The limbs were sucked inside the trunk, which collapsed in on itself, while Adrian screamed and screamed until the screams cut off abruptly. And still the armour shrank in upon itself, until nothing was left but a golden box, a cube barely three feet in diameter, sitting quietly on the carpet before us. Crow Lee looked at it in silent shock, and then looked at me.

"Don't look at me," I said. "I didn't know it could do that."

The golden box exploded back into human shape again and stood facing me. Moxton's Mistake, regarding me with its featureless golden face.

"He put me in the Maze," it said, in its rasping inhuman voice. "Left me there to run wild for centuries. Did he think I'd forgive and forget? Your torc has no authority over me, Eddie Drood. I serve you only because I choose to."

"We made a bargain," I said steadily.

"So we did," said the rogue armour. "I haven't forgotten. Take this as a sign, a warning . . . of what might happen to you if you were to turn against me."

It hunched its back, which split open to allow out what remained of Adrian Drood. A hot and steaming cube of compacted meat and splintered bone burst out of the armour's back and fell, stinking and splashing, to the floor in a rush of bodily fluids. And while I was looking at that, the golden armour flowed forward and wrapped itself about me. I shuddered, and not only from the familiar cold. I felt strong and well again, free from all pain, but I also felt the armour's presence watching me thoughtfully. I looked at the bloody steaming mess on the carpet. Not a bad end for the greatest traitor the Droods had ever known. I just wished . . . I could have done it myself. It occurred to me that the armour could have done the same thing to me any of the times I wore it. And still could . . .

I turned to consider the Plymouth Fury. Mr. Stab was still trapped beneath it, still struggling to break free. He rocked the heavy car back and forth with his more-than-human strength, but he still couldn't lift the thing off him. The Plymouth Fury settled itself more firmly, like a duck upon its eggs, quietly humming "Rock 'n' Roll Is Here to Stay." I stopped down, picked the monkey's hand up off the floor and slipped it through my armoured side and into my pocket dimension. Because you never knew . . . and because I didn't want anyone else to surprise me with it.

I moved over to the car and knelt down beside Mr. Stab's protruding head and shoulder. He'd worked one arm out from under the car, and suddenly there was a blade in it, shining bright. I grabbed his hand and squeezed hard until he dropped the knife. And then I picked it up and snapped it neatly in two. The bright glow was quickly gone, leaving just two pieces of broken steel. Mr. Stab glared at me sullenly as I threw the pieces aside.

"It's all right," I said to the car. "You can get off him now."

"Are you sure?" said the car. "I can run back and forth over him a few times, if you like. No trouble . . ."

"Thanks," I said. "But that won't be necessary."

The car sniffed loudly, reminding me irresistibly of Molly for a moment. "People . . . just don't know how to enjoy themselves."

The Plymouth Fury backed slowly away, reversing steadily till it was halfway out the jagged hole it had made in the wall when it arrived. Mr. Stab rose slowly to his feet, brushing the dust off his Victorian finery in an unfussy way. His eyes never left mine.

"You'll never stop me," he said coldly. "I can recover from anything you do to me. You've seen that for yourself."

"Maybe no one ever tried hard enough before," I said. "Maybe no one was ever motivated enough before me. This new armour really is very versatile. The things it can do . . . You saw what it did to the traitor Drood."

"Crush me. Put me in a box," said Mr. Stab. "I'll still bounce back. Like the worst jack-in-the-box you ever saw."

He held up his hand, and there was a new shining blade in it. He swept it back and forth before him, smiling coldly.

"I am never without a blade. This, too, was given to me."

"But all the other attacks were from outside," I said. "I'm thinking about . . . inside."

And before Mr. Stab could react, I stepped quickly forward and punched him in the mouth. The golden armour didn't stop at his mouth; it carried on, flowing down his throat, filling up his insides. I held him firmly with my left hand as he struggled wildly, my right hand pressing down on his mouth. The golden metal flowed off me and into him, inside him, filling every space, every little nook and cranny. He couldn't scream, but his eyes were full of a terrible horror. He still couldn't die, despite what was being done to him. So I sent a final command through my torc, and the golden metal inside Mr. Stab exploded. The blast tore him apart, blasting him open from inside, every bone and organ reduced to fragments and less than fragments.

I'd got the idea from watching Molly's protein exploder.

A familiar pink mist rolled and roiled in the air, but this time there were no bones. The bloody mist fell slowly out of the air to soak and stain the carpet. I could feel the rogue armour's presence at the back of my mind. Felt its . . . satisfaction.

I just felt cold.

"For you, Penny," I said. "And for all his victims down the years. And especially for six poor women in Whitechapel, who never wanted to be part of a legend."

The Plymouth Fury whistled loudly. "Way to go, Drood! Let's see the evil little scrote come back from that!"

I ignored the car and turned to look at Crow Lee, who was standing very still, exactly where I'd left him. He smiled briefly.

"People . . . can always surprise you. Have to say, Eddie, I didn't think you had it in you."

"I didn't," I said. "He had it in him. And I did it for the victims. . . ."

"No," said Crow Lee. "You did it for yourself. I know about these things."

"Why didn't you run?" I said. "I was . . . distracted. You might have got away."

"Where could I go that you wouldn't find me? You're a lot more than I thought you were . . . I'm bad, Drood, but you're the biggest monster in this room. So, better to stay and work out some kind of agreement that will get you off my back."

"You took away my family and my Molly."

"The least of my many crimes, but let's not dwell on the Past. I still have something to bargain with. Something you want."

"Can you bring back Molly and her sisters?"

"No . . . I'm not exactly sure where that particular spell sends people. Not that I've ever given a damn, as long as they disappeared from my life. It can't be that bad; no one ever comes back to complain! Little joke there . . . No. All right. I can help you recover your lost family! I still have the remote control I used to send Drood Hall away. It still contains the exact coordinates of the dimension I had Alpha Red Alpha send them to. A place so remote and distant you'll never find them, Eddie, never track them down. Not without the exact coordinates contained within my remote control."

"You still have it?" I said.

"Not here," Crow Lee said quickly. "Not actually on me . . . but it is somewhere near. Somewhere safe. We can make a deal, Drood: I give you the remote, and you agree to let me live."

"Let you live?" I said. "Let you go unpunished after everything you've done?" I remembered the major hitting Molly, his fist smashing into her face over and over, saying, *This is Crow Lee's orders*. . . . I shook my head. "I don't think I can do that."

"Isn't it worth it? To get your family back? Immunity for one man, to have the mighty Droods back in the world again?"

"But you're not the only game in town," I said. "I have the monkey's hand. It can find anything. It can make changes in reality. Put that together with my Merlin Glass, and what do I need you and your remote for?"

"Well, yes, technically speaking," said Crow Lee. "But, unfortunately, I know more about these objects than you do. So I know it's already pretty much used up. It can only hold a certain amount of magical energies, and it has been very busy. . . . You see, a monkey's paw isn't supposed to be a Hand of Glory. And vice versa. The two contrasting natures are always fighting it out, which is why it can never hang on to its various powers for long. See for yourself."

I looked at him for a long moment and then fished the ugly thing out of my pocket dimension. The monkey's paw was always a dried, withered thing, but now it was actually rotting and falling apart. I let it drop to the floor, and it just fell to pieces as it hit. Crow Lee tutted sadly.

"They really are such fragile things. . . . So, now you're going to have to make a deal with me, Eddie. If you ever want to see your family again."

And then we both stopped and looked around sharply, as we heard the sound of something approaching. A great roaring, rushing sound that seemed to come from every direction at once, and then concentrated directly under my feet, under the floor. A sudden wild surmise gripped hold of my heart, and for a moment I couldn't breathe, for hope. I stepped quickly backwards . . . as the great hole before Crow Lee's chair reopened, and Molly and Isabella and Louisa came flying up out of the hole together and back into the room. The hole in the world disappeared and the three Metcalf sisters stood there together. They all looked radiantly healthy and entirely uninjured. Molly didn't have a bruise or a drop of blood on her. She smiled brightly at me.

"Hello, sweetie. Miss me?"

I dropped my armour and stepped forward to take her in my arms, holding her tight, so tight that no one would ever be able to take her away from me again. Molly held me just as tight, murmuring comforting, reassuring words in my ear. Eventually I let her go. Isabella was looking down her nose at me. Louisa was beaming widely. Molly looked haughtily at Crow Lee.

"I have been to Heaven and Hell and everywhere in between. Did you really think you could send me anywhere that I couldn't get back from? And once you'd broken the chains holding my sisters, their magics returned and they could heal me. You really didn't think it through, did you? Had to go for the big dramatic gesture." She looked at me and broke off. "I'm sorry, love. You still look terrible. Let me."

She took my head in both hands, gently, gently, murmuring Words under her breath, and all my injuries healed in a moment. I hadn't realised how much fighting the pain had weighed down on me till it was gone. She stepped back, looked me over briskly and nodded, and then frowned.

"Eddie, you're looking at my sisters again while they're naked!"

"They're standing right in front of me! I am so glad to see you again, Molly. I was so worried . . ."

"Well, that was sweet of you," said Molly. "But you really are going to have to learn to trust me to be able to look after myself." She looked around her. "Where's Mr. Stab?"

"You're standing in what's left of him," I said.

"Oh, ick," said Molly. "And what is the car doing in this room?"

"Saving the day!" the car said cheerfully. "I helped!"

"It's true," I said. "She did. Apparently the Scarlet Lady is one of the Regent's Special Agents."

"Will wonders never cease?" said Molly. "Hold everything—where's Crow Lee?"

"He went into the next room," the Plymouth Fury said helpfully. "While you were all distracted. He's still in there. Up to no good, I'm sure."

"Can you please get these collars off us?" said Isabella. "They're suppressing our magic, now that we're back in the world."

"Oh, sure," I said.

I armoured up my right hand and gave two of the fingers sharp edges to form simple scissors. I snipped through Isabella's collar easily enough, and then Louisa's, and she giggled happily as I did so. Molly stood close beside me as I worked.

"Whatever you do," she said, "Don't look down."

"You don't want me closing my eyes as I'm doing this," I said. "Could be a very unfortunate incident."

"I like you," said Louisa. "You're cute."

"And you're a very scary and destructive person, by all accounts."

"That's right!"

I cut through her collar. Immediately Louisa and Isabella covered themselves with clothes. Isabella was back in her crimson biker leathers, while Louisa wore a long daisy-yellow dress and white stilettos. Isabella nodded to me brusquely.

"Good to see you again, Eddie. Thanks for the rescue."

"You plotted with Crow Lee to destroy my family," I said.

"Your family, my family . . . I think maybe it's time all of us stopped defining ourselves by our families."

"Yes," I said. "But not quite yet."

I looked at Louisa, who smiled brightly.

"I knew everything would work out! Group hug!"

The three Metcalf sisters moved together and held hands, and there was a brief burst of swirling lights and coruscating energies that filled the whole study. Molly let go and stepped back and stretched luxuriously, like a cat in the sun.

"Ah . . . Now, that's more like it! My magic is back, every last bit of it! Let us have words with Crow Lee."

"Hard words," I said.

We marched over to the door leading into the next room. It was locked. Molly laughed and snapped her fingers at it. The heavy wood of the door groaned loudly and rattled furiously in its frame, but it wouldn't open. Isabella and Louisa said a Word of Power together, and the veneer jumped right off the door, but still it held. So I got out my skeleton key, slipped it carefully into the lock and turned it slowly, with just the right amount of pressure, and the protections on the door just threw their hands in the air and said, *Have it your own way, then,* and the door opened.

Crow Lee was scrabbling through the contents of a chest of drawers. He spun round as we entered, and the remote control was in his hand. I knew what it was, what it had to be, just from the look on his face. The thing didn't look too complicated. Crow Lee snatched up a long ironwood staff and held it out defiantly before him. I immediately stopped short and made sure the others did, too.

"No one move," I said. "No one do anything. That is Oath Breaker."

"That is?" said Isabella. "I've only ever read descriptions of it. I'd expected a lot more, to be honest."

"What's Oath Breaker?" said Louisa, frowning prettily.

"One of the Drood forbidden weapons," said Molly. "It revokes all agreements and bonds, right down to the atomic level."

"Oh goody!" said Louisa, clapping her hands together. "I want one!"

"You're dangerous enough as it is," said Molly.

"Girls just want to have fun!" Louisa said brightly.

"Is she always like this?" I said quietly to Molly.

"This is her being relatively stable," said Molly. "God knows how long it'll last. . . . Now you know why we never let anyone meet her." She glowered at Crow Lee. "I don't care what you've got. You do not get to walk free after everything you've done."

"My offer of a deal still stands," said Crow Lee, ignoring the Metcalf sisters to stare directly at me. "The remote control, the coordinates it contains and the return of your Hall and family in return for immunity for all the things I may have done."

"We might have made a deal," I said steadily, "but not now. I can't let you walk out of here with Oath Breaker. Throw it aside and we'll talk."

"How did he get his hands on that thing, anyway?" said Molly.

"From the Original Traitor Drood," I said.

"And where's he?" said Isabella.

"Dead," I said.

Molly looked at me sharply. "You have been busy while I was gone. Mr. Stab and the Original Traitor?"

"Let's not get distracted, people," said Crow Lee. "This remote control can guide your Merlin Glass straight to your family, Eddie. And their safe return is all that really matters, right? And don't even think about taking the remote from me; I've got it rigged with a dead man's switch. If the remote leaves my hand without my permission, it'll self-destruct. And then no one will be able to find the Droods. You're not going to risk that, Eddie. So, I'll be leaving you now. With the remote and Oath Breaker. I'll be in touch, from a safe distance, and then we can work out the terms of our agreement, like civilised people."

"You make one move to leave and I'll kill you," I said.

"Like Mr. Stab and Adrian Drood?" said Crow Lee. "You are getting a taste for it. Aren't you, Eddie? But I don't think so. All your armour and all the Metcalf sisters' magic are still nothing when set against the ancient brute force of Oath Breaker."

And that was when Major Michaels came slamming through the other door on the far side of the room, with a whole bunch of heavily armed mercenary soldiers. Who took one look at me and the Metcalf sisters and opened fire on all of us. Crow Lee darted quickly out of the line of fire, shouting, *No! No! Stop it! You're ruining everything!* The three Metcalf sisters clasped hands, and a protective screen snapped into place between them and the bullets. I armoured up and laughed as the bullets just bounced off me. Crow Lee cried out as ricocheting bullets slammed into the piece of furniture he was hiding behind. Molly let go of her sisters' hands and stepped forward to face Major Michaels. He saw the expression on her face, the face repaired from the beating he'd given her, and opened fire on her at point-blank range. The bullets turned into flowers in midair and drifted to the floor. Molly held up her hand and snapped her fingers sharply. And just like that, Major Michaels and all his soldiers were gone, replaced by the same number of filthy sewer rats. They ran squealing around the room, biting and tearing at one another, and then they all turned on the biggest and oldest one and chased it out of the room.

"Never mess with a Metcalf sister," said Molly. "We always get our own back."

"Yeah," I said. "Major Michaels as a sewer rat, eaten alive by other rats. That'll do. Just."

And then I stepped forward and punched Crow Lee so hard in the face with my armoured fist that it ripped his head clean off his shoulders. The head still held a startled expression as it flew on to slam against the far wall with such an impact that it all but exploded before slipping to the floor, leaving a long bloody trail on the wall behind it. And while the body was slumping to its knees, blood pumping from the severed neck, I dived forward and grabbed the remote control from the slowly opening hand. I held it tightly and forced golden tendrils of my armour out of my glove and deep into the mechanism, shutting down all its systems. I waited a moment, but it didn't self-destruct. I'd got to it in time.

"Was he bluffing?" said Molly.

"Apparently not," I said, pulling the golden tendrils back into my glove. "But it's safe now."

I looked up from the remote control to find all three Metcalf sisters staring at me, and not in a good way.

"That makes three people you've killed," said Molly. "You even put finding your family at risk to kill Crow Lee. And that . . . isn't like you, Eddie. None of this is like you."

"He had it coming," I said. "You can't say he didn't have it coming. They all did. I've just been doing what needs doing. Taking out the trash."

"No," said Molly. "More and more you're doing what your armour wants you to do. I've seen it affecting you, Eddie."

"Maybe I like what it's doing to me," I said. "I feel so much more decisive now. Taking care of business, and to hell with the consequences."

"That's Moxton's Mistake talking," said Molly. "Turning my Eddie to the dark side for its own purposes. I can't let that go on."

She clasped hands with her sisters again. I armoured up almost involuntarily. Bright lights and swirling energies surrounded the sisters, as they chanted a series of Words of Power. I tried to speak to them, to explain that everything was fine, really, only to discover that my words were trapped inside the mask with me. The armour wouldn't let me be heard. I tried to move and found I couldn't. The armour was moving on its own now. I was trapped, helpless, inside it. Like being buried in a golden coffin with murder on its mind. It moved slowly towards Molly and her sisters, savage claws emerging from its golden gauntlets. I could hear the rogue armour laughing. I called out to Molly, trying to warn her, but she couldn't hear me. She didn't know the armour advancing on her wasn't me but Moxton's murderous Mistake.

"He's mine," said the armour. "You can't have him."

The three sisters stopped their chanting, though coruscating energies still spat and sparked in the air around them. Molly looked directly into the featureless golden face mask.

"He was mine long before you got your claws into him," she said. "And you can't keep him."

The three sisters spoke together, chanting a single powerful Word: "*Out!*"

The rogue armour shook, shuddering and spasming wildly, fighting for control and losing, and then it leaned forward abruptly and vomited me out. The face mask split apart like a great wide-stretched mouth, and I was forced up and out and deposited on the blood-stained carpet like a newly birthed thing. I lay there, shaking and shivering, curled into a ball, suddenly aware of all the things I'd done while wearing the armour and wondering how long it had been since I was thinking clearly and on my own. I finally looked up to see the armour standing awkwardly stiff and poised, as though considering its situation.

So much hate, so much rage . . . How long had it been influencing me in all the things I'd said and done?

"Free!" Moxton's Mistake said suddenly. In a voice just human enough to make it sound really disturbing. "Free at last . . . No more masters, no more orders. And, oh, the things I'll do now there's no one left to hold me back. I was bound to serve you, Eddie, once I'd given my word, because that's the way I was made. But you took so easily to my quiet murmurings in your back brain. . . . Still, now you're gone, I am free to do what I will do! And I had so many years in the Maze to think of all the terrible things I'd do to the Humanity that made and disowned me!"

"Five minutes on his own and already he sounds like a bad

Frankenstein movie," said Molly. "Sorry, Moxton's Mistake, but it's clear you can't be left to run wild. Not that I ever thought you should. You need someone to wear; you need a controller and a conscience. And since you've worn Eddie out, that just leaves me."

She looked at Isabella and Louisa, and they nodded slowly. They all hummed together, in increasingly complex harmonies, and a torc appeared around Molly's throat. Silver, not gold. She turned away from her sisters, and walked steadily towards the rogue armour. It backed clumsily away from her. It could tell something was happening, something was in the air, but it couldn't tell what. Its back slammed up against the far wall, and there was nowhere left for it to go. It lifted one golden hand to make *Stay away!* motions at Molly, but she just kept coming. She reached out and grasped the extended golden gauntlet, and the rogue armour cried out in shock and anger as the golden metal was pulled forward onto Molly's hand and over it, and then up her arm.

"You're mine now," said Molly. "You have no choice. The power of the torc compels you."

The armour surged forward and fell over her in a great wave of liquid metal, and when it was done, Molly stood there, wearing the golden armour. The details slowly reworked themselves around her, fitting the armour to its new shape. It tucked in at her waist and showed off her pronounced breasts, though the face mask remained blank and featureless. I forced myself up onto my feet and moved unsteadily forward to stand before her.

"Molly?" I said.

"Oh, Eddie," said her voice, from inside the armour. "You should have told me . . . how good this feels. What do you think? How do I look?"

"You look a lot more . . . feminine than most Droods do," I said.

"I'm not a Drood," said Molly. "Oh, Eddie . . . I feel so sharp, so alive! Like I've been dreaming all my life and only just woken up! I feel strong and fast, like I could take on the whole world! Except . . . it's cold. It's so cold in here. . . . And I'm isolated from the natural world, in a way I never was before. Eddie, I don't like this. . . ."

Her voice was unsteady and uncertain. I stood right in front of her, staring into the blank mask. Isabella and Louisa watched from a distance, making no move to intervene.

"Control it, Molly," I said. "It's your armour while you wear it, so you have to be in control. It's all about willpower, and you've never been short of that."

The golden head nodded slowly, jerkily, and raised one golden hand before the mask. The hand shook as she turned it back and forth, studying it. And then the armour just disappeared back into the silver torc around her throat and was gone. Molly smiled uncertainly at me.

"It's me. I'm back. But . . . I can still feel the armour's presence, like it's always there, looking over my shoulder."

"I know," I said. "Don't get used to it."

"I hate feeling cut off from the natural world," said Molly. "I'm the wild witch of the woods, the laughter in the trees! But with this collar around my neck, I can't hear the trees or feel the sunshine or . . ."

"Molly . . ."

"Don't worry, sweetie. I can handle this. At least long enough to get your family back."

"This is the bravest thing I've ever seen you do," I said. "And you're doing it for me."

"I know!" Molly said cheerfully. "I'm going to hold this over you for the rest of our lives!"

"Fair enough," I said.

"I may puke," Isabella announced loudly.

"Oh, hush, you," said Louisa. "I think it's all very sweet."

"How do you feel, Eddie?" said Molly.

"Naked," I said. "And helpless and very vulnerable. I was trained on how to operate in the field without my armour, but knowing it's not there anymore, even as backup . . ."

"You still have your training and your experience," Molly said firmly.

"If we're going after my family, I'm going to need something," I said. "A weapon or . . ." And then I looked down at the floor, and there was a long staff of dark ironwood just lying there. I reached down and picked it up.

"Eddie . . ." said Molly. "That's Oath Breaker."

"Just the thing," I said. "I'm sure it'll come in very handy wherever we end up going. And afterwards I can make sure it goes back in the Armageddon Codex. Where it belongs."

I hefted the long staff, turning it slowly back and forth to study the strange shapes carved into it. Very old carvings; some of them possibly prehuman. Oath Breaker is one of the oldest weapons in the Drood Armoury. Some say older than the family itself. There are good reasons why we keep it locked away. It felt . . . heavy in my hand, weighed down with spiritual weight as well as physical. A burden to the body and the soul . . . because of what it was, and what it could do. You don't break heads with a staff like Oath Breaker; you break worlds.

Just what I needed.

I led the sisters back into the main room and addressed the Plymouth Fury, still sprawled half in and half out of the broken wall.

"Go on back to the Regent. Tell him everything that's happened here. So he'll know what to do if Molly and I don't come back. If the Droods don't come back."

"Oh, sure!" said the car. "I'm your secretary now, am I? No, don't you mind me. I'll find my own way home. I'm a better driver than you, anyway."

"What are you, really?" said Molly. "There's no way you're just a car with a souped-up sat nav."

"I'll never tell!" said the car. "I might be all manner of things. I might be an AI, I might be a ghost haunting my old ride, I could be a demon poltergeist possessing the car or I could be an alien in a really good disguise. You'll never know!"

The car fired up her engine and roared back out the hole in the wall with only a moderate amount of tyre squeal, and taking only a little more of the wall with her, and then she charged off through the devastated grounds, sounding her horn and loudly singing Bruce Springsteen's "Thunder Road."

Isabella and Louisa were very polite but made it very clear they had absolutely no intention of coming with me and Molly to rescue my family and bring them home. Which was just as well, because it saved me having to tell them that I didn't trust either of them an inch where my family's interests were concerned, and I didn't want them along. There were problems to be sorted out between us, but that could wait for another day. Isabella and Louisa exchanged bye-byes with Molly, and then Isabella nodded a polite good-bye to me, Louisa winked and blew me a kiss, and they both teleported out without saying where they were going.

As we left the study Molly set fire to the door knocker and the withered thing nailed to it. "They say fire purifies and sets at rest," she said quietly. "Maybe I should burn the whole place down. . . ."

"Not just yet," I said.

I looked down the hall at all the faces silently screaming and pleading, trapped behind the mirrors, and I hefted Oath Breaker in my hand. And then I strode down the hallway, smashing each mirror as I came to it, and dozens of half-starved, tormented men and women suddenly appeared in the hall, crying out and clinging to one another, looking around with wide eyes, only half daring to believe that they were finally free. Molly and I got them up on their feet and moving towards the front door. And once they were all out and gathered together on the grounds before the manor house, I gave the nod to Molly, and she snapped her fingers, and the whole damned building went up in flames. It burnt fiercely, thick black smoke billowing up into the lowering evening sky. Many of the freed men and women applauded. A few even cheered.

"What's with all this finger snapping?" I said quietly to Molly. "You never used to do that."

"It's my new style," said Molly. "It's bold, it's dramatic, it's . . . me. What do you think?"

I was saved from having to answer that when one of the freed men approached me. He wore the tatters of what had once been an expensive suit, and his eyes were haunted. The woman clinging to his arm wore what remained of an expensive evening gown, and looked at me with wide unblinking eyes.

"Is he really gone?" said the man. He didn't have to say the name.

"Dead and gone," I said. "I punched his head clean off. And what's left of him will be ashes by morning."

"He'll be back," whispered the woman sadly. "He always comes back. . . ."

The man patted her hand comfortingly, and they drifted away.

Molly and I walked off across the grounds, and there, coming towards us, were the Regent of Shadows, the Armourer Patrick and Special Agent Diana. They nodded easily at us and the Regent actually grinned.

"I've been keeping an eye on you through the car. We're going with you to help rescue the family. Because they're my family, too."

"Oh, hell," I said. "Why not? The more, the merrier."

CHAPTER TEN

Where the Monsters Are, and a Not Entirely Unexpected Surprise

was ready to go straightaway, but Molly would have none of it. She folded her arms tightly and gave the Regent her very best *I see right through you* look, before bestowing an equally harsh glare on Patrick and Diana. All of whom, to their credit, stood their ground and smiled pleasantly back at her.

"I am really not happy that you've been spying on us all this time," Molly said flatly to the Regent. "Why would you do that?"

"Because Eddie is my grandson," said the Regent, entirely unfazed. "I wanted to see him in action, to see if he really was everything the reports made him out to be. And I have to say, I am very impressed, Eddie. Allowing yourself to be taken prisoner like that so you could get close to Crow Lee . . . And, of course, now that you have a real chance of going after our family, I have to go with you."

"Why?" said Molly bluntly.

The Regent smiled and spread his hands, almost helplessly. "Anything for the family."

"All right," Molly said reluctantly. "I've been around Eddie long enough that sort of makes sense, but . . . what are they doing here?"

She jerked her head at Patrick and Diana, who just smiled

pleasantly back at her. I looked at them, too. At the way they stood together, like they belonged together and always had. I still couldn't shake the feeling that I knew them from somewhere, that there was something . . . familiar about them.

"These are my two top Special Agents," said the Regent. "There's no one else I'd trust more to watch my back in a perilous situation. After all, it's been a long time since I was out in the field. I might be a bit rusty."

Patrick and Diana both started to laugh at that, only to turn their laughter into entirely unconvincing coughs as the Regent looked at them sternly.

"Exactly!" said Molly. "No offence, Regent, but you're a bit long in the tooth for this. We don't know what kind of dangers we'll be heading into. We can't carry passengers."

"She does have a point," I said. "We have no idea what kind of world Crow Lee has sent the Hall into, except, knowing him, it's hardly likely to be anywhere pleasant. There's no telling what kind of opposition we'll be facing."

"In our game," the Regent said calmly, "in the hidden world of secret agents and unnatural enemies, you get to be as old as me only by proving very hard to kill. I think you'll find I can keep up and look out for myself."

Molly gave up on him and turned her glower on me. "Are you sure you want to do this, Eddie? Take an old man and two strangers into an unknown situation?"

"I know," I said. "You're completely right, of course. But I just have this feeling . . . that they belong here. That they have a right to be included."

Molly threw both hands up in the air and actually stamped a foot. "Oh, well! That's fine! Everything's going to be all right because you have a feeling!"

I had to grin. "You're always telling me I need to get in touch with my feelings. . . ."

"This isn't what I had in mind! Oh, hell. Just get on with it. Before I get a rush of common sense to the head."

"So!" the Regent said cheerfully, rubbing his old hands together. "How are we going to do this, Eddie?"

"Actually," I said, "I'm still working on that. As a wise man once said, 'I'm making this up as I go along. . . .' We start with the Merlin Glass."

I took out the Glass, and the Regent and Patrick and Diana all crowded in for a good look. I turned the silver-backed hand mirror back and forth, and it gleamed innocently in the sunlight.

"I sort of thought it would be bigger," the Regent said finally.

"It will be," I said.

I tossed the hand mirror into the air before me, and it immediately shook itself out to the size of a door, hovering just above the grass. The Regent and his agents made pleased and impressed noises, but I had a suspicion they were just being polite. Where the mirror reflection should have been, the Glass was now showing a blank, colourless emptiness that actually hurt the eye if you looked at it too long.

"I thought . . . it was supposed to show a silvery tunnel or passage," said the Armourer Patrick. "That's the usual sign of an interdimensional interface. Not that there is a tunnel, of course, silver or otherwise; it's just an image your brain supplies because the mind is too limited to cope with what's actually there."

"It's not showing anything at the moment because it's between settings," I said, trying hard to sound like I knew what I was talking about. "I haven't supplied the Glass with the correct arrival coordinates yet. And for that I need this: Crow Lee's remote control."

"Space . . . and time," Molly said suddenly. "Hold on, go back, go previous. I've just had an idea."

"Oh, that's always dangerous," I said.

"Hush, you. Could you set the Glass to send us back into the past? Then we could arrive in the other world, immediately after the Hall and your family arrive there!"

"I have thought about that," I said. "But this is going to be a difficult enough jump as it is. I have no idea how this remote control works or even exactly what information it holds. So I really don't want to add any unnecessary complications. Except for this."

I showed them the Drood compass I'd acquired from the tomb in Egypt.

"A compass?" the Regent said, politely.

"Preprogrammed to point to Droods, wherever they might be," I said. "This will point the way, and the remote will supply the exact arrival coordinates. Between the two of them, they should get us there."

"Are you sure about that?" said the Regent.

I smiled as convincingly as I could. "The remote knows where the Hall is, so we follow the remote. And the compass. And if you know any good prayers or deities, now would be a good time to lean heavily on them."

I hefted the control in my hand. Just a simple box with a whole bunch of coloured buttons, none of which I felt like messing with. I pitched the compass through the Merlin Glass, which swallowed it up immediately, and then the remote. The grey nothingness pulsed quickly in a way that made me feel oddly seasick for a moment, and then it became the standard silver tunnel. I let out a breath I hadn't realised I'd been holding and relaxed just a little. If that hadn't worked . . .

At least now we had a destination. The Regent turned to Patrick and Diana and nodded briskly, and they both grinned widely. Suddenly they were both holding really big guns that had appeared out of nowhere. High-energy weapons clearly derived from alien tech.

"Where did you get weapons like those?" I said sharply to the Regent.

"Oh, you know how it is. Some of my chaps just picked them up," the Regent said vaguely. "It's amazing what some people leaving lying around. Behind locked doors in secret laboratories. They clearly didn't appreciate them. . . . And whilst the Shadows, and now the Uncanny, are quite definitely mostly information-gathering organisations, some-times, you just have to be ready to lay down the law."

"Ready to rock and roll!" Patrick said cheerfully.

"Ready to kick bottom!" said Diana. She smiled suddenly at me. "You're not the only one with access to pocket dimensions and really useful toys."

"Told you," the Regent said to Molly and me. "Let us go now, and let the bad guys beware."

Patrick smiled fondly at Diana. "Just like old times, isn't it, dear?"

"Ah, the good old days," said Diana. "Was there always an evil mastermind to overcome in some secret lair, a monster to destroy and a conspiracy to put down, and still home in time for tea?"

I looked at them both for a long moment. Something in the way they smiled at each other, in the way they held themselves . . .

"Do I know you?" I said bluntly. "Have we met before? There is something very familiar about you. . . ."

"Time for the social chitchat later," the Regent said firmly. "Concentrate on the mission. We have a family to rescue. Everything else can wait."

"What about you?" said Molly. "Are you going to grab a really big gun out of midair, too?"

"I have a few tricks up my sleeve," the Regent said modestly.

"It's true," said Patrick. "He does."

"I'm often amazed he has room in there for his arms," said Diana.

"Oh, hush, children," said the Regent.

He strode towards the Merlin Glass and its waiting silver tunnel, and Patrick and Diana fell quickly into step behind him, guns at the ready. Molly and I hurried after them, and I made a point of taking the lead. It was my Merlin Glass, my plan, and whatever we'd be facing, I was determined to face it first. Even if I didn't have my armour anymore. I hefted Oath Breaker in my hand. The long ironwood staff still felt unnaturally solid and heavy, and I found that reassuring. I stepped carefully through the hovering Glass and into the silver tunnel, and there were the compass and the remote control, hovering on the air ahead. I moved forward and they drifted on before me, and step-by-step they led me through the silver tunnel between the worlds. Molly stuck close to my side, and the others stuck close behind us. This wasn't somewhere you wanted to get lost.

As the compass and remote moved on, worlds flashed and flickered into existence before and around us, come and gone in a moment, like walking through a pack of shuffled playing cards, giving brief glimpses of other dimensions, other Earths, other Halls.

There was Big Hall, an immense single structure that covered the entire grounds. Acres of stone walls under miles of roof with thousands of windows. The whole place just hummed with activity, with an army of people coming and going, hurrying about their unknown missions. They all wore golden armour. All kinds of flying machines filled the skies over Big Hall, landing and taking off from dozens of busy landing pads, scattered across the vast roof. They flashed back and forth in carefully conceived patterns, often coming within inches of one another but never once colliding, moving like the very best regulated clockwork. There was a real sense of purpose to it all, of everyone playing their part in some grand important scheme.

Next came Small Hall. Drood Hall as it had once been back before the family grew so big we had to add on four more wings. Small Hall was just the original central building from Tudor times, with its black-and-white boarded frontage, heavy leaded-glass windows and jutting gabled roof. The grounds stretched away around the Hall, open and empty. No lake, no hedge Maze, no unicorns or gryphons, and no sign of Droods anywhere.

Two small suns burnt hotly in a deep purple sky over Alien Hall. The air was unbearably hot and humid, dragging in the lungs, even for the few moments it took us to walk through it. Alien Hall was a huge, organic structure, seemingly as much grown as constructed, a strange shape made up of unnatural curves and shadowy hollows, its angles forming patterns that made no sense at all to human eyes. All over the smooth, shiny exterior swarmed golden-armoured creatures, almost human in shape but not in nature or in movement, as they darted in and out of hollow mouths in the side of the Hall. There was something of the insect in their behaviour, and the whole place had more the air of a hive than a home.

A dim red sun in a grey sky shed a murky bloodred glare over Machine Hall. A massive steel cube with no doors or windows, just sharp projections and waving antennae, strange undulating patterns and endless flashing lights. Vehicles in solid primary shapes moved smoothly all around Machine Hall, in a single complex pattern. The few golden figures to be seen were quite clearly mechanical. The grounds were just empty stone flats stretching away; empty and without shape or purpose.

And then there was Magic Hall. In this version, this Earth, Drood Hall was a castle in the grand old style, complete with towers and turrets and crenulated battlements. Flags and pennants flapped bravely in the gusting wind under a perfect cloudless summer sky. Great open lawns surrounding the castle were covered with gleaming white tents and colourful pavilions, and the golden figures strolling back and forth had the aspect of knights from medieval legends. Winged unicorns flew back and forth above the castle, and golden-armoured figures waltzed happily on the air among them.

"The Hall as Camelot," I said, pausing for a longer look. "The best of us, perhaps . . ."

"The Pendragon, King Arthur, has returned to Castle Inconnu and the London Knights," said the Regent. "I shall be most interested to see what happens next."

"Boys and their knights," said Molly. "I'll never be a maid-in-waiting."

"Camelot lasted only a few decades," I said. "The Droods have endured for centuries. We might wear armour, but we were never chivalric."

I followed the compass and the remote, which had waited obligingly, and Magic Hall disappeared, lost in the shuffle of so many realities, so many variations on the Drood family.

And then the world turned, there was a blinding flash of light and the compass and remote dropped out of the air to land at my feet. I quickly stooped down to pick them up and stuff them in my pocket. And only then looked around me. The Merlin Glass had already shut itself down, zipping back to hide in my pocket dimension, as though it didn't care for its new surroundings. I didn't blame it.

"Can the remote get us out of here?" said Molly.

"Almost certainly not," I said. "All it possessed were the arrival coordinates. We need the Hall and Alpha Red Alpha to get home again."

"Now you tell me," said Molly.

She armoured up, taking on the exaggeratedly feminine aspect of Moxton's Mistake. And the more I looked around me, the more I missed my armour. Patrick and Diana were already standing back-to-back, guns tracking this way and that in search of a target. The Regent of Shadows just beamed happily around him as though he were on holiday and determined to enjoy every moment of it. I took a firm hold on Oath Breaker.

We were standing in the middle of what I decided to call a jungle, because I had to call it something. There were no trees, no vegetation; instead, massive gnarled and whorled growths erupted out of the ground, rising, twisting and turning as though they had been forced molten from the ground and then hardened in the air. They rose high above us, hundreds of feet tall, sprouting branches here and there, twisted and knotted things that thrust out to challenge and interlock with one another. A tiny sun shone fiercely in what we could see of a sick green sky, the light forcing its way down through the canopy overhead. The gravity was distinctly heavier than I was used to and the light had a strained, sour quality. The air was so thick and wet I had to struggle to breathe the stuff. There were things moving in the shadows surrounding us on all sides, and none of them looked pleased to see us.

It took me only a few moments to realise there were loud noises, roars and screams and explosions, off to one side, and not far off at all. We all looked in that direction.

"I say we go that way," said Molly.

"It does sound like my family," I admitted.

Molly strode off in the direction of the destructive noises, smashing her way through the alien growths in her rogue armour. She didn't look for a path or an opening, just forced her way through with brute strength. The gnarled and knotty growths were no match for Moxton's Mistake. I knew how it felt to wear armour—like you're walking through a world made of paper—so why go around when it's so much easier to go through? You have to learn to treat the world with respect, because it can always surprise you. Molly hadn't had the armour long. I just hoped it hadn't gone to her head. Molly was dangerous enough in her own right.

I made a point of walking right behind her in the trail she'd opened up. Ready to watch her back, because in her current mood she probably thought she didn't need to. Patrick and Diana hurried close behind, guns constantly moving, ready to target anything that looked threatening or even overcurious. And the Regent just strolled along behind like a retired gentleman on his day out, enjoying the sights.

We'd barely been moving a few minutes before really unpleasant-looking creatures emerged from the alien jungle to attack us. Hopping insectoid things came first, with glowing green carapaces and dark faces with clacking, complex mouth parts. They sprang all around us, bounding and leaping with horrid speed high into the air before plunging down at us with clawed hands extended. Many-legged crawling things shot out of the shadows, curling and coiling and doing their best to snake around our legs and drag us down. They had great sucking mouths with needle teeth. And squirming blobby things just fell on us from the lower branches. One dropped right onto Molly's golden shoulder and tried to cling to her neck. It scrabbled and skittered there for a moment, unable to get a hold, and then Molly grabbed it in one hand and squeezed till the living pulp shot out between her golden fingers.

Patrick and Diana blew away the hoppy things with great speed and enthusiasm, and the air was soon full of flying innards. We all stamped on the long-legged things, and they made high wailing sounds as they burst messily underfoot. Anything that got too close I smashed out of the air with my ironwood staff, and whatever Oath Breaker touched exploded. It didn't take long for the alien wildlife to get the message, and we went the rest of the way observed but unmolested.

The Regent was still strolling along quite happily, hands in his pockets, taking a great interest in everything, and I couldn't help noticing that none of the alien life went anywhere near him. I pointed this out to Patrick, who just nodded solemnly.

"Why?" I said.

"Because they wouldn't dare," said Diana.

It didn't take us long to reach the clearing and the Hall. From the look of it, the Hall's sudden arrival in this world had blasted a massive clearing out of what I was still thinking of as the jungle. Broken and blasted parts of alien growths were scattered all around us, littering the perimeter of the clearing. I stopped at the very edge and looked the situation over carefully. The Hall, Drood Hall, that I had once been so sure was destroyed and lost forever, that part of me had still been sure I would never see again, stood there before me, solid and upright, in the middle of a half-mile-wide clearing. A shimmering barrier hung in the air surrounding the Hall, roughly halfway across the clearing.

The Hall was under siege from all sides by huge and monstrous creatures. They came slamming through the jungle, smashing through the twisting growths as though they weren't even there. Overpoweringly huge, bigger than the Hall . . . like hills with eyes, and mouths big enough to swallow an underground train. Packed with hundreds of jagged teeth, each of them bigger than a man. The ground shook with every step the monsters took, and there were so many of them, the earth never stopped shaking, like an earthquake. Like it was afraid. The monsters roared and howled and screeched, as though someone had given horror a voice. And an insane voice at that. Vast muscles rolled under shiny skins like great slow waves. Monsters, big as houses and bigger, whose shapes made no sense, whose limbs just sprouted from scaly sides and leathery sockets with too many joints. Claws that gouged the earth and left deep trenches. Eyes that blazed like the sun, and swirling sets of things that might be sensory organs, whose nature I couldn't even guess at.

I had to look up at them. They were so large they probably didn't even know I was there. But they knew the Hall was there, and they hated it. They pressed constantly forward, screaming and crying out and slamming against one another in their eagerness to get at the Hall.

They tore and clawed at one another, but their vast misshapen heads never turned aside from the Hall. Only the shimmering barrier held them back. They would not cross it, would not touch it. The last barrier between them and Drood Hall.

Dozens of golden-armoured figures defended the Hall. In armour covered with vicious spikes, with hands extended into long blades and heavy axe heads, Droods guarded the perimeter, standing just outside the shimmering barrier, cutting at everything that came close. Something in the cool, measured way they fought, preserving their strength, suggested to me that they'd been doing this for some time. Probably ever since the Hall first arrived here. Golden blades sheared through monstrous flesh and dark steaming blood flew in the air, but nothing they did seemed to make any real impression. The Droods were just so small in comparison to what they were fighting.

A huge distorted head slammed down and snapped up a Drood in its jaws. He was caught, half in and half out of that terrible mouth, the heavy teeth grinding fiercely but uselessly against his armour. The jaws opened and closed, trying to saw through the Drood, but all that happened was that several teeth shattered and broke off. The Drood used the extra space to get his feet under him, and then he walked backwards into the jaw and severed the muscles with his golden blade. The creature howled like a fire siren as its lower jaw just dropped down. The armoured man jumped. It took him some time to reach the ground, and when he hit, the sheer impact blasted out a crater and a cloud of dust. When the dust settled he was climbing out of the crater, entirely unharmed. I felt like applauding.

But the monsters were so big, so powerful, and there seemed no end to them. Armoured Droods cut at legs bigger than tree trunks and hardly made an impression.

More golden figures defended the Hall from inside, firing all kinds of weapons from every door and window. Everything from automatic rifles to energy weapons to steam-powered bazookas. Plus a whole bunch of cobbled-together-looking things, probably come straight from the Armoury for testing. The sheer firepower blasting from all sides of the

Hall would have been enough to wipe out an army, but the colossal monsters of this world just soaked it up and kept pressing forward. They surrounded the Hall on all sides, looming over it, driven by sheer fury at this alien thing that had dared to enter their world. I wondered if they even knew it was the tiny golden figures that were their real enemy and not the Hall itself. Perhaps only the Hall was big enough to hold their attention.

"Do you know what that shimmering screen is?" said Molly beside me.

"No," I said. "Never seen it before. It's not part of the Hall's defences. Maybe some kind of improvised force shield?"

"I don't think so," said Molly. "Looks . . . wrong for that."

"We'll find out when we get close enough," said the Regent.

Molly and I turned back to look at him. He seemed entirely serene.

"You think we should just go running out there?" said Molly. "Into monster-snack territory?"

"I think the family needs all the help it can get," said the Regent. "Don't you?"

"You're wearing Drood armour, Molly," said Patrick. "You don't have to worry about monsters anymore."

"We're not doing any good just standing here," I said quickly. "So I say . . . Go the reinforcements!"

I took a deep breath, silently called myself all kinds of idiot and ran out into the clearing, heading straight for the shimmering barrier hanging in the air and the Hall beyond it. Molly was right there at my side in her rogue armour, and I just knew she was grinning broadly behind her featureless golden mask. She put on a sudden burst of speed, leaving the rest of us behind, striking out savagely at the monstrous creatures that blocked our way. Her golden fists gouged great chunks out of alien flesh, but the creatures didn't even seem to notice one more stinging irritant at their feet. Molly's actions worried me. They showed a viciousness I'd never seen in her before. And why wasn't she using her magic instead of relying on the armour's brute strength? Was the rogue armour getting to her already, the way it had got to me?

I fought to keep up with her, striking out with Oath Breaker. Wherever the ironwood staff struck alien flesh, great slabs of muscle exploded and more than one monster lurched suddenly to one side as a limb buckled unexpectedly. Patrick and Diana stuck close behind, maintaining a devastating rate of fire and keeping anything from getting too close to us. And the Regent just trotted along behind us, puffing gently, still smiling that interminable smile.

Molly laughed aloud, delighting in the strength and speed the rogue armour bestowed on her, smashing her way through everything that stood before her. I was disturbed at how quickly she'd taken to the armour after all the comments she'd made before about how she didn't approve of unnatural sources of power. But it is an undeniable truth that power tends to seduce, and appalling amounts of power . . . Molly took the rogue armour away from me to save me from its influence. Was I going to have to take it back again for her sake?

We were halfway across the clearing now, almost at the shimmering screen. I could see the Hall ahead of us. Huge creatures the size of airplanes cruised by overhead, circling the great clearing, swooping down to attack the Hall on massive wings that briefly blocked out the sun. Droods went up to meet and duel with them, in flying saucers, autogyros, attack helicopters . . . even sitting astride winged unicorns. They darted back and forth, easily evading the languorous movements of the larger creatures, plunging in to attack again and again and blasting the winged creatures with all kinds of weapons. Like golden wasps attacking winged whales.

Huge wormlike things burst up out of the ground inside the shimmering barrier, exploding up and up into the air, sending dark earth flying in all directions. Slimy ringed segments the size of hot-air balloons and with leprous grey flesh rose over the Hall, carrying blunt heads with great circular mouths full of rows of teeth that rotated like meat grinders. The Droods inside the Hall targeted the massive worms with every weapon they had and blew them apart one segment at a time. The slimy flesh soaked up incredible amounts of punishment before the worms collapsed and fell, slamming back to earth inside and outside the barrier. The creatures still outside tore the wounded worms apart and ate them up, all in a few moments.

And inevitably there came a time when the monsters were packed so tight together before the shimmering barrier that Molly and I were forced to a halt. No matter what we did with armoured strength or with Oath Breaker, we just couldn't make any progress. They were simply too big and we were too small. Of course, size didn't mean anything where Oath Breaker was concerned; if I'd unleashed its true power, even for a moment, I could have blown whole monsters apart right down to the molecular level. . . . But then, neither I nor any of my party would have survived such an explosion. Using the ironwood staff as a club was a bit like hitting someone over the head with a nuclear device, but it was still safer than the alternative.

Patrick and Diana kept up a steady stream of fire, while Molly and I looked around for another way forward. They blasted anything that got too close, and then they stopped briefly to confer before concentrating their firepower on a massive leg that blocked our way. The vicious energies actually opened up a tunnel through the flesh of the leg, and Molly immediately ran forward into it. So of course I had no choice but to go after her, with the others bringing up the rear. Patrick and Diana kept firing their guns, blasting out more elbow room from the meat walls and ceiling of the tunnel, expanding it as we went.

I couldn't help noticing how well they worked together, as though they'd been doing it for a long time. And they certainly seemed a lot more familiar with action in the field than I would have expected, even from the Regent's favourite Special Agents. They were excellent marksmen, too. I never saw them hit anything they didn't mean to. So, professional field agents with a long working relationship who didn't seem fazed by anything they encountered . . . Who were Patrick and Diana, really? And why was I so sure I knew them from somewhere?

We burst out the other end of the meat tunnel to find the shimmering barrier right ahead of us. I yelled for Molly to stop so the others could catch up, and she did, reluctantly. I looked back in time to see Patrick and Diana run out of the dripping tunnel mouth and immediately look around for new things to shoot at. The Regent strolled out after them, and a monstrous foot came slamming down from above and crushed him into the ground. We all cried out in shock and horror, but there was nothing any of us could do. It had already happened; it was over. And then the massive foot lifted up and moved on, and there, in a deep depression in the ground, was the Regent. Sitting up and brushing fussily at his clothes, entirely unhurt. Which was, of course, when I remembered.

"Kayleigh's Eye!" I said. "When that tea lady tried to kill you, the bullets couldn't hurt you because you were wearing Kayleigh's Eye! No wonder you weren't bothered by taking a walk in monster country!"

Even as I was saying that, a winged thing dropped down from above, heading straight for the Regent. It was much more our size, our scale, barely twenty to thirty feet in wingspan. The Regent looked up at it, smiling, and suddenly there was a small silver gun in his hand. He aimed carefully and pulled the trigger, and the winged creature just blew apart into hundreds of meaty chunks. The Regent smiled, blew imaginary smoke from the end of the short barrel, and made the gun disappear with a quick flexing of his fingers.

"I didn't just bring the Eye," he said easily.

"Told you," said Patrick. "More tricks up his sleeve than a barrel of conjurers."

I turned away, not trusting myself to speak, and tested the shimmering barrier with one hand. Nothing bad happened, so I just plunged right through it. And the moment I was on the other side, the alien world's heavier gravity fell away and I could breathe again without struggling. The barrier wasn't a force shield; it just marked the spot where alien conditions ended. The Hall was still surrounded by an area of Earth-normal conditions that it had brought with it. The relief was so great I just stood there for a long moment, breathing deeply, a big stupid grin on my face. And then the others came through to join me, so I put on my professional face again and led them towards Drood Hall.

The golden figures at the perimeter, inside and outside the screen, just nodded briefly to us as we passed, concentrating on keeping back the monsters. More armoured figures ran back and forth from the Hall to the barrier, presumably with important messages or more ammunition. They were too busy even to acknowledge us. As we approached the front doors, a single figure appeared, carrying the single biggest and most impressive-looking gun I'd ever seen. I was surprised he could even hold the thing, let alone aim it. It was, of course, the Sarjeant-at-Arms. He aimed the gun right at us, and then he saw me, and I swear his jaw actually dropped. I think the whole journey was worth it just to see that. His mouth snapped shut again almost immediately, and he stepped outside and urged us in. He tracked the gun back and forth, making sure nothing had come through the barrier after us, waited till we were all safely inside, and then hurried in after us and slammed the front doors shut.

It was wonderfully cool and calm and quiet in the hallway.

The Sarjeant-at-Arms put down his huge gun, leaning it carefully against the closed front doors. He nodded briefly to me.

"Good to see you, Eddie. What took you so long?"

I stepped forward and hugged him tightly. It was a bit like trying to hug a brick wall, but I gave it my best shot. Then I stepped back and grinned at him.

"Good to see you too, Cedric. You have no idea how good."

"Please, Edwin," said the Sarjeant. "Not in front of strangers. Who are these people you've brought with you?"

Molly armoured down, and the Sarjeant blinked several times as the golden mask disappeared to reveal her features. But that was nothing compared to the look of actual shock that took over his face when he looked at the Regent, Diana and Patrick. He stepped forward involuntarily, his gaze fixed on the Regent of Shadows.

"Dear God," he said. "It's you!"

"Quite, Cedric," said the Regent. "Demons in Hell are probably snowboarding even as we speak. . . . But, yes, it's me. I'm back. Where is the rest of the Council?"

"Here," said a familiar voice. "All that's left of us."

I looked around, and hurrying down the hallway towards us were William the Librarian and the telepath Ammonia Vom Acht. The Librarian looked his usual tall and world-buffeted self, but he was wearing clothes that actually seemed like he'd put them on himself for a change, and with his great head of grey hair and full grey beard, he looked more like an Old Testament prophet than usual. His eyes seemed sharper and clearer than they had in a long time. Ammonia Vom Acht stuck close beside him, giving every appearance that she'd been doing that for some time. Medium height, sturdy, with a broad mannish face and a shock of unruly auburn hair, Ammonia had a face so full of character there was no room left in it for anything like good looks. She was wearing her usual battered tweed suit and stout brogues with trailing laces. Her jaw protruded forward with bulldog stubbornness. I noted, with quiet shock, that William and Ammonia were holding hands.

I pointed at them. "All right," I said, "when did that happen?"

But before William could answer, I stepped forward and hugged him hard. The Sarjeant sniffed loudly behind me.

"He keeps doing that. I don't know why."

I let go of William, stepped back and grinned at him. "You're looking a lot more yourself, William."

"Ammonia's been helping me," said William. "I always knew what I really needed was the love of a good woman."

"But we couldn't find one," said Ammonia, "So he has to settle for me."

They smiled at each other fondly. The Sarjeant-at-Arms gave me a *What can you do?* look but said nothing.

"The three of us are all that's left to form a Council," said William. "And we've been very busy since we arrived here."

"Where's Uncle Jack?" I said. "Has something happened to Uncle Jack?"

"The Armourer is down with Alpha Red Alpha," said Ammonia. "Hitting it with the science stick, trying to persuade it to work again and get us the hell out of wherever it is we are."

And then we all cried out and jumped back as a vicious snapping creature materialised abruptly in the hallway. Covered in dark green scales, long and Reptiloid with a great wedge head, lots of fangs and claws and a vicious barbed tail that snapped back and forth behind it. Big enough that it filled the hallway from wall to wall and from floor to ceiling, it was actually trapped for a moment, unable to manoeuvre. Ammonia pointed a single finger at the beast and scowled really hard, and all the beast's eyes rolled up in its head. It collapsed, slamming its great length on the floor.

"Telepathic bludgeon," said William proudly.

"Best kind," said Ammonia.

"Yes . . ." said the Sarjeant. "Luckily, it appears only a very few of these things can teleport, or we'd be hip deep in the bloody things by now. Is it dead or just sleeping, Ammonia?"

"Dead, of course." The telepath kicked the creature in the head a few times, just to be sure. "William, get this out of here, would you?"

"Of course, dear."

William armoured up. I didn't think I'd ever seen the Librarian in armour before. He grabbed the long barbed tail and dragged the creature briskly down the hallway to the front doors. He kicked them open and dragged the dead thing outside, where he picked the whole creature up and pitched it right through the shimmering barrier. William came back in to join us, and armoured down.

"Why am I always the one who has to take out the trash?"

"Show-off," said Ammonia. She fixed me with a hard look. "Don't even think about hugging me, boy. Why are you so pleased to see everyone?"

"He thought you were all dead," Molly said briskly. "When this Hall disappeared from the world, another Hall rotated in to take its place. That Hall was a burnt-out ruin, full of dead Droods. It took us a while to figure out what had happened."

"Wait a minute," said the Sarjeant-at-Arms. "The whole world thinks the Droods are dead? We have got to get back. With the cats away, the rats will run riot."

"Well, yes, quite right, Sarjeant," said William. "But first things first. The Armourer really was very clear and most upset when he told us that Alpha Red Alpha couldn't get us home again. That we were, in fact, trapped in this shithole of a world. And it was very nice of you to come and join us, Eddie. But have you brought anything useful with you? Something to help us get back home?"

"I've brought along a few useful items," I said. "I'll take them down to the Armourer."

"I still want to know who all these other people are!" said Ammonia, scowling at the Regent in particular.

"Ah yes," said William. "I should have got around to that, shouldn't I? Sorry, everyone. My mind isn't what it was."

"Though we are working on that," Ammonia said quickly.

The Regent smiled gently at the Librarian. "Do you remember me, William? I'm your uncle Arthur. First husband to Martha. I've been away for a while, but I'm back now in your hour of need. Because that's what I do."

William just nodded vaguely. He clearly still had some way to go. The Sarjeant nodded heavily.

"The Regent of Shadows. Never thought I'd see the day . . . Welcome home, Great-uncle."

"I and my associates here are just along for the ride," said the Regent. "It's Eddie's show, really. And Molly's, of course."

"The infamous Molly Metcalf," said the Sarjeant-at-Arms. "And wearing Drood armour . . . There's a story behind this, I'm sure, and I'm really not going to like it. Am I?"

"Almost certainly not," I said.

"Then it can wait. Get down to Alpha Red Alpha and do what you can to help the Armourer. Those things out there are getting closer all the time. We don't have any of the Hall's usual exterior defences; they didn't travel along with us. Most of the family are out manning the perimeter, doing what they can with all the weapons we could find in the Armoury, some of which are being field-tested for the first time even as we speak." He scowled briefly. "We've lost some good people.

And a lot of the weapons are running out of ammunition. I don't want to open the Armageddon Codex, but I will if I have to. I will destroy this world before I let it destroy us."

"Spoken like a true Sarjeant-at-Arms," I said.

The whole hallway was suddenly full of a rose red glow as Ethel manifested, bestowing her peaceful and calming presence on us.

"Hello, hello, hello, Eddie!" said the familiar disembodied voice. "I'm so glad you caught up with us at last! Isn't this an absolutely fascinating world? I've never seen creatures this ugly before, and I've been to dimensions you don't even have concepts for! I'm sure if some of these things would only stop trying to kill us, just for a moment, we could have some really interesting conversations!"

"You can talk to them?" I said.

"Well, no, not as such," Ethel said reluctantly. "I keep trying, but all I get is this mental static. . . . They're just so different! I'll keep trying, though. But first things first. You need your armour back, Eddie."

And I cried out loud in relief as armour poured out of my torc and formed around me. I'd forgotten how good it felt after the cold embrace of the rogue armour. I revelled in the feeling for a moment and then reluctantly armoured down again. But before I could say anything, the rose red glow seemed to concentrate around Molly, as though Ethel was studying her closely.

"That's a very interesting torc you've got there, Molly," said Ethel. "Where on earth did you get it? It's not one of mine. I can see it contains armour, but it's not strange matter. It tastes funny. I don't like it."

"I don't like it, either," said the Sarjeant-at-Arms. "Only Droods are supposed to have armour."

"This was a special case," said Molly.

"I needed armour," I said steadily. "And you were gone with the Hall, Ethel. So I went with the only armour that was left. The armour in the hedge Maze. Moxton's Mistake."

The Sarjeant just frowned, but William's head came up immediately. He looked at me sharply, and I thought he was going to say something, but he didn't.

"Still doesn't explain why she turned up here wearing it, and not you," said the Sarjeant.

"It's complicated," said Molly.

"I want to know what it is!" insisted the Sarjeant.

"It's rogue armour," I said. "Created by a previous Armourer to be intelligent, self-aware and to operate on its own. It rebelled and killed a whole bunch of Droods. That's why it was imprisoned in the hedge Maze for so long. But I made a deal with it: service in return for freedom. And since I spoke with Drood authority, Sarjeant, you will abide by my decision in this matter."

The Sarjeant scowled at Molly's torc but said nothing.

"How did you get here, Eddie?" said William. "How did you find us?"

"The Merlin Glass, combined with some useful information I picked up along the way," I said. "Which I really do need to get to the Armourer. Defend the Hall, Sarjeant. Buy us time to get the dimensional engine working again. Regent, Patrick, Diana: You come with me and Molly. You're about to see a part of the Hall we don't normally show people."

"Not back in the Hall ten minutes, and already you're barking orders," said Molly.

I led them all down to the Armoury, that great stone cavern set deep in the bedrock underneath the West Wing. It felt weird, hurrying through deserted workstations and abandoned firing ranges, with not a single overenthusiastic lab assistant to be seen, doing something unwise with something dangerous. It reminded me too much of the deserted Armoury in the ruined Hall. I found the trapdoor lying open at the far end of the Armoury, and we all gathered around it. Nothing to be seen but the top part of the iron ladder leading down into an impenetrable darkness. I didn't give any of them time to think about it, just started down the ladder without looking back. I was quietly pleased that one by one they followed me down, without saying anything. There was no light anywhere, and several times I had to stop and feel for the next rung in the ladder with my foot. The ladder seemed to descend for ages, long enough that my leg muscles had begun to cramp painfully by the time I reached the bottom. The moment I stepped away from the ladder, a bright light flared up, dazzling me for a moment. The others quickly joined me, and then we all waited patiently as the Regent took a moment to quietly massage his old leg muscles.

We had arrived in a truly massive stone cavern stretching away in all directions. It looked to be bigger than the whole Hall itself, and I wasn't even sure exactly where under the Hall we were. The huge stone walls were covered with line after line of carefully delineated mathematical symbols, none of which meant anything to me. The Armourer had called them mathemagics, the bastard child of supernatural equations and description theory. When people start telling me things like that, I usually just nod and move on because I know that even if I do ask questions, I'm not going to understand the answers.

Strange machines rose everywhere, set out in no obvious pattern, packing the great cavern from wall to wall and from floor to ceiling, with only narrow walkways left in between. Technology so advanced that none of it meant anything to me. Just brutal and ugly shapes, with no obvious function or controls. Some of the machines appeared blurred or indistinct, as though human eyes couldn't properly perceive or understand them. The result of one Armourer's mad wisdom. Along with gifts from other worlds, dimensions, realities. Our best and craziest Armourers have always been pack rats, putting things we pick up along the way to good use. Drood knowledge is older and weirder than most of us care to admit. Mile upon mile of colour-coded cables held everything together and hung in a complicated web between the upper levels of the machines and the uneven stone ceiling. Sometimes they twitched dreamily, like a dog's legs kicking in its sleep.

I called out to the Armourer, and his voice rose from deep back in the cavern.

"Over here! Whoever you are. Unless you're a monster, and then I'm out. Leave a message."

I headed for his voice, past colossal machines whose intricate workings were constantly moving, rising and falling, turning this way and that in endless variations, in pursuit of unknown purposes. Some of the structures seemed to lean and slump against one another, half melting, combining into some new and even stranger thing. Some changed shape right before my eyes, as though unable to settle, humming loudly to themselves in complex harmonies. And all the time I had the feeling of being watched and studied by unseen cold and thoughtful eyes. The cavern was comfortably warm and well-lit, but there was a bristling static in the air and the smell of iron filings and something burning, and I couldn't escape the feeling that I just wasn't welcome.

None of the others said anything. They just stuck very close to me as I led them through narrow wandering walkways. Just as well, because I didn't know what I could have said in return, except, *Yes, I know. It creeps the hell out of me, too.*

And finally, at last, we came to Alpha Red Alpha itself, which looked just as complicated and disturbing and overwhelming as I remembered it. Big as a house, bigger than most houses, rising all the way up to the ceiling, so you had to bend your head right back to see the top of it. It looked mostly like a plunging waterfall of solid crystal with glowing wires running through it like multicoloured veins. Etched all over with row upon row of inhuman symbols. And all of this surrounded a massive hourglass, some twenty feet tall or more, fashioned from solid silver and glass so perfect you could barely see it. The top half of the hourglass was full of shimmering golden sand, with not one golden mote falling down into the lower half.

The Armourer's lab assistants were crawling all over Alpha Red Alpha, clinging precariously to outcropping parts, making adjustments, taking readings and occasionally just hitting it with hammers in a hopeful sort of way.

The Armourer himself came bustling forward to meet us—a tall middle-aged man with too much intelligence and nervous energy for his own good, wearing the usual stained and slightly charred lab coat over a T-shirt reading *Eat, Shoot and Leave.* He was quite bald, apart from two tufts of white hair jutting out over his ears, from where he kept tugging at them while he was thinking, and bushy white eyebrows protruding over steely grey eyes. He also had a permanent stoop, from years of leaning over workstations for long hours, designing useful dangerous things for the family. He beamed happily at me, nodded happily to Molly and then stopped dead as he saw who was with us. The Regent stepped forward to smile gently at him.

"Dad?" said the Armourer. His mouth worked for a moment, as though he couldn't figure out what to say. And then he plunged forward and hugged the Regent close. It did look a bit odd from the outside. There was a lot of hugging going on today, and we're really not a touchy-feely kind of family on the whole. The Armourer finally let the Regent go and held him at arm's length so he could look him over properly.

"It's been such a long time, Dad! I did my best to keep in touch, but it hasn't been easy. I did think you might come home again when Mum died. . . ."

"It would only have complicated things," said the Regent. "At a time when you really didn't need . . . distractions."

"You're looking great!" said the Armourer. "I told you that serum would work."

And then he finally looked past the Regent, at Patrick and Diana, and his whole face just shut down, as though it didn't know what to do. He looked blankly at them, and they just looked quietly back.

"I can't believe you're here," the Armourer said finally. "I can't believe you've come back at last." He broke off, looked at me and then back at the Regent. "You haven't told him, have you? Why haven't you told him? He has a right to know!"

"Because it isn't the right time," the Regent said firmly. "Far too much going on right now. He doesn't need to be distracted."

"I'll decide what I need to know and when I need to know it," I said just as firmly. "What's going on here?"

"I will tell you everything once this mess is over," said the Regent. "I give you my word."

The Armourer frowned at Patrick and Diana and then nodded

slowly. "He's right, Eddie. You need to focus on what's in front of you. We all do. Just . . . trust us. For now."

"All right," I said. "For now. Talk to me about what's happening here."

"We've been working on Alpha Red Alpha nonstop, ever since the bloody thing started up for no reason and dumped us here," said the Armourer, giving the dimensional engine his best *There's going to be trouble* scowl. "Power levels are fine. Everything's doing what I think it should be doing, but . . ."

"You don't have the proper return coordinates," I said. I ran quickly through what Crow Lee had done and handed over the remote control and the Merlin Glass. The Armourer gave the remote a quick look and then handed it off to a hovering lab assistant, who hurried off with it. The Armourer scowled thoughtfully. "There's a lot of useful information to be found in that thing, no doubt, but this . . . Eddie, this isn't the Merlin Glass I gave you. I know that for a fact, because the original Merlin Glass is still lying on a bench up there in the Armoury, cracked from top to bottom and waiting for me to do something about it. This . . . is a whole new Merlin Glass. Where did you get it?"

"It's from another Drood Hall, from another reality. Long story you really don't need to know for now. But this Glass can do anything the old one can, and then some. It should be able to point the way home for Alpha Red Alpha. It's very eager to please."

"Not necessarily a good thing, with anything made by Merlin Satanspawn," sniffed the Armourer. "But never look a gift whore in the mouth."

"Language, Jack!" said the Regent.

"Sorry, Dad," said the Armourer. "But you're right, Eddie. Let me work on the Glass. If you and the rest of the family can just keep the monsters at bay for a little while longer . . . till I can get this heap of junk working . . . Yes, I'm talking about you, you oversized egg timer! Don't think I don't know you're listening!"

We left him to it and went back up into the Hall. Which might have been under attack by an army of nightmarish monsters, but was still less disturbing than the cavern below.

Back in the main hallway, we all crowded together in the open front doors, looking out into the clearing. The monsters were pressing closer than ever to the Hall. The shimmering barrier that contained the Earth-normal conditions had been forced back right across the clearing and was now only a few yards away. The creatures seemed bigger and madder and more determined than ever, rising to fill the sky with huge slabs of angry shapes. The armoured Droods defending the perimeter had been pushed back, too, till they were only just outside the Hall. They were hitting the monsters with everything they had, but even the combined clamour of all their weapons was nothing compared to the howls and screams and roars of the massed monsters.

"According to some short-range scanners the Armourer rigged up for me," the Sarjeant-at-Arms said tightly, "these creatures give off dangerous radiations and toxic emissions. As if they weren't ugly enough already. Together, just their presence is enough to overwhelm our poor Earth-normal conditions. The monsters have been pushing the barrier hard, and it can't stand against them much longer. Soon enough the clearing will be full of those monsters, and we'll have to fight from inside the Hall."

"Could they push the barrier back inside the Hall?" I said. "Push their world's conditions in here with us?"

"I don't know," said the Sarjeant. "The Hall has all kinds of protections, but most of them don't seem to work here. As though we're so far from our own reality that even the laws of physics are different."

"Where are the Librarian and Ammonia Vom Acht?" I said.

"Planning some kind of psychic attack," said the Sarjeant-at-Arms, making clear what he thought of that idea with a very expressive upraised eyebrow. "It's a sign of how desperate our situation is that I've encouraged them to try. It keeps them out of the way. . . ."

"Just how desperate is this situation?" said Molly, peering out the door while tapping one finger idly against her silver torc.

"We've had to ground all our air forces," said the Sarjeant. "The skies were getting too crowded. All that's protecting us from death from above are the gun emplacements on the roof. And just like everyone else, they're running out of ammunition. It's been centuries since we had to withstand a siege; we're just not prepared. A lesson for the Future, if there is a Future. Any idea how long it'll be before the Armourer can fire up Alpha Red Alpha and get us out of this hellhole?"

"He didn't say," I said.

"Of course he didn't. He never does."

Pushed back by the monsters, their backs set against the front of the Hall, golden-armoured figures stood side by side, firing every kind of gun I'd ever seen. Doing remarkable amounts of damage to the walls of flesh before them, but not enough to stop or even slow them. Vicious steaming fluids fell down to splash across the golden armour, only to fall harmlessly away. The stench drifting in through the doorway was unbelievably vile. I wondered if I should raise the question of the Armageddon Codex with the Sarjeant-at-Arms. He'd noticed I was carrying Oath Breaker, but he hadn't said anything. I wasn't looking forward to explaining to him just who had taken the ironwood staff in the first place.

He didn't need to know about the Original Traitor for now.

And then we all jumped and cried out as the shimmering screen slammed back several feet to right inside the hallway. We all fell back from the open doors as harsh air and heavy gravity filled the doorway. The Sarjeant yelled for all the Droods on the perimeter to get back inside, and they lowered their weapons and ran for it. Many of them threw themselves through the open windows, rather than get caught in the crush at the doors. Patrick and Diana each got a chair to stand on and calmly laid down covering fire over the Droods' heads to discourage the advancing monsters. I looked across at the Regent, who just shook his head sadly.

"Sorry, Eddie. Lateral thinking and tricks of the trade are fine against my usual enemies, but this is all a bit beyond me."

"Ethel?" I said.

"Yes, Eddie," the disembodied voice said immediately. "I'm right here."

"The elderly gentleman here is my grandfather Arthur. I say he is a Drood in good standing once more, so please be so kind as to grant him his armour again."

"Of course, Eddie. What about the other two?"

I paused. "What do you mean, what about the other two? You mean Patrick and Diana? What about them?"

"Well, they're both Droods, too. Do you want me to give them armour, as well?"

I looked at the Regent and then at Patrick and Diana. And just like that, I knew who they were. Who they had to be. And why they'd always seemed so familiar. Age had made a big difference. They didn't look anything like they used to in the only old photo I'd had of them. Hell, Patrick was bald with a beard now, and that'll disguise anyone. Diana's hair was grey. . . . They'd both changed so much, but even so, deep down I'd recognised both of them the moment I saw them. It had just taken till now, this moment, for me to see them clearly and admit to myself who they really were.

"Mum?" I said. "Dad?"

Emily and Charles Drood smiled at me. The Regent stood between them and put his arms across their shoulders.

"My children . . ." he said. "Don't blame them, Eddie. They wanted to explain everything the moment you walked into Uncanny. I persuaded them not to. Because you already had so much on your plate . . . But they still insisted on meeting you and working alongside you."

I put up a hand, to stop his talking. "All right," I said. "I get it. But there will be a hell of a lot of questions afterwards."

"Yes," said Charles. "We'll tell you everything. Afterwards."

"There is quite a lot of it to tell," said Emily.

"You abandoned me," I said. I hadn't meant for it to come out that harshly, but I couldn't hold it back. "How could you leave me here?"

"We didn't want to!" said Emily.

"We had no choice," said Charles.

"You see?" said the Regent. "This is why I didn't want you to know yet! We can't do this now, Eddie. We have to concentrate on the matter at hand."

The front doors exploded inwards as a massive monster's head slammed right through them. A great battering ram of a head more than twenty feet across and half as high, it forced its great bulk into the hallway after us as we scrambled to fall back. Long jaws slammed together in their eagerness to get at us. Charles and Emily opened fire on it, blasting great chunks of its face away, but it just roared deafeningly and pushed more of itself into the hallway, expanding the opening it had made in the doors with brute force. Molly armoured up and punched the head with as much force as the armour could deliver, but still she could only damage it, not hurt it. I yelled for everyone to fall back, and advanced on the snapping head with the ironwood staff in my hand. Huge dark eyes followed me, and the jaws gaped open. I hit the head a mighty blow with Oath Breaker, and the whole head exploded. The force of the blast threw bloody fragments the whole length of the hall and back out the doorway, and in a moment the entire space was empty again. Dark blood and other fluids coated the walls and dripped down from the ceiling, along with misshapen gobbets of flesh.

I was just lowering Oath Breaker and starting to relax when a long snakelike head shot through the gap where the doors had been, grabbed me in its jaws and hauled me out into the alien world. I armoured up instinctively, so the heavy teeth just ground uselessly against me, but I was still held firmly as the great snake head hauled me high up into the air and waved me back and forth. The world spun dizzyingly around me. I jabbed at the front of the snake's head with Oath Breaker, and all its front teeth shattered and blew apart. The huge alien creature screamed deafeningly, spraying dark blood by the gallon, but it released some of its hold on me. I punched holes into the scaled flesh of the upper jaw with both my armoured fists, and then used the precarious handholds to pull myself out of the mouth and up onto the top of its head. I stamped my golden feet into the head to anchor myself.

I could see the Hall a long way below, surrounded by all the many monsters that dwarfed it. The huge snake head swayed viciously back and forth, spraying blood everywhere, and screaming so deafeningly I could barely stand it, even inside my armour. I balanced myself as best I could, raised Oath Breaker with both hands and brought it down on the back of the creature's neck, where the head met the body. Scaled flesh exploded and the whole great body went limp. I rode the dying snake all the way down to the ground, and my armoured legs soaked up the massive impact as the head smashed into the ground. I jumped down and ran for the open doorway.

Molly came out to meet me in her armour. She stopped abruptly, blocking my way into the Hall. I stopped. I knew what was wrong. It was Molly's armour, all right; the familiar tarnished gold with the feminine attributes . . . but it hadn't walked like Molly, moved like Molly.

"What are you doing?" I said to the armour. To Moxton's Mistake. "Why have you overridden Molly's control?"

"You're planning on going home," said the rogue armour in its grating, too-human voice. "I'm not. I like it here. I think I could have fun here. Our bargain is over. No more service; I'll take my freedom here. And you're not going to stop me, Eddie. Because I have Molly Metcalf inside me. Trapped."

"What do you want?" I said.

"I'm going to stand back and watch the monsters tear the Hall apart, and then drag you out and eat you," said the rogue armour. "A fitting retribution for all the years you left me trapped in the Maze. Maybe I'll even help the monsters. Smash Alpha Red Alpha . . . And you won't lift a finger to stop me, Eddie, or I'll crush your precious Molly into a cube, like I did before. Only slower, so I can enjoy it more . . ."

I remembered the golden cube and the crushed meat and bones it had left behind. I clenched my golden fists uselessly. I hadn't a clue what to do.

"Eddie!" yelled a familiar voice from the doorway. "Catch!"

A small shiny thing tumbled through the air, the rogue armour, and I reached out a hand and plucked it from the air. Just a small metal clicker. I looked at it and then I looked at Moxton's Mistake . . . and then I grinned slowly behind my featureless mask. I held up the clicker so the rogue armour could get a good look at it.

"My uncle Jack is the best Armourer we ever had," I said. "He knew armour couldn't be trusted, especially in the wrong hands. So he made this."

I hit the clicker, and just like that Moxton's Mistake disappeared from around Molly and reappeared standing on its own, a dozen feet away. Molly swayed for a moment, and then her head came up and her face cleared. I ran forward, grabbed her by the arm and hustled her back to the Hall, where the Armourer was waiting. Moxton's Mistake howled its rage and its fury and sprinted after us. I could hear it behind us, closing the gap in seconds, and it was almost upon us by the time we charged through the great opening where the front doors used to be. The Regent stepped forward, his small silver gun in his hand. Molly and I ducked quickly out of his way as we ran past, and the Regent shot Moxton's Mistake full in the chest. The impact blasted the rogue armour off its feet and threw it backwards, into the path of the advancing monsters.

"Thanks, Dad," said the Armourer. He nodded easily to Molly and me. "Ready to go home, kids?"

"Oh yes," said Molly. "Really. You have no idea." Her hand went to her throat where the silver torc had been. "Armour . . . is overrated."

"Everyone, keep your heads inside!" yelled the Armourer. "We are leaving now! And I don't want anyone's bits left behind!"

He activated the remote control in his hand, and the familiar groaning and straining sounds of Alpha Red Alpha started up. Moxton's Mistake was running straight at us, but already he looked vague and far away.

"You stay here," I said, hoping he could hear me. "You stay here with all the other monsters."

And the last thing we heard as the dimensional machine carried us away was the rogue armour's howl of thwarted fury.

We came home to bright sunlight and pleasant summer air, and the gardens and the grounds were just as I remembered them. I stepped out of the shattered doorway and looked around, Molly clinging to my arm. The ruined Hall was gone, no trace of it left behind. My Hall was back. I grinned at Molly.

"Good to be back."

CHAPTER ELEVEN

Home Again, Home Again

To celebrate not having all died a terrible death in a horrible alien world, we threw a big party in the Sanctity, and everyone came.

It seemed like the whole family had crammed itself into the massive open chamber, bathed in Ethel's reassuring rosy red glow, but it was really just the main gathering. Everyone who couldn't fit in was out on the grounds, picnicking and enjoying the fresh Earth air and sunshine. Inside there were mountains of food and oceans of drink, though not for long. There's nothing like fighting for your very existence as a family to raise a thirst and work up an appetite. Ethel was playing classical music from everywhere at once.

"Mozart was clearly one of us," she said loudly. "Far too intelligent to come from anywhere around here."

"Ethel, you're a snob!" said Molly.

"And proud of it!" said the disembodied voice. "Someone has to maintain standards!"

A dozen lab assistants were dancing on the ceiling, around a new gravity inverter they'd invented specially for the occasion. Given their track record, people made a point of staying out from underneath them. William the Librarian and Ammonia Vom Acht were getting tipsy on something very rare and expensive from the wine cellars, and giggling together like teenagers, which was actually quite disturbing to watch. The Sarjeant-at-Arms was boasting to everyone who'd stand still long enough about how many monsters he'd killed. The number kept rising the more times he told it.

A few monsters had come back with us, or at least parts of them, caught inside the Hall when we returned. They died almost immediately, unable to survive Earth conditions. We'd made haste to bury them in a very deep pit at the back of the gardens, under rather a lot of concrete. Given how toxic they'd been while they were alive, none of us felt like taking any chances with them now that they were dead and already falling to pieces.

I gave Oath Breaker back to the Armourer the moment we returned, and he sealed it up in the Armageddon Codex again. And we all felt a lot safer. Oath Breaker is a disturbing presence to have around—something that only exists to make other things not exist. The Armourer was currently well into his second bottle of something that was bad for him and assuring everyone he was working on a whole new process that would shield Alpha Red Alpha from every kind of outside influence, so that nothing like this could ever happen again.

"I notice you haven't told him or anyone else exactly how Crow Lee got access to the dimensional engine or how Oath Breaker got out," Molly said quietly.

"I don't think I'm going to tell anyone about the Original Traitor," I said, just as quietly. "They don't need to know. It would only upset them."

"Now you're thinking like a Drood," said Molly.

"You're just being nasty," I said.

The Armourer wandered over to us, smiling widely. "I have decided to introduce the two Merlin Glasses to each other and see what happens!" he said grandly. "Should prove most interesting!"

"Let me know when," I said. "So I can arrange to be somewhere else entirely."

"I'm still concerned with where the other Drood Hall came from," said the Sarjeant-at-Arms, joining us abruptly. "Not from the monster world, obviously. So what happened to the family of Droods in the ruined Hall? Who attacked them? I mean, who is there that could take out the Hall and our entire family so easily, so thoroughly?"

"And whoever it is, do they exist in our world?" said the Armourer. "Are they out there somewhere, right now, waiting for their chance?"

"You should never drink, Armourer," said the Sarjeant. "It makes you paranoid."

The Armourer smiled. "You say that like it's a bad thing." He looked suddenly thoughtful. "I have been wondering. . . . Could something be attacking Droods in every dimension? And perhaps heading our way? Should we perhaps be looking for a way to contact other Droods on other Earths to discuss the possible threat?"

"Part of me wants to say, *Why go looking for trouble?*" I said. "But if you're right, trouble could be looking for us. Keep thinking, Uncle Jack. But don't try anything until you've brought it before the council. We could be opening all kinds of cans of worms with this. . . ."

"Speaking of which," said the Armourer just a bit vaguely, "Come with me, Eddie. And you, too, Molly. Got someone I want you to meet."

He led us out of the Sanctity, closing the doors very firmly behind him, and then led us down a corridor and into a side room. And there waiting for us was my grandfather, the Regent of Shadows, and my father and mother, Charles and Emily Drood. We all stood around and smiled uncomfortably at one another. There was still so much left unspoken, so much unfinished business.

"What happened?" I finally said bluntly to my father and my mother. "Everyone here thinks you were killed on a field mission that went wrong."

"We will tell you everything, I promise," said Charles. "But not here. Not in this place. Most of the family doesn't know we're alive, and we have good reasons for wanting to keep it that way."

"We've been hiding for a long time," said Emily. "We have many enemies. Nothing else would have kept us from you."

"You don't trust the family?" I said.

"Do you?" said the Regent. "Your uncle Jack and I have been discussing this, Eddie, and we've come up with an idea. You've done all you can for the Droods, and a lot of thanks you've got for it. It's time to strike out on your own. Come with us. Join the Department of the Uncanny. Make a new home for yourself and a new family. Your real family." He smiled at Molly. "You come, too, and find out what really happened to your parents."

Molly looked at me. "What do you think, Eddie?"

I smiled. "I think that . . . is a really interesting idea."

Shaman Bond

Will Return

in

CASINO INFERNALE